Through her marriage to Reggie Kray, Roberta Kray has a unique and authentic insight into London's East End. Born in Southport, Roberta met Reggie in early 1996 and they married the following year; they were together until Reggie's death in 2000.

ROBERTA KRAY

DANGEROUS PROMISES

sphere

SPHERE

First published in Great Britain in 2015 by Sphere

1 3 5 7 9 10 8 6 4 2

ISBN 978-0-7515-5381-9

Typeset in Garamond by M Rules
Printed and bound in Great Britain by
Clays Ltd, St Ives plc

Papers used by Sphere are from well-managed forests
and other responsible sources.

MIX
Paper from
responsible sources
FSC
www.fsc.org   FSC® C104740

Sphere
An imprint of
Little, Brown Book Group
Carmelite House
50 Victoria Embankment
London EC4Y 0DZ

An Hachette UK Company
www.hachette.co.uk

www.littlebrown.co.uk

1

Sadie Wise was a girl on a mission. She tapped her feet impatiently against the floor and beat out a rhythm on the table with her fingertips. Unfortunately the 3.45 from Liverpool Street didn't share her sense of urgency. Could the train go any slower? It was crawling along the tracks, stopping and starting as if it couldn't make up its mind as to what to do next. 'Come on, come on,' she murmured. At this rate it would be dark before she even got to Kellston.

She stared through the window at the slums of London's East End, her gaze taking in the derelict warehouses, the high-rise blocks and the depressing rows of old brick terraces. A pall of despair hung over the area, a greyness that was down to more than the fading light. She began to wonder if this was yet another wild goose chase. Eddie was as slippery as an eel. If he got so much as an inkling that she was on to him, he'd be on his toes and out the door before she could even say the word 'divorce'.

Sadie gave a sigh, determined not to give up before she'd properly begun. In another fifteen minutes – if they ever managed to get going again – she'd be there. She refocused her gaze, staring briefly at her reflection in the glass: an oval face framed by pale blonde hair, a pair of wide hazel eyes and an expression that was perhaps stupidly hopeful. *Don't wish for too much*, she told herself, trying to stay grounded. After all these years, the chances of catching up with her husband were slim.

Sadie pulled her coat around her. The heating wasn't working properly and a blast of cold air swirled around her feet. She felt the train give another jolt as it continued its slow progress along the line. At that very moment a girl came walking up the aisle, her eyes darting left and right as if searching for a spare seat even though the compartment was almost empty. In her early twenties, she was small and slim, elfin-faced with short black spiky hair. She was wearing jeans and a black suede jacket with a fur collar. Stopping by Sadie, she threw her a smile and slid into the seat on the opposite side of the table.

'Sodding train! At this rate we're never going to get there.'

'I know,' Sadie said. 'What's wrong with it? There was some kind of announcement, but I couldn't hear a word.'

'Signals,' the girl said. 'Something to do with signal failure.' She sat back and immediately sat forward again. 'Where are you going, then?'

'Kellston.'

'Oh, right. I'm the stop after.' She glanced at her watch. 'God, my dad's going to do his nut. He's waiting to pick me up.'

'It's not your fault if the train's late.'

'He won't see it like that. He'll have a go. He always does. He's the type who expects you to get out and push if the damn thing isn't going to get there on time. You've got no idea what he's like. He's a pig, a complete bastard.' She paused and then added, 'He's a huge fan of Thatcher,' as if this political allegiance was the final nail in the coffin when it came to his damnation.

2

Sadie's eyebrows shifted up a fraction. Unsure as to how to respond, she decided to say nothing. Her silence, however, didn't put the girl off.

'Not that he actually is my dad. I don't reckon so, anyway. Knowing my mother, it could be any number of blokes. She was never the faithful sort. Bit of a slapper, if you get my drift. Can't blame her for it, though. Being married to *him* is enough to drive anyone to drink – and the rest.' She stopped to take a breath and smiled again. 'I'm Mona, by the way, Mona Farrell. May as well introduce myself as we seem to be stuck on this nightmare journey together.'

Sadie reflected that they wouldn't actually be there together if Mona hadn't deliberately sat down opposite to her, but there was little she could do about it now. The girl was definitely odd, hyped up, but it was difficult to tell whether this was her natural personality or if she was under the influence of something. 'Sadie.'

'Hi, Sadie.' She glanced at Sadie's holdall that was sitting on the seat next to her. 'Do you live in Kellston, then?'

'No, just visiting.'

'Strange place to visit.'

'Is it?' Sadie studied the girl's face, the very pale skin and the small rosebud mouth that had been painted bright red. She wasn't pretty exactly, but there was something striking about her, a certain force behind the eyes. A whiff of perfume floated in the air – it might have been Chanel – accompanied by the faint smell of alcohol. 'I don't think I'll be there for long.'

'Nobody stays in Kellston for long, not if they can help it.' Mona glanced down at the file that was lying open in front of Sadie. 'Sorry, are you trying to work? I know I can go on a bit. Just tell me to shut up if I'm disturbing you.'

Although Sadie thought the girl strange, she was also a

distraction, and anything was better than her own company at the moment. 'It's okay,' she said, placing her hand on the private investigator's report. She'd read it so many times she virtually knew it off by heart. 'I'm finished here. I'm all done.'

Mona's gaze settled on the photo that was clipped to the top page. She leaned in to get a closer look. 'Who's that then?'

'His name's Eddie Wise. He's my husband. Although I'm hoping he won't be for too much longer. I'm trying to track him down, sort out a divorce.'

'What, done a disappearing act, has he?'

'Yes, well, he did that years ago – and cleaned me out while he was about it.' Sadie wasn't sure why she told the girl this. It was just an impulse, a combination of anger and frustration. Sometimes the mere thought of Eddie was enough to make her hackles rise. 'He emptied our joint bank account, every last penny, and then cleared off without a word.'

Mona gave a snort. 'No way! What a bastard!'

The last private detective Sadie had employed had traced Eddie to Southampton, to Portsmouth and then to East London, where the trail had finally gone cold. Or had it? She wasn't completely convinced. The investigator had been a sly, patronising sort of man and perhaps not entirely trustworthy. It was possible that Eddie had bunged him a few quid to keep his mouth shut. 'I think he may be in Kellston. It's where he grew up.'

'Can I have I look?' Mona asked, pointing to the upside-down photo. 'I may have seen him around.'

Sadie glanced at the picture, finding it hard to believe that this was the face she'd woken up to every morning for seven years. A handsome face – there was no denying it – but not an honest one. The photo had been taken a few weeks before Eddie had done a bunk. That had been almost five years ago, on New Year's Day, 1981; the date was forever engraved on her memory. She turned the file around and pushed it across the table. 'Help yourself.'

Mona inclined her head and stared hard at the photograph. 'No,' she said after a while. 'Can't say I recognise him.' Her eyes skimmed through some of the other information on the top sheet of paper before rising to meet Sadie's again. 'How long were you married for?'

'Too long,' Sadie said. They called it the seven-year itch, didn't they? Except Eddie had always been scratching, right from the moment they'd exchanged their wedding vows.

'So when did you start looking for him?'

'Ages ago, but he's always been one step ahead. He's probably worried that I'll want my money back, but I don't. I don't care about it any more. I just want to be free of him.'

'Maybe he doesn't want to be free of you.'

'No, I'm sure he doesn't.' Sadie gave a rueful smile. 'Although not because he still cares. It's probably so that no other woman can get her claws into him. I'm the perfect excuse for why he can't tie the knot with someone else.'

'That's the thing about men. They don't care about anyone but themselves.'

Sadie glanced out of the window again, her thoughts tumbling back to the past. Of course she'd been asking for trouble, rushing into marriage when she was only nineteen. Head over heels in love, young, crazy and blindly romantic. Although she couldn't deny that it had been fun at the start – one long round of pubs and clubs and concerts – the novelty had soon faded. As she'd started to grow up, things had altered between them. For Eddie, life was a party and that was never going to change. Mention getting a regular job and he'd let out a groan. Paying the monthly rent was always at the bottom of his list of priorities. Ducking and diving was what he was best at, although as it turned out he wasn't particularly good at that.

Sadie recalled the loan sharks who'd come knocking at the door only days after he'd left. Eddie had been running up debts right, left and centre, leaving her to face the music when his fragile house of cards eventually collapsed. The final straw had come a month later when Theresa Rimmer showed up at the flat, heavily pregnant and looking for the daddy. Sadie might have felt sorry for her if it wasn't for the fact that the cow had been shagging her husband behind her back. It was at this point that she'd decided she'd had enough, packed her bags and headed up north.

'Sadie?'

Sadie turned her head to look at Mona again. 'Sorry, I was miles away.'

'I was just saying, what about his family? Don't they know where he is?'

'I'm sure they do, but they're not telling me. Covering his back as usual.' She was maybe revealing too much, but it didn't really matter, did it? Chances are she'd never see the girl again and it was an opportunity to vent, to get some stuff off her chest. 'His parents live over in Essex, Romford way, and I've told them that all I want is a divorce, but they still keep insisting that they don't know where he's living.'

'I hate men,' Mona said, worrying on her lower lip. 'They're all bastards, the whole damn lot of them.'

'Not all of them,' Sadie said, thinking of Joel. He was a gem, sweet and smart and understanding. She still couldn't believe her luck. After all the miserable years with Eddie, she'd wondered if she would ever be happy again. But she was happy now, except for one small fly in the ointment. She really needed this divorce. Once she'd legally disentangled herself, she could have a fresh start in a marriage that was based on something deeper than a mutual appreciation of real ale and The Clash.

'Have you met someone else?'

Sadie nodded. 'Yes. He's a nice guy, really nice. I just want to get the papers signed and move on with my life.'

Mona pulled a face as if to imply there was no such thing as a nice guy, before returning to her earlier subject. 'My dad's a control freak, wants to know what I'm doing every minute of the day. It's weird. He's weird. Actually he's worse than that. He's fat and vile and disgusting.' She put her elbows on the table and stared at Sadie. 'I wish he was dead.'

Sadie looked back at her, startled. 'You don't mean that.'

'I'd kill him myself if I could get away with it. I'd creep up on him in the middle of the night and slit his throat from ear to ear.' She made a cutting motion with the side of her hand. 'Straight through the arteries. It wouldn't take long. He'd be dead in minutes.'

Sadie gave an involuntary shiver. Was she serious? There was a smile tugging at the corners of the girl's mouth, but there was also a malevolent glint in her eyes. 'You'd spend a long time inside for that.'

'Only if I got caught. That's the trick you see, *not* to get caught.' Mona paused, her forehead creasing into a frown. 'People do get away with murder. Have you ever seen that film, *Strangers on a Train*?'

'I've read the book,' Sadie said cautiously.

'Oh, is there a book? I don't read much. I don't like reading. But it was the perfect plan, don't you think? You get a total stranger to kill the person you hate and because they've got no motive, there's no reason for the cops to ever suspect them. It's a done deal. You could kill my father and I could kill Eddie.'

Sadie shifted in her seat. The conversation was starting to unnerve her. 'Except I don't want Eddie dead. All I want is a divorce.'

'But what if he won't sign the papers? You might have to wait years to get it sorted. By then your new guy could have lost interest. And anyway this Eddie sounds like a real piece of work. I mean, what sort of bloke behaves like that? It's sick.'

Sadie pulled the file back across the table, snapped it shut and stored it in her holdall. 'It didn't work, though, did it?' she said in what she hoped was a suitably dismissive tone. 'In the book, I mean. The two of them didn't get away with it. And one of them didn't even want his wife dead.'

'Sometimes people don't know what they want. And the plan only went wrong because Bruno was a drunk and didn't stick to the rules. If there's no communication, there's no connection. The cops wouldn't have anything to go on.'

Sadie had the feeling that this wasn't the first time Mona had thought about such an arrangement. The girl, she decided, was a fantasist. Did that make her dangerous? Probably not, but it still didn't make for comfortable listening. Thankfully the train had picked up speed again and would soon be arriving in Kellston. She tried to steer the conversation back on to neutral territory. 'So where do you live, then?'

'Hampstead, 12 Constance Avenue. You can't miss it. It's a bloody great mansion, got turrets on the roof and everything. Tennis courts, swimming pool, eight bedrooms – and there's only the three of us living there. How ridiculous is that? And there are marble floors everywhere. I hate it. The place is like a goddamn mausoleum.'

Sadie's eyebrows shifted up again. 'I dare say there are worse places. I've lived in some real dives in my time.'

But Mona, even if she'd heard, didn't take any notice. 'You know how he gets his money, don't you? He makes guns and rockets and stuff, shit for people to kill each other with.' Her face took on a hard, angry expression. 'People like him shouldn't be allowed to live. All he brings is pain and misery. I'd be doing the world a favour by getting rid. Of course the house is alarmed – he's bloody terrified of anyone breaking in – but I know the code. I could easily turn it off.'

Sadie began to gather her things together, willing the train to get into the station. Mona was freaking her out. The sooner she was away from her the happier she'd be. She knew that the train wasn't going anywhere near Hampstead and so she asked, 'You're not on your way home then?'

'Of course not. I'm going to see . . .' Mona hesitated. 'I have to go somewhere, see someone. He doesn't trust me on my own so he always picks me up and takes me there. He's paying by the hour, you see, so he can't bear to be late. He's a fucking millionaire but he hates the thought of wasting a penny.' Mona scratched at the skin on her wrist with her scarlet fingernails. 'It's a joke. It really is.'

Sadie didn't push her on who she was going to see. She didn't want to know. She had already learned more about Mona Farrell's life than she wanted. 'Right,' she murmured. Feeling the train beginning to slow, she breathed out a sigh of relief. Quickly she rose to her feet and grabbed her holdall. 'Well, nice to meet you. Take care.'

'I hope you find him.'

'Thanks.' Sadie made her way through the compartment, resisting the urge to glance over her shoulder. She had a sudden fear that the girl might decide to follow her, like one of those stray dogs that attach themselves and refuse to go away. It was only when the doors opened and she was about to step out on to the platform that she risked a quick look back. The seat was empty. Mona was gone. And suddenly the whole strange encounter felt like a figment of her imagination.

2

A bitter wind blew the length of the platform, making Sadie shiver. She turned up the collar of her coat as she hurried towards the steps that would take her out of the station. Now all she had to do was find somewhere to stay, somewhere cheap she could use as a base until she caught up with Eddie. She couldn't afford to waste money on a fancy hotel. The private detective had cost her a fortune, although whether it had been cash well spent remained to be seen. Maybe Eddie had already moved on, concerned that she was snapping at his heels.

As she emerged on to the small but busy concourse, her eyes automatically raked the faces as if by some miracle her husband might be in the crowd. But of course it would never be that easy. She felt a wave of tiredness wash over her as she contemplated all the pubs and clubs and cafés she would need to check out over the next few days. And what if it was all a waste of time? No, she couldn't afford to think like that. She had to stay positive, to believe that she would eventually find him.

Sadie's knowledge of Kellston was slight. She had only been here once before, years ago when Eddie had shown her the place where he'd been born. What she did remember, however, was the row of guest houses on Station Road. As she walked through the exit, she was relieved to find that they were still there.

The big red-brick Victorian houses, once home to the wealthy middle classes, had long since fallen into disrepair, the exteriors shabby, the interiors divided and subdivided into as many money-making rooms as possible. Most of them had a *Vacancies* sign in the window.

Sadie crossed the road, weaving between the cars that were waiting for the traffic lights to change. She hurried along the row, peering at all the houses. Which bell was she going to ring? There was plenty of choice, but little way of knowing what the actual accommodation would be like. With the cold nipping at her face and fingers, she decided to take pot luck and plumped for one called Oaklands, purely on the grounds that there was a light on in the porch.

The woman who answered the door was elderly, small and thin with a tight, blue-tinted perm. 'Yes?'

'Hello,' Sadie said. 'I'm after a room for a few days. A single. Do you have anything available, please?'

The woman looked Sadie up and down as if she'd come for a job interview, her beady eyes raking her body from head to toe. 'I only rent out by the week. That any good for you?'

'How much is it?'

She gave the price, paused and then added, 'That includes breakfast and a change of sheets.'

Sadie hesitated. It was hardly extortionate but she could, perhaps, find something cheaper if she kept on looking. And would she really need it for a whole week? The cold, however, was starting to creep over her and all she wanted was to get inside and get warm. 'Okay,' she said. 'That's fine.'

'I'll be needing the money up front.'

Sadie reached into her bag, took out the purse and passed the notes over. Only then did the landlady step aside and allow her into the hall.

'What name is it?'

'Sadie, Sadie Wise.'

'Right, well, I'm Mrs Cuthbert. The house rules are: no visitors, no noise and no food in the rooms. Breakfast is available from seven to nine-thirty.' She waved a hand in the general direction of the far end of the hallway. 'Along there, in the dining room. Cereal and toast. If you want something hot there's a café on the high street.'

'Okay.'

'It's the second floor,' said Mrs Cuthbert, pulling a key out of her pocket. 'Number six, on the right off the landing. I won't come up with you, dear. I've got the arthritis and these stairs play buggery with my knees.'

Sadie gave a nod, took the key and began to climb upstairs. 'Thank you.' The inside of the guest house was clean, if somewhat down at heel. The décor probably dated back to the Fifties, the paintwork was chipped and the rail of the banisters worn to a shine by the number of palms that had travelled along it. As she made the ascent her thoughts flew back to the girl on the train. It had been a strange meeting and one that she was glad to put behind her. There had been something highly disturbing about Mona Farrell.

Sadie reached the second landing and quickly found number six. As she put the key in the lock, she could hear the tinny sound of a radio coming from the room opposite: Jennifer Rush's 'The Power of Love'. She pushed open the door and flicked on the light, her heart sinking a little as she saw what lay beyond.

The room was about twelve foot square, sparsely furnished with a single bed, a ramshackle wardrobe, a chair and a chest of drawers. The beige carpet was threadbare and the faded flowery wallpaper was peeling in places. It smelled musty, as if it had been unoccupied for a while. She took a deep breath, refusing to be downhearted. What did it matter? She wouldn't be here for long.

Sadie went in, threw her bag on the bed and walked over to the window. The room overlooked the main road, and to the right she could see the station and to the left a pub called the Fox. A roar of traffic came through the glass, a rush of cars, buses and taxis. Every now and again, as the lights changed, the noise dropped to the more gentle sound of engines ticking over.

It was cold in the room and there was no central heating. She quickly turned, crouched down and tried to light the gas fire. For some reason it wouldn't come on. Was it broken? She twisted the switch but again nothing happened. It was then that she heard the voice behind her.

'It's on a meter, hon. You'll have to pop in a 50p.'

Sadie looked over her shoulder to where a woman was standing in the open doorway. She was tall, in her forties, and was wearing a short brown leather skirt, cream blouse and knee-high boots. 'Oh, right. Thanks, I didn't realise.'

'The Cuthbert didn't tell you, huh?'

Sadie stood up and smiled. 'No, she didn't mention it.'

'Must have slipped her mind. She gets mighty forgetful when it suits her. You don't get nothin' for nothin' in this place.' The woman gave a snort. 'I'm Velma, by the way. The room across the hall.'

'Hi, I'm Sadie.'

'Nice to meet you, Sadie. So what brings you to Oaklands?'

Sadie got her purse out of her bag and began to search for the money. 'It's a long story, but I'm only going to be around for a week or so.'

'That's what I said, hon. And twelve years later I'm still here.'

'Twelve years?'

13

Velma gave a rueful smile. 'Well, it might not be cheerful but at least it's cheap. You need a 50p, babe? I've probably got one.'

'No, it's okay.' Sadie finally found a couple of coins and bent down again to slip them into the meter. This time when she turned the switch the fire gave a pop and roared into life. 'That's better,' she said, rubbing her hands in front of the flames.

'You look frozen. Fancy a cuppa? I've just brewed up.'

'God, I'd love one. It was icy on that train.' Sadie followed her neighbour across the landing. This room was much bigger with pale blue walls and a pair of heavy, dark blue velvet drapes drawn across the window. It was warmer too with the fire on full blaze. There was a sink, a double bed, a table, an armchair, a portable TV and even a few plants.

Velma turned the radio down and busied herself with the teapot. 'Where are you from then?'

'Haverlea. It's a small town up north, near Liverpool.' Saying it reminded Sadie of Joel and she made a mental note to give him a call from one of the phone boxes outside the station. Already she was missing him and counting down the days until she could go home.

'This your first time in London?'

'No, I've been here before. I lived in Tufnell Park for a few years.'

'Milk and sugar?'

'Just milk, thanks.'

'You take the chair,' Velma said, passing her a mug. 'I can sit on the bed.'

Sadie sat down and took a welcome sip of tea. 'Lord, I needed that. Thanks very much.'

'That's okay, hon. Anything you need, you only have to ask.'

Sadie hesitated. 'Well ...'

'Go on. What is it?'

'Well, the reason I'm here is that I want to find my husband

and get him to sign the divorce papers. I don't suppose you've got any brilliant ideas on that, have you? He's avoiding me. In fact, the bugger's been avoiding me for years.'

'What's his name, love?'

'Eddie, Eddie Wise.'

Velma gave a shake of her head. 'Can't say I've heard of him. You could try the Fox across the road. The landlord, Tommy Quinn, knows most people round here, all the regulars anyway. Or you could ask his missus, Moira. What makes you think he's in Kellston?'

Sadie told her story as she drank the tea. Up close, she realised that Velma was probably in her fifties rather than her forties. The woman was wearing a lot of make-up, a thick layer of foundation and heavy eyeliner. Her hair, long and wavy, was a solid, unnatural-looking black. She had a kind face, however, the sort that invited confidences.

'You got a picture of this Eddie?' Velma asked.

'Hang on a sec.' Sadie stood up, went to her room and retrieved the photo from her holdall. She came back and passed it over. 'This was taken almost five years ago but I don't imagine he's changed that much.'

'Good-looking guy,' Velma said, holding the picture at arm's length.

'And doesn't he know it.'

Velma smiled. 'Yeah, they're the worst. Bit of a ladies' man, huh?'

'You could say that.'

'They're not worth the trouble, babe. You're better off without him. What does he do in the work line?'

'Good question,' Sadie said. 'About as little as he can get away with, usually. He doesn't do nine to five, and whatever it is, it'll probably be dodgy.'

Velma gave her back the photo. 'Ah, right, then you might

15

want a word with Nathan Stone. He knows all the faces round here.'

'Nathan Stone?'

'Terry Street's right-hand man.' Then seeing Sadie's blank expression, she added, 'Terry runs this manor. There's not a villain farts round here without him knowing about it. If Eddie's working for someone, Nathan will be able to tell you who. He's usually in Ramones between six and eight. It's a bar round the corner. Turn right out of the house and then left at the lights. You can't miss it. He'll be sitting at the back.'

Sadie pulled a face, not exactly relishing the prospect of approaching a local gangster. She'd met a few iffy characters in her time with Eddie, but no one in this kind of league. 'Why should he tell me, though? Blokes tend to stick together and he doesn't know me from Adam.'

'Yeah, he's a bloke, hon, so use your charms. It's not as though you're the law or anything. All you want is to get a few papers signed. Be persuasive and I'm sure he'll see it from your point of view.'

'Persuasive?' Sadie echoed, raising her eyebrows.

'You know what I mean. Just be nice, flutter your eyelashes and play the little girl lost. You'll be fine. Nathan's got a weakness for blondes so it shouldn't be too hard.'

'You think?' Sadie didn't feel entirely comfortable with the idea. 'And what if he tells me that he doesn't know where Eddie is and then tips him the wink as soon as I'm out of sight? The weasel's going to be gone from Kellston in five minutes flat.'

Velma gave a shrug. 'So what's the alternative? You could visit every pub and club in the district and still not find him. At least this way you've got a chance, and you could save yourself a lot of legwork too.'

'I suppose.'

16

Velma put down her mug and glanced at her watch. 'I'd come with you only there's somewhere I've got to be. Sorry.'

Sadie, taking the hint, quickly rose to her feet. 'Oh, that's okay. Thanks again for the tea – and the tip about Nathan.'

'No worries. Good luck, then. Let me know how it goes.'

'I will.'

Sadie went back to her room, closed the door and walked over to the window. It was ten to five and dark outside. She stood and watched the traffic, mulling over what Velma had told her. Should she go and see Nathan Stone? She found the idea daunting, but she wasn't overjoyed at the thought of slogging round all the local pubs either. Perhaps, all things considered, it was the lesser of two evils.

She pulled the curtains across and began to unpack. It didn't take her long. All she'd brought with her were some clothes and toiletries, the file on Eddie and a couple of books. As she shoved her things into a drawer, she hoped her stay would be a short one. The room was small and depressing and already the walls were closing in on her.

After a while, she heard Velma's door click shut, followed by the sound of footsteps on the stairs. Sadie felt a pang of guilt that she'd spent ten minutes offloading all her own problems and not asked the woman anything about herself. It was hardly polite, was it? Well, she'd have to find a way to make it up to her, maybe take her for a drink at the Fox once this business with Eddie was sorted.

Sadie sighed into the silence of the room. She felt that peculiar loneliness that often comes from being in a large city, surrounded by millions of people but not really knowing anyone. Joel had offered to take a few days off work and come with her, but she'd passed on it. Even though Eddie didn't have a faithful bone in his body, he'd still get the hump if she turned up with someone else. He was perverse like that. And anyway that hadn't been the only reason she'd wanted to come alone. Eddie was the past and Joel was the future, two different parts of her life that she preferred to keep separate.

'Time to move on,' she murmured.

And there was only one way to do that. She rummaged in her bag, took out her make-up and prepared to meet Nathan Stone.

3

Sadie was feeling a mix of emotions as she emerged from the phone box and began to walk towards the high street. Just hearing Joel's voice again was enough to cheer her up, but it also reminded her of how much she missed him. In her head, she could see him standing in the workroom with the phone pressed against his ear. She could see his mop of tawny hair and his kind brown eyes. She could almost smell the cherry and the oak and the maple, all the woods he used to make his beautiful furniture.

Sadie loved that room with the floor covered in shavings, the tall windows and flood of light. She loved to watch Joel work, to see his strong hands plane and turn and shape the wood. He was a craftsman and an artist. There was something almost spiritual in his acts of creation. He was a religious man, although not in a bible-thumping kind of way; he went to church, helped out in the community, but never forced his views on to anyone else. She knew that he brought out the best in her, that she had become a nicer and a kinder person through knowing him.

The only point he wouldn't compromise on, however, was

the two of them having kids before they married. And at thirty, Sadie's biological clock was starting to tick. She wished she'd been smarter and cut the ties with Eddie years ago. Why had she wasted so much time on him? The main reason – and she wasn't especially proud of it – was that she hadn't wanted to be proved wrong. And she especially hadn't wanted to hear her mother say, *I told you so.* A part of her had gone on believing that one day she would change him. Ha! If false pride was a sin then she was definitely guilty of it.

The temperature had dropped a few degrees and despite her warm jacket, jeans and jumper, Sadie was still cold. She hunched her shoulders, turned the corner and began to walk south along the high street. A freezing wind whipped around her head, making her teeth chatter. She hadn't mentioned Nathan Stone to Joel, thinking he would only worry about it. Going to visit a local gangster hadn't exactly been on her list of things to do when it came to searching for Eddie, but if that's what it took . . .

It was another twenty yards before she came across the blue neon sign of Ramones. She stopped outside and peered through the glass. The place was quiet with just a couple of girls sitting at the bar. She hesitated, nerves causing butterflies to flutter in her stomach. Was she doing the right thing? God, she didn't even know what the guy looked like. And what if he point blank refused to help her? Well, there was only one way to find out.

Sadie put on her confident face as she pushed open the door and stepped inside. The room was dimly lit with soft jazz music playing in the background. The two girls turned to stare at her and the barman glanced up from the paper he was reading. Ignoring all three of them, she headed towards the rear, hoping her courage wouldn't drain away before she got there.

She wasn't sure what she feared most as she wound her way

between the tables – that Nathan Stone would be there, or that he wouldn't. And what was she going to say to him if he was? She should have worked that out before she came inside. But it was too late now. She'd just have to play it by ear.

As she looked around, her gaze fell on a grey-haired man seated at a corner table under one of the meagre lights. He was alone and was bent over what looked like a ledger, busily totting up figures on a calculator. She stopped and stared, wondering if this was Nathan Stone. Surely it had to be. But now was possibly not the best time to approach him. She hesitated, uncertain whether to advance or retreat. As she was still pondering her options, the man raised his head, looked at her and raised a quizzical eyebrow.

Sadie walked over to the table. 'Mr Stone?'

The man didn't answer her directly. 'And you are?'

'Sadie,' she said. 'Sadie Wise. I'm sorry to disturb you, but I was wondering if I could have a word.'

'Now?'

She lifted her shoulders and dropped them again. 'Would you rather I came back later?'

He thought about this for a moment, but then flapped a hand towards the chair on the opposite side of the table. 'Seeing as you're here.'

Sadie sat down and cleared her throat. 'Thank you. I appreciate it.'

'So what can I do for you?'

'I'm looking for someone,' she said. 'His name's Eddie Wise. I was told that you might be able to help.'

Nathan Stone placed his hands on the table, linked his fingers together and gave her a long hard look. 'And who told you that?'

Sadie was reluctant to mention Velma's name in case it got her into trouble. 'Someone in a pub. They said you knew everybody in Kellston.' She took the photo out and slid it across the table. 'This is him.'

Stone looked at the photo but his expression, impassive, gave nothing away.

Now that she was up close she could see that despite the grey hair he was only in his early forties. His face had a fine, almost ascetic quality with pronounced cheekbones, a long aquiline nose and deep-set grey eyes. Not how she imagined a gangster to look, although in truth she didn't have much to go on other than the TV and the movies. 'I'm not here to cause trouble. I give you my word. All I want is a divorce, nothing else.' As if to prove her point, she plucked the papers from her bag and pushed them across the table too. 'His signature, that's all I'm after.'

But Nathan Stone seemed singularly uninterested in the paperwork. He sat back, folded his arms across his chest and stared at her. 'Why?'

She didn't really see how that was any of his business but answered him anyway. 'Well, we've been separated for years and we're never getting back together again so—'

Stone quickly interrupted her. 'No, I mean why should I help you?'

Sadie frowned. 'Why shouldn't you?'

'Because it's usually a mistake to get involved in other people's relationships.'

'Except you wouldn't be. All I want is an address or a place I can find him. That's not getting involved. It's just . . . just being helpful.'

Stone pulled a face. 'Helpful to *you*,' he said. 'What's in it for me?'

'What do you want?' she asked, although as soon as the words were out she had a feeling she might regret them.

A small smile tugged at the corners of his mouth. 'What are you doing tomorrow night?'

'Why?'

'Ever been to the dogs?'

'What?'

Stone's grey eyes bored into her. 'The dogs,' he said again. 'The races. Greyhounds. Four legs, brain the size of a peanut. Would you like to go?'

Sadie stared back at him. 'Why would I want to do that?'

'As a favour,' he said. 'I do something for you and you do something for me. You want to know where Eddie is, don't you?'

'Do you know where he is?'

'I can find out.'

'But you won't do it unless I come out with you.' Sadie, recalling what Velma had told her about Stone's preference for blondes, narrowed her eyes. 'Are you hitting on me?'

He gave a low mocking laugh as if the very idea was beyond ridiculous. 'No, love, I'm not. Like I said, I'm just asking for a favour. I have to meet a guy, a possible investor, him and his missus. The girl who was going to come with me can't make it, and I need someone to keep the wife occupied while I talk business.'

'You must know lots of girls. Why me?'

'Why not? It's short notice and I need someone presentable.' Stone gave her a dubious look. 'I take it you can do presentable?'

Sadie bristled. 'You're not exactly selling it to me.'

'Your choice,' he said with a shrug.

'Then the answer's no,' she said. 'Sorry, but I can't.'

Stone pushed the papers and the photo back across the table. 'Can't or won't?'

'Both,' Sadie said firmly, shoving the documents into her bag. She refused to be manipulated into doing something she didn't feel comfortable with – and spending an evening with Nathan Stone was pretty much at the top of the list.

'Shame,' he said slyly, 'because now I come to think about it, your old man does look kind of familiar. I think he may well live round here. Still, if you're not interested . . . '

Sadie stood up, intending to leave, but then hesitated. What if she was throwing away her best chance of finding Eddie? And all for the sake of a few hours down a dog track. What was the worst that could happen? It wasn't as if she'd even be alone with him; Mr Investor and his wife would be there too.

Stone bent his head over the ledger again, running a finger down one of the columns. After a while, aware that she was still standing there, he glanced up again and said, 'I'm sorry, was there something else?'

'Tomorrow night. Strictly business, yes?' she asked.

'Absolutely.'

'And then you'll tell me where Eddie is?'

Stone gave a nod. 'I'll do my best.'

Sadie wondered if she could trust him. Well, of course she couldn't, but there was probably more chance of tracking down Eddie with his help than without it. 'Okay,' she said. 'You've got a deal.'

Nathan Stone's expression was smug. 'Where are you staying then?'

'Oaklands, opposite the station.'

'Fine. I'll pick you up at seven.'

As Sadie walked away, she couldn't work out whether she'd just been very smart or very stupid. On balance, she suspected it was the latter. Still, it was done now. There was no turning back. Whatever the consequences, she would have to live with them.

4

Mona Farrell watched as her father walked across the living room, went to the cabinet, gazed at the bottles for a moment and then proceeded to pour a stiff scotch. There was a chink of ice cubes against glass as he carried the drink back to his armchair and sat down. She studied him while pretending not to, her fingers flicking through the pages of the magazine while her eyes made their careful scrutiny.

She was trying to work out which part of him she hated most: the curved dome of his paunch straining against the cotton of his white shirt, his heavy, jowly face with its piggy eyes or his abnormally small feet sheathed in a pair of brown leather brogues. Then, of course, there was his hair, thin and sandy coloured, brushed back from a wide forehead. Or his fleshy fingers with their neat manicured nails. And that was just the physical stuff. When it came to personality, she hardly knew where to begin.

It was quite remarkable, she thought, that one man could be in possession of so many ugly traits. He was arrogant, controlling, overbearing, greedy and callous. He was conceited and quick-tempered. He was a snob. Already he was eagerly looking forward to the New Year's Honours list when he would, or so he'd been assured by people in the know, be receiving a knighthood for services to industry. She gave an inner hiss. Services? Since when did manufacturing arms count as a bloody service? It was a disgrace, a crime against humanity. And when he became *Sir* Paul Farrell he'd be even more pompous than he already was.

It was hot and stuffy in the room, the radiators blasting out a fierce heat. The curtains were pulled across but, even above the noise of the television, she could hear the sound of the rain battering against the windows. Her mother was staring at the screen with a glazed expression on her face. Beside her, on the small mahogany table, was a glass of vodka and tonic. Not the first of the day, and probably not even the third or fourth.

Once, a long time ago, Christine Naylor had been considered a catch. In her twenties she'd been a socialite, a tall willowy blonde, a model who had appeared on the front cover of *Vogue*. Now, although still slim and attractive, there was something brittle about her, something fragile and damaged. *He* had done that. *He* had made her weak and shallow and stupid.

Mona returned to studying her father, aware from his scowl that he still had the hump with her. They'd been late, almost twenty minutes late, for the appointment and he hated wasting money. It was Dr Lund's policy to charge for the whole hour no matter what time his patients arrived – a nice arrangement for him, but not so agreeable to those who had to struggle with the vagaries of London's public transport system.

'It wasn't my fault,' she said, for the tenth time that night.

'You should have got an earlier train.'

'Why? I'm not psychic. How was I to know there were going to be signal problems?'

'Nothing's ever your fault, Mona. One day, perhaps, you'll start taking responsibility for your actions.'

Oh, here it comes, she thought, another damn lecture. He just couldn't help himself. She wrinkled her nose and closed her ears, letting the words wash over her. *Responsibility ... disappointment ... duty ...* It was always the same. He was like a stuck record repeating the same pathetic complaints over and over.

Of course if it hadn't been for that unfortunate 'incident' a year ago, she'd never have been forced to see Lund in the first place. He was an unpleasant skinny man with a protruding Adam's apple and a reddish beard. A psychoanalyst. At least that's what he called himself. Money for old rope was what she called it. All he did was sit there in that black leather chair, asking stupid questions about her childhood and making odd little bobbing gestures with his head.

Perhaps Lund thought the beard made him look like Freud. She wasn't up to speed with Freud's theories, but had an idea that he'd believed the root of most women's problems lay in some kind of sexual neurosis. But then he would have believed that, wouldn't he? He was a man and all they thought about was sex. Well, sex and money. Lund was probably of the opinion that deep down she wanted to sleep with her father whereas all she really wanted to do was to kill him.

Lund had only asked her once about the fire. Had it been an accident or ...? And she had told him the truth, or at least as much of the truth as she'd felt like telling him, that the house was a Gothic monstrosity, a blot on the landscape, and that she'd been doing Hampstead a favour by attempting to raze it to the ground. She was not sure if he'd taken her seriously. What she hadn't mentioned – she didn't trust doctors or their confidentiality clauses – was that she'd been hoping to dispatch her father at the same time.

'Are you listening to me?'

Mona gazed at her father and raised her eyebrows. 'I don't need to listen. I know it all off by heart.'

'And I'll go on repeating it until you finally start to take some notice.'

'You could have a long wait.'

Her father gave a grunt and leaned forward to retrieve the *Financial Times* from the coffee table. She saw his eyes flash with anger as his gaze fell on the copy of *Socialist Worker* she had deliberately left lying underneath. On the front cover was a tirade about Neil Kinnock's suspension of the Liverpool District Labour Party after a Trotskyite militant group had tried to take control.

'What's that rag doing here?' he snarled. 'What have I told you about bringing that rubbish into this house?'

'It's not a rag,' she replied calmly. 'Just because you don't agree with its views, doesn't make it worthless. Anyway, if I was you I'd be keeping a close eye on the enemy. It's always good, don't you think, to know what they're up to?'

'What they're up to, my dear, is anarchy. And come the revolution, they'll be chopping off your head as well as mine.'

'Maybe,' she said. 'Maybe not.'

He gave a thin, mirthless laugh. 'Imagine they'll spare you, do you? Well, I wouldn't be too sure. In case it's slipped your mind, you're living in this house too, using its electricity and gas and water, eating the food I put on the table and happily spending my money. And that, my darling daughter, is what is known as collaboration.'

Mona gave a shrug. 'We'll see.' In truth, she wasn't exactly gripped by the far left either. Although she'd briefly dabbled, she'd found the people tedious and, in their own way, as egotistical as her father. She only feigned an interest in order to wind him up.

As he flicked to the back of the *Financial Times* and began studying the share prices, Mona's thoughts drifted away from her father and on to Sadie Wise. They were going to be good friends, the best, she was certain of it. It wasn't often that you met someone and felt an instant connection. They had understood each other right from the off, creating a bond that could never be broken.

It had been an impulse to jump off the train and follow her out of the station and on to the street. But it had been the right thing to do. Now she knew where Sadie was staying, she could arrange to accidentally bump into her again. They could go for a coffee or a drink in the pub. Maybe she could even help her look for Eddie. Yes, it would be fun, the two of them searching together.

But then Mona frowned. Of course she couldn't do that. What if someone saw them? It would blow the whole arrangement out of the water. She had to be cautious, careful, to tread softly. Still, there was nothing to stop her from going to Kellston and checking that Sadie was okay. She would just have to keep her distance, that's all.

Mona's gaze slipped back towards her father. A tiny smile played around her lips. She felt the usual shudder of revulsion but this evening, at least, her disgust was moderated by the knowledge he would soon be dead.

5

Sadie woke up on Saturday morning, surprised that she had slept so well. The traffic had eased off after midnight and she'd fallen asleep shortly after. She stretched out her arms and yawned. Suddenly the pleasure she felt at being well rested was replaced by a dull feeling of dread as she recalled the arrangement she'd made with Nathan Stone. What had she been thinking? But there was nothing she could do about it now. She couldn't cancel. She didn't even have a phone number for him.

Shivering in the cold morning air, she got out of bed and turned on the fire. Then she grabbed a towel and her wash bag before padding along the landing to the shared bathroom. Thankfully it was empty. Her plans for taking a shower, however, were instantly thwarted by the discovery of yet another meter. If she wanted hot water, she was going to have to pay for it.

Sadie muttered a soft curse and trotted back to her room, hoping no one would nip in and take her place while she was gone. Apart from Velma's and her own, there were two other rooms on this floor but she had no idea if they were occupied or not. From the bowels of the house, she could hear a thin clink of cutlery and the clatter of plates. Breakfast was being served.

The bathroom was still vacant when Sadie got back. She fed the meter and turned on the shower, disappointed but not entirely surprised to find that the flow was hardly torrential. After locking the door, she stripped off and stepped into the water. At least it was hot and she was able to have a proper wash. She'd meant to shower last night – there was something about trains that always made her feel dirty – but hadn't got around to it. She'd felt so tired that she'd just had a wash and gone to bed.

Once she was scrubbed clean, she dried herself off, brushed her teeth, pulled on her pyjamas and scurried back to her room. Quickly she got dressed, wondering what she was going to wear that night. What did people wear to the dogs? All she'd brought with her were jumpers and jeans and they weren't going to be suitable. What was it Stone had said? *Presentable.* Which meant she was going to have to go out and buy something new, an added expense she really didn't need.

Her stomach gave a rumble, reminding her that she hadn't eaten last night. She'd intended, despite the no-food rule, to grab a sandwich from the high street and take it back to Oaklands, but in the end she hadn't bothered. After the meeting with Stone, her appetite had gone.

Downstairs, she made her way to the dining room. It was a dim, rather gloomy room with a lot of dark brown furniture. The wallpaper was brown too. The only other person there was a plump bespectacled middle-aged man. He lifted his eyes from his copy of *The Times* and gave her a nod. 'Morning.'

'Hi,' she said.

'Not much of a day,' he said, glancing towards the windows.

'No. It looks cold out there.'

There were six square tables in the room but only two of them were set for breakfast. Sadie hesitated, but then chose the empty one. She didn't want to be rude but she wasn't in the mood for making small talk either. There was a packet of cornflakes on the table, a jug of milk, a few slices of toast, butter and marmalade. No sooner had she sat down than Mrs Cuthbert appeared.

'Tea is it?' she asked.

'Thank you,' Sadie said.

Mrs Cuthbert retreated to the kitchen. And then the only noise was the gentle rustle of the man's newspaper. Sadie poured some cornflakes into a bowl and added milk. As she scooped the cereal into her mouth, she gazed around the room again. There were two long windows, their panes spattered with rain, and a lamp in the corner with a beige tasselled shade. The worn carpet had a swirling pattern of browns and fawns. With little else to occupy her mind she found herself thinking about Eddie. She wondered where he was and what he was doing now. Sleeping off a hangover, probably, if past history was anything to go by. When they'd been together he'd rarely got up before eleven.

A few minutes later, Mrs Cuthbert came back with a stainless-steel pot of tea. She placed it on the table without a word and instantly disappeared again. Sadie finished her cereal, buttered a piece of toast and poured the tea. She was hoping that Velma might come down so she could pick her brains about Nathan Stone. But then again, maybe there were things it was better not to know. She wasn't looking forward to the evening. It loomed ahead like some terrible ordeal.

Sadie was also feeling bad about not saying anything to Joel as regards the meeting. It wasn't a big deal, she told herself, and when she'd talked to him on the phone she hadn't even known about going to the dogs. But would she tell him about the night out? She was aware that she ought to, that in a good relationship there were no secrets, but she also suspected that he wouldn't be happy about it. She had the feeling that when it was said out loud it would sound much worse than it actually was. Here she was, in Kellston for barely five minutes, and already she was going out with another man. It might be 'strictly business' but, no matter how she explained, it would still sound dubious.

'Eddie,' she muttered. 'This is all your damn fault.'

'I'm sorry?' the man behind her said.

Sadie turned, smiled and shook her head. 'Nothing, I was just ... It's nothing.' She gazed out of the window as she finished her tea. When it became obvious that Velma wasn't coming, she left the dining room, went back upstairs, collected her jacket and prepared to face the dismal weather.

Outside, the icy wind and rain blasted her face as she walked to the corner. She put up her umbrella and pushed her chin down into her scarf. There had been a market, she remembered, when she'd been here with Eddie. Perhaps she could pick up something smart and cheap – if those two things ever went together – for tonight. Would they be under cover at the track or standing around outside? She had no idea but didn't much relish the thought of watching a load of dogs run round in circles while she slowly froze to death.

The high street was shabby and dilapidated with a lot of the shops boarded up. At the far end, three tall concrete towers loomed over the area. Even from a distance they seemed cold and inhospitable, like high-rise cells for the poorer residents of the area. She presumed they had been built in the Sixties but they were already showing signs of wear, the exteriors stained a dirty shade of grey from the traffic fumes.

It didn't take her long to find the market and once she'd got into the centre of it her spirits began to rise. There was music and life here, hustle and bustle. The mingling smells of frying onions, soup and curry wafted in the air. Many of the stalls were selling festive decorations, tinsel and baubles, glittery angels, snowmen, stars and dancing Santas. There were strings of fairy lights, crackers and candles. She couldn't help but smile as her gaze took it all in.

She and Joel would be spending Christmas together, and maybe – if everything went according to plan – it would be their last Christmas before they became Mr and Mrs Hunter. *Sadie Hunter.* She repeated the name to herself, liking the sound of it, liking the way it made her feel.

The market had a temporary cover stretched over the top, providing much-needed shelter from the elements. She walked up and down the aisles, feeling the warmth of the crowd as she drank in the atmosphere. There were plenty of clothes stalls and she rummaged through the goods on offer, checking out the prices.

After an hour of looking at skirts and shirts and dresses, she eventually settled on a pair of black trousers and a silky, rose-coloured, scoop-necked sweater. She suspected they'd both fall to bits after a few washes, but they'd do for tonight. The trousers were smart enough and the sweater was pretty without being too revealing. She paid over the money, took the carrier bag and pondered on what to do next.

It was as she was making her way back towards the high street that she first felt it, a hot prickling sensation on the back of her neck. Someone was watching her. She stopped, quickly turned her head and stared, but the crowd was thick and dense and constantly shifting. She scanned the faces, searching for the one. Maybe it was her imagination. Maybe she was just jumpy about tonight, her nerves playing tricks on her. And yet . . . She automatically rubbed her neck, still unable to escape the feeling that someone's eyes were on her.

For a while she stood there, rooted to the spot. She felt assailed by something cold and menacing. A shiver ran down her spine. She wanted to get away but it took an effort to force her legs to move again. With her mood abruptly altered, she hurried out of the market, crossed the road and took sanctuary in a café called Connolly's.

The place was packed, full of Saturday shoppers, and it smelled of fried bacon, cigarette smoke and wet coats. But at least it was warm and dry. A few seconds passed before she finally spotted a free table. She glanced towards the door, checking that no one had followed her in. Of course they hadn't. She was stressing over nothing. What was wrong with her? But she knew what was wrong. In her desperation to free herself from Eddie, she had made a deal with a total stranger and now that decision was starting to scare her.

When the waitress came, she ordered a coffee and tried to relax. Her worries, however, refused to go away. Instead they tumbled in on her, making her pulse race and her hands go clammy. What if Nathan Stone was some kind of psychopath? Maybe there wasn't any business meeting tonight. Maybe it was all a set-up so he could lure her to some lonely place and . . .

Sadie took a deep breath, willing herself to calm down. She was overreacting. Velma would never have sent her to see him if he was that much of a danger. Her heart skipped a beat. Unless Velma was in on it too. It wasn't as if she really knew the woman. Maybe she worked with Stone, procuring girls for him. Maybe she—

Sadie's thoughts were interrupted by the arrival of coffee. She thanked the waitress, lifted the mug to her lips and took a grateful gulp. The caffeine seemed to restore some sense of balance to her mind. No, she didn't really believe that her neighbour was involved in anything sinister. Sometimes you had to trust your instincts and hers were saying that Velma was sound.

Her gaze roamed around the room, settling on this person or that before quickly moving on. There was no one she recognised.

Why should there be? She was a stranger here. And hopefully, before too long, she'd be back on that train and heading for home. If Stone came up with the goods tonight, she might even be able to see Eddie tomorrow. She could imagine the expression on his face when he opened the door to find her standing there.

The rain was lashing against the steamy windows. Sadie took her time over the coffee, not wanting to leave before she had to. She felt safe in the café now that her anxiety had started to recede. Everything would be okay if she kept her head and didn't panic. She could handle Nathan Stone. He was just a bloke like any other. If she'd tolerated Eddie for all those years she could manage one evening with a lousy jumped-up gangster. Couldn't she?

The rain had eased a little by the time she left. As she sloshed through the puddles, she tried to maintain her restored sense of calm. For some reason she couldn't fathom, she still felt the urge to keep glancing over her shoulder. It was like a nervous tic she couldn't quite shake off.

'Stop it,' she murmured. 'There's no one there.'

Still, she was glad when she turned the corner on to Station Road and the guest house was in sight. She broke into a trot, eager to get inside. Oaklands was unlocked and she stepped into the empty hallway, closed the door firmly behind her, jogged up the two flights of stairs, opened her room, dropped her bags on the bed, leaned her wet umbrella against the wall and went over to the window.

Sadie folded her arms as she gazed down on the street, watching the people pass by. It was still hours before she was due to meet Nathan Stone. She decided that the sensible thing to do was to let Velma know about the arrangement. That way there would be at least one other person in the world aware of who she was with tonight.

She was about to do just that when her gaze suddenly fixed on a girl going into the station. She couldn't see her face, only the back of her head, but the short spiky hair was familiar and so was the black suede jacket. She gave a start. Was it? Could it be? She leaned forward, pressing her nose against the glass, but already the figure had passed through the entrance and disappeared from view.

Sadie continued to stare, a frown gathering on her forehead. It had been Mona Farrell, she was sure of it, except ... no, she couldn't be certain. Lots of girls had that punk hairstyle these days. Lots of girls had black jackets with fur around the collar. And what would Mona be doing in Kellston? Other than the market – and she couldn't really see Mona shopping there – the area didn't hold much in the way of attractions.

Sadie's hand instinctively rose to the back of her neck again. She felt a stirring in her guts, a twisting. Was it possible that ... But quickly she pushed the thought aside. The girl couldn't have followed her here. Why would she? That was just crazy. And yet she had seemed a bit crazy, unbalanced at the very least. All that talk of her father and how she wanted to ...

With a small shake of her head, Sadie turned away from the window. She was on edge, that was all, nervous and jumpy. A passing resemblance was what it had been. Nothing else. She had enough real-life problems without inventing new and imaginary ones.

6

By a quarter to seven, Sadie was dressed, her hair combed and her make-up done. Now all that was left was to wait for Nathan Stone to put in an appearance. She'd already turned off the fire and a thin chill was starting to creep over the room. She rubbed her arms, impatient for him to arrive. The sooner he got here, the sooner it would be over. Butterflies had invaded her stomach again, making her feel almost queasy.

She was back by the window, watching out for the car. According to Velma, it was a black Daimler, and there couldn't be many of those around Kellston. The only place he could pull in was at the bus stop and she kept her eyes firmly fixed on the spot. She intended to get downstairs the minute he showed. She didn't want him coming to the door like he was picking her up on some kind of date.

Velma had thrown back her head and laughed like a drain when she'd told her about Nathan coercing her into going to the dogs. 'And you agreed? You actually said yes?'

'What else was I supposed to do? I need to find out where Eddie's living.'

'Er, how about just bunging him a tenner for his trouble? That's the normal routine, love. Money talks round here.'

This option hadn't even occurred to Sadie. 'So why didn't you tell me? *Flutter your eyelashes*, you said. *Be nice to him.* You didn't say anything about giving him money.'

'Sorry, hon. I just presumed you'd realise.'

'And now I'm stuck with him for the whole damn evening.'

Velma had laughed again. 'Oh, come on, it could be worse. Look on the bright side. You get a free night out with supper and drinks thrown in. It's hardly the end of the world. To be honest, I wouldn't mind a bit of that myself.'

'Good. You can go instead of me.'

'If I was twenty years younger.'

Sadie had let out a groan. 'I don't even know anything about this guy. Is he . . . I mean, is he okay when it comes to women?'

'As okay as any of them are, hon. No better or worse than most of the other blokes I've come across. I can't say I've ever seen him with the same girl more than a couple of times, but then you're hardly looking for love and romance.'

'So he's a bit of a player?'

Velma had given a shrug. 'More of a loner, I'd say.'

Sadie hadn't been especially reassured by this piece of information. Weren't loners usually the ones with troubled pasts and dark secrets? Or maybe she'd just been reading too many crime novels. She was still dwelling on this when she saw a shiny black motor cruise past Oaklands and then pull in. Quickly, she grabbed her bag and headed for the stairs.

By the time she was on the street, Nathan Stone was just getting out of the car. He was taller than she'd realised, an inch or so over six foot, and was dressed in a stylish grey suit, white shirt, no tie. He leaned his elbows on the roof of the car and grinned at her.

'Didn't change your mind, then?'

'Why should I? We made a deal, didn't we?'

Stone smirked as he got back in the Daimler. 'People don't always stick to them.'

Sadie climbed in too and pulled across her seatbelt. The interior, with its soft leather seats and generous leg room, was probably the most luxurious car she had ever been in. She made an effort not to look impressed. 'And you?'

He raised his eyebrows in a quizzical fashion. 'Me?'

'Do you always stick to your side of the bargain?'

'Sure.' He paused. 'Nearly always.'

There was a short silence while he manoeuvred the car into the line of traffic and set off along Station Road. Sadie could smell his aftershave, something subtle and expensive. She had meant to play it cool, but couldn't stop herself from asking, 'So have you found out where Eddie's living?'

'Yes.'

Sadie's heart gave a leap as she turned to stare at him. 'You're kidding?'

'No one's that hard to find if you know where to look.'

She waited, but he didn't say anything more. 'Aren't you going to tell me?'

'Not until the end of the evening.'

'You don't trust me?'

Stone grinned again. 'I figure this way you won't do anything to spoil the night.'

'I wouldn't.'

'Well, who's to say? Maybe you would, maybe you wouldn't. I prefer to keep things simple – that way there can't be any misunderstandings.'

'I gave you my word, didn't I?'

His lips twitched as he glanced at her. 'You haven't met Cheryl Moss yet.'

'Oh,' Sadie said. 'Is she the wife?'

'Yeah, she's Barry's missus.'

'So what's wrong with her?'

'Nothing, babe, nothing much. She can be a little . . . loud, that's all.'

Sadie frowned. 'In what way?'

'In a loud kind of way.'

Sadie shrugged. In all honesty, she didn't much care about Cheryl Moss. In a few hours, she'd have Eddie's address and tomorrow she could go and see him. That meant – if she could persuade him to sign the papers – she could be on her way home before Sunday was through. Anything was worth putting up with for that. 'And Barry? What's he like?'

'Oh, Barry's sound. He's a builder, got a big construction firm over Shoreditch way. We're trying to put a deal together, a new development in Kellston.'

'Houses, you mean?'

'Yeah, houses and flats. Where the old asylum is. Do you know it?'

Sadie shook her head. 'No.'

'It's round the corner from where you're staying. Silverstone Road. The place used to be the local Bedlam. It's been derelict for years. There's a lot of land there just going to waste.'

'Sounds like a project.'

'It is. Or it could be.'

'And if Barry's not interested?'

'Barry is interested. If there's money to be made, he'll have his snout in the trough.'

Sadie gazed out of the window as they passed through the streets of Kellston. The area, with its litter-strewn pavements and graffiti-covered walls, had that air of desolation that comes from high unemployment and long-term poverty. 'It's a risky time for that sort of investment.'

'People need places to live. That's never going to change.'

41

Sadie wondered how dodgy the deal was. Very, she imagined, seeing as Nathan Stone worked for Terry Street and Terry was, apparently, the top-dog villain round here. 'But interest rates are high at the moment. What if people can't afford to buy the houses you build?'

'You giving me business advice now?'

'Just making conversation.'

'I didn't realise you were an expert.'

'You don't need to be an expert to offer an opinion.

'Well,' he said dismissively, 'maybe you should stick to commenting on things you actually know something about.'

Sadie gave a snort of derision. 'What, like shoes and handbags? Or what to make for dinner?'

Stone lifted and dropped his shoulders. 'You said it, darling, not me.'

Sadie suspected he was deliberately goading her. She gave him a long hard stare. 'You do realise that it's 1985?'

'Meaning?'

'Meaning that we're not living in the dark ages any more.'

'No need to get snippy,' he said. 'What are you, some kind of feminist?'

'Depends what you mean by feminism. But I reckon women are as smart as men – given the opportunities.'

'You won't be saying that after five minutes with Cheryl.'

Sadie huffed out a sigh. 'And that doesn't help.'

'I'm not trying to help. Just warning you, babe. It's always best to be prepared, don't you think? That way you don't get any nasty surprises.'

'So why me?'

'Why you what?'

Sadie lifted her hand in a vague wave of exasperation. 'Why ask me to come along tonight? You barely know me and this meeting's clearly important.'

'It's just a jolly,' he said. 'Something to oil the wheels, make things run a little more smoothly.'

'You mean a bribe?' she said caustically.

Stone shook his head. 'Hardly that. It'll take more than a night out to get Barry Moss on board.'

'So why bother?'

'Because it's to do with building trust, getting to know someone better. You think those flash guys in the City seal their deals over the boardroom table? No, they do it at the Ivy or the Savoy with a big juicy steak and a bottle or three of champagne.'

Sadie raised her eyebrows. 'And you're taking Barry to the dogs?'

'Barry likes the dogs.'

'Just my luck,' she said. 'And you still haven't answered the question. Why me? Why ask me to come along?'

'I already told you. The girl who was coming got sick.'

'And so you thought you'd ask a total stranger. That doesn't make sense.'

Stone gave a nod. 'Sure it does.

'And how do you figure that?'

'Because you've got something to lose if it doesn't go well.' Stone reached into his pocket with his left hand, took out a slip of paper and flapped it around. 'Eddie's address. I've got it and you want it. Therefore . . .'

Her eyes followed the slip of paper, resisting the urge to try and snatch it from him. 'Therefore, you think I'll do anything to get it.'

'Not *anything*,' he said. 'Just this one thing. You help me make tonight run smoothly and in return I'll give you what you want.' He put the address back in his pocket and grinned at her. 'That's fair, isn't it?'

'In your world, maybe.'

Stone's grin stretched a little wider. 'It's good to know we understand each other.'

'Couldn't be clearer.' Sadie looked away, returning her attention to the outside. The rain had stopped but the pavements were still wet, shimmering in the orangey light of the street-lamps. Where were they now? Somewhere in Hackney, she guessed. Her resentment at being forced into the arrangement had returned. Stone was too smug for his own good. Sharply, she turned her face towards him again. 'How do I know you're even telling the truth? You could have any old address written on that piece of paper.'

'You'll just have to trust me.'

'And why should I do that?'

'Because how else are you going to find him? Kellston's a big place. You could be tramping the streets for months.'

'Maybe I'd prefer that.'

'You want me to stop the car? You can get out now if you like.'

Sadie knew that he was calling her bluff. She was almost tempted to go through with it, to tell him to stop, but then she thought about Joel and what it would mean to go home empty-handed. 'I didn't say that.'

'That's settled then,' he said with a triumphant smile.

A few minutes later they drew up outside the brightly lit stadium. Sadie gazed out through the windscreen, looking at all the people milling about. As Stone killed the engine, she took a deep breath and prepared to face the night ahead.

'Ready?' he asked.

'As I'll ever be.'

'You could try and look more cheerful about it.'

Sadie painted a fake smile on her face. 'Will this do?'

Stone gave a shrug. 'If it's the best you can manage.'

Sadie gritted her teeth as she got out of the car. Had she ever disliked anyone more than Nathan Stone? She doubted it. Just a few hours, she told herself, and it would all be over.

7

Mona Farrell sat on the edge of the bed, watching as her mother put on her make-up. She twisted the silky cover of the eiderdown between her fingers and picked at the gold and turquoise threads of the embroidered peacocks. 'Where are you going?'

'Dinner with the Jensons.'

'The Jensons are boring. Stay here. We can watch TV together.'

Christine Farrell dabbed some powder on her nose before reaching out for the vodka and tonic that was always by her side. 'Don't be silly, darling. Your father can't go on his own.'

'Why not? Tell him you don't feel well. It's only a stupid dinner.'

'We won't be late.'

Mona gave a sigh. 'The Jensons are boring,' she said again. 'You know they are. All they ever talk about is how much money they've got. You'll have to sit and listen to them droning on for hours and hours and hours.'

'It's not just the four of us. There's going to be other people there.'

'They'll be boring too.'

Christine Farrell inclined her head and stared at her daughter in the mirror. 'So what have you been up to today?'

'Nothing special,' Mona said. 'I went to see a friend.' She tried to keep her voice calm even though she felt tumultuous inside. It had been the best thing she'd done in ages, following Sadie around. She'd felt like her protector, her guardian angel, making sure that nothing bad happened to her on the mean streets of Kellston.

'That's nice, dear. Anyone I know?'

'No. She's someone ... someone I was at college with. I bumped into her again and we were just hanging out. Coffee and that. Her name's ...' She paused, wanting to say it out loud – *Sadie, Sadie, Sadie* – but forced herself to bite her tongue. 'Sheila. That's her name. She's called Sheila.'

'It's always nice to have friends,' her mother said. 'You should invite her round.'

Mona, thinking of the plan that was starting to take a more solid form, gave a nod. Her lips parted in a small secret smile. 'Maybe I will one day. She's kind of busy at the moment, though. She's getting married next year.'

'Oh, she'll have a lot to do then.'

'It won't be a big do or anything. Nothing flash. They're not those sort of people.'

The conversation was interrupted by the sound of her father's voice booming from outside the door. 'Christine? Are you ready?'

'Five minutes.'

'We haven't got five minutes. I told you we were leaving at seven. The car's here. Get a move on.'

Christine gave her face one last look in the mirror, made some minor alterations to her hair and rose to her feet. She leaned over her daughter and kissed her on the top of her head. 'Have a nice evening, darling.'

'It'll be nicer than yours.'

'We'll be back by midnight.'

As soon as she'd gone, Mona got up and fetched the glass from the dressing table. With her back against the headboard, she sipped on what remained of the vodka and tonic and gazed around the room. She liked it in here. It was pretty and warm and as comforting as a cocoon. Above all, it was the one place in the house, apart from her own room, that was completely devoid of *him*. Her parents slept separately, had done for years, although sometimes – usually when he was drunk – the fat bastard would lurch across the landing to claim his conjugal rights.

Mona pulled a face. Tonight, she suspected, would be one of those nights. She would hear the padding of his heavy feet on the landing, the two clicks of the door as it opened and then closed again. Why did her mother put up with it? She could have got a divorce years ago, got the hell out of here with a decent settlement and the freedom to do what she wanted. Lots of people got divorced these days. It was no big deal.

The problem was that her mother lacked courage. She had been beaten down, stripped of her ability to think for herself. She was weak and vulnerable and didn't believe she could survive on her own. Well, all that was about to change. Mona would be brave enough for the two of them. And when it was done, they could sell this vile house and get themselves a nice comfy apartment in the West End, maybe in Bloomsbury or Covent Garden. They'd be happy there, just the two of them.

Her thoughts shifted naturally on to Sadie Wise. She knew that Sadie still used her husband's surname because she'd seen it on the sheet of paper that the photo of Eddie had been attached to. She had memorised her address too: 67 Buckingham Road, Haverlea. So even if Sadie suddenly left Oaklands and went home, she'd still know where to find her.

It had been surprisingly easy to follow her this morning. The worst bit had been hanging around in the cold waiting for her to come out of the guest house. She had waited in the doorway to the station for over an hour. Still, it had been worth it just to see her again. And as soon as she had, she'd known that she was doing the right thing.

Mona thought about Sadie's soft hazel eyes and the sweep of blonde hair that fell around her face. It was fate that had brought them together. What else could it be? They'd been destined to meet, to form a bond, to make a commitment that could never be broken. Although she still hadn't figured out what Sadie had been doing at the market. Wasn't she supposed to be looking for Eddie? Unless that's where she'd expected to find him. But she hadn't shown anyone the photograph and hadn't talked to anyone other than the stallholder she'd bought the clothes from.

Mona took another sip of vodka. A pair of black trousers and a pink sweater. What had she wanted those for – or had they just been an impulse buy? Sadie had looked at the Christmas decorations too, at all the baubles and tinsel. But what kind of Christmas would it be if Eddie didn't play ball? And even if he did, it still wasn't right what he'd done. The guy was a user, a nasty piece of work just like her father.

Mona knew what Sadie wanted her to do without her having to spell it out. An understanding had passed between them on the train. But she couldn't go through with it until she found out where Eddie was. She smiled as she remembered how Sadie had suddenly turned in the market and scanned the faces of the crowd, as if she was searching for her, as if she knew somehow that she was there. And for a second Mona had thought about stepping out, revealing herself, but had managed to stop just in time.

No, she had to stick to the rules and not do anything rash. Later, when this was all over and the dust had settled, it would be different. Until then she had to keep her distance. Wasn't that what Sadie had said? That the big mistake was … She stared into the bottom of the glass. Or maybe that hadn't been Sadie. She couldn't quite remember. But never mind, it would all come good in the end.

She had followed Sadie from the market to Connolly's. That had been another boring bit, having to hang around in the rain while she drank her coffee or her tea or whatever she was drinking. It wasn't as if she could even see her. Sadie had gone to sit somewhere at the back and the café was packed. For the next forty minutes she'd had to pace up and down the street, waiting for her to come out again. But it had been worth it. Of course it had. Patience, that's what it was all about. Tomorrow morning, she'd go back to Kellston and give it another go. Perhaps this time, fingers crossed, Sadie would lead her to Eddie Wise.

8

It didn't take long for Sadie to understand what Stone meant about Cheryl Moss. She was a short, loud brunette who laughed like a hyena. She had a Barbie-doll figure with boobs like melons, a tiny waist and no hips. Tonight she was dressed in a clingy, low-necked, glittery dress that showed off her cleavage to its full advantage.

They were watching the races from the warmth of the restaurant where the wide windows overlooked the floodlit track. As the dogs whipped around, Cheryl screeched out. 'Come on, Golden Boy! Come on!'

Although the racing was more fun than she'd expected, Cheryl's screaming was enough to give anyone a headache. Sadie's jaw was starting to ache from having to smile all the time. She threw Nathan Stone a glance and he grinned back at her. It was the kind of grin that made her want to slap him.

When the race was over, Nathan got up and said, 'We're just going to the bar. You girls be all right for a minute or two?'

'We'll do our best,' Sadie said.

As soon as they'd gone, Cheryl turned to her and said, 'So,

are you a natural blonde, hon? Course you are. I can tell. I used to be a hairdresser. I had my own salon before I met Barry.'

'Don't you miss it?' Sadie asked.

'Miss what?'

'Working for yourself? Being your own boss?'

Cheryl widened her eyes. 'Are you kidding me? I couldn't wait to stop. Too many long hours. I was dead on my feet most days. No, I love being married, hon. Barry's a real sweetheart.'

Sadie looked towards the bar where Barry Moss was deep in conversation with Stone. He was a great bear of a man, almost as tall as Nathan but twice as wide. He didn't say much, but his wife more than made up for it. 'So, how long have you two been married?'

'Ten years now, almost eleven.'

'You got any kids?'

'One boy. He's eight. I'd have liked another, but after Jimmy . . . Well, it turned out I couldn't have any more. I'd have loved a girl, but you've got to be grateful for what you've got. How about you, hon? You got any?'

Sadie shook her head. 'Not yet.'

'But you'd like to?'

'When the time's right.' Sadie thought of Joel and smiled. 'Yeah, that'd be nice.'

'How long have you and Nathan been together?'

'Er . . . ' Sadie hesitated, not quite sure how to respond. Was she supposed to be his girlfriend or just a friend? Nothing had been made clear during the introductions. *This is Sadie*, he'd said and not a word more. 'Not long.'

'Early days, huh? You don't want to go rushing into anything.'

'Yes, early days,' Sadie agreed.

'I think you two make a nice couple though.'

51

Sadie's eyebrows shifted up. Quickly, she tried to change the subject. 'Do you come here a lot then?'

'Only now and then. It's more Barry's thing than mine – he likes a flutter – and I don't mind. It's a bit of a laugh.' Cheryl glanced towards the bar and lowered her voice. 'I suppose it can't be easy for him, after what happened and all.'

'Barry?' Sadie asked.

'No, Nathan, you know with . . . Well, it's been a few years now but it's not the sort of thing you get over in a hurry.'

'No,' Sadie said, keeping her tone neutral. She didn't have a clue what Cheryl was going on about and wasn't sure if she wanted to. This was a strictly business arrangement and Stone's personal life was of no concern to her. She wasn't interested, not in the slightest . . . Well, maybe just a little bit. Curiosity nagged at the edge of her indifference. 'He doesn't really talk about it.'

'No, well, it's probably still hard for him. Guys aren't good when it comes to talking about feelings, are they? They keep it all bottled up inside. My Barry's just the same. Any problems, he keeps them to himself. Says he doesn't want to worry me, but that's the whole point of being together – sharing the bad as well as the good. Don't you think?'

Sadie was saved from answering by the return of the two men. Stone slid into the seat beside her and said, 'So, what have you two been talking about? Should my ears be burning?'

'No,' Sadie said.

'I was just saying what a nice couple you two make,' Cheryl said.

Sadie would have raised her eyes to the heavens if Cheryl hadn't been right in front of her. Instead she threw Stone a quick cold look that was meant to convey her utter dismay at the notion.

'So you *were* talking about me,' he said smugly. 'To be

honest, Cheryl, I think I'm still on trial. Sadie's not entirely sure that I'm her type.'

Cheryl let out one of her loud penetrating laughs. 'Oh, you just need to work a little harder, hon. Take her on holiday. Take her somewhere nice. A girl likes to feel the sun on her face.'

'Sadie doesn't like the sun,' he said. 'She prefers a cooler climate. Don't you, babe?'

Sadie smiled thinly back at him. 'It depends on the company.'

'There you go,' Cheryl said, completely oblivious to the undercurrent. 'A week away, a couple of weeks. How about the mountains? How about Switzerland? What could be nicer?'

Stone rubbed his chin as if he was giving it some genuine thought. 'Yeah, somewhere with lots of snow and ice. That'd make a change.'

'I prefer the warm myself,' Cheryl continued. 'Mind, you've got to go a long way to get any decent sun at this time of year.'

Barry put his elbows on the table and grunted. 'Don't go getting any ideas. I've too much work to be thinking about a holiday right now.'

The conversation moved on, food was eaten, wine was drunk, bets were placed and the dogs continued to run round in circles. Nathan Stone was genial, charming and attentive to his guests. From time to time, Sadie gave him a sidelong glance. Although he appeared on the surface to be completely absorbed, completely at ease, there was a distance in his eyes, almost as if he was just going through the motions. But then he probably was. The wining and dining was simply something he had to put up with in order to secure a deal with Barry Moss.

It was shortly after ten when the two couples parted company and went their separate ways with handshakes and pecks on the cheek and suggestions they should do it again some time. Sadie climbed into the Daimler, sat back and sighed. The night hadn't been that bad but she was still relieved it was over. She had been on edge throughout the evening, worried that she might say or do something wrong and that Stone would change his mind about giving her Eddie's address.

As he started the motor and swept out of the car park, Sadie examined Stone's lean, enigmatic face. He was hard to read, the type of man who didn't give much away. 'So how did it go? Do you reckon he's up for it?'

'Maybe.'

'Only maybe?'

'It's a big job,' he said. 'Barry's not the impulsive sort, but he knows a good deal when he sees it. He'll think it over, check out the site and do the sums. Hopefully, he'll say yes, but even if he doesn't it's not the end of the world. There's plenty more builders out there.'

Sadie found herself wondering how much Barry Moss knew about Stone's connections to the underworld. But of course he knew – how could he not? Anyway, it was none of her business. After tonight, she'd never see any of these people again. Her part in it all was finished.

'And you?' he asked.

'Me?'

That grin tugged at the corners of his mouth again. 'How was it for you?'

She threw him one of her cooler looks. 'An experience,' she said.

'Well, that's what life's all about, huh? It would be mighty boring if every day was the same.' He stopped at a set of red traffic lights and tapped his fingers on the wheel while he waited for them to change. 'And actually, I think Cheryl quite liked you.'

'There's no need to sound so surprised.'

'Well, you can be a bit . . . '

'A bit what?'

He paused for a few seconds as if searching for the right word. 'Snippy,' he said eventually.

Sadie released a waspish breath. 'Yeah, well, you'd be a bit snippy too if you'd been forced into doing something you didn't want to do.'

'Jeez, we're not back on that again, are we? I thought we'd got that sorted.'

'You thought wrong.'

'And, as it happens, I haven't forced you to do anything. I offered you a deal. You accepted.'

'As if I had a choice.'

'There's always a choice. Maybe you should learn when to let things go.'

'Maybe you shouldn't put people in a position where they need to let things go.'

'Ah,' he said. 'You think I should be *nicer*.'

Sadie heard the mockery in his voice and answered in a similar tone. 'Why not? It's always good to try new things.'

Stone barked out a laugh. Then he leaned down and rudely switched on the radio, turning it up loud to effectively drown out anything else she might have to say.

Sadie averted her face and gazed out through the side window. For the rest of the journey they didn't speak again.

By the time Stone pulled up outside Oaklands, the atmosphere between them was positively frosty. The upside to this, Sadie thought, was that at least she didn't need to worry about him making a move on her. There wouldn't be any funny business tonight. It was perfectly clear that he couldn't stand the sight of her and the feeling was mutual. He was cold and arrogant and sarcastic. Any charm he had was entirely superficial and reserved purely for those who could be useful to him.

As if Stone didn't want to hang around any longer than he had to, he kept the engine running while he reached into his pocket and took out the slip of paper. 'Here,' he said, thrusting it into her hand.

Before getting out of the car, Sadie unfolded the piece of paper to check the address. She peered through the gloom and the words that might be about to change her future. All it said, in neat sloping handwriting, was: 93 Carlton House.

Stone began his impatient rhythmic tapping on the steering wheel again. 'What's the matter now?'

'Where is this?' she asked. 'Is it in Kellston?'

'The Mansfield,' he said. 'The estate. The three towers, yeah? Just walk up to the top of the high street and you can't miss them. You don't want to go at this time of night, though. It's rough enough in daylight, but you've got to have a death wish to go there after dark.'

Sadie felt her heart sink. 'Okay.' She put the slip of paper in her bag, reached for the handle of the door and then hesitated. Frowning, she turned towards him again.

'What?' he asked.

'How do I know this is really where Eddie lives? You could have written down any old address.'

'I could,' he said wearily, 'but I didn't. Just go and check it out, yeah?'

'I will, but if you're lying to me—'

'You'll do what?' he said. 'Hunt me down and kill me?'

Sadie gave a small shake of her head. He was impossible. 'Goodnight, then. I'd like to say it's been a pleasure but it hasn't.'

'Likewise.'

She got out of the Daimler and slammed the door. Seconds

later the car screeched away, accelerated up the road and disappeared round the corner. Sadie stood for a while on the pavement, feeling the relief wash over her. Nathan Stone was gone and with luck she would never have to see him again. She breathed in the damp evening air and thanked God for small mercies.

9

Sadie woke on Sunday morning with a dull pain in her temples and a jumble of emotions running through her head. She felt a mixture of anticipation, hope and dread – today was the day she might finally track down Eddie – but what if she met with disappointment again? He might not be there and, even if he was, there was no saying he'd cooperate. He could be bloody-minded at times, awkward just for the sake of it.

It was still dark outside and she scrabbled around for the switch on the lamp. She screwed up her eyes as the light came on and then reached for her watch, peering at the hands on the face. A quarter to seven. Way too early to think about going over to the Mansfield. Dragging Eddie out of his pit wouldn't be an ideal start. No, she'd leave it until about eleven, that window of opportunity when he should be out of bed but hadn't yet gone to the pub.

She put the watch down and turned off the light. But her mind was too busy for her to go back to sleep. Instead she lay on her back and stared into the darkness. Outside, an occasional car went by but for the most part it was quiet. She wondered how it would feel to see Eddie again after all these years. The anger had not entirely gone away, but it had been diluted by time to a thin, simmering resentment. Only a coward, a stupid feckless coward, would have left the way he had without so much as a goddamn note. But that was Eddie all over. The only person he ever thought about was himself.

Sadie sighed into the silence of the room. There was no point in dwelling on the past. What was done was done and no amount of accusations, of bitterness or bad feeling, could change it. And perhaps, after all, Eddie had done her a favour. If he hadn't walked out on her, she'd never have gone back to Haverlea, and if she'd never gone back she'd never have met Joel Hunter.

Thinking of Joel caused her conscience to start niggling again. She knew she wasn't going to tell him about last night and the knowledge made her feel guilty. What kind of woman lies to their intended? Except she wouldn't be lying exactly – he was hardly likely to ask her straight out – only being economical with the truth. This, she knew, didn't make it right but she couldn't think of another way round it.

Last night had left a sour taste in Sadie's mouth and it wasn't only down to the wine she had drunk. Nathan Stone had used her and she'd allowed him to. She had made a pact with a local villain, a criminal, a man who must be involved in all kinds of nastiness, just so she could get what she wanted. She had allowed her sense of what was right and wrong to become distorted in her selfish quest to be free of Eddie Wise.

'It doesn't matter,' she whispered, trying to still that other voice. 'You only did what you had to do.' And it wasn't as if anything sordid had happened. The two of them hadn't even touched, not so much as a brush of a hand. It had all been entirely innocent. But no matter how much she protested, the feeling remained that in some way she would be made to pay for the deceit.

Still unable to go back to sleep, Sadie put the light on again, picked up her book from the bedside table and tried to read. But the words swam in front of her, letters that danced into dots and sentences that merged together. No matter how hard she tried to, her mind refused to concentrate. Instead she found herself thinking about greyhounds running round in circles, about Nathan Stone, Barry and Cheryl, a black Daimler that smelled of leather and aftershave and guilt.

At half past seven she got up, went to the bathroom and had a shower. Yet she still felt dirty, as if what she had done had left a residue of grime that could never be washed away. She paused on the landing outside the bathroom and listened. There was no sound coming from behind Velma's door. She had heard her come in at about two in the morning, heard the key in the lock and the gentle click of the door closing behind her.

At eight o'clock, Sadie went down for breakfast and found herself alone in the dining room. Even the middle-aged man with *The Times* was absent. She poured out some cornflakes and ate them even though she wasn't feeling especially hungry. The two Anadins she'd taken hadn't done much to dent her headache. After five minutes Mrs Cuthbert shuffled in with some toast and a pot of tea and plonked them on the table.

'It's quiet this morning,' Sadie said, just for the sake of saying something.

'Sunday, ain't it? No one comes down before nine on a Sunday.'

Sadie wasn't sure from her tone whether this was meant as a fact or an admonishment. She had, perhaps, disturbed Mrs Cuthbert in her own breakfast. 'Oh,' she said. 'I didn't realise.'

'No matter. Will you be wanting anything else?'

'No thanks.'

Mrs Cuthbert gave a grunt and shuffled off again.

Sadie finished her cereal and forced herself to eat a slice of toast. If she was going to confront Eddie later she'd need all the sustenance she could get. She drank two cups of tea while she thought about what she'd say to him. Stay calm, she told herself. Don't lose your rag or you won't get anywhere.

She checked her watch again, but it was still only twenty past eight. What was she going to do for the next couple of hours? They stretched ahead of her like a great yawning chasm. Too restless to stay put, she decided to go for a walk. Anything was better than sitting in Oaklands watching the minutes tick by.

Sadie went up to her room, put on her jacket, grabbed her bag and went downstairs again. Outside the air was cold, the sky low and grey as if snow might be on the cards. She turned up the collar of her coat and tramped towards the high street. There were a few people around, but not many. Even the station was eerily quiet. Her plan was to head for the Mansfield, make sure she knew where Carlton House was and then have a wander around Kellston until eleven.

As Nathan Stone had told her, the place wasn't hard to find. The three tall towers were visible from just about everywhere in the area. Within fifteen minutes she was standing at the entrance staring down the long wide path that led into the estate. She could see Carlton House almost directly in front of her, a concrete monstrosity covered with graffiti. As she gazed up at the rusting balconies, the boarded-up doors and endless grey windows, she felt a shiver of dismay run through her.

Sadie shifted from one foot to the other. In truth, places like this made her nervous, ever since the Brixton riots, and then the trouble at Broadwater Farm in Tottenham only last month. These estates were all on a knife-edge, steeped in poverty, desperation, anger and despair. The shabby walkways were lawless

61

and the police were the enemy. All it would take was a single spark and . . .

Still, there wasn't much sign of life at the moment. She watched a teenage boy scuttle along one of the paths, his shoulders hunched, the hood of his jacket pulled over his head. He ducked into a doorway and disappeared. Across the far side of the estate, a couple of kids were throwing a football about.

Sadie turned and began to walk back along the street again. And then she stopped. What was she doing? The idea of kicking her heels for the next couple of hours was ridiculous. It wasn't as if the shops were even open. And the longer she waited, the later she would get home tonight. It would be better, surely, to get it over and done with. Eddie might not take kindly to being dragged out of bed, but he would just have to live with it.

She stood there for a while in two minds as to what to do next. If she waited until eleven, she might catch him in a better mood, but what if she missed him completely? He might go out and not get back before midnight. And then she'd be stuck in Kellston for another day.

No, she was going to do it now. With the decision made, she took a deep breath, retraced her steps and walked boldly on to the estate. She tried to look confident as she made her way down the main path, keeping her head up and her shoulders back. Looking nervous or wary was only asking for trouble. It was too early, perhaps, for muggers to be on the prowl but she wasn't taking any chances.

At the entrance to Carlton House she checked the numbers and found that 93 was on the ninth floor. She pushed open the door and entered the foyer, a chilly space that stank of piss and dope. The tiled walls were covered in spray-painted tags and the floor was littered with empty cans, cigarette butts and old crisp packets.

There were four lifts to her left, all with their doors open, and she viewed them dubiously. Two of them had pools of urine in the corner, but they all smelled bad. She hesitated, unsure as to what was worse: taking the stairs or taking her chances in one of the stinking metal boxes. What if the lift broke down and she was trapped inside? On the other hand, she wouldn't be in much of a state to do anything by the time she'd climbed up nine flights.

On balance, Sadie decided that the lift was probably a better option. She chose the least noxious one, stepped inside and punched the button. As the doors closed, she felt a brief flurry of panic and was tempted to jump out again. It was only by gritting her teeth, by telling herself she *had* to do it, that she managed to stay put.

The lift slowly heaved its way up to the ninth floor as if every inch was an effort. Sadie held her breath, trying not to inhale the awful smell. When the doors finally opened again, she leapt out, went quickly to the edge of the landing and gulped in the cold morning air. She stayed there for a while, gazing down on the estate while she gathered her thoughts together.

'Please God, let him be here,' she muttered. She didn't think she could bear the disappointment if the address was fake or if Eddie had taken off somewhere. And what if Nathan Stone had already tipped him the wink, warned him that she was on her way? Her not-so-beloved husband would have exited the building like a bat out of hell.

She frowned at the thought but then swept it aside. Better to stay positive, she decided, as she pushed away from the railing and began to walk towards the flat. She checked the numbers on the doors until she reached the one that said 93 Then without much more than a moment's hesitation, she leaned forward and pressed the bell.

There was a short delay before the door was answered by a

63

slender, hard-faced blonde in her early twenties. She stared at Sadie with suspicious eyes. 'Yeah?'

'Is Eddie in?'

'Who are you?'

'Just tell him Sadie's here.'

If the name meant anything to the girl, she didn't show it. Instead she yelled over her shoulder. 'Eddie! It's for you.'

Sadie felt a wave of relief. So Nathan Stone hadn't screwed her over after all. The feeling was quickly followed by a tumble of others: hope and anxiety and anger. Her hands clenched into two tight fists in her pockets. *Keep your cool,* she told herself. *Don't blow it.*

The girl continued to stare with undisguised hostility until Eddie appeared beside her. He didn't look that different from the last time Sadie had seen him. His hair was a little longer and he'd put on a few pounds but otherwise he was the same old Eddie.

'Sadie!' he said. There was a look of shock on his face, although he rapidly tried to cover it up. 'Hey, how are you? What are you doing here?'

'Can I come in?'

He hesitated but then beckoned her inside. 'Sure.'

Sadie followed him and the girl through to a living room that was littered with cups and plates, pizza cartons, overflowing ash-trays, cans and newspapers. The room smelled of old food and fag smoke. Eddie, never a domestic god at the best of times, had clearly decided to give up trying.

'You want a coffee?' he asked.

'No thanks. I'm not staying long.'

Eddie waved towards the sofa. 'Take a pew then.'

'You're not an easy person to find,' Sadie said as she perched on the edge of a grubby blue sofa. 'Or have you just been avoiding me?'

Eddie assumed his Mr Innocent expression. 'Why would I do that?'

'I can't imagine.'

The girl looked from one to the other before her gaze finally settled on Eddie. 'What's going on, babe? Who is she?'

Eddie grinned. 'This is Sadie,' he said. 'I've told you about her. She's the missus.'

'But hopefully not for much longer,' Sadie said.

The blonde girl narrowed her eyes as if whatever Eddie had said about his married life hadn't been good. Still, that didn't come as any surprise to Sadie. Eddie was an expert at rewriting history, especially when it came to painting himself in a good light. He probably hadn't mentioned robbing her blind or the fact that he'd done a moonlight flit.

'Look, Kelly,' he said, 'why don't you go on home and I'll give you a bell later?'

'What for?' she asked sharply.

''Cause I've got stuff to talk over with Sadie here.'

Kelly looked less than happy at the prospect of leaving the two of them alone. Perhaps she was worried that an old spark would be rekindled. 'What kind of stuff?'

'Divorce kind of stuff,' Sadie said bluntly.

'About time,' Kelly said. 'Eddie's been—'

'Come on, babe. Don't start,' he quickly interrupted. Picking up Kelly's coat from where it had been thrown over the back of a chair, he handed it to her. 'I won't be long. Be a love and just give us some space, huh?'

Kelly's mouth pursed. For a moment, Sadie thought she was going to refuse to leave, but then she shrugged on the coat and flounced out of the room. A few seconds later the front door slammed shut.

Sadie looked up at Eddie. 'Still bringing joy to the ladies, I see.'

He sat down in the chair, flashing her one of his wide smiles. 'You're looking good,' he said, 'really good. But then you never had to try that hard.'

Sadie raised her eyes to the ceiling. 'Oh, let's skip the bullshit, shall we? I'm not in the mood. You know why I'm here so let's just get on with it.' She delved into her bag, took out the divorce papers and passed them over. 'Here. All you have to do is sign and then I'll leave you in peace.'

As if the papers were red hot, Eddie immediately dropped them on to the coffee table. 'So what have you been up to? How are things going? Are you still living at—'

'Eddie,' she said impatiently, 'I haven't come for a chat. I haven't even come to ask for my money back. I don't want an explanation of why you did what you did. All I want is to be legally separated. That's not too much to ask, is it?'

He took a cigarette from the pack on the arm of the chair, lit it and exhaled a thoughtful stream of smoke. 'Maybe we shouldn't rush into anything.'

'Rush? Are you kidding me? It's been almost five years.'

He pulled on the cigarette again and frowned. 'Has it? It doesn't seem that long.'

Sadie leaned forward and nudged the papers closer to him. 'Just sign, please, and then we can draw a line under it all.'

'I can't.'

'What do you mean, you can't?'

'I need to read it first.'

'Fine,' she said. 'You go ahead and do that. I'll just sit here and wait.'

But Eddie didn't seem too keen on this idea either. 'I can't do it now.'

'Why not? It'll only take five minutes. There's no money involved. It's a straightforward split. I don't want anything from you apart from your signature.'

Eddie pulled a face as if she was asking him for a kidney rather than a divorce. 'I need to think about it.'

'There's nothing to think about.'

He gave a sly smile. 'Why don't you leave it with me, babe? I can post the papers back to you.'

'What, in another five years? Come on, Eddie, I know what you're like. As soon as I'm out of this flat, you'll dump them in the bin and that's the last I'll ever see of them.'

'I won't. I swear.'

'Why don't I believe you?' The question, of course, was purely rhetorical. Eddie couldn't be trusted to come home of an evening, never mind complete some basic paperwork. She could feel the irritation growing inside her. 'For God's sake, you were the one who walked out on me, on our marriage. At least have the decency to finish things properly.'

Eddie gave a sigh, picked up the papers and stared at them. 'Shit, babe, there's a lot of words here.'

It occurred to Sadie, as she watched his eyes glaze over, that rather than being up early, Eddie probably hadn't even been to bed yet. He had made a habit of all-nighters when the two of them were together and she suspected things hadn't changed much. 'Long night?' she asked.

'We went to see a band in Camden and then . . .' As if his memory was blurred he pondered for a moment before giving a shrug. 'A few bars, a party, and then back here with some mates.'

Sadie gave a wry smile. Yes, it was the same old Eddie all right. Still living for the day and partying every night. He'd still be doing the same thing, she suspected, when he was drawing his pension.

Eddie dropped the papers again and jumped up from the chair. 'I need coffee,' he said. 'I can't do this without coffee. Do you want one? Go on, you may as well.'

'All right,' she said, realising that nothing was likely to happen in a hurry. 'Milk, no sugar.'

'You don't need to tell me. I remember.'

'Things change,' she said.

He stopped by the door, turned and looked at her. 'Some things,' he said, 'not everything.'

While he was gone, Sadie had time to deliberate on how she felt about seeing him again. She was surprised by her lack of animosity. Somehow, now that they were face to face, she couldn't summon up the energy to be really mad any more. Eddie was weak and feckless and selfish. He would always be that way. He was incapable of fidelity or honesty, and complaining about it was as pointless as complaining that the sea was wet.

She glanced around the room, which didn't improve on a second inspection. A layer of dust covered everything, the carpet was stained and a pall of cigarette smoke hung in the air. There was a poster of The Clash pinned to the wall, one corner curling where the drawing pin had fallen out.

Eddie came back with two mugs of coffee and placed one on the table in front of her. 'So, are you with anyone now?'

Sadie didn't answer his question. 'So, is it serious with Kelly?'

Eddie gave one of his shrugs. 'She's a laugh.'

Sadie found it hard to believe how intensely she had once loved him. It had been a young, mad passion, a fire that had blazed too brightly. In those heady days she had not been able to imagine life without him. She took a sip of coffee, staring at his face from over the rim of her mug. Where had all those feelings gone? There was nothing left but resignation and a soft lingering resentment. 'Well, so long as she's a laugh.'

Eddie sat back, watching her carefully. 'I got in a bit of a mess, to be honest.'

'Huh?'

'Back then, when we were together. I shouldn't have done a runner like that. It just all got on top of me.'

'Poor Eddie,' she said.

'I'm a bit strapped at the moment but I'll pay you back, every penny . . . when I get some cash.'

'I won't hold my breath.'

'Since when did you get so cynical?'

Sadie widened her eyes. 'Do you really want to go there?'

Eddie put out his fag and immediately lit another. 'Still, we had some good times, didn't we? It wasn't all bad.'

'No,' she said. 'Just most of it.'

Eddie flashed another of his wide smiles, placing his free hand on his heart. 'Ah, don't say that, babe. I'll tell you what, why don't we go and grab some breakfast and have a proper catch-up?'

'Because I've got a train to catch. Just sign the papers, will you?'

Eddie flicked his cigarette in the general direction of the ashtray. 'You know, I don't think I've actually got a pen in the flat.'

Sadie took a biro out of her bag and threw it into his lap. 'Here.'

But still he procrastinated. 'Are you sure you really want to do this?'

'I'm sure.'

He tapped the pen against his teeth. 'It's kind of final, though, isn't it?'

'That's the point.'

'I dunno,' he said. 'Maybe this isn't the right time.'

Exasperated, Sadie decided to resort to desperate measures. 'Have you been in touch with Theresa?'

Eddie assumed his innocent expression again. 'Who?'

'Theresa Rimmer. You remember – the girl who lived down the street in Tufnell Park, the girl you were shagging behind my back. Well, one of them anyway. Or maybe you can't remember all their names.'

Eddie glanced away, his eyes shifty.

'She came looking for you,' Sadie continued, 'but then she would, wouldn't she, her being pregnant and all.'

'I doubt if it was mine,' he said. 'She'd fuck anything, that one.'

'Two of a kind, then.'

Eddie smirked. 'It was a mistake. C'mon, we all make mistakes.'

'You could always do a paternity test, sort it out once and for all. Perhaps I should give her a ring, let her know where you're living now.'

Eddie's face paled, his smirk quickly fading. 'You wouldn't.'

Sadie gave a nod. 'Why not?' There was something cheap, something low, about blackmailing him over an unwanted child, but she couldn't see any other way of getting him to cooperate. If she had to play dirty, she would. She stared meaningfully towards the divorce papers. 'I mean, it's not as though you're doing anything to help me.'

And finally Eddie gave up the fight. Snatching up the papers he signed on the dotted line and thrust the document gracelessly into her hand. 'Since when did you become so hard, Sadie Wise? You used to be a nice sweet girl.'

'No, I used to be a nice sweet *gullible* girl.' She stashed the papers in her bag and smiled. 'Thanks. I appreciate it.'

As she rose to her feet, Eddie said, 'You're not going, are you? Stay a while. Finish your coffee at least.'

Sadie shook her head. 'Sorry. Like I said, I've got a train to catch.'

He followed her into the hallway and leaned against the wall as she opened the door. 'Don't I even get a proper goodbye?'

Sadie paused, gazed at his face for a moment – one last

memory – and then put her fingers to her lips and blew him a kiss. 'Bye, Eddie. Take care.'

'I'll see you around.'

But Sadie knew that was never going to happen. This was the last goodbye. She was moving on. She was finally closing the door on the past.

10

Mona Farrell turned the Beretta around in her fingers, feeling the smooth coolness of the metal. It was a small, neat, light-weight gun that could easily be carried around in a handbag. Point and shoot. That's all you had to do. What could be easier? She aimed the gun at the pottery dog sitting on the mantel-piece.

'Bang bang,' she said. 'You're dead.'

Mona smiled. She'd had the gun for three years now, ever since the burglary. She kept it under the floorboards in her bed-room, safely hidden, only taking it out when she knew she wouldn't be disturbed. Some people might view it as chance that she had found the weapon lying in the hall, dropped by the thieves who had swept through the house (relieving her mother of her jewellery and her father of his extensive gun collection), but she saw it as fate. God had wanted her to have it. So she had picked it up, put it in her pocket and no one had been any the wiser.

Mona wandered over to the window and gazed out at the snow that had been falling for hours. A white blanket covered the garden. Usually Sundays were boring, long and slow, tainted by the knowledge that Monday was to follow. And Mondays, historically, had always meant school or college or work. She had not got on well with any of these things. They simply didn't suit her. She'd been expelled from more schools than she cared to remember, dropped out of numerous courses and been sacked from every job she'd ever been hired for.

It was no big deal, though. She was only twenty-three. Why should she be shackled to a desk for the rest of her life? Her father banged on about responsibility, but she couldn't see what was responsible about blowing another human being limb from limb. No, she would find her own way in her own time. Maybe she'd start her own business. Maybe she'd go into business with Sadie. That would be fun, just the two of them.

Mona pressed her nose against the glass. Thinking of Sadie reminded her of what she'd done that day, of what had made this Sunday different to all the others. It was a good thing she'd got to Kellston early or she might have missed the boat. She'd only been there ten minutes when Sadie had come out of Oaklands and headed for the high street. Following her hadn't been so easy this time. The road had been quiet, almost deserted, and she'd had to keep her distance.

Still, it had worked out well in the end. And in a way it had added to the thrill. Every step she'd taken, she'd been worried that Sadie would glance over her shoulder and spot her. But her friend must have had other things on her mind. Unlike at the market when Sadie had definitely felt her presence, this time she'd been completely oblivious.

Sadie had hesitated when she'd reached the Mansfield. Mona had been able to tell that she didn't want to go in there, and who could blame her? It was clearly a sink estate with nothing to recommend it other than cheap accommodation and a constant supply of marijuana. It wasn't the kind of place that any self-respecting girl would want to venture into.

And then … and then … Sadie had turned around and started walking straight back towards her. That had been a moment! She could still recall how her heart had almost leapt out of her chest. There was nowhere to go. Sadie was going to see her. She had to. And when she did, how the hell was she going to explain what she was doing there?

But then Sadie had stopped and thought, before retracing her steps. It had been like a miracle, like victory snatched from the jaws of defeat. And that was when Mona had known that it was meant to be. Of course it was. It was a sign that she was doing the right thing, that God was on her side.

She had hung back as Sadie walked up the path to Carlton House and went through the front door. That had been another tricky moment. She'd had no idea whether Sadie would take the stairs or the lift or which floor she was visiting. All she could do was watch the tower, hoping that Sadie would appear behind the railings at some point.

Mona had passed an anxious couple of minutes, concerned that she wasn't watching the right side of the building. What if Sadie came out round the back? In the event, she needn't have worried. Her friend had suddenly surfaced on the ninth floor, stood for a while gazing out at the estate and then continued walking to the left.

The door had been answered by a blonde girl. Mona could see the brightness of her hair but couldn't make out her features clearly. There had been a brief conversation before a man appeared and that man, she had known, was Eddie Wise. She wondered what had made her so sure. Well, it had to be, didn't it? Why else would Sadie be visiting this crummy estate? Mona had counted off the doors from right to left so she would know how to find the flat again.

Fifteen minutes later, Sadie had come out and walked straight back to Oaklands. She hadn't been there long before she'd reappeared with her holdall and crossed the street to the station. She'd looked happy, relaxed, as if she'd got what she'd wanted. Mona had watched her leave with a mingling of sadness and regret. It was a shame that she was going, but it wouldn't be for ever.

Mona moved away from the window and sat down on the bed, placing the Beretta beside her. She ran her finger along the cool metal barrel. It would be easy for Sadie, she thought. It would be quick. To kill with a gun was a straightforward way of disposing of someone. One tiny pull on the trigger and it was all over. Nothing prolonged, nothing messy. You didn't even have to look into your victim's eyes.

'Bang bang,' she murmured again.

For her, it had not been so straightforward. Worried that the police might be able to link the two murders through forensics or ballistics or whatever it was called, she hadn't dared use the Beretta. Anyway, it was too risky to fire a gun in a tower block – the sound would echo through the thin walls and floors – so she'd gone instead for something more discreet. Eddie Wise, who hadn't thought twice about inviting a stranger into his flat, had looked more surprised than afraid as she'd slid the blade between his ribs.

Mona glanced down at the gun, a smile creeping back on to her lips. There was a certain irony to the fact that in a month or two her father would be murdered by his own weapon. And that, she thought, was a shining example of divine justice.

11

Sadie woke, rolled over and stretched out her arm but the other side of the double bed was empty. She gave a sigh, wishing that Joel was there. The smell of him was still on her, the feel of his touch imprinted on her skin. The memory of last night, of every kiss, of every gentle caress, lingered in her flesh. He must have left for work. Yes, she had a vague recollection of him leaning over to kiss her goodbye. Even though he wasn't with her, there was something comforting about knowing he wasn't far away. His workroom was only downstairs. Two flights of stairs and she could see his face again.

A thin whitish light slipped through a gap in the curtains, telling her that the snow was still lying. She snuggled into the warmth of the blankets. Soon she would get up, but there wasn't any hurry. Anticipating that it would take longer than it had to track down Eddie, she'd taken the whole week off work and now had seven free days to do with as she wished.

Sadie yawned and smiled, luxuriating in the pleasure of being back in her own bed. It was odd how journeys made her feel so tired, as if they sucked out all her energy. She had spent most of yesterday on trains and tubes and buses. She thought back to her visit to the Mansfield estate and the satisfying outcome. She still found it hard to believe that Eddie had finally signed the papers. The first thing she was going to do today was to pop them in the post to her solicitor.

Sadie's only regret was that she hadn't had the chance to say goodbye to Velma. She had knocked gently but got no response. Aware that her neighbour had come in late, she hadn't persisted. Instead she'd slipped a note under the door thanking her for all her help.

Mrs Cuthbert's response on hearing that she was leaving Oaklands had been quick and sharp. Her rheumy eyes had flashed defiantly. 'There's no refunds, dear.'

'That's okay.'

'We let the rooms by the week so—'

'It's fine. I understand.' Sadie had been in too good a mood to quibble over a few wasted quid. It was a price worth paying to get away from Kellston.

Mrs Cuthbert had given her a hard stare as if the combination of an early departure and no argument over a refund was virtually unknown and therefore highly suspicious. 'Not in any kind of trouble, are you?'

'No, no trouble at all. I just had something to sort out and I've done it faster than I thought.'

Sadie had left for the station immediately after this brief conversation. Travelling on a Sunday was a pain – there had been long tedious waits between connections – but she was still glad that she had done it. Being back in Haverlea, back with Joel, was the best feeling in the world.

Sadie stayed in bed for another five minutes before forcing herself to get up. She took a hot shower and got dressed in her old faded jeans and a cream sweater. In the kitchen she wrapped her hands around a mug of coffee and gazed out of the window at the snowy landscape.

She was still standing there, basking in happiness, when she heard the sound of the key in the lock. It had to be Joel. She put the mug down and rushed through to the living room, smiling widely, but then stopped dead in her tracks when she realised he wasn't alone. There were two uniformed officers with him. The smile froze on her lips. Joel had an odd expression on his face, his eyes anxious, his mouth twisted into a grimace.

'Sadie,' he said. 'It's the police. They want to talk to you.'

'What?'

The older of the two men took out his ID and held it up. 'Inspector Gerald Frayne.' He gestured to his left. 'And this is my colleague, PC John Turner.'

Sadie felt a wave of panic wash over her. 'What's happened? Is it Mum? Has something—'

'No, it's not your mum.' Joel rushed forward and put his arm around her shoulder. 'It's not your mum. She's okay. She's fine.'

Relief flooded through her. She might not always see eye to eye with her mother, but the thought of . . . 'Then what? What is it?'

'It's about Eddie,' Joel said.

Sadie looked at him and then at the two officers. 'Eddie?'

Inspector Frayne gave a nod. 'We've got bad news, I'm afraid. Perhaps you'd like to sit down.'

'Just tell me,' she said. 'Please.'

The inspector looked her straight in the eye. 'I'm afraid Mr Wise was found dead in his flat in London.'

Sadie felt her knees go weak. 'Dead?' she murmured. He couldn't be. It was impossible. The blood rushed from her face as the shock of it sank in. 'But how . . . what . . . I don't understand.'

Joel led her over to the sofa. 'Come on, sit down. Sit here.'

Sadie sank on to the cushions, her head swimming. This was unreal, a bad dream. It couldn't be happening. Joel sat down beside her and she automatically reached for his hand. Dead? How could Eddie be dead? She'd only seen him yesterday. The image of him sprang into her mind, him leaning against the wall, smiling at her. *Don't I even get a proper goodbye?*

Inspector Frayne settled into the only armchair while the constable took a chair from the dining table and positioned it on the other side of the sofa. Sadie, as she gradually recovered her senses, was aware of the two men watching her carefully.

'Perhaps some tea?' the inspector suggested.

Joel glanced at Sadie and squeezed her hand. 'I'll do that, shall I? Will you be all right?'

She gave a nod.

There was a short silence while Joel left the room. Then Frayne said, 'I'm sorry. It must be a dreadful shock for you.'

Sadie leaned forward, placing her hands on her thighs. Her hands curled into two fight fists. 'I don't understand,' she said again. 'What happened to him? Was it an accident?'

'Mr Wise was murdered,' Frayne replied softly.

Sadie felt the response like a blow to her chest. Her heart missed a beat and then began to race. 'No,' she said hoarsely, her mouth suddenly dry. 'When? How? Jesus, why would anyone . . . ' Her voice trailed off into nothing. She swallowed hard. A lump the size of a marble had lodged in her throat.

'We can go down to the station if you'd rather.'

'No,' she said, shaking her head. 'Why would I . . . ?' She saw the inspector's eyes dart towards the kitchen and instantly understood. 'Oh, no, you can ask whatever you want in front of Joel.' She stared at Frayne and a shudder ran through her. She had been in London. She had been with Eddie. Did they consider her a suspect? They couldn't. It was mad, crazy. 'When was he killed?'

The inspector didn't reply directly. 'We've been told that you went to see Mr Wise yesterday.'

'Yes.'

'Perhaps, if it's not too hard for you, we could talk about that.'

Sadie wanted to scream that it *was* too hard for her, that she still hadn't absorbed what she'd been told, that her head was still spinning. But she knew she didn't have a choice. Their questions would have to be answered and she may as well get it over and done with. 'I-I went to London, to Kellston, on Friday. I wanted to see Eddie to get our divorce papers signed.'

'That's a long way to go. Couldn't you have posted them to him?'

'I could have if I'd known where he was living.' As soon as the words were out of her mouth, she wished she could take them back. Why hadn't she just said that she'd wanted to make sure he signed, that he had a habit of putting things off? Now she was going to have to explain how she'd actually found him.

The inspector frowned. 'So you travelled all the way to London without an address?'

Sadie shifted on the sofa, knowing that it sounded odd. Quickly she tried to justify her actions. 'Well, I'd heard that he was in Kellston. He's got friends there and I thought he wouldn't be too hard to find.'

'Really? Kellston's a big place. You could spend a long time searching for someone.'

'Eddie is ... was ... a creature of habit. He liked a drink. I figured I'd find him in one of the pubs.'

'A long shot.'

'Not that long,' she said.

Frayne gave a thin smile. 'Go on.'

Sadie lifted her shoulders in a shrug. 'I booked into a guest house, a B&B called Oaklands. It's just opposite Kellston station.

And then I started looking. I went to a few local pubs but didn't have any luck.'

At that moment Joel came back with a pot of tea, four mugs, milk and sugar on a tray. His arrival created a natural break in the conversation and while he organised the drinks, Sadie tried to fight her way through a fog of disbelief to invent a credible tale for the police. She didn't want to mention Velma and she certainly didn't want to mention Nathan Stone. The latter, she was sure, would not welcome a visit from the cops. And seeing as she hadn't even mentioned him to Joel ... Her heart was thumping in her chest. She didn't like lying but what else could she do?

12

Sadie took a sip of tea and looked at the inspector. 'I found out where he lived on the Saturday,' she said, trying to keep her voice steady. 'I bumped into an old mate of Eddie's in a café on the high street.'

'That was lucky,' Frayne said dryly.

Sadie shrugged again. 'Not really. Eddie knows . . . knew a lot of people.'

'And what was this mate's name?'

Sadie plucked a name from the air. 'Dave,' she said. 'I don't remember his surname. It's been years since I last saw him. He told me Eddie was living on the Mansfield.' She gave Joel a sideways glance, glad now that she hadn't gone into any detail when she'd got home yesterday. The vague story that she'd given him pretty much tallied with this one. And he hadn't asked any difficult questions. Joel was a trusting kind of guy, not the sort to probe.

'Dave,' the inspector repeated.

'Yes.' Sadie noticed the young officer scribbling in his notepad. Would the waitress remember her being in Connolly's?

It was doubtful. The place had been busy, chock full of customers. But even if she did, there was no way she could swear that Sadie hadn't talked to anyone else.

'So, this Dave gave you the address and then what did you do?'

Sadie thought there was a distinct scepticism to his tone, but carried on regardless. What choice did she have? 'I went over there but there was no one in. I didn't want to hang about and so I went back to the guest house.'

'You didn't try again later?'

'No. It was Saturday and I didn't think there was much chance of him getting back until late. When Eddie goes out he usually stays out.' She paused and took another sip of tea. 'I decided to wait and have another go first thing in the morning.'

'And what time was that?'

Sadie reflected for a second, remembering Mrs Cuthbert's comment about most people not coming down for breakfast before nine. 'It must have been around twenty past eight when I left Oaklands so I probably got to the Mansfield about fifteen minutes later. I wanted to go early, to catch him in case he went out again.'

'And this time he was there?'

Sadie nodded. 'Yes, he was there with his girlfriend.'

'And how was that?'

Sadie stared at Inspector Frayne over the rim of her mug. 'What do you mean?'

'How did he react to you turning up out of the blue? Was he happy, angry, irritated, confused?'

'I don't know. Surprised, I guess, but not angry. He was all right about it.'

'And what happened next?'

'Kelly left and we sat down and talked.'

'Talked or argued?'

Sadie felt alarm bells going off in her head. 'Why would we argue? We've been separated for years. The divorce was just a formality.' But already she knew that the police must have spoken to Eddie's parents. They'd have told him about the bad blood between her and Eddie, about how he'd walked out on her and fleeced her in the process. Although she was sure they'd have put a different slant on it. 'What's going on here?' she asked defensively. 'Are you accusing me of something? Am I a suspect?'

'Of course you're not!' Joel exclaimed. He looked at Frayne. 'Tell her. Tell her she isn't.'

Inspector Frayne skirted around the request. 'This is a murder inquiry. I'm sorry but there are questions we have to ask.' He shifted his gaze on to Sadie. 'You may have been the last person to see Eddie Wise alive.'

Not the last, Sadie thought. That would have been the person who . . . 'I didn't kill him, if that's what you're thinking. We might have had our differences but they were in the past. I'd never have . . . I wouldn't. I *couldn't*.'

'But the split was acrimonious.'

'He walked out on me, if that's what you're saying. But the marriage was over anyway. We hadn't been getting along for months. And it was all a long time ago, almost five years now. I didn't hate him. I wasn't even angry at him any more. He took some money but I didn't want it back. I just wanted to get the divorce sorted and move on.'

Frayne's eyes bored into her. 'So you're saying the conversation was an amicable one?'

'Yes. I was only there for . . . I don't know, it can't have been more than twenty minutes. He signed the papers. I've got them right here.' She jumped up off the sofa, went over to the table, picked them up and thrust them into the inspector's hands. 'I got what I wanted so why would I . . . There wouldn't be a reason, would there?' She sat back down on the sofa beside Joel. 'He was fine when I left. I swear he was. He was absolutely fine.'

Frayne glanced down at the papers. 'Do you mind if I hold on to these?'

Sadie was about to say that she needed them, that she had to send them to the solicitor, when she suddenly realised that none of that was necessary now. Eddie was dead. Legally, she was a widow. The reality of his murder, the horror, hit her again and she leaned forward and put her head in her hands. Bile rose into her throat. She had wanted to be free but not like this. She had never wanted it to end in this way.

'Do we really have to do this now?' Joel asked the inspector. 'Couldn't you come back later or tomorrow? It's been a shock. It's all too much.'

Sadie raised her head and rubbed at her face. 'No, it's all right. I'm okay. I'd rather get it over with.' She nodded at Frayne. 'What else do you want to know?'

Frayne kept his eyes on her, sharp brown eyes that held more than a hint of intelligence. 'Where did the conversation take place between you and Eddie? Whereabouts in the flat?'

'In the living room.'

'And did you go anywhere else while you were there – to the bathroom perhaps, or the kitchen?'

Sadie shook her head. 'No. Eddie went to the kitchen to make coffee but I didn't go with him.' She noticed the constable glance up from his scribbling and sensed that the question was an important one. 'He was only gone a few minutes.'

'And you definitely didn't follow him, not even to the doorway?'

'No, I stayed on the sofa. I didn't move from there until I left.'

'And that would have been at what time?'

Sadie frowned. 'I can't say exactly. It was probably around nine. I don't think I was there for more than twenty minutes.'

'Where you wearing gloves?' Frayne asked.

The question surprised her. 'What? No, no I wasn't.'

'We'll need you to come down to the station at some point so we can take a set of prints. Do you remember what you touched while you were in the flat?'

Sadie racked her brains, trying to recreate the scene in her head. 'The coffee table, I suppose. I'm not sure. I put the papers down on it. And the mug I drank from. And the front door; I opened that on the way out. Otherwise, I don't ... Oh yes, there was a pen too. I leant him a biro, one of those yellow Bic ones, and forgot to take it back it again.' Had there been anything else? 'I think that's it, apart from the sofa and the cushions.'

Frayne sat back and crossed his legs. 'What kind of a mood would you say Eddie was in? I mean, generally. Did he seem worried about anything?'

'No. He was just ... just Eddie. I think he had a bit of a hangover, but that was nothing unusual.'

'Can you think of anyone who might have wanted to hurt him, anyone who held a grudge?'

'No,' she said again. 'But like I told you, I haven't seen him for years. I don't know who he was hanging around with, what he was doing. I don't know anything about his life now.' No sooner had she said it than that icy shock ran through her again. There was no life now. Eddie was dead. He was gone for ever. Quickly she added, 'Eddie had his faults but on the whole people liked him. He was an easy-going sort of person, probably too easy-going. Nothing ever bothered him. He wasn't the type to go looking for trouble.'

'And so you left the flat at about nine o'clock. What did you do then?'

'I walked back to Oaklands, packed my things and told Mrs Cuthbert – she's the woman who runs the guesthouse – that I was leaving. I suppose by then it was about ten to ten. I went straight to the station but I had to wait for a train to Liverpool Street. It was Sunday service so they weren't that frequent. From there I caught a tube to Euston, changing at King's Cross. Then I had another wait until I could get a train to Manchester. I took the one that left just after midday.'

'And that got in at?'

'Around two-forty. I caught the next train to Haverlea and then got a bus back here. I was home at about a quarter to four.'

'Quite a journey. Do you still have your ticket from London?'

'No, I had to hand it in at the station.'

'Did you talk to anyone on the train?'

Sadie shook her head. 'No, I don't think so.' It was then, suddenly, that she remembered Mona Farrell and the crazy conversation she'd had with her on the way to Kellston. Her heart gave a jolt. But she couldn't have had anything to do with this. The girl had been odd, there was no denying it, but it had just been talk. She couldn't have killed Eddie. She didn't even know where he lived.

Frayne must have seen a change in her face because his gaze grew more intense. 'Are you sure?'

Sadie hesitated. Should she tell him? But then she thought about how weird it would sound, like some ludicrous story she'd made up in order to deflect suspicion from herself. And the only reason she'd do that was because she had something to hide. No, she was better off keeping quiet. 'Only the guy who punched my ticket. We had one of those meaningless exchanges about the weather. He might remember me. I don't know.'

The inspector continued to stare at her as if he knew that she was lying.

Sadie forced herself to meet his eyes, to feign an honesty she wasn't feeling. But to tell him would make matters worse. They already suspected her – she was sure of it – and mentioning Mona Farrell would only muddy the waters.

There was a short silence before Frayne turned his attention to Joel. 'And you, Mr Hunter? What were you doing yesterday?'

Joel was startled by the question. 'Me?'

'If you wouldn't mind.'

'Why do you want to know that?'

Frayne gave him a wry smile. 'We're investigating a murder, Mr Hunter. We want to know everything.'

And Sadie instantly understood why they were asking. They thought Joel might be involved, that they had killed Eddie together.

'I was here,' Joel said. 'I mean, I was in Haverlea. I went to church in the morning, St Matthew's on Bench Street, then lunch with my parents, and in the afternoon I did the VAT.'

PC Turner took all this down in his notebook. Sadie knew that they would check the alibis, that they'd ask the vicar and Joel's parents. It wouldn't be long before everyone heard about the murder of Eddie Wise and the small-town gossips would have a field day. She wasn't bothered on her own account, but it wasn't fair on Joel. He was about to be dragged into something that had nothing to do with him.

'Do you live here together?' Frayne asked.

'Yes,' said Sadie, at exactly the same time as Joel said, 'No.'

Frayne's eyebrows arched.

'Not exactly,' Joel explained. 'I've got the flat downstairs and work space on the ground floor, but we spend most of our free time here.'

'And do you have a job?' Frayne asked Sadie.

'The bookshop in town,' she said. 'Peterson's. But I've got the week off. I'm not going back until next Monday.'

Frayne studied them both for a moment and then slowly rose

to his feet. 'Well, thank you for your time. I think that's about it for now. We may have some more questions so please don't leave Haverlea without informing us.'

'How did . . . how did Eddie die?' Sadie asked, standing up too as the inspector headed for the door. 'What happened to him?'

Inspector Frayne turned and looked at her. 'He was stabbed through the heart.'

Sadie closed her eyes, her mouth twisting. Had he suffered? Had he been in pain? These were questions she couldn't bring herself to ask. Not yet. She needed time for it all to sink in first. When she looked again, the two officers had left the room.

Joel saw them out, hurried back and wrapped his arms around her. 'Are you all right, love? Sorry, of course you're not.' He held her close and stroked her hair. 'It'll be okay. We'll get through this together.'

'They think I had something to do with it.'

'No one who knows you could ever think that.'

But she hadn't told the truth, not all of it. Withholding information wasn't the smartest move in the world, especially in a murder inquiry. And Eddie was dead. How was that possible? He'd never crack any of his bad jokes again, never laugh, never smile. For Eddie it was all over. She felt tears prick her eyes and buried her face in Joel's chest.

'They'll find out who did it,' he said. 'They will.'

Sadie wanted to believe him. She knew she was innocent but that didn't stop her from being scared. She had a feeling deep inside her, a dark kind of premonition, as if everything good was about to be ripped apart.

13

Wayne Gissing winced as Kelly burst into yet another flood of tears. He felt sorry for his little sister but all the crying was getting him down. He wasn't comfortable with this excess of emotion. What was he supposed to do? In truth, he felt out of his depth. He didn't know what to say to comfort her. Anyway, she was inconsolable, so there wasn't much point in trying.

He paced the room, glancing at his watch for the tenth time in five minutes. Where the fuck was his mother? The train from Bournemouth only took a couple of hours. She should be here by now. He had things to do, people to see – the world didn't stop turning just because Eddie Wise had got himself killed – but he couldn't go out and leave Kelly in this state.

It was only eleven o'clock but he went to the cabinet, took out a bottle of brandy and poured a couple of stiff ones. He needed something to take the edge off. Perhaps a drink would help calm Kelly too. Taking the glass over to the sofa, he leaned down and pushed it into her hand.

'Here, have this.'

She stopped crying long enough to look up at him through red-rimmed panda eyes. 'What is it?'

'Brandy.'

'I don't like brandy,' she snivelled.

'Drink it,' he said. 'It'll help.'

'Where's Mum? Why isn't she here yet?'

'She'll be here soon.' Wayne tried to sound confident, hoping that she hadn't changed her mind. He'd called her earlier that morning, got no reply and presumed she was on her way. Of course, her coming would create as many problems as it would solve. On the one hand, she'd be able to take care of Kelly, but on the other there was going to be fireworks when Sharon – his father's second wife – got home to find her here. But what else could he do? At times like these a girl needed her mother.

Wayne gulped down the drink and poured another. Yesterday had been a bloody nightmare. Kelly had gone over to the Mansfield at six o'clock when Eddie still hadn't rung her and wasn't answering his own phone. She hadn't been that worried then, presuming that he'd crashed out and was still sleeping off the excesses of the night before. The flat had been in darkness and the front door, oddly, had been unlocked. She'd turned on the lights, gone into the bedroom, tried the living room and then . . . Eddie had been lying on the kitchen floor with a knife through his heart. They must have heard her screaming across the whole estate.

'That bitch did it,' Kelly spluttered. 'She must have. It had to be her. Do you reckon the filth have charged her yet?'

'If they've found her.'

Kelly wiped the snot from her nose with the back of her hand. 'That bitch killed my Eddie. She hated his guts. She couldn't get over him dumping her. She was always hassling his mum and dad, trying to find out where he was. The evil cow wouldn't leave him in peace.'

Wayne gave a nod. 'Yeah.' He wasn't really listening. She'd been saying the same thing for hours, over and over, as if she was caught in a loop she couldn't escape from. He felt bad for her but at twenty-two she was young enough to get over it, to find someone else. And it wasn't as if Eddie had been any great shakes. Personally, he hadn't thought much of him.

'So why haven't they called?' she whined. 'Why ain't I heard nothin'?'

'Huh?'

'The filth,' she said.

'Give 'em time, Kel.' Wayne was hoping she was right, that this was a straightforward domestic, a row that had got out of hand and ended badly – but he had his doubts. That's why he wanted to get out of the house and down the pub, to find out what other people thought, what the word was on the street.

'How long does it fuckin' take? All they have to do is arrest the bitch.'

Wayne swigged at the brandy. 'Maybe they already have.' He went over to the window and gazed up and down the road. There was another possibility. What if Eddie had been wasted by Terry's mob? They'd had a few run-ins recently, the last only a few days ago. During a bust-up in the Hope and Anchor, Vinnie Keane had got stabbed. It hadn't been serious – nothing that a few stitches couldn't put right – but he was one of Terry Street's boys and Wayne wondered if this was retribution.

Kelly curled up in the corner of the sofa, her long fair hair falling over her face. She wrapped her arms around her knees and rocked back and forth. 'She killed my Eddie. How could she do that?'

Wayne gave a long sigh. It seemed to him that everything had been going wrong over the past few months. First the old man had been sent down for a five-stretch, then he'd had to leave his flat and move back in here – his dad had asked him to, saying it wasn't safe the two women being on their own, although really he reckoned it was just so he could keep an eye on Sharon to make sure she wasn't shagging anyone else – and now this. It was just one bloody thing after another.

As soon as his mother arrived, he intended to make himself scarce. He didn't want to be around when Sharon returned from visiting the old man at Highpoint and found wife number one back in residence. He probably should have mentioned it, but he'd known she'd do her nut and who needed that first thing in morning? It would have been easier to take Kel down to Bournemouth but she wasn't allowed to leave London until the cops had finished their investigation.

Wayne considered rolling a joint – maybe that would calm Kel down a bit. Or would it make her worse? Hell, there was no way of knowing at the moment. His thoughts slid back to Eddie Wise. Yeah, the tart had probably killed him. It was the most likely explanation. Hadn't he walked out on her? Didn't he owe her money? But if it was Terry, that was a whole different ball game. That would be a declaration of war. Wayne might not have liked Eddie much but he'd still been Kel's boyfriend. And that was like being family – well, almost.

Kelly finished the brandy and slammed the glass down on the coffee table. 'I shouldn't have left him on his own. I should have guessed she was a fuckin' psycho.'

'And how could you have known that? Don't start blaming yourself, Kel. None of this is your fault.'

'If I knew where she was, I'd kill the bitch myself.'

And Wayne reckoned she would too. She was crazy enough to do anything at the moment. 'Yeah, well, she'll get what's coming to her. She'll spend the next twenty years banged up.'

'What if she's done a runner? She could be miles away by

93

now. She could be in bloody France or Ireland or fuck knows where. She ain't gonna hang around to be picked up by the filth.'

Wayne was trying to think of something comforting to say when a black cab pulled up outside the house. Thank God. His mother was here. Finally, she was here.

14

As Petra Gissing stepped out of the cab, suitcase in hand, she glanced down the path towards the grey brick semi. The house had been her home for over twenty years until Roy had dropped the bombshell that he was dumping her for a cheap little slut who couldn't keep her legs shut. That had been three years ago, but the betrayal still rankled. It was her pride that had been hurt more than anything else. She'd stuck with that man through thick and thin – and most of it had been thin – and then he'd gone and done the dirty on her.

The old resentments rose to the surface as she approached the front door. She'd fed the bastard, washed his clothes, raised their kids, lied to the filth for him and never missed a visit when he got sent down. And what thanks had she got for it? A goddamn divorce petition three days after her fiftieth birthday. Still, there was one consolation: the old git was serving a five-stretch now and it served him bloody right.

Petra started hauling the heavy suitcase up the driveway. She had probably packed more than she needed but she didn't know how long she'd be staying for. A week? A month? That depended on Kelly. The poor kid was bound to be a mess and she didn't plan on leaving until she could take her baby with her.

Wayne appeared before she was even halfway along the drive, which saved her the indignity of having to ring her own front doorbell. 'Give us a hand with this case, will you, love. It weighs a ton.'

'What took you so long?' he snapped. 'We've been waiting all morning.'

Petra threw him a sharp look. 'It's good to see you too. And I'm in Bournemouth, not bloody Bethnal Green. I've been up since the crack of dawn.'

'Yeah, sorry. Sorry, Mum. It is good to see you. It's just all been . . . ' He picked up the case and carried it the rest of the way and over the threshold into the hall. 'Kel's been asking for you.'

'How is she?'

'Hysterical,' he said. 'She hasn't stopped crying since she found him. And last night they kept her down the nick for hours.'

Petra closed the door behind her and frowned. 'They can't think she had anything to do with it.'

'She's a Gissing, ain't she? The filth don't think twice about stitching any of us up.'

'Well, they'd better not try it with her. Did you get her a brief?'

'Yeah, course I did. Tony Marshall. He was with her when they did the interview.'

'And what does he reckon?'

'Says it's early days. The pigs are still trying to work out exactly when Eddie died. And the only alibi Kel's got is that after leaving the Mansfield in the morning she was home all day with Sharon.'

Petra flinched a little on hearing the name of the tart who'd taken her place. 'But you said his wife did it, that she was there when Kelly left. Why would they—'

'I'm not saying they do. I'm just not saying they don't either.' Wayne pulled a face. 'Let's wait and see what happens, huh? Kel's in the living room. You go through and I'll take your case up. Will you be okay in the spare room?'

'Have I got a choice?'

'Well, you can have my room, if you'd rather. I don't care where I sleep.'

'No, that's fine. Put it in the spare.'

As her son walked up the stairs, Petra hurried along the hall and into the living room. 'Kelly? I'm here now, love. I'm here.'

Kelly raised her tear-stained face and wailed, 'She killed him, Mum. She killed my Eddie. What am I going to do?'

Petra sank down on to the sofa and took her daughter in her arms. 'I know, baby. It's a terrible thing. Don't you worry, sweetheart. Mummy's here. You'll be all right. I'm going to take care of you.'

It was another ten minutes before Wayne came downstairs again. By then Petra had managed to calm Kelly down a bit. She looked up at her son. 'Make us a brew, will you? I'm spitting feathers here.'

'I've got to go out.'

'What's so urgent that it can't wait five minutes?'

Grumbling under his breath, Wayne disappeared into the kitchen.

Petra gave Kelly another hug. 'I won't be a minute, love. I just need a word with your brother.' She got up, crossed the room and leaned against the door with her arms folded across her chest. 'Want to tell me what's going on?'

'You know what's going on.'

Petra moved inside the room, closed the door and lowered

97

her voice. 'Don't give me that, Wayne Gissing. What aren't you telling me?'

'Nothin'.'

'You're a bloody awful liar. Come on, spit it out.'

Wayne turned his back on her, playing around with the mugs and the tea. 'It's probably nothin'.'

'And what's that supposed to mean?'

Wayne looked over his shoulder. 'There's been a bit of bother with Terry Street.'

'What kind of bother?'

'Just a scrap at the Hope. It was a few days back.'

Petra raised her eyes to the ceiling. Like father, like son, she thought. Neither of them was capable of keeping out of trouble for more than five minutes. 'And what's that got to do with Eddie?'

'Did I say it had anything to do with him?'

'Does it?'

He hesitated before replying. 'It could have. Maybe. Things got kind of . . . Well, Vinnie Keane got knifed, nothing serious but maybe Terry decided . . . But he wouldn't, would he? Eddie was never one of the firm so it don't make sense. Except with him getting stabbed same as Vinnie . . . '

'An eye for an eye,' Petra said, knowing exactly how Terry Street's mind worked. He wouldn't have taken kindly to Vinnie being hurt. The two blokes went way back. They'd both worked for Joe Quinn all those years ago and they'd been tight ever since. 'What the hell were you doing at the Hope in the first place?'

'I can drink where I want, can't I?'

Petra placed her hands on her hips and let out a sigh. 'Not in Terry's pub. That's just asking for it. Was Eddie with you?'

'Nah, course not.'

'Are you sure?' She stared hard at her son. 'Wayne?'

'He was waiting outside, okay. He was keeping the motor ticking over in case . . . '

'Oh, for fuck's sake,' she muttered.

Wayne's face took on a surly expression. 'It's not my bleedin' fault. He offered. I didn't make him do it. Anyway, that tart's still in the frame, Eddie's missus. It was probably her did for him.'

'And if it wasn't?'

Wayne turned back to the counter, slopped some hot water into the mugs and gave the tea a stir. 'Then I'll sort it.'

Petra stared at him. He was the image of his dad in every way, short and solid with the same sharp face and thin lips. She loved her son but he wouldn't win any beauty contests. All the Gissing men were ugly – it was in their genes – and most of them were nasty too. 'Yeah, and that'll really help. Who's going to run things if you get banged up?'

Wayne dropped the teabags into the bin, added milk and sugar to the tea and handed her the two mugs. 'The same invisible man who's doing it now while I'm wasting time talking to you. I need to get out there, Mum, and do some digging.'

'When are you coming back?'

'How should I know? Later. This evening probably.'

Petra gave her a son a steely look. 'Don't do anything stupid, huh?'

Wayne picked up his jacket from the back of a chair and shrugged himself into it. 'You just worry about Kel, I'll take care of the rest.'

It was another few hours before Petra was finally able to persuade her daughter to take a sleeping pill and go to bed. She sat beside her until she fell asleep thinking that the hardest thing about being a mother was seeing your kid in pain and not being able to take that pain away.

Since moving to Bournemouth, Petra missed Kelly more

than anyone else. Perhaps she should never have gone away, but after being ditched by Roy, the thought of staying in Shoreditch, of constantly bumping into him and his tart, was just too much for her. Not to mention the pitying looks from the neighbours. *Oh, have you heard about poor Petra Gissing...* No, she couldn't have borne it. What she'd needed was a fresh start, a new beginning.

Once she was sure that Kelly was out for the count, Petra took the opportunity to have a snoop round the house. A few changes had been made since she'd been living there and none of them were to her taste. She wrinkled her nose at the deep-pile cream carpet and red walls of the master bedroom. The sheets on the king-size bed were black silk, the cover a deep shade of scarlet. Like a tart's boudoir, she thought, although it didn't come as any great surprise. Sharon was as common as they came.

Petra went into the bathroom and noticed that it needed a good clean. She ran a finger along the window ledge, picking up a smear of grease and dust. 'Lazy cow,' she muttered. The loo didn't look too sparkling either. She'd have to give the whole place a good going over if she was going to stay for a while. There were enough germs in this one room to start a bloody epidemic.

Petra was on her way downstairs to get some cloths and a bottle of bleach when the front door opened and wife number two stepped into the hall. Sharon, a small busty blonde, looked up and stopped dead in her tracks, her jaw dropping.

'What the ... what the fuck are you doing here?'

Petra scowled at her. 'Taking care of my daughter. You got a problem with that?'

'I've got a problem with you being in my house.'

'I think you'll find that it's Roy's house, darling. How is he, by the way? Enjoying a bit of peace and quiet I should imagine.'

'Get out!' Sharon ordered, jerking her thumb towards the door. 'Get your bloody coat and fuck off!'

Petra shook her head. 'Oh, I don't think so, love. Kelly's in a state, in case you hadn't noticed, and I'm going nowhere until she's back on her feet again.'

'You ain't staying here!'

'And who's going to stop me?'

Like two cats preparing to fight over territory, the women glared at each other, their hackles up and their claws out. Petra was the first to make a move. She swept down the stairs and pushed her face into Sharon's. 'If you want me out, you're going to have to throw me out.'

For a moment Petra thought she was actually going to try – the slut was certainly stupid enough – but quickly she backed off, resorting instead to empty threats.

'You wait 'til I tell Roy about this.'

'Yeah, and what's he going to do about it?'

'He ain't going to be happy.'

'Try talking to someone who gives a shit.' Petra strode off towards the kitchen with a wide smile on her face. Ding dong. First round to her. But she didn't intend to get complacent. The fight, she suspected, was only just beginning.

15

It was after nine before Gerald Frayne finally made it home and sat down at the table to eat his dinner. He sipped on a glass of beer while his better half dished out the beef stew she had kept warm for him. He was lucky, he knew, to have a wife like Nina, a partner who never whined or complained about the antisocial hours he often had to keep. Since their move his workload had, naturally, lessened considerably – Haverlea was hardly the crime capital of the north – and although a part of him missed the faster pace of London it was a sacrifice worth making to keep Nina happy.

For over twenty years, she had put up with the stress and fear of being a cop's wife, of wondering whether he would be another statistic, the subject of the next news flash, the one who never came home. His being part of the Flying Squad hadn't done much for her peace of mind either. Now, as he neared retirement, he was content to return to uniform and spend his days dealing with less dangerous adversaries.

Still, he had to admit that this morning's phone call had set the adrenalin flowing. DI Ian McCloud, an old colleague, had rung from Cowan Road station to tell him about a murder that had taken place in Kellston, and a possible suspect living in Haverlea. Sadie Wise had apparently paid a visit to her estranged husband and later he'd been found stabbed to death in his flat.

Nina laid the plate in front of him and sat down on the opposite side of the table. 'So what did you think of her?'

Gerald dug hungrily into the stew, chewing on a mouthful while he considered his answer. Although it would probably be frowned upon in certain circles, the two of them often discussed cases and he always welcomed her input. Nina was smart and insightful and very discreet. He valued her intelligence and her judgement. 'She seemed genuinely shocked, but then she could be an excellent actress. If she did do it, she had twenty-four hours to prepare for our visit.'

'Don't they know what time he died?'

'Not exactly – they're still waiting on the autopsy – although they think it was between ten and one.'

'Which puts her in the clear, doesn't it?'

'Probably,' he said. 'She claims she left the victim's flat at around nine and the landlady of the guesthouse confirms that she checked out at about ten or just before.'

Nina placed her elbows on the table and put her chin in her hands. 'But?'

'But there's nothing to say she didn't return to the Mansfield. She might not have gone straight to the station. Perhaps she changed her mind and went back over to her husband's flat instead. Perhaps she was still unhappy about something. There's no proof that she actually caught the train she said she caught . . . or that she got home at the time she said she did.'

'Apart from the boyfriend. Do you think he's lying?'

Gerald tapped his knife against the side of the plate. 'In all honesty, I don't know. He seems a decent type but people do all kinds of stupid things for love.'

'Like moving to Haverlea,' Nina said, grinning.

Gerald smiled back at her. 'That was smart, not stupid. I get to see a lot more of you, don't I?'

'Ah, well batted, Frayne.' She paused and then added, 'I think I know her. Sadie Wise, I mean. Did you say she worked in Peterson's?'

'That's right.'

'A pretty girl, yes? Blonde?'

'Is she?'

Nina grinned again. 'Don't pretend you didn't notice. I've seen her in the bookshop. She seems nice.'

'Even nice people do bad things sometimes.'

'I suppose. What was this Eddie Wise like?'

Gerald took a sip of beer before replying. 'It's all a bit sketchy at the moment. No criminal record, but he might just have been lucky. He'd been dating a girl called Kelly Gissing. Her dad's inside for robbery, doing a five-stretch. Mind, that's nothing new for him; Roy's been in and out of nick all his life – just like his brothers. The Gissings are what you'd term habitual criminals. She was the one who found Eddie.'

'But she's not a suspect?'

'She's not been ruled out, but it seems unlikely.'

Nina inclined her head, her face becoming thoughtful. 'Maybe Eddie got involved in something dodgy. This might not have anything to do with either of the women.'

'Now you're just being sexist.'

She smiled again, her brown eyes creasing at the corners. 'It's possible, though, isn't it?'

'It's also possible that if Sadie Wise didn't do it herself, she got someone else to.'

'What, straight after she'd been to see him? Why would she

104

put herself in the frame like that? It's not very sensible. If she was going to hire a killer, wouldn't she wait a few days, a week, a month? Enough time, anyway, for her visit to seem disconnected from the murder.'

'I know,' Gerald said. 'But there's . . . I can't quite put my finger on it. It's just a feeling. Maybe I'm wrong, but I sensed she was holding back, hiding something.'

'Gut instinct.'

'Pretty much.' He felt his nose starting to run, gave a loud sniff and got up to fetch a tissue. 'Perhaps I need to talk to her when the boyfriend isn't there.'

'Are you all right? It sounds you're coming down with a cold.'

Gerald blew his nose, feeling a dull headache tugging at his temples. He threw the tissue in the bin and sat back down at the table. 'I'll be fine. I'll take an aspirin before I go to bed.'

Nina gave him a concerned look. 'You've been up since six. Maybe you should have an early night.'

'I might just do that.' He stretched out his arms and yawned. The long day was finally catching up with him. When he was a younger man, he'd been able to work all sorts of ridiculous hours, but now they took their toll on him. The idea of an early night was tempting, although he probably wouldn't be able to sleep. The interview with Sadie Wise threatened to keep revolving in his head while he tried to figure out why he was certain she was lying.

'So will you see her again tomorrow?'

'Maybe. It depends what news there is from London.'

'Poor girl. It must be dreadful for her.'

'Not as dreadful as it is for Eddie Wise.'

'Yes,' she said solemnly, 'you're right. But I hope she didn't have anything to do with it. She seems such a nice girl. I can't imagine her . . . And how awful to just throw your life away like that. All those years in prison and for what?'

'Revenge?' he suggested. 'A woman scorned and all that.'

'If that's true then she waited a long time.'

'Maybe she's the patient sort.'

'Do you really believe that she's capable of murder?'

Gerald wasn't sure exactly what he believed right now. His gut might be telling him one thing, but his head was full of doubts. Maybe he was searching for guilt where there wasn't any, something juicy to get his teeth into, something more challenging than the usual petty crimes of a small seaside town. 'Well, we'll find out soon enough.'

'I don't suppose she'll be getting much sleep tonight.'

'No,' he agreed. 'I don't suppose she will.'

16

Sadie felt like her head was full of fog, as thick and dense as the morning air. A mist had swept in off the sea and covered the town in a cold shroud of grey. Beneath her boots, she heard the crunch where the snow was turning into ice and felt the threat of the slippery surface. Twice now she had almost fallen, her feet skidding out from under her. It was madness, she knew, to keep on walking, but she didn't want to go home yet.

Last night she had barely slept, slipping only occasionally into a doze from which she had woken with a start, her mind full of Eddie, the image of his dead body as clear as if she had actually seen it. She shuddered at the memory. Who had done that to him? Who had felt such hate, such anger, that they'd put a knife through his chest? The girlfriend perhaps. Kelly had to be a suspect too.

It was unnerving, scary, being under suspicion. *A murder suspect.* Sadie recoiled from the thought. What if the police got it wrong? What if they arrested her, charged her, put her on trial? Innocent people had gone to jail before. She wished now that she had never gone to London. If she could only turn back time, she would.

The ordeal of the fingerprint taking was over at least. She had been embarrassed, humiliated, when less than an hour ago the officer had placed her fingers one by one in the ink and made the black marks on the piece of card. She had felt like a criminal. It was the first time she had ever been inside a police station and she had no desire to repeat the experience.

It wouldn't be long before everyone in Haverlea knew. She could imagine the looks she would get, the things that would be said about her. Joel had called his parents yesterday to break the news about Eddie and to warn them that the police would be round. Sadie had listened as he'd given them a clear and concise summary of the situation. And then he had said, 'Would you like to speak to her?'

Sadie had frantically flapped her hands, shaking her head and mouthing the word 'no'. She liked the Hunters and wanted them to believe in her innocence but she hadn't been able to face the inevitable questions and expressions of sympathy.

'Actually,' he'd said quickly, 'we'll be seeing you soon anyway. We can have a proper catch-up then.'

After he had put the phone down, Sadie had apologised. 'Sorry, I just . . .'

'It's all right, I understand.'

Joel was the only person keeping her going at the moment. So long as he believed in her, what did it matter about anyone else? She had to stay positive, keep her head held high. The investigation was only beginning. Eventually the police in London would find out who the murderer really was. Wouldn't they?

She walked to the front and stood on the promenade peering through the mist at the sea. The waves pummelled the shore, the surf grey and scummy. The cold air crept around her, slipping under the collar of her coat and sliding down her spine. She pushed her hands deeper into her pockets.

Last night, after Joel had rung his parents, she had bitten the bullet and called her mother too. The response had been pretty much what she'd expected, a concern more with what the neighbours would say than the horror of Eddie's death or what Sadie might be going through. Jean Wilson was a narrow-minded woman who took pleasure in finding fault in others. She was most often to be found lurking behind the net curtains, watching the road and looking out for something to disapprove of.

'I don't see why you had to go to London in the first place. Couldn't you have got a solicitor to sort it out?'

'That's what I've been trying to do for the past five years.'

'I still don't see why the police want to talk to you.'

'Because I was there, Mum. I was in his flat on the day he died.'

'Yes, but it's not as though you had anything to do with it.'

'Well, they don't know that, do they?'

'And how's Joel taking it?'

'What do you mean?' Sadie asked, although she knew perfectly well what she meant. Her mother lived in a perpetual state of worry that having found a respectable man Sadie would find a way of screwing it up. She had never liked Eddie and had made her feelings clear from the beginning. Looking back, Sadie knew that this had just made him even more attractive to her.

'It can't be easy for him, having the police round and all.'

Sadie had sighed softly down the line. 'It's not easy for me either.' And then, before they could start to bicker, she had promised to keep her up-to-date, said her goodbyes and rung off.

The sea made an angry swooshing sound as the waves tumbled in. Sadie thought about her mother. She found her exasperating but tried to be patient, knowing that her life hadn't been a happy one. Sadie's father had died before she was two, leaving her mum to bring up a child on her own. It hadn't been easy for her. Bitterness had always tugged at the edges of her existence, a sense that she'd been hard done by, that she'd been dealt a bad hand of cards. Had she married again, it might have been different, but the opportunity had never come her way.

An elderly man walking his springer spaniel gave Sadie an odd glance as he went past. A few days ago, she'd have thought nothing of it, but now she found herself wondering if he recognised her, if he was thinking: *That's the girl who killed her husband.* She inhaled a quick breath of air, the cold sharpness hurting her throat. No, she was getting paranoid. He was probably just musing on what the hell she was doing standing in the freezing cold staring out at the sea.

With that thought in her head, Sadie turned and headed for home. On the way back she went into a newsagent's and bought a paper. As she turned the corner into Buckingham Road, she half expected to see a panda car parked outside the house. Finding the space occupied by nothing more than Joel's blue van, she heaved out a sigh of relief.

She opened the front door and heard the sound of the radio playing. The song was 'Dancing in the Street' by David Bowie and Mick Jagger. For some reason it reminded her of Oaklands, of Velma, of Nathan Stone. It reminded her of the mistakes she had made and the lies she had told. But they had only been white lies about how she had found out where Eddie was living. They had nothing to do with his murder. She wished, though, that she'd had the courage to be more honest.

Instead of going straight upstairs she veered to the right to where the music was coming from. The ground floor had been converted so that Joel could use half the space to work in and the other half to exhibit his furniture. It was a slow process but he was gradually building up a client base. Some people still valued craftsmanship.

Sadie stood in the doorway, watching as he planed a piece of oak. He had his back to her and she studied the curve of his spine, his strong shoulders and slender artistic hands. She envied him his talent and his passion for what he did. He knew exactly who he was, what he was and where his place was in the world. While she walked vaguely through life, taking this path or that, his road was long and straight and direct. Although she enjoyed working in the bookshop, she didn't see it as a job for ever. Perhaps one day she would find a niche of her own.

Joel was so absorbed in his work that he remained oblivious to her presence. Not wanting to distract him, she turned away and started to climb the stairs. She passed the door to his flat, wondering what they would do with it after they were married. The house was owned by his parents and at the moment she and Joel were paying rent on two separate apartments as well as the ground floor space. It would be a help, financially, if they could let out one of the flats. Maybe they should move into his and rent out the top floor so that the tenant wouldn't be disturbed by the noise from the workroom.

Even as she mused on these plans, Sadie's stomach did a flip. It felt dangerous to plan too far ahead as if she might be tempting providence. What if ... But she quickly shut down the thought. She wouldn't get through the day if she gave in to her fears. She wished she had a solid faith, a belief like Joel's, but for her God seemed a capricious creature, rarely there when you needed him and decidedly picky as to who he would help and who he wouldn't.

She unlocked the door to her flat, went through to the kitchen and put on the kettle. While she was waiting for it to boil, she took off her coat and hung it over the back of the chair. The wool was damp from the mist and had a slightly salty smell. Sitting down at the table, she opened the paper and flipped through the pages. She checked all the stories but there was nothing about Eddie. His death, at least for the moment, didn't warrant as much as a column inch.

She made a coffee and sat down again. Her fingers turned over the pages of the paper but she barely registered the words she was reading: Margaret Thatcher being urged to call a General Election, unemployment figures, the assassination of Gérard Hoarau, an exiled political leader from the Seychelles killed by a gunman on the doorstep of his London home. Another murder, and one that got more publicity than Eddie's.

It was only when she came to a piece about Bob Geldof and Live Aid that her head shifted back into gear. The concert had taken place that summer and she had watched it on TV with Joel. A roll call of the most memorable artists slid through her head: Queen, The Boomtown Rats, U2, The Who and Elvis Costello. She could remember searching the faces at Wembley Stadium, looking for the familiar features of her runaway husband, convinced that Eddie must be in the crowd somewhere. She had forgotten to ask when they'd met on Sunday. And now the time for asking was over.

Half an hour later Joel came upstairs. 'Hey, I didn't realise you were back. How did it go?'

'Not bad, thanks,' she said. 'It didn't take long.' He had offered to go with her to the police station but she had turned him down. There were some things, she thought, that you had to face on your own.

'This came for you,' he said, brandishing a small package. 'The postman just dropped it off.'

'Oh, thanks.' Sadie took the Jiffy bag from him and examined the front. She didn't recognise the handwriting on the label, a round, almost childlike scrawl. Who was it from? What was it? She wasn't expecting anything. Turning the packet over, she saw that there was no return address. She ripped open the flap and pulled out the contents.

Inside was a slim paperback and as she caught sight of the title the blood drained from her face and her hands began to shake. *Strangers on a Train.* As if the book was red hot, she quickly dropped it on the table.

'What is it?' Joel asked. 'What's wrong?'

But all Sadie could think about was Mona Farrell and a mad conversation on a train. *You could kill my father and I could kill Eddie.* And now . . . this was a message, wasn't it? The crazy girl had sent the book because she'd actually gone through with it. Suddenly, she felt nauseous.

'Sadie?'

She looked up at him, her mouth dry, her heart pounding in her chest. Sweat prickled her forehead. Now was the time to come clean, to tell him everything. But as she gazed into his trusting brown eyes, she still couldn't bring herself to do it. What was stopping her? She knew what it was: a fear that he might not believe her side of the story. The tale was so incredible, so bizarre. What if a tiny seed of doubt started growing in his mind? What if he thought that she'd agreed to the arrangement?

'It's nothing,' she said, snatching up the paperback again and flicking through the pages to see if there was a note inside. There wasn't. But Mona must have sent it. Who else could it have been? Glancing up again, she saw the puzzled, concerned expression on Joel's face. 'I was . . . I was just thinking about Eddie.' The lie was out of her mouth before she could stop it. 'He bought me a copy of this book once. It gave me a shock, you know, seeing it again.'

Joel placed a hand on her shoulder. 'It'll get easier. It's hard now but . . .'

'I know,' she said, forcing a smile and trying to affect a

calmness she didn't feel. She put the book down and pushed it away. 'I leant it to a friend ages ago. I didn't think I'd ever see it again.'

Joel leaned over and picked it up. 'It looks brand new,' he said. 'I don't think it's even been read.'

'Maybe she lost it and bought me a new one.'

'That was nice of her.'

Sadie gave a vague nod while her thoughts continued to race. How could it be Mona? The girl didn't even know where she lived. Except . . . God, yes, she might have mentioned Haverlea when they were talking. And then there was the private investigator's report with Eddie's photo clipped to it. Her address had been written at the top. Had Mona memorised it? It was possible; she had spent a long time staring at the picture.

'Would you like a drink?' Joel asked, putting the book down and walking across the kitchen to turn on the kettle.

'No thanks. I've just had one.' Suddenly, Sadie felt like the walls were closing in on her. She couldn't breathe, couldn't think straight. She had to get out. Quickly, she rose to her feet and put on her coat. 'I promised Mum I'd pop in and see her. I'll catch you later, yeah?'

'Okay. Say hello from me.'

'I will.'

It took every inch of her will power to walk calmly out of the room but once she was free of the flat she sprinted down the stairs, taking them two at a time before launching herself through the front door and out into the street. She gulped in the cold air as she half walked, half jogged to the corner. Where was she going? She had no idea. She just needed to be alone, to try and figure things out.

Sadie's breath flew from her mouth in small misty clouds. Maybe she was getting it all wrong. It was possible that Mona had read about Eddie's death in one of the London papers and sent the book as a joke. But what kind of joke was that? You'd have to be sick in the head to do something so bizarre. But then Mona wasn't exactly normal. She'd gathered that much even from the short amount of time they'd spent together.

Sadie's legs felt unsteady as if her knees might give way, but she pushed on, tramping through the thin layer of snow. 'She couldn't,' she muttered, 'she wouldn't.' And Mona hadn't even known where to find Eddie. But then she recalled looking out of the window at Oaklands and seeing the dark-haired girl going into the station, only the back of her head but familiar enough to give her a jolt. Not to mention that sensation she'd had in Kellston market, the feeling that someone's eyes were on her. Was it possible that Mona had followed her there?

Sadie could feel a sense of panic rising in her chest. If it was true, if Mona really had done it, then she had to go to the police. No matter how crazy it sounded, she had to tell them. With her stomach churning she set off for the station, determined not to bottle it this time. She would ask for Inspector Frayne and tell him everything.

With her clenched hands deep in her pockets, Sadie walked with her shoulders hunched and her head down. She could imagine Frayne's face when she told him what had happened – incredulity and disbelief. And the inevitable question: Why hadn't she mentioned it before? She tried to figure out what she'd say: that she hadn't thought anything of it, that she'd thought Mona was just sounding off. But then she'd received the book through the post and ... and what? That she now thought Mona Farrell must be the killer?

The longer Sadie walked, the less convinced she became that Mona could have done it. The girl was half the weight of Eddie and why would he even let her into the flat? And to kill someone in cold blood like that, to take a knife and plunge it into a stranger's chest – it beggared belief. And what if she was wrong?

115

The police would turn up in Hampstead and there would be all sorts of trouble.

When she reached Queen Elizabeth Road, Sadie slowed her pace. It would be the second time today she'd been to the police station. She stared at the low, grey brick building, wondering if Frayne was inside. Already she could feel his eyes boring into her. As she grew closer, her nerve began to fail and she wondered if she was doing the right thing. What if it turned out that someone else had killed Eddie? Maybe it had been Kelly or a dubious business associate. It could even have been a robbery that went wrong. If she hung on for a day or two, she might know more.

What to do? She couldn't decide. If she wasn't careful, she could end up being accused of wasting police time. Mona's words, *It's a done deal,* came back to haunt her, but she pushed them away, not wanting to hear. 'I'll wait,' she muttered. 'Shall I wait?' She wasn't sure if her indecision was based on rational thought or pure cowardice, although she suspected the latter.

Sadie stopped as she drew level with the police station. She gazed across the road at the building, its edges made blurry by the mist. She stamped her feet on the ground, trying to keep warm. Yes or no? Once she walked through those doors and asked for Inspector Frayne there would be no turning back. She would start a ball rolling over which she'd have no control.

Perhaps it wouldn't hurt to wait a while. Only fools rush in. The arrival of the book had thrown her into panic. She hadn't thought things through properly. She should give it forty-eight hours and see if there were any developments. Maybe by then Eddie's killer would have been caught. Or maybe not.

Sadie worried on her lower lip. Whatever decision she made she could come to regret it. She was stuck between a rock and a hard place. She knew what Joel would say: Tell the truth, be honest, get it all out in the open. But she wasn't Joel. She never

116

saw things in the same black and white way that he did. Her life was filled with tones of grey.

The door to the police station opened and a couple of uniformed officers strolled out. Their appearance gave her a start as if they might be about to arrest her. She turned and quickly walked away. 'You're innocent,' she muttered under her breath. 'You've got nothing to fear.'

But she was afraid. The fear seeped through her, infecting her bones, her nerves, her reason. She was terrified of speaking the words out loud – *Mona Farrell might have killed Eddie* – in case they turned out to be true.

17

Gerald Frayne sat at his desk, trying to concentrate on the papers in front of him. He had woken full of cold with a runny nose, aching sinuses and a throbbing head. There was even a dull ache running the length of his spine. He'd been tempted to stay in bed, to call in sick, but he was curious about the Eddie Wise case and wanted to know if there were any developments.

A number of faxed sheets had come through from Ian McCloud at Cowan Road, including the autopsy report on the victim. No big surprises there. Killed instantly by a single stab wound to the heart. Rigor mortis had already set in by the time the body was found and the estimated time of death was between ten and twelve on Sunday morning.

The report from forensics didn't shed any fresh light on the situation either. No prints on the weapon – the assailant had probably been wearing gloves – and Kelly Gissing claimed that she had never seen the knife before and was certain that it didn't belong to Eddie. It was a brand new run-of-the-mill kitchen knife available in lots of stores all over the country.

Multiple sets of fingerprints had been found in the flat –

most of them unidentified – and they probably went back weeks, even months. The flat, apparently, was often full of people and Eddie clearly hadn't been the most domesticated man in the world. The prints from Sadie Wise had been forwarded to Cowan Road and Gerald would have to wait to see if they turned up in the kitchen or anywhere else they shouldn't be.

PC John Turner, who was sitting on the other side of the desk, stared at his boss with concern. 'You don't look well, guv.'

'It's only a cold,' Gerald said, blowing his nose again. His head felt hot and he thought he might be running a temperature. It would be just his luck to go down with a dose of flu in the middle of what could turn out to be the most interesting investigation that had come his way in a while. Mind over matter, he told himself, trying to staying focused. 'Anything more on Eddie Wise?'

Turner shuffled the papers on his knee. 'He worked part-time in a pub in Kellston, the Speckled Hen. He was into music, bands, that kind of thing. Nothing much from the neighbours. They knew him by sight but that was about it.'

This didn't surprise Gerald. Whether Eddie had been the angel Gabriel or the Devil incarnate, the residents of the Mansfield estate would keep shtum about it. Talking to the law – whatever the subject – was liable to get you branded a grass. 'And what about Sadie Wise? None of them saw her arrive or leave?'

'No, guv.' Turner frowned as he flicked through another of McCloud's reports. 'Eddie's parents weren't a big fan, though. They claim she wouldn't leave them alone, that she was always calling them up, hassling them for his address. They reckoned it was more than a divorce she was after, that she wanted her money back too.'

'How much are we talking about?'

Turner shook his head. 'Doesn't say.' He paused and then asked, 'Do you really think she had something to do with it?'

Gerald gave a shrug, causing a thin ache to run across his shoulders. 'Can't rule it out.'

'Only the guesthouse woman, Mrs Olive Cuthbert, has verified that she left at the time she said she did. They've found the ticket collector, too, and he thinks he remembers her. Not a hundred per cent but he's pretty sure.'

Which blew Gerald's theory about her going back to the Mansfield out of the water. He felt a faint rush of disappointment. Still, just because she hadn't wielded the knife herself didn't mean that she was innocent. He was still pondering on this when Turner pushed a faxed copy of a newspaper report across the desk.

'This was in the *Evening Standard* yesterday.'

The report of Eddie's murder was brief but it was accompanied by a photograph of him and Sadie on their wedding day. The couple were standing on the steps of Finsbury Town Hall, all smiles. He was kitted out in a very Seventies-looking brown suit and she was wearing a short pale dress that might have been cream – it was impossible to tell exactly what colour from the fax – and knee-high boots. Her fair hair was longer than it was now, reaching almost to her waist. He wondered where the London paper had got the picture. From Eddie's family perhaps? 'Well, I suppose it might jog someone's memory.'

'And Joel Hunter's alibi pans out. Unless his parents *and* the vicar are covering for him.'

Gerald smiled. 'What are the chances?'

'So what next? Do we go and to talk to Sadie Wise again?'

'No, not right now. She's got something on her mind, but she's not prepared to share it yet. Let's leave her to stew for a while.'

PC John Turner furrowed his brow. 'I don't get it, though. If it was a spur-of-the-moment thing, a row about the divorce, that would make sense, but it can't have been . . . well, not if the autopsy's right about the time of death. And if she got someone else to kill him . . . why on earth would she do that? Surely she can't have hated him that much? It's been years since he left her and she's with someone else now. There's no life insurance so she wouldn't benefit financially. I don't get what the motive is.'

Gerald gave a shrug. Turner was young and enthusiastic, eager to make a mark in his chosen career. He liked the man and knew he was bright, but suspected that he wouldn't stay long in Haverlea. Once the constable had passed his sergeant's exams, he'd be looking for bigger challenges than this seaside town could offer him. 'Just because we can't see the motive yet, doesn't mean there isn't one.'

'So how do we find it?'

Gerald sneezed loudly and reached for the box of tissues. When he'd finished mopping up his nose, he threw the damp tissues into the bin. 'We keep digging,' he said, 'until we find out where the secrets are buried.'

18

Petra Gissing was on her hands and knees keeping up a stream of muttered imprecations as she scrubbed at the kitchen floor. 'Slut ... bitch ... cow ... whore ...' How could anyone let this amount of dirt accumulate? The lino was sticky and thick with grime. She had not been able to find any rubber gloves and already her hands were turning red from the bleach.

For years Petra had kept this house spotless and now it was more like a squat than a family home. It was no longer her job to keep the place clean, but what choice did she have? She wasn't prepared to live in squalor, no matter how much she resented doing Sharon's job for her. The little tart had gone out first thing this morning and still hadn't come back. God knows where she was – probably screwing some other poor sucker for whatever she could get out of him. Cash would be tight now that Roy was inside and Sharon wasn't the type to go without.

As Petra worked her way around the edges of the oven, she reassured herself with the thought that the relationship wouldn't last. Roy was a pain in the arse when he was banged up –

demanding, paranoid and spiteful. She'd give it six months before Sharon bailed and found herself an easier ride. And then . . . well, Roy would be left high and dry with only Wayne to rely on. And much as she loved her son, he wasn't exactly the sharpest knife in the drawer. He wasn't overly keen on prison visiting either, especially when it involved a long slog to Suffolk. Roy would be lucky to see him once a month.

A plan was gradually forming in Petra's head. Bournemouth was nice enough but she had never really settled there. London was her home, where she belonged, and it tugged on her heart like an old lover. Not that she wanted Roy – that ship had sailed long ago – but she did want her house back and to be closer to her kids. To some the old backstreet semi might only seem like bricks and mortar, but for her it held a thousand memories.

She dunked the cloth in the hot water, wrung it out and wiped down the front of the oven. Her knees were starting to ache and she shifted position, trying to get more comfortable. Roy had given her a decent settlement – it was shortly after the Hatton Garden job – and she'd taken the money and run. She regretted it now. She should have held out for the house and forced him and his fancy piece to find somewhere else to live.

But it wasn't too late, she thought. With Roy out of the way, there was an opportunity to get back what was rightfully hers. And possession was nine-tenths of the law. All she had to do now was to get rid of the slut and she'd be laughing.

The back door opened and she raised her head, hoping it was Sharon. She was just in the mood for another scrap. Instead it was Wayne who came in, shedding snow from his boots. 'Oh, it's you.'

Wayne gave her a look. 'Who else were you expecting?'

'Take those boots off. I've just cleaned that bit.'

He frowned as if the concept of cleanliness was an alien one, but still did as he was told. 'It ain't your job to wash the floor.'

'Oh yeah? And who's going to do it if I don't? I'm surprised you lot ain't dead by now. Filthy this place is, a bleeding disgrace.'

'How's Kel?' Wayne asked, dumping a carrier bag on the table. He pulled out a chair and sat down. 'Where is she?'

'Upstairs, having a lie-down.'

'You think it's good for her, taking all those pills?'

Petra heaved herself to her feet and sloshed the bucket of dirty water down the sink. 'You think it's good for her, crying all day? She needs some rest. Poor kid doesn't know whether she's coming or going. The shock's been too much for her.'

Wayne sat back, folding his arms across his chest. 'You making a brew then?'

'Why? You lost the use of your legs all of a sudden?'

'I've been working.'

'And you think I haven't?' Petra glanced at the clock on the wall. 'It's only half twelve. What are you doing back so early?'

'Lunchtime, ain't it?' Wayne tapped the carrier bag. 'Anyway, I need to drop the books off with Stacky.'

'What are you using him for?' Eric Stack was a local accountant, as bent as they came and happy to cook the books for a price. 'The man's a creep. I'm sure the bastard charges more than he ever saves you. You want me to take a look at them instead?'

'You?'

Petra put her hands on her hips. 'Why not? I always used to do them.'

'Yeah, *used to*. I don't think the old man would be too happy about it now. He told me to give them to Stacky.'

'Your choice, love. I just figured things might be a bit tight now your dad's inside. No point in throwing money away, is there? Anyway, what he doesn't know isn't going to bother him.'

Wayne thought about this for a while, weighing up his

father's displeasure – should he ever find out – against the cash he could save. 'I suppose it wouldn't do any harm.'

Petra turned away to hide her smile. It was just a single step but it was an important one. Over the next few weeks she planned to make herself indispensable in every way. She and Wayne hadn't always seen eye to eye – unlike Kelly, he hadn't exactly stuck up for her over the whole Sharon business – but then he'd always been under his father's thumb. Now Roy was out of the picture, everything was going to be different.

'Fancy a sandwich then?' she asked. 'I was just going to make one for myself.'

'Wouldn't say no.'

'So how's it going at the yard?'

'So so.'

Petra got out a loaf of bread and began buttering the slices. Roy's scrapyard was fifty per cent legit but the other half was decidedly shady – nicked lead, copper and anything else the local opportunists could get their thieving mitts on. She glanced over her shoulder. 'Things a bit slow since your dad went inside?'

Wayne gave a shrug. 'It'll pick up.'

'Better had or you'll be getting it in the neck. You know what he's like. I suppose you're having to hand over half the takings to Her Royal Highness. And what the hell does she even do round here? She's a waste of space if ever there was one.'

'Don't start, Mum. And as it happens, she does have a job.'

'Oh yeah?'

'Yeah, she's doing shifts at JoJos.'

Petra gave a snort. 'And we all know what kind of place that is. Still, I can't imagine anyone paying to see *her* take her clothes off.'

'She's not . . . She's working behind the bar.'

'And the rest,' said Petra, unable to resist the temptation to stick the knife in. Everyone knew that JoJos was full of tarts and hookers. 'I don't suppose your dad's best pleased.'

'How would I know? It's between the two of them, ain't it? Nothing to do with anyone else.'

Petra scowled, resenting the fact that Wayne clearly wasn't prepared to slag Sharon off. How wrong was that? He was her son and should be on her side. A little loyalty was all she asked for. 'If you say so.'

Eager to change the subject, Wayne opened the carrier bag and pulled out a newspaper. 'Billy gave me this. It's yesterday's *Standard.*'

After wiping her hands on her apron, Petra went over to the table. 'He's still working at the yard then?'

'When he feels likes it.'

'There's a surprise. He never was a grafter that one.' Billy was Wayne's cousin, the son of Roy's brother Lennie. 'If he's not pulling his weight, you should get shot of him.'

'He's family.'

'And since when did anyone round here care about family?'

Wayne, ignoring the comment, flicked over the pages of the paper. 'There's a bit in here about Eddie.'

'Let's see it then.'

'I'm looking, all right?' He shoved the paper across the table, jabbing at the article with his forefinger. 'There . . . there it is.'

Petra leaned over to read it. The report was short and didn't tell her anything she didn't already know, but she stared hard at the photograph. 'So that's her.'

'Yeah, that's the wife.'

'They arrested her yet?'

'Not that I've heard.'

'And Terry Street?'

'What about him?'

Petra gazed at her son wondering if he was being deliberately obtuse or if he'd already forgotten about the conversation they'd had. 'You know what. Have you found out if he had anything to do with Eddie's murder yet?'

'No.'

'And?'

Wayne gave a shrug. 'I've put the word out. If it was down to him, I'll hear about it.'

'I want to know, right? As soon as you find out one way or the other.'

'Sure.'

'Jesus, at least try and say it like you mean it.'

Wayne heaved out a sigh, his heavy shoulders drooping. 'I promise, okay? That good enough for you?'

Petra folded the paper over and picked it up. 'And I don't want Kelly reading this. The last thing she needs is to see a picture of that murderous cow.' She was about to put it in the bin but then thought better of it. Instead she hid it the back of the cupboard under the sink. There might come a time when she would need to be reminded of what Sadie Wise looked like.

19

It was three days since Sadie had been informed of Eddie's murder and with every hour that passed her fear receded a little. They must have checked out her story by now, confirmed that she'd been telling the truth about when she'd left Oaklands and the time of the trains she'd caught back to Haverlea. If she was still a suspect they would have come back to question her again, maybe even taken her down the station.

She pushed her hands deep into her pockets as she trudged towards home. Despite the cold, she'd done a lot of walking in the past few days. Too restless to stay in, she'd wandered aimlessly around the streets, her mind full of dread, her thoughts burdened by what might happen. At night she slept badly, tossing and turning, her brief snatches of sleep haunted by the face of Eddie standing in the hallway of his flat.

It was dark by the time she turned the corner into Buckingham Road. She could see the lights on in the top window of the house and knew that Joel must have finished work. She had lost all track of time. Peering at her watch, she saw that it was a quarter to six; the hours had slipped by without her even noticing.

Where had she been? She remembered walking down by the golf course, but that had been this morning. Since then it was all a blur.

On the doorstep, Sadie kicked the snow off her boots before going inside. She wearily climbed the stairs, her legs feeling like lead. The flat was warm and she gave an involuntary shiver as her cold body met the heat. In the kitchen, Joel was rooting through the cupboards. He turned as he heard her come in and smiled.

'Hey, how are you doing? Nice walk?'

'Yes, thanks.'

'What do you fancy for tea? Cheese on toast or . . . beans on toast?'

Sadie realised that she hadn't eaten since breakfast and that her stomach felt hollow. 'Sorry, I should have done some shopping.'

'You've got enough on your mind.'

'And you've been working all day. You need more than a slice of cheddar to keep you going. I'll nip down the corner shop.' She looked at her watch again. 'There's still time. It doesn't close until six.'

'I'll come with you.'

'No, it's okay. You put the kettle on. I could do with a coffee.'

'Are you sure?'

'I'll only be five minutes.'

Joel closed the cupboard door and said, 'Oh, I almost forgot. You just missed a call. Anne rang about ten minutes ago.'

'Who?'

'Anne,' he repeated.

Sadie frowned, shaking her head. 'I don't know anyone called Anne.'

'Yes you do.' Joel gave her a patient smile as if recent events had addled her brain. 'The girl who sent you the book, remember? I told her that it got here safely.'

129

Sadie gave a start. 'W . . . what?' she stammered. She could feel the blood rising to her face and her cheeks began to burn. 'What did . . . what did she want?'

'Just to see if you were okay. She'd heard about Eddie. She was worried about you.'

It was Mona. It had to be. Anne Faulkner was the name of the girl in the book. 'But I barely know her.'

Joel looked confused. 'I thought you said she was a friend.'

'When did I say that?'

'When you got the book. You said you'd leant it to a friend.'

Feeling herself caught out in a lie, Sadie reddened even more. 'Oh, well, she was never really a mate, just a friend of a friend. It was years ago.'

'She said she'd call back later.'

Sadie glanced towards the living room as if the phone might suddenly spring into life. Her heart had started to thump. How had she got the number? But then she realised that Mona had her name and address and all she'd had to do was ring Directory Enquiries.

'Are you all right?'

She forced a smile, a nod, as all her old fears swept over her again. There was only one reason why Mona would be ringing and it wasn't a good one. 'I'm fine. Just a bit tired, that's all.'

'She left a number. It's written on the pad by the phone.'

I don't want to talk to her, don't make me talk to her is what she wanted to say, but the words caught in her throat. 'Thanks,' she said instead, fighting hard to keep her voice steady. She picked up her bag and made for the door. 'See you soon. I won't be long.' On the way out she ripped off the note on the pad and stuck it in her pocket.

As Sadie ran down the stairs her fingers closed around the slip of paper. She couldn't ring from the flat, not with Joel there, but there was a phone box she could use on the corner. Did she

130

have any change in her purse? She had to call. She had to do it. She had to find out if Mona really had killed Eddie. But the thought of asking filled her with dread.

She went to the shop first, hurrying along the aisles and throwing items into a basket: milk, eggs, bread, mince, mushrooms, onions and a tin of tomatoes. She did it all unthinkingly, her mind preoccupied by other things. She still wanted to believe that this was some sort of sick mind game Mona was playing and that she hadn't really committed murder. You couldn't just go and kill a man like that. You'd have to be crazy, deranged, a psychopath. But then maybe she was. And maybe Sadie had made the worst mistake of her life by not telling the police about her.

She paid for the food, grabbed the bags and went back out into the cold evening air. The wind whipped around, the icy air stinging her face. How was she going to ask that all-important question? She tried to choose the words as she walked. It wasn't the kind of thing you could come right out and say. Even the thought of broaching the subject made her feel sick inside.

Sadie stepped inside the phone box and placed the carrier bags by her feet. Her heart was pounding again as she took the slip of paper from her pocket and laid the coins out on the ledge. All she had to do was to establish whether Mona was guilty or not. And if she was, if she definitely was, then Sadie would go and see Inspector Frayne and tell him everything. She may have bottled it before but this time would be different.

Carefully, she dialled the number. As she stood there listening to the phone ringing, she muttered a prayer that this nightmare would soon be over. *Please God.* The phone rang eight times before it was eventually answered.

'Hello?'

Sadie pulled in a breath, her lips feeling dry. The pips went and she quickly pushed the change into the slot. 'Mona?'

'Hey, Sadie. Hello. How are you?'

Mona sounded so bright and breezy, so *normal*, that Sadie felt a wave of relief wash over her. 'I'm all right.'

'Thanks for calling me back. I'm glad you got the book.'

'Yes, but I don't really understand why . . . why you sent it to me.'

'Because you said you liked it. On the train. Don't you remember?'

'I said I'd read it.'

'But you wouldn't have read it if you didn't like it.'

Suddenly Sadie caught an edge of slyness in the girl's voice. 'Oh, I see.'

'Did you enjoy your walk this afternoon?'

'What?' Surprised by the question, Sadie glanced over her shoulder as if Mona might be watching her. 'How did you . . .'

'Joel told me,' Mona said softly. 'And you're right. He is nice. We had a long chat. He mentioned how upset you were about Eddie.'

Sadie swallowed hard. 'I am upset,' she said. 'We might have had our differences but I never wanted him dead.'

There was a short pause on the other end of the line before Mona spoke again. 'I've got something else to send you.'

'Why would you send me anything else?'

'I'll put it in the post tomorrow.'

'What is it?'

But Mona didn't answer directly. 'Your picture was in the paper. Did you know?'

'What? What picture?'

'You and Eddie on the day you got married. It was in . . . I don't know, one of the evening papers, the *Standard* or the *News*. Would you like me to post it to you? It's no trouble. I can send it with—'

'No,' Sadie said sharply. 'I don't want you to send it. I don't want you to send anything else.'

'Oh,' Mona said. She left a short pause before adding, 'Right, yes, I understand. That was silly of me.'

Sadie wasn't sure what she meant. That it was insensitive or something else entirely? She took another deep breath, knowing that she had to ask but not entirely sure how to do so. 'Look, er ... do you know anything about how Eddie died?'

'Of course,' Mona said.

Sadie felt her heart miss a beat. Her hand tightened around the phone. 'You do?' she croaked.

'It says in the paper that he was stabbed. But they don't always tell the truth, do they? Most journalists make it up as they go along.'

'How did you hear about it?'

A soft sigh floated down the line. 'In the paper,' Mona said. 'Didn't I just tell you that?'

'So you didn't ... I mean ...' But Sadie didn't have the nerve to ask her outright. 'You haven't ...'

'Haven't what?'

'The police came to interview me,' Sadie said. 'I'd been to see Eddie just before he was murdered.'

'Had you?' Mona paused again. 'But they can't think that you had anything to do with it.'

'Why not? I was the last person ... *almost* the last person to see him alive.'

Mona released a peel of laughter. 'Even the cops aren't that stupid. Why would you do it? You don't have a motive.'

'I wanted a divorce.'

'You don't kill people because you want a divorce. Anyway, if they thought it was you, you'd be locked up by now. And you're not. You're a free woman. There's nothing to worry about.'

'There's plenty to worry about.'

133

'You're not too upset, are you? About Eddie, I mean.'

Sadie frowned. 'Of course I am.'

'It's probably just the shock. But there's no point crying over spilt milk, is there? What's done is done. You just have to get on with your life.'

Sadie couldn't believe how blasé the girl was, as if the murder of a husband was nothing more than a temporary inconvenience. *Spilt milk?* Mona didn't seem affected at all by the enormity of what had happened. Was that because she had killed him or because she wasn't capable of any kind of empathy? Both, perhaps.

'Are you still there?' Mona asked.

'Yes.'

'It went all quiet there for a while. What were you thinking?'

'Nothing,' Sadie said. She shuffled from foot to foot, exasperated by her inability to reach the truth. 'Nothing much.'

'When are you coming back to London?'

'I'm not. I mean, I haven't got any plans. Why would I—'

'No,' Mona quickly interrupted. 'Maybe you're right. Best not, I suppose.'

The pips went and Sadie put another ten pence in. Her frustration was reaching breaking point. 'Mona?'

'Yes?'

But still Sadie couldn't find a way to ask the all-important question. It hung on the tip of her tongue like a drop of poisoned water. With her left hand, she raked her fingers through her hair. 'I thought I saw you,' she said eventually. 'When I was in Kellston, I thought I saw you going into the station.'

There was a silence on the other end of the phone. And then that odd laugh came again, more of a giggle this time. 'Who, me?'

'Yes.'

'How strange.'

'So you weren't there?'

'Why would I be there?'

'I don't know,' Sadie said, defeated. 'Look, I have to go. I'm almost out of money.'

'Bye then,' Mona said. 'Take care of yourself. And don't forget.'

'Forget what?'

But Mona had already hung up.

Sadie replaced the receiver, aware that she was no closer to learning the truth than when she'd picked the damn thing up. She ran through the conversation in her head as she gazed out through the smeared glass panels at the street. Mona had not said anything that directly implicated her and yet . . .

As she bent to lift the carrier bags, Sadie had a sudden thought. Perhaps there was another way of finding out about Eddie. She stood upright again and rummaged in her bag for a pen. Failing to find one, she had to resort to an eyeliner pencil. Then, after flipping over the piece of paper with Mona's details on, she dialled Directory Enquiries.

'Yes, could I have the number for Ramones, please? It's a bar on Kellston High Street. That's Kellston, East London.'

There was a short pause before the number was relayed to her. Sadie quickly scribbled it down, said thank you and hung up. She took out some more change from her purse and picked up the receiver again. Would he be there? She glanced at her watch. It was after six now and so hopefully he would be.

The phone was answered smartly after only a couple of rings. The pips went, Sadie put her money in and a male voice said, 'Ramones.'

'Hello, is . . . er . . . is Nathan Stone there, please?'

'Who's calling?'

'Tell him it's Sadie.'

'Hang on. I'll see if he's here.'

Sadie hung on. She could hear music in the background, Marvin Gaye singing 'I Heard it Through the Grapevine'. Kind of apt, she thought, hoping that Stone might have heard something too. The seconds ticked by and she began to wonder if he was ever going to come. She was also starting to wonder if this was a smart thing to do. The last time she'd seen him they hadn't exactly parted on the best of terms.

Eventually she heard a murmur of voices and then the phone was picked up. 'Yeah?'

'Mr Stone?'

'Yeah.'

'It's Sadie,' she said. 'Sadie Wise.'

'I know. What the hell do you want?'

Sadie bristled at his rudeness. 'Well, I can see your manners haven't improved much.'

'Unlike your marital status.' Stone gave a loud snort. 'Thanks for getting me involved in all this by the way. I really appreciate it.'

'I didn't get you involved. All I did was to ask for his address. And anyway, there's nothing to be involved in. *I* didn't do it. *I* didn't kill him.'

'Oh, yeah? Try telling that to Wayne Gissing.'

Sadie gave a start. 'What? Who?'

'He's Kelly Gissing's brother. Kelly was the girl who was going out with Eddie when—'

'Yes, I know who she is but I don't see what that's got to do with anything.'

'Don't you?' Nathan Stone made a harsh clicking noise in the back of his throat. 'Well, you should. The Gissings are the family from hell and they're not best pleased about what's happened.'

'But—'

'But nothing,' he said. 'You know what? I really don't want to discuss this over the phone.'

'So how else are we supposed to discuss it?'

'The usual way. Come and see me. We'll talk face to face.'

Sadie gave a sigh. 'And how am I supposed to that? I'm two hundred miles away.'

'So get in a car, get on a train. It's not that hard.'

'I can't. The police don't want me to leave Haverlea.'

'You've got a problem then.'

Sadie, gritting her teeth, tried to keep her voice polite. 'Look, all I want to know is whether you've heard anything, any rumours about who might have murdered Eddie.'

'Apart from you, you mean.'

'It wasn't me.' She felt a sudden flurry of panic in her chest. 'Is that what people are saying? That I did it?'

'How would I know what people are saying?'

'I thought you knew everything.'

'Not everything,' he said, 'just enough.'

Sadie felt like banging her head against the phone box. 'Okay, put it this way. If I was to come and see you, could you tell me anything useful?'

'Define useful.'

'You know what I mean.'

'Maybe,' he said.

'Do you have any idea of *why* he was killed?'

Nathan Stone gave a grunt. 'Sadie, I've already told you. I'm not talking about this over the phone. I've got to go, okay?'

'Can't you just—'

But the line had gone dead. Sadie slowly replaced the receiver. What was it with people hanging up on her today? She thought about calling him back but decided it would be a waste of time. Nathan Stone wasn't going to give her any more than he already had – which was very little. There was only his comment about the Gissings to think about, a comment that made the hair on the back of her neck stand on end. *The family from hell.* Did they really believe that she'd killed Eddie? It wasn't the most comforting thought.

Sadie picked up her carrier bags and left the phone box. She had made two calls but was no further forward than when she'd started. Joel would be wondering where she was; it didn't take this long to buy a few groceries. It was time, regretfully, to tell a few more lies.

20

It was dark and cold outside and the snow, although it had more or less cleared from the streets, was still lying on the garden. Mona smiled as she made her second circuit of the grounds, her Wellingtons crunching on the ice. She hadn't been sure if Sadie would call – some people had a habit of reneging on their promises – but now she felt guilty about ever having doubted her. A deal was a deal and Sadie Wise wasn't the type to go back on her word.

Mona thought about the day they'd met on the train. She couldn't say exactly what it was that had drawn her; it was something she couldn't quite put her finger on, a feeling deep inside, an instinct, a gut reaction. And it hadn't just been that Sadie was attractive – there were plenty of pretty girls in the world – but because she had a kind of aura about her. Fate, she decided, had thrown them together.

'Fate,' Mona uttered into the silence of the garden. Now that was something else her so-called father didn't believe in. It could be added to a long list that included coincidence, premonition and even chance.

'You make your own luck in this world, Mona. If you work hard, you'll get rewarded. Nothing's going to fall into your lap.'

'Well, we'll see,' she murmured.

It had to be fate that she'd seen that film a few weeks before bumping into Sadie. It was an old Hitchcock movie, black and white, and she'd only stayed up to watch it because she wasn't feeling sleepy and had nothing better to do. But gradually she'd got drawn in, fascinated by the plot. The perfect murder. What could be more compulsive viewing than that? And while she'd been watching, the seed of an idea had started to grow inside her.

Mona scuffed up the snow with the toe of her right boot. Sending the book to Sadie had been a nice touch, she thought. It had taken her a while to find it in the shop as she hadn't had a clue as to who the author was. After searching for ten minutes, she'd asked an assistant for help, a plain girl with glasses and stringy brown hair. The girl had gone straight to a shelf and passed the book over to her.

'Is this the one you're looking for?'

It turned out the writer was called Patricia Highsmith, an American author Mona had never heard of. She'd made a quick scan of the synopsis on the back just to make sure that it was the right novel. Even reading the description had given her a kick, as if she was studying the blueprint for her own future plans.

'Yes, this is the one.'

While she'd been paying, she had wondered if the assistant would remember her. But why should she? And even if she did, there was no reason why she would ever make the connection between the purchase of a crime novel and two murders committed months apart and in completely different areas of London. No, that wouldn't be a problem. She was sure of it.

Mona had used the name Anne when she'd called Sadie's flat because that was the name of the girl in the book – and because she hadn't wanted to reveal her real identity to Joel. And Sadie had realised of course. Sadie had got it straight away. That was because they were on the same wavelength. Their understanding went beyond mere friendship; they were bound by mysterious threads, by ties that could never be broken.

Sadie was smart too. Of course she couldn't come to London. Not right now. And it wouldn't be sensible for Mona to send the Beretta through the post. What if it got lost or Joel was there when she opened the package? God, that would be a disaster. She would have to find another way of getting the gun to her.

Mona strode on towards the high wall that surrounded the garden. As she tramped around the perimeter, she took a half bottle of vodka from her pocket, unscrewed the lid and took a swig. Various schemes were revolving in her head. Over the past few days she had drawn numerous maps of the house and grounds, trying to work out the best way of Sadie gaining access. When the time came there could be no room for error; everything had to be perfect.

She had dropped the idea of simply turning off the alarm. It would look too suspicious. And anyway, there was nothing to say that her father wouldn't notice and turn it on again. No, it wouldn't do. It was a sloppy, careless plan that could too easily go wrong. Plus, the slightest hint that it was an inside job and the police would immediately turn the spotlight on the family.

Mona drank some more vodka, feeling the rush as it hit the back of her throat. She would have to make sure that both she and her mother had cast-iron alibis for the time the bastard was despatched. A Thursday would be good because that was the night her mum went to play bridge; she'd be out from seven until after eleven. And as for herself? Well, she could always arrange to meet some friends in a bar, up West perhaps or in Chelsea.

But that was all detail, stuff that could be sorted later. What she really needed to figure out was how Sadie was going to get into the house. It might be possible to smuggle her in during the day while her father was out at work, for her to hide her in Mona's bedroom until everyone else had gone out, but that would be risky. What if one of the neighbours saw them together or they bumped into her mother on the stairs? And then, of course, a break-in would need to be faked. She pulled a face. It was overly complicated. There had to be a better way.

Slowly, she made her way back across the lawn. She paused by the pool, empty of water now it was winter, and gazed into the eerie oblong of black. There were blue tiles on the bottom but they had merged into the darkness. The hole was like a giant grave waiting to be filled. Lifting her eyes, she looked across at the timber chalet, the place where people changed into their swimming things when it was warm enough to bathe. And it was then, suddenly, that the germ of an idea came to her. Her fingers tightened around the bottle and her lips slid into a smile.

Mona turned away and hurried through the snow towards the back of the house. There was a light on in one of the ground-floor rooms – the study – and as she grew closer she could make out the figure of her father. He was there every night after dinner, on the phone or sorting through his papers. He was a man of habit, never changing his routine.

She slowed when she was a few yards away, moving as quietly as she could. She could see him clearly now. The desk was at right angles to the wide mullioned window and he was hunched over, reading through some documents. Would he realise she was there? She waited, holding her breath, but nothing happened. He didn't even lift his head.

With the bright light on in the study, Mona guessed she was invisible. Even if he did glance up, all he would see in the panes of glass was a reflection of the room. Smirking, she raised her hand and pointed with her forefinger. *Bang bang.* How easy would that be? The bullets would pass straight through the window and into his fat, disgusting flesh.

Mona stepped to one side, making sure her feet didn't crunch in the snow. This was the way, wasn't it? Her heartbeat had accelerated, her pulse starting to race. Sadie wouldn't even need to be inside the house. She could shoot him from out here. If Mona got a copy of the key to the back gate – the one the gardener used – Sadie could come through the grounds and wait in the pool house until the time was right. Then, when she left, she could lock the gate behind her again. It was simple, perfect. All they'd have to do is to make it look as though someone had come over the back wall.

Mona grinned as she imagined coming home and finding the cop cars parked outside the house, their blue lights flashing. How would she react when she heard the news? There would have to be a show of shock, of grief, of tears. *Her poor daddy murdered in his own home.* Well, she could manage that. She could manage just about anything when she put her mind to it.

21

It was Sunday morning and Petra Gissing had already been up for four hours before her son finally dragged himself out of his pit and staggered downstairs. She had heard him come in late, pissed and cursing, banging against the furniture as he tried to negotiate the living room. Now, as he slumped down at the kitchen table, she showed no mercy in noisily clattering the saucepans together.

'Jesus,' said Wayne, rubbing his bloodshot eyes. 'What's with the racket?'

'You want to eat, don't you?'

'Do I look like I want to eat?'

'You look like something the cat dragged in.' She gave an exaggerated sniff. 'Come to mention it, you smell like it too.'

'Ta very much.'

'Just saying it like it is.'

'Well, don't bother. I'm not in the mood.'

Petra began chopping the carrots, hammering the knife rhythmically against the board. 'What's the matter? Got a headache?'

'So I had a few bevies. Since when did that become a crime?' He gave a thin groan. 'For fuck's sake, do you have to do that right now?'

'I could have asked the same thing of you at two o'clock this morning.'

Wayne peered at her. 'What?'

'When you came in. You were making enough noise to wake the bleedin' dead.'

'It wasn't that bad.'

Petra gave a snort. 'As if you can remember. I'm surprised you even found your way home.'

'Yeah, well, I needed a drink after what I'd heard.' He paused and glanced around the kitchen and then towards the living room. 'Where's Kel?'

'She's gone to Romford to see Eddie's parents. What did you hear?'

'I'll tell you if you give me some peace and quiet for five minutes.'

Petra put down the knife. 'Well?'

Wayne leaned forward and placed his elbows on the table. 'Seems that Sadie girl ain't quite as innocent as she makes out. You know that picture in the paper, the one of her and Eddie?'

'What about it?'

'Old Pym recognised her. He reckons she and Nathan Stone are at it. Says he saw them together down the dogs the night before Eddie got wasted.'

'And you believe him?'

'Why not? Makes sense, don't it? She and Stone are in this together. She wanted Eddie out of the way and so Stone got one of Terry's boys to take him out.'

Petra pulled out a chair and sat down. She put her chin in her hands and thought about it. Pym was a skinny furtive bloke who had once worked – albeit in a lowly position – for Terry Street's predecessor, Joe Quinn. He dealt in information, in rumour and gossip, in anything that might earn him a few bob from interested parties. 'How can he be sure it was her?'

'You know Pym. He's good on faces. He swears it was. Says the two of them were all cosied up, having a meal with some other couple. Can't be a coincidence, can it?'

'Does the law know?'

Wayne gave a shrug. 'You think we should tell Kel?'

Petra shook her head. 'Not right now.' It was only a week since Kelly had found Eddie's body and she was still all over the place, ranting and raving one minute, crying uncontrollably the next. 'Let's keep it to ourselves until we're sure. There's no saying what she'll do if she gets wind of this.'

Wayne gave a belch, expelling his beery breath across the table. 'I told you, didn't I? This has Street's name written all over it.'

'Not exactly,' said Petra, grimacing as the smell invaded her nostrils. 'What you said is that it could be payback for Vinnie Keane.'

'Same difference.'

'It's not though, is it?'

'And how do you figure that?'

Petra, knowing that her son hadn't been blessed with a surfeit of brains, had to spell it out for him. 'If Sadie Wise wanted rid of her husband and got Stone to arrange it for her, Eddie's death has nothing to do with what happened to Vinnie Keane. You're making a connection where there isn't one. You're taking it personal.'

'Of course I'm taking it bleedin' personal,' he protested. 'Whatever the reason, Eddie was still Kel's boyfriend.'

Petra gave a shrug. 'It wouldn't have lasted. Come on, you know what Eddie was like. He was hardly the faithful type; a girl couldn't walk into a room without him giving her the eye. You didn't even like the bloke.'

'So what?'

'So you're planning on going to war over some guy you didn't give a damn about. Where's the sense in that?'

'It's the principle,' Wayne said.

'Well, it's a shit principle.' Petra knew there would only be one winner if the Gissings took on Terry Street – and it wouldn't be Wayne and his cousins. It was over ten years since the murder of Joe Quinn, and Terry Street's rise to the top had been meteoric. Within a few months of his former boss's death, he'd taken over the firm and been running Kellston ever since. He was smarter than Joe, less brutal but just as ruthless. Although Terry didn't go looking for trouble, he would never back down from it either.

'That's your opinion.'

'You should have a word with your dad before you do anything.' Petra didn't say this out of any respect for Roy's judgement – he didn't have any – but purely as a delaying tactic. It would be another week before a visiting order became available and a lot could happen in seven days.

'He'll say the same as me.'

'Maybe. Maybe not. But there's no point in going off half-cock before you've got the whole picture. If Terry did organise this hit, then you can get the law to do your dirty work for you.'

'What do you mean?'

'Well, if someone was to tip them the wink about Sadie's involvement with Nathan Stone, then she might finally get arrested. And as soon as that happens, she's going to start trying to shift the blame on to Stone and Terry Street. She'll be singing like a canary, no doubt about it. With a bit of luck they could all go down for a long stretch and you wouldn't have to lift a finger.'

Wayne's befuddled brain was clearly struggling to come to terms with the concept of a different kind of revenge. His mouth opened a little and his eyes narrowed into two tight slits. 'If Terry Street wasted Eddie, I'll deal with him myself.'

Petra raised her own eyes to the ceiling. 'And then you'll be the one doing the stretch. Is that what you want? Maybe you and your dad can bunk up together. That'll be nice, a real family reunion.' She knew it was all to do with male pride, with machismo and respect – but none of those things meant anything to her. 'What's wrong with doing it the smart way for a change?'

'You saying I'm stupid?'

'I'm saying there's more than one way to skin a cat.' Petra was aware that all the Gissing men were the same; subtlety wasn't their strong point. Respect was everything and they tried to earn it with their fists. However, violence could only take you so far in this world; if you really wanted to succeed you needed guile and a little bit of finesse. 'Just think about it,' she urged, not wanting to find herself in the middle of a war with Terry Street's firm.

'Think about what?' asked Sharon, suddenly appearing in the kitchen.

Petra glared at her. The younger woman was still in her dressing gown, a pale pink silky wrap hanging open at the front to show a good deal of cleavage. 'None of your business.'

'Still here then?' she snarled at Petra.

'Where else would I be?'

'Back in your own bleedin' house where you belong.' Sharon pushed past her, switched the kettle on and then, aware of the silence, turned, folded her arms across her ample chest and said, 'Don't stop on my account.'

'We were just talking about Eddie,' Wayne said.

Sharon gave a sigh. 'Yeah, poor bloke. It's a right shame. I liked him. He was a good laugh.'

Petra threw Wayne a dirty look – why couldn't he take her side for once? – but he didn't bat an eyelid. He didn't even notice. Despite the hangover, his gaze was firmly fixed on Sharon's tits. She felt her stomach shift with revulsion; there was something disgusting about watching her son lech over the woman who'd replaced her. 'Ain't you got stuff to do?' she said to him.

'Like what?'

'Like finding out what else Pym might know.'

'He don't know nothin' else.'

'You sure about that?'

'He'd have said.'

'That little creep always knows more than he lets on. You should have another word.'

The kettle boiled and Sharon looked at Wayne. 'Fancy a brew, babe?' she asked, deliberately ignoring Petra.

'I wouldn't say no. Ta.'

Sharon gave Petra a triumphant smile as she reached for the mugs.

Petra's gaze fell on the knife that she'd been using to chop the carrots. For a few brief seconds she thought it would be almost worth doing the time just to wipe the smug smile off the bitch's face. She took a few deep breaths before moving away from the counter and heading for the door. 'See you later.'

'Where are you going?' Wayne asked.

'Out.'

'Out where?'

But Petra didn't bother to answer. In the hall, as she put on her coat and scarf, she could still hear them talking.

'So what's going on with that Sadie?'

'Fuck knows,' Wayne said. 'But I'll tell you something, if I could have five minutes with the murderous cow I'd get the truth out of her.'

'So why don't you?'

'Because I don't know where she lives.'

'You can find that out easy enough.'

'You reckon?' Wayne asked.

'Sure. I bet Eddie's parents have an address. Why don't you ask Kel to get it for you?'

Petra pursed her lips. She knew the kind of damage her son could inflict in five minutes. What was the stupid bitch playing at? Did she want to see Wayne behind bars? Jesus, the slut was only making things worse.

Petra opened the front door and slammed it closed behind her. There was a phone box round the corner. If no one else was going to ring the filth, she would. She'd muffle her voice with the scarf and give them the lowdown on Sadie Wise and Nathan Stone. With any luck, they'd get to her before Wayne did.

22

Sadie didn't normally go to church with Joel on a Sunday but this morning she had considered it, wondering if she should, if it was the right and proper thing to do after Eddie's death. Shouldn't she go and say a prayer or something? And yet it felt kind of hypocritical, bearing in mind that she rarely went near the place. She wasn't even sure if she believed in God, even though – like most people – she was prone to ask for his help in times of trouble. And Eddie had never been religious. If heaven did exist, he'd have to use all his charm to get through those pearly gates.

In the end, she had decided to walk down to the front instead. Now she stood watching, her hands deep in her pockets, as the grey angry waves lashed against the shore. She thought about the man she'd married all those years ago, of the fun they'd had before it all turned sour. If felt like another age, another lifetime. She tried to conjure up the love she'd once felt for him, but all that remained was a thin kind of sadness.

As the cold wind whipped around her, Sadie toyed – not for the first time – with the idea of ringing Eddie's parents. She felt that she ought to, but wasn't sure if they'd welcome the call. Since her separation from their son, they hadn't been on the best of terms. That, however, wasn't the only reason she'd been putting it off; she was worried that they might suspect her of murder, that in looking for someone to blame their fingers would point in her direction. And what could she do about that? Swear that she was innocent, that she'd had nothing to do with it? That could make her appear even guiltier.

The ongoing silence from the police filled her with as much uneasiness as it did relief. It was a week now since Eddie's murder, a week since she had gone to the Mansfield estate and asked him to sign the divorce papers. Why hadn't they arrested anyone yet? For as long as the killer remained on the loose, her name would not be cleared and a cloud of suspicion would continue to hang over her.

Sadie felt a pang of guilt at even thinking of herself at a time like this. Eddie was dead, gone for ever, and she was fretting over her own situation. The truth would come out eventually, wouldn't it? But sometimes the truth wasn't what you wanted to hear. Every time the phone rang, she jumped, wondering if it was the cops or another call from Mona. She wasn't sure which would be worse.

In her head, she continued to replay the two conversations she'd had with Mona Farrell, going over and over everything that had been said on the train, everything that had been said on Thursday evening. She still couldn't believe that the girl was crazy enough to have killed. And yet ... well, it wasn't impossible.

'Oh, Eddie,' she sighed. 'You may have been trouble but you didn't deserve this.'

The wind caught her voice and snapped it away. She gazed out towards the horizon where the sea merged into the sky in a fine line of grey. A few drops of rain were starting to fall. She wished she could talk things over with Joel, that she had been more honest with him since returning from London. Why hadn't she mentioned the strange meeting with Mona? But she knew why not. Because she hadn't wanted to dwell on what had happened in London, not on any part of it. She had wanted to brush it all under the carpet.

Glancing down at her watch, Sadie saw that it was past eleven. The church service would be over by now. It was time to go home and tell the truth. The burden of lies was getting too much for her. She would come clean and tell Joel everything. She shivered a little at the thought of *everything*. Well, perhaps there wasn't any need to tell him about Nathan Stone. What if he thought that something iffy had gone on between them? What if he started having doubts about her fidelity?

'Damn it,' she said, closing her eyes for a moment. Already she was backtracking, trying to think up reasons for being economical with the truth. Perhaps, like her mother, a part of her feared that Joel would suddenly wake up, see the real Sadie Wise and decide that he didn't much like her.

And whose fault would that be?

'My own stupid fault,' she murmured.

Sadie took a deep breath, tasting the salt in the back of her throat. She gave the wild grey waves a final look before turning away, bowing her head against the wind and heading for home. While she walked she rehearsed what she would say in her mind, searching for the words, for an adequate explanation as to why she hadn't been completely honest in the first place.

It wouldn't be easy but as long as Joel trusted her, *really* trusted her, it would be okay. When she reached Buckingham Road, she suddenly got a song in her head, 'I Got You Babe', the version by UB40 and Chrissie Hynde. She sang along to the lyrics under her breath, drawing strength from the sentiments, starting to believe – finally – that she was on the right path.

By the time she reached home, Sadie was as eager to divulge her secrets as a sinner queuing at the confessional. She hated hiding things from Joel; it made her feel deceitful and lonely. She took the stairs two at a time, eager to get it all out in the open, to get it over and done with. But as she opened the door to the second-floor flat she heard the murmur of voices coming from the living room. Immediately, her heart sank. Joel must have brought some friends home from church. She had wanted to talk to him in private but now it would have to wait.

Sadie hung up her coat on the peg in the hall, painted on a smile and went on through. Joel was in one of the easy chairs and a girl was perched on the edge of the sofa with a mug in her hand. They both turned their heads to look at her.

'Look who's here,' Joel said.

'Hi, Sadie. How are you?'

It took a few seconds for the girl's face to properly register, for Sadie to realise who it actually was. She stopped dead in her tracks, paralysed by shock and horror. The intake of her breath must have been clearly audible. It wasn't. It couldn't be. But no amount of denial could change the fact that Mona Farrell, bold as brass, was sitting right in front of her. 'W-what are you doing here?' she stammered.

'I hope you don't mind,' Mona said. 'I probably should have called, but I was in the area and thought I'd just pop in and see how you're doing.'

Sadie stared at her, her thoughts beginning to spin as the adrenalin kicked in. *Fight or flight?* What she wanted to do was turn on her heel and make a run for it. Her heart was banging in her chest, her pulse racing. She could feel the dryness of her lips as she forced a few words out. 'I didn't realise you knew anyone round here.'

'Yes, I've got an aunt in Liverpool.'

'Really?' asked Sadie brusquely. 'You never mentioned it.'

'Didn't I? Well, she hasn't been living there for long.'

During this brief exchange, Sadie became aware that Joel was looking puzzled, probably wondering why she was being so abrupt. But she couldn't help herself. How could she be polite to this woman? How could she welcome her into her home? But she couldn't throw her out either, not without looking like a prize cow. She inwardly cursed the fact that she hadn't got back earlier, that she hadn't had the opportunity to talk to Joel before Mona turned up.

'Anne's been telling me how you met,' he said.

Sadie felt her blood run cold. 'What?' If she was going to speak out, she had to do it now before the chance slipped away for ever. She had to say: *This girl isn't called Anne, she's called Mona Farrell and I only met her ten days ago. This girl's crazy and I think she might have murdered Eddie.* But even as the words sprang on to her tongue, she quickly swallowed them down. The only person who would end up looking crazy was herself.

Mona smiled at her. 'In that pub, remember? The one on the South Bank.'

Sadie's gaze flew between the two of them. Mona, she noticed, appeared different to when they'd met on the train. Her spiky black hair had been smoothed down and the bright red lipstick replaced by a more subtle shade of pink. Instead of wearing black, she was dressed in a demure navy blue dress with a cream cardigan. 'Was it?'

'Yes, you were with Eddie and the two of you—'

But before Mona could embellish her imaginary tale, Sadie lurched forward on unsteady legs and made a dash for the kitchen. She felt like she was going to be sick. Leaning over the sink, she closed her eyes and clung tightly to the cool metal edge. Her throat contracted but only a thin dry retching sound came out.

Joel hurried in after her and placed an arm protectively

around her shoulder. 'What's wrong? What's the matter? Are you ill?'

Sadie's lips parted and she tried to speak but couldn't.

'You look as white as a sheet,' he said.

She felt hot and feverish. Quickly she ran the tap and splashed some cold water on her face. The nausea passed leaving in its wake a dull, ugly dread. She knew she had to pull herself together, try and stop herself from falling to pieces. 'It's nothing,' she said. 'I just . . . It must have been something I ate. I'm okay now. I'm fine.'

Joel passed her a tea towel. 'You don't look fine.'

Sadie dried off her face, glanced towards the living room and lowered her voice. 'How . . . how long has she been here for?'

'Not long. Only twenty minutes or so. She was at the front door when I got back.' He paused and then added, 'We've been having a chat. She seems nice.'

Sadie flinched at the word. Nice? He had no idea what he was talking about. And he had no idea either that her sudden desire to vomit had been a reaction to finding Mona Farrell in her living room. 'I don't understand what she's doing here.' And then, because that came out sounding petulant, she quickly continued, 'I mean, I don't know her that well. It's not as though we're best friends or anything. Why would she turn up out of the blue?'

He gave a shrug. 'I think it's like she said. She was just in the area. She'd heard about Eddie and wanted to make sure you were okay.'

And Sadie knew that if she was going to tell the truth, now was the time. If she didn't, there would be no going back. 'Joel,' she began, 'there's something—'

But before she could even start to explain, Mona's voice came from the doorway. 'Are you all right, Sadie?'

Sadie glared back at her. 'I'm fine.'

'Are you sure? Is there anything I can do?'

Yes, Sadie wanted to scream, *you can get out of my flat and leave me alone.* But instead she simply shook her head and muttered, 'No, no I'm all right.'

'Maybe we should leave this afternoon,' Joel said. 'I'm sure Mum won't mind.'

It was only at that moment that Sadie remembered they were supposed to be going over to Joel's parents' house for his mother's birthday celebrations. It was an event she hadn't been looking forward to, even though she liked Frank and Emily Hunter. She knew that the local gossips would have been busy whispering about Eddie's murder and didn't relish the prospect of being the focus of their attention. On the other hand, if she didn't attend, it might look like she had something to hide. 'Of course we have to go,' she said, feigning more enthusiasm than she actually felt. 'It's her birthday.' And also, she thought, it would be a good excuse to get rid of Mona.

'Oh, I should get off,' Mona said. 'I didn't realise you had plans. I don't want to be in the way.'

And Joel, forever polite, then said the last words Sadie wanted to hear. 'You're not. You should come along if you've nothing else to do.'

Sadie threw him a pleading look but it was already too late. The invitation had been made and couldn't be withdrawn.

'Are you sure?' Mona asked. 'I wouldn't want to intrude.'

'You wouldn't be. Lots of people are coming. You're more than welcome. Isn't she, Sadie?'

Sadie, having been put on the spot, could hardly say no. 'Yes,' she mumbled. 'Of course.'

'Good. That's settled then. We'll all go together.'

'I'd better get changed,' Sadie said. 'I won't be long.' She hurried out of the kitchen, her eyes briefly meeting Mona's as she passed. There was, she thought, a gleam of triumph in them.

With a sinking heart, she went through the living room and into the bedroom.

'No, no, no,' she muttered as she closed the door behind her. She sat down on the bed and put her head in her hands. Jesus, why had Joel had to do that? Why did he always have to be so damned pleasant? Now they were stuck with her for the whole afternoon. Mona Farrell was a loose cannon and God knows what she might come out with at the party.

There was still time to do something. Sadie stared towards the door, knowing that all she had to do was to open it and give Joel a shout. All she had to do was to sit him down and explain. Except she didn't have any evidence, nothing solid at least. The story was so strange, so bizarre, that he might end up thinking that *she* was the one who had lost her marbles. It wasn't as if Mona had actually confessed. What if the girl was just living out some delusional fantasy?

Sadie had to find out – and she had to find out fast.

23

Half an hour later, Sadie was in the front of the white van, squashed between Joel and Mona. She was sitting stiffly, trying not to let her left arm or leg touch Mona's, but was still close enough to hear the other woman's breathing and to smell the distinctive scent of Chanel No. 5.

As the van headed towards Shore Road, Sadie glanced down at the dress she had chosen, plain and grey and not especially flattering. She had spent ten minutes going through her wardrobe, dismissing her black cocktail frock as being too dramatic – wouldn't it look like she was in mourning? – and all the brighter ones as being too frivolous. The grey, she hoped, would help her blend into the background.

While Joel made small talk, Sadie tried to figure out what she'd say to Mona once she got her on her own. Direct questions, she decided, no more beating around the bush. She had to know for sure what her involvement had been – if any – in Eddie's death. It wasn't the kind of conversation that she wanted to have at a birthday party, but then there wasn't really a good time or place to broach the subject.

Sadie wished that she was somewhere else, anywhere else but stuck in this van with Mona Farrell. The girl gave her the creeps; she was weird and unnerving. And suddenly her head was full of *if onlys* again: if only she hadn't gone to London, if only she hadn't chosen Oaklands to stay at, if only she'd never met Nathan Stone.

'So what's your line of work?' Joel was asking Mona.

'I'm working in an antique shop at the moment, just a small one. It's nothing much but I'm hoping to learn the trade, maybe have a place of my own one day. I'm doing night classes too in Art History.'

'That's interesting.'

'Yes, I'm enjoying it.'

Sadie didn't believe a word she was saying; none of it rang true. Mona was either a consummate liar or she'd already rehearsed her answers. Probably both. The girl was doing her best to ingratiate herself with Joel, to come across as perfectly normal when she was about as far from that condition as a person could be. A wave of panic flowed over her. What the hell was she doing? If Mona was a killer, then Joel could be in danger too. She'd never forgive herself if anything happened to him.

Sadie stared out through the windscreen, making a mental effort to stop her hands from clenching. If Mona had killed one man then what was to stop her from . . . But there was a part of her that still refused to believe it. Wasn't it more likely that the girl was just unhinged, playing a weird psychological game? For some obscure reason Mona had latched on to her and wasn't prepared to let go.

Five minutes later they drew up outside the large detached house on Shore Road. Already people were milling around the entrance, laughing and joking, kissing each other on the cheek and shaking hands. Usually, Sadie would have looked forward to a do like this but today she wished she was anywhere but here.

'Are you sure this is okay?' Mona asked. 'I feel like I'm gate-crashing.'

'It's fine,' Joel said. 'Half the town's going to be here. One more won't make a difference.'

As soon as they stepped into the grand reception area, Joel's mother swept across the room and embraced Sadie, making the point – should there be any doubters observing – that she for one believed wholeheartedly in her future daughter-in-law's innocence when it came to Eddie Wise's murder.

'Hello, darling. It's wonderful to see you. I'm so glad you could make it.'

'Happy birthday, Emily.'

'You're looking lovely as always. How are you bearing up? Oh, poor you. It must be dreadful. You know we're always here for you, don't you? Just pick up the phone if ever you need any-thing.'

Emily Hunter was a kind, sociable woman in her mid-fifties, generous and open-hearted. Sadie knew that she meant well, but the effusive welcome only succeeded in drawing unwelcome attention. She could feel the eyes on her, the raised brows and the weighing-up stares. In a small town like Haverlea, gossip spread like wildfire. Speculation would be rife as to whether Sadie Wise had actually disposed of her husband.

Sadie, making an effort to smile, wondered if she appeared as nervous as she felt. 'Thank you,' she murmured. If it hadn't been for Mona's presence, it would have been easier to brazen it out, but she was worried about what the girl might say and to whom. And where was she now? By the time Sadie had disen-tangled herself from Emily's embrace and Joel had taken her place, Mona had disappeared. She scanned the crowded room but there wasn't any sign of her.

Worried, Sadie set off in search, but was intercepted by Frank Hunter before she'd taken more than a couple of steps.

'Sadie,' he said, putting a paternal arm around her shoulder. 'How are you doing? Rotten business all this stuff with Eddie. I hope Joel's taking good care of you.'

Sadie fought to maintain her shaky smile. Frank was a big, bluff, old-fashioned guy, the type who still believed that women were the weaker sex and that it was a man's duty to protect them. 'We're surviving.'

'Glad to hear it.' He lowered his voice a fraction. 'If you need a good solicitor, I've got a number you can have.'

'I'm hoping I won't need one.'

Frank pulled a face. 'I hope so too, love, but sometimes the police get the wrong end of the stick, if you know what I mean, so it's always smart to have a fallback position. You hear about all these miscarriages of justice, about innocent people spending years in prison and—'

'Dad!' Joel interrupted.

'What?'

'Sadie doesn't need to hear this. She hasn't done anything wrong and there won't be any miscarriages of justice.'

'I was only saying . . . '

'Yes, I know what you were saying but there's no need. It's fine, okay? Everything's fine.'

While this exchange was taking place, Sadie was aware of the people around them halting their own conversations and leaning in to listen. She had a sudden scary image of being led away in handcuffs, pleading her innocence while the crowd looked on.

'So have the police been in touch again?' Frank asked.

'No,' Sadie said. 'Not since I promised not to leave the country.'

Frank gave her shoulder a squeeze. 'Well, I'm sure it will be okay.'

'It *will* be,' Joel insisted.

Sadie turned to him and asked, 'Have you seen—' She only just stopped herself from saying Mona. 'Do you know where Anne is?'

'I think she's gone to get a drink.'

'Sounds like a plan. I'll see if I can find her.'

Sadie squeezed her way through the crowd, saying fleeting hellos to people she passed but not stopping to talk to anyone. Her eyes darted left and right as she sought out the girl in the navy blue dress. A buffet had been laid out on a long table in the kitchen: cold meats, coleslaw, sausage rolls, sandwiches and plates full of cheese cubes and pineapple squares on sticks. To the right was another smaller table with bottles and glasses.

Sadie poured herself a large glass of wine – she was in desperate need of one – took a gulp and then looked around again. After a while she spotted Mona chatting to a middle-aged guy in the corner, a man she recognised as a journalist on the local rag. Royston, his name was, Peter Royston. Her heart missed a beat. She felt a tightening in her chest as she approached. What was Mona saying? What was she telling him?

She gave a vague nod towards the reporter before addressing Mona. 'Here you are,' she said brightly. 'I've been looking for you.' She put out a hand, intending to pat her on the arm, but then withdrew it again. Somehow she couldn't bear the thought of touching her.

'Sadie, isn't it?' asked Royston. 'So sorry to hear about your troubles.'

Sadie gave him a thin smile. 'Should my ears be burning?'

Royston was a plump oily man with an ingratiating manner. His cheeks were threaded with red veins and long strands of lank brown hair were ineffectively combed over a balding skull. 'No, no,' he insisted. 'Not at all. I was just telling Anne here about the delights of Haverlea.'

'I didn't realise there was a fairground,' Mona said. 'We should go. I love the fair. Don't you, Sadie? Don't you just love it?'

'It's all right.' Sadie glanced at her. There was something about her face, the tone of her voice and her body movements which suggested that if not already drunk she was certainly close to it. But how could she be? She'd only been here for ten minutes. Unless she'd had a few before turning up at the flat. Dutch courage perhaps ... or something more like a habit? Sadie remembered the train and the faint smell of alcohol that had wafted off the girl.

'The waltzers and the stalls and the candy floss. And is there a big wheel?' Mona asked. 'I like those.'

'It's not very big.'

Mona laughed. 'Still, we should go. It would be fun. Why don't we? Just the two of us. What do you think?'

'It's a bit dull in the winter. Besides, it's only open on a Saturday.'

Mona's face fell. 'Is it? Oh, that's a shame. There's something ... I don't know, kind of magical about them. Don't you think? Especially at night. They remind me of being a kid. All the best films have fairground scenes in them.'

'Do they?' Royston asked. He thought about it for a second and then added, 'Which ones?'

Mona put her empty glass down on the window ledge and reeled off a list, ticking them off on her fingers: 'There's *Brighton Rock*, *The Third Man*, *The Lady from Shanghai*, *Saturday Night and Sunday Morning*, *A Taste of Honey*, *Paper Moon*. Oh, there are loads of them.'

'You're a fan of old movies then?'

'Yeah, they're the best. There's another one too.' Mona looked at Sadie and frowned. 'I can't recall the title. Do you remember? We were talking about it just the other day. It's to do with these two guys who meet—'

Sadie instinctively grabbed hold of Mona's elbow, squeezing it hard as she interrupted. 'You really must come and meet Joel's parents.' She smiled at Royston. 'Sorry, I hope you don't mind. I promised I'd introduce them.'

'Of course not. Nice to meet you,' he said to Mona. 'Will you be coming back to see us again soon?'

Mona smiled widely. 'Yes, I'm sure I will.'

Sadie quickly propelled her away. 'What the hell are you doing?' she hissed under her breath.

Mona giggled. 'There's nothing to worry about. He wouldn't guess, not in a thousand years.'

'He's a reporter, for God's sake.'

'I know.'

Sadie kept her voice low as she forged a way through the crowd. Even though music was playing and the room was full of chatter, she wasn't taking any chances. And then the full meaning of what Mona had said suddenly sank in: *He wouldn't guess.* Was she still playing games or was she serious? 'You're crazy. I don't even know what you're doing here.'

'You invited me. Well, as good as.'

'What?'

'You said you couldn't come to London so I knew I had to come to you. I mean, we need to talk, don't we?'

'Yes, I think we do.'

'I need a drink first.' Mona gazed down at her hand as if surprised to find that a glass wasn't in it. She turned abruptly and headed for the kitchen. 'Come on.'

Sadie trotted behind, not wanting to let her out of her sight. It had been her intention to be in control, the one asking questions, the one putting Mona on the spot, but somehow the balance of power seemed to be shifting. She felt fear flutter in her chest. Now that the moment of truth was drawing close, she wasn't entirely sure that she wanted to hear it.

While Mona poured herself a vodka and tonic, Sadie tried to think of somewhere they could talk in private. The conservatory, she decided, was the best option. Rather than going through the living room where she was bound to bump into people she knew, she led Mona through the back door and into the garden instead.

'It's cold,' Mona said, glancing up at the sky. 'It's going to snow again. Don't you think? I like the snow. It makes everything seem . . . different.'

But Sadie wasn't interested in the weather. 'What's going on?'

Mona looked at her, wide-eyed. 'What do you mean?'

'You know exactly what I mean.' Sadie expelled a sigh of frustration, her breath emerging as a cloud of mist in the icy night air. 'Sending the book, calling me at the flat, turning up here and pretending to be my friend. I don't understand. I don't get it.'

Mona frowned. 'I'm not pretending anything. We are friends, aren't we?'

'How can we be? We've only met once. We had a five-minute conversation.'

'It was longer than that.' Mona sipped on her drink as she walked. 'And anyway, it only takes five seconds to know if someone's going to be your friend or not. We hit it off. You can't deny it. There's a connection between us.'

'No, there isn't.'

'Of course there is.'

Sadie pushed open the door to the octagonal conservatory. It was furnished with rattan chairs and tables and filled with plants, mainly tall potted palms that cast long shadows in the gloom. A thin light came from the living room along with the sound of laughter and the chink of glasses. There was a temporary pause in the music – maybe someone was changing the tape – and then it started up again: the Drifters singing the Sixties hit, 'Under the Boardwalk'.

Sadie quickly glanced around, making sure they were alone before speaking again. 'I don't know what you want from me.'

Mona stepped in behind her and closed the door. She sipped on her drink, keeping her sly eyes on Sadie. 'Sure you do.' A smile flickered at the corners of her lips. 'Hey, I know it's kind of scary but you can do it.'

'Do what?'

'You know what.'

Sadie swallowed hard. 'I-I don't,' she stammered. 'Tell me what's going on.'

A frown settled on Mona's forehead and a look of distrust crossed her face. She paced to the left and the right as if it might be a set-up and the police were lurking in the undergrowth. She poked among the palms and peered into the corners. When she was sure that they were the only two people in the conservatory, she returned to Sadie and said very softly, 'I've done mine and now you have to do yours.'

Sadie forced herself to utter the words. 'Are you ... are you saying that you killed Eddie?'

Mona smiled again, a chilling smile that didn't quite reach her eyes. 'A deal's a deal. You can't go back on it now. Not after I've kept to my side of the bargain.'

Sadie gulped what remained of her wine, still desperately hoping that the girl was bluffing. 'I don't believe you. I don't believe you did anything.'

'He's dead, isn't he?'

'That doesn't mean you did it.'

'Who else?' Mona whispered.

'Then prove it,' Sadie said, still grasping at straws. She had that vile sick feeling in her guts again. It couldn't be true. It couldn't. She wanted to grab hold of Mona and shake her like a rag doll. But what if she wasn't lying? A trembling ran through her bones, a seismic fear that drained the blood from her face.

Mona pursed her lips. 'What do you want to know?'

Sadie shrugged, struck dumb by terror.

'The Mansfield estate,' Mona said. 'Carlton House, Number 93.' She gave another of her weird giggles. 'Eddie wasn't very house-proud, was he? The place was a real tip, cans everywhere and it stank of fag smoke. You'd think he'd tidy up every now and again. Still, that's men for you; dirty bastards, all of them.'

Sadie stared, her heart thumping. Mona couldn't know any of this unless she'd been to the flat. 'No,' she muttered, shaking her head. 'You couldn't. You—'

'Oh, come on. It's not as though you even liked the guy. He was a shit, Sadie, a user. He got what he deserved. It's pointless to get all sentimental over him now.'

'You're crazy!'

Mona's face took on a hurt expression. 'Don't say that. I only did what we agreed.'

'We didn't agree *anything*.'

'Of course we did. And you can't go back on your word.'

'What?' Sadie felt as if the whole exchange was surreal, a nightmare that she wasn't able to wake up from. 'I never promised anything. I didn't want Eddie dead. Why would I?'

Mona inclined her head and gazed at her for a moment. Eventually a smile slid on to her lips. 'It's okay. You're just scared, right? I get it. But there's no need. I've got it all planned out. You won't get caught, I promise. It's foolproof. You won't even have to go into the house.'

'No, I won't. Because I'm not going near it. I'm not having any part of this. Do you understand? I don't ... I don't want anything more to do with you.'

'It's a bit late for that.'

'I want you to go away and leave me alone.'

Mona sipped on her vodka, leaving a pale pink stain of lipstick on the rim of the glass. 'I know what you're thinking,' she said. 'As soon as my back's turned, you'll go to the cops and tell them what I did.'

'I won't,' Sadie lied. 'I swear. I promise.'

A malevolent gleam crept into Mona's eyes. 'The thing is,' she said, 'if you do that then I'll have to tell them everything: how we met on the train, how you told me about your husband and I told you about my father, how we hatched a plan to get rid of them both. Except after I did Eddie you got cold feet and tried to double-cross me.'

'They won't believe you. Why the hell should they?'

'No, you're the one they won't believe. I mean, why would I do away with Eddie Wise? I didn't even know the guy. And if you thought I'd murdered him, if you had even the slightest suspicion, then why didn't you go straight to the cops? But you didn't. Not even when I turned up on your doorstep. No, instead you brought me to a birthday party.' Mona pulled a face. 'It's not going to look good, Sadie. It's not going to look good at all.'

'I'll ... I'll just say that I thought you were crazy, that I thought you were making it up.'

'And what about Joel?'

'What about him?'

'He's going to wonder why you lied.'

'I didn't.'

'You didn't tell him the truth.'

'He'll understand.'

Mona wrinkled her nose. 'Are you sure? Only he's bound to question it all, isn't he? Why you didn't tell him straight out that we'd never met before or that I'm not really called Anne. Why would you keep that from him? And when he hears about the plans we made—'

'We didn't make any plans.'

'It's all going to look very odd. Yeah, he's going to ask some

169

awkward questions, like why you didn't say anything when you came back to find me at your flat today or why you brought me here to his parents' home when you thought I might be a cold-blooded killer.'

Sadie knew she was right. She could feel her chest growing tighter, the breath being squeezed out of her lungs. 'I'll explain,' she said hurriedly. 'I was confused, scared. I'll tell him how I didn't believe you'd actually done it.'

'And you think he'll be okay with that?'

'He trusts me.'

'For now.' Mona leaned in close to Sadie, so close that their faces were almost touching. 'But I don't think the police will be as understanding. No, they'll take a different view entirely. They'll think you've been hiding something – and they'll be right.'

'Maybe I'll take my chances.'

'I don't think so,' Mona snapped. 'You're way too smart for that. You grass me up and we'll both go to jail. I'll swear to God that we were in this together. If I go down, Sadie, I'm taking you with me.'

Sadie stepped back, unable to bear the proximity of the girl. It was like standing too close to the Devil. 'Why are you doing this to me? It's not right. I never agreed to . . . You know I didn't.'

Mona's voice suddenly changed again, switching from a threatening tone to one that was almost wheedling. 'Hey, it'll be all right. You see if it isn't. We'll be okay. In a week or two every-thing will have settled down. The cops have got more important crimes to worry about than who killed a nobody like Eddie Wise.'

'He wasn't a nobody. He might not have been perfect but—'

'By Christmas they won't even remember his name.'

Sadie, battling against an ever growing panic, knew that any further remonstrations were pointless. You couldn't argue with a crazy person and Mona was deranged. It was better, surely, not to antagonise her. What if she made a habit of carrying kitchen knives around? One wrong word and she might flip. No, it was better to try and keep the girl sweet until she could figure out a way of getting shut of her, of getting her away from the house. 'Maybe,' she said softly. 'Maybe you're right.'

Mona gave a triumphant smile. 'See? I knew it. I knew you'd come round eventually. I've got so much to tell you.' She put down her glass, reached into her shoulder bag and pulled out a few folded sheets of paper. 'It's all here, all the details and there's a map as well. You'll have to wait a few weeks of course, perhaps even a month but—'

'Not now,' Sadie interrupted, quickly waving away the papers. 'Not here.'

But Mona, insistent, pushed them into her hand. 'Go on. You'll need them.'

Reluctantly, Sadie put them in her own bag. What choice did she have? At the same time she glanced towards the glass partition to make sure they weren't being observed. 'We shouldn't be seen together.'

'Oh, don't worry about that. No one's going to remember me.'

'They might. It's too risky. You should go. I think it's for the best.'

Mona glanced over her shoulder towards the crowd gathered in the living room. 'But the party's just getting started.'

'There'll be other parties, better ones. Please, just leave.'

Mona gave a sigh. 'If that's what you really want.'

'It is.'

'We can meet up tomorrow.'

'No,' Sadie said. 'You have to go back to London. You have to go back straight away.'

'So when will I see you again?'

'Not for a while.' Then, before Mona could think of more reasons for staying, Sadie walked determinedly towards the door that led out into the garden. 'Come on,' she urged. 'Quickly!' And fortunately Mona followed her. They crossed the lawn and went along the path that ran adjacent to the side of the house until they came to the front gate. 'There's a taxi rank on the corner, right at the end of the street. You can pick up a cab there.'

'It's not far to the hotel. I'll walk.'

'Where are you staying?'

'The Bold.'

Sadie knew the hotel, a large white building on the promenade. She could call the police and get them to arrest her. Did she dare? Mona's threats were still revolving in her head, a spinning whirl that made her feel almost dizzy. One call could change everything. But if she made the wrong decision . . .

'Why don't you come with me? We could have a drink together.'

Sadie's fingers tightened around the glass of wine she was holding. 'I can't leave the party. Look, I have to go. I'm sorry. Joel will be looking for me.'

'Okay.'

'And don't ring me at the flat again. It isn't safe.'

'So how—'

'I'll call you,' Sadie lied. 'But not right away. We need to wait. We need to wait a while.'

'If that's what you want.'

'It's for the best.'

'All right,' Mona said. She turned to go but stopped again. 'Oh, I almost forgot. I left something for you at the flat.'

'What?'

Mona's lips slid into that familiar smile. 'It's a surprise. It's in the drawer in your bedside table.' She raised a hand and gave a breezy wave. 'Bye then.'

Sadie clutched the gatepost as she watched Mona walk away. Despite the cold, she could feel the sweat running down her back. Now she knew for sure who'd killed Eddie, she had to do something about it. The right thing, the moral thing, would be to put aside all thoughts of her own precarious position and go straight to the police. But what if that meant being arrested too? The more she thought about her own story, the less convincing it appeared to be.

Sadie could hear the sounds of the party drifting from the house. She felt removed from it all. She felt like she was standing on quicksand, that the world as she knew it was shifting and changing, that she was being sucked down into a filthy squelch of lies and horror and madness.

24

Wayne Gissing loved his mother, but he loved her more when she was a hundred miles away. Having her around all the time was proving to be a pain in the arse. If she wasn't on his back about the scrapyard or the hours he spent down the pub, she was nagging about wet towels left on the bathroom floor, dirty mugs or overflowing ashtrays. And then there was the constant sniping between her and Sharon; it was like living in a bloody war zone. He couldn't wait for the day she packed her bags and cleared off home to Bournemouth.

However, there wasn't much chance of that happening any time soon. It was only six days since she'd got here but already her feet were well and truly under the table. Of course it was handy having her to look over the books and provide hot meals every day – no one made a better steak and kidney pie than his mother – but the cons still outweighed the pros. He wanted his life back and the only way to achieve that was to sort out Kelly's problems. His little sister needed to know for sure who'd killed Eddie, and the filth weren't exactly making progress.

'It's been a bleedin' week already,' Kelly said. 'What's the matter with them? Why isn't the bitch locked up?'

'I dunno,' Wayne mumbled. It was a question she never stopped asking, as if by constant repetition she would eventually get a satisfactory answer. He flicked over the pages of the road atlas until he came to the one he wanted. 'Here it is: Haverlea. Shit, it's fuckin' miles away. It's up by Liverpool.'

'So?' Kelly asked.

'So it'll take hours to get there.'

'Who cares. You got something better to do?'

Wayne had plenty of better things to do, but he didn't want to piss her off. 'I'm not saying that, Kel. All I'm thinking is that we don't know for sure that she's even there at the moment. We could drive all the way and find she's cleared off some place else.'

'I don't care. I'm sick of sitting here doing sod all. It's doing me head in.'

'Maybe he's right, love,' Sharon butted in. 'It's a long way to go and even if she is there she might not talk to you.'

Kelly's face grew hard. 'I'll make her bleedin' talk to me.'

Sharon shared a conspiratorial look with her stepson. 'Maybe there's a better way of doing it.'

Kelly glanced at her. 'Like what?'

'Like saving yourself the bother of driving halfway across the country. Why don't you get her to come to you instead?'

Kelly slammed her palms down on the table, her face twisting with anger and frustration. 'And how the hell am I supposed to do that? Give her a bell and ask if she'd like to pop down for a chat?'

'Not exactly. Didn't you say that Eddie's body is going to be released soon?'

'Yeah, next week probably. What of it?'

'So then there'll be the funeral.'

Kelly still didn't get it. 'And? She ain't going to come, is she?'

'Why not?' Sharon said. 'If she's as innocent as she claims, if she's got nothing to hide, then why shouldn't she pay her last respects?' She gave a small smile. 'Especially if Eddie's parents invite her along. Do you reckon they'd do that?'

Kelly, who had been to see Stan and Marcie Wise that morning, thought about it for a moment. 'I dunno. I suppose they might.'

'Well then. Why don't you ask them? After that, all you have to do is wait a while and she'll be here in London.'

Wayne put his elbows on the table and rubbed his chin. 'Sounds like a plan, Kel. What do you reckon?'

'What if she doesn't turn up?'

'Then I'll drive you up there and we'll have it out with her. She can't hide for ever.'

Kelly gave a sigh, disappointed at the prospect of not being able to take immediate action, but aware that this was probably a better option. She rose to her feet and shrugged on her jacket. 'I'm going round to Tina's for a while. I'll see you later.'

'See you, love,' Sharon said.

Wayne waited until the front door had closed before speaking again. 'You really think that Sadie bird's going to show?'

'Why not? She's the widow, ain't she? And if Stan asks her she won't have much choice. It'd look kind of weird if she refused. No, she'll be here, you mark my words.'

'And then?'

'And then what?'

Wayne rubbed at his face. 'What do we do with the bitch when she does show up?'

A smile crept on to Sharon's lips. She lowered her voice and asked, 'Where's your mother?'

'Out.'

'Are you sure?'

'Listen,' he said, cupping a hand to his ear. 'Can you hear anything?'

'No.'

'So she's definitely out.'

Sharon grinned. 'Well, this is what I'm thinking: that Nathan Stone, he's got a few bob, ain't he?'

'What of it?'

'So he owes you. Well, he owes Kelly and it's the same thing. Family's family. You can't let people take the piss. You play this right and you could earn yourself a few quid. We could *all* earn a few quid.'

'And how's that going to happen?'

'She's Stone's tart, ain't she?'

'What of it?'

'So he's not going to want to see her get hurt.'

Wayne thought about this for a while, the effort creating furrows on his forehead. 'But if the two of them are at it, he'll be watching out for her.'

'Yeah, well, he can't watch her twenty-four hours a day.'

Wayne gave a nod. 'Pym reckons she was staying at a guesthouse near Kellston station. Oaklands, it's called. She might book in there again if she does come down. We could always—'

'I'll tell you how we're going to do it, hon.' Sharon leaned across the table, her eyes bright and greedy. 'Listen to me. I've got it all worked out.'

25

Gerald Frayne shook the snow from his shoes and brushed the rain from the shoulders of his heavy overcoat before stepping inside the pub. A blast of noise hit him as he opened the door, a mixture of conversation, laughter and music from the jukebox; the White Swan was popular with the locals and this evening it was doing a brisk trade.

He made his way to the bar and while he was waiting to be served took the opportunity to look around. The usual faces were in evidence, including a few minor villains chatting in the corner. It was the kind of pub where the women dressed to impress – there were lots of miniskirts, plunging necklines, big hair and shiny costume jewellery on view – and the men, more casually attired in shellsuits or jeans and T-shirt, quite blatantly eyed them up.

It was a habit of Gerald's to have a drink in the Swan from time to time. This wasn't because he was particularly fond of the place – he wasn't – but it was where the gossip did the rounds and he liked to keep his ear to the ground. It was surprising how much you could learn in the twenty minutes it took to drink a pint.

'Evening,' the barman said. 'Nice to see you again. The usual?'

'Thank you.'

'Still raining is it?'

'A little.'

While the Guinness was settling, a middle-aged man sidled over from the other side of the bar. He drew close to Gerald, lifted his pale blue eyes, smiled and gave an almost obsequious nod.

'Ah, Inspector Frayne. Fancy seeing you here. Great minds think alike.'

Gerald didn't much care for Peter Royston. Some reporters he could get along with, the ones that played fair and didn't twist the truth, but this man was a scandalmonger; he liked to dig the dirt and didn't give a damn about the consequences. Despite his antipathy, Gerald smiled back. It didn't do to let your personal feelings get in the way of the job and Royston often had useful snippets of information. 'Nasty evening,' he said. 'It's good to get into the warm.'

Royston sipped on his drink, watching Gerald with a sly expression on his face. 'I hear you've been busy.'

Gerald lifted his eyebrows, already suspecting where this was going. 'We're always busy. No rest for the wicked.'

'You're investigating the Eddie Wise murder, aren't you?'

Gerald had long since ceased to be amazed at how quickly news travelled in a small town like Haverlea. 'I wouldn't go that far. We're just helping with a few enquiries.'

'And is there likely to be an arrest soon?'

'I really couldn't say.'

Royston put his glass down on the counter. He cleared his throat and ran his tongue over his plump fleshy lips. 'I saw her this afternoon over at the Hunters'.'

'And who was that?' replied Gerald, feigning ignorance.

'Sadie Wise, of course. She was at Emily Hunter's birthday bash. I'm surprised you weren't there.'

Gerald gave a shrug. 'Too busy, I'm afraid.' He had received an invitation but had graciously declined, claiming – untruthfully, as it happened – that pressure of work meant he was unable to attend. The Hunters were one of the more influential families in Haverlea and he'd suspected that either Frank or Emily would try to bend his ear about the innocence of their future daughter-in-law. Although he would have been interested in seeing Sadie Wise again, he had decided, on balance, that he was better off keeping his distance. It could be awkward, after accepting the Hunter's hospitality, if he later had to arrest the girl.

'It's an interesting case.'

Gerald, although he was of the same opinion, gave a light shrug. He was always cautious around Royston. Any comment he made could be taken and twisted and splashed across the front page of the next edition of the local rag.

'She's a pretty girl,' the reporter continued, undeterred by the lack of feedback. 'A bit jumpy, though. She looked positively horrified when she saw me talking to her friend. I wonder why that was?'

Gerald lifted his pint of Guinness, took a long draught and put the glass back on the bar. 'Everyone is horrified when they find you talking to their friends, Peter. It's a natural reaction.'

Royston sniggered. 'Now that's not a nice thing to say, Inspector. It's lucky I'm not the sensitive sort.'

'No one could accuse you of that.'

'Odd thought though, a slip of a girl plunging a knife into the chest of her husband. Still, appearances can be deceptive. You wouldn't think she was capable but—'

'Good do, was it?' Gerald asked. 'Many people there?'

'Not bad. Not bad at all.' Royston, who was used to people trying to deflect him, carried on regardless. 'Still, a woman scorned and all that. I hear he walked out on her a few years back. Must have been tough to take. Is it true that he stole from her too?'

'I couldn't possibly comment.'

'Of course Emily Wise made a point of showing her support, but then she would, wouldn't she?' Royston paused for a few seconds before adding, 'You had any of the nationals sniffing round, the *Sun* or the *Mirror*?'

'Not yet.'

'That's something, I suppose. If you do make an arrest—'

'We'll be sure to let you know.'

Royston rubbed his hands together in gleeful anticipation of what might be to come. 'I'd appreciate it. You don't often get a decent story round here. It'd be good to have a head start on the London boys.'

Gerald gave a thin smile. 'Of course. I understand.'

'Well, I'll leave you to enjoy your pint in peace.'

As he watched Royston lumber away, Gerald's smile quickly vanished. The man reminded him of one of those cane toads, large and ugly and toxic to anything that got too close. Still, at least he hadn't got wind of the news that had come through from McCloud this morning. Gerald frowned as he thought about it. There had been an anonymous phone call to Cowan Road police station insisting that Sadie was involved with a man called Nathan Stone, a villain who worked for the Kellston gangster Terry Street. But was it the truth or was someone just trying to stir up trouble?

'She was seen with him, apparently, down the dogs last Saturday night.'

'Any way of verifying that?' Gerald had asked. 'She certainly didn't mention it to me.'

'We're working on it.'

They'd had a brief discussion as to whether Gerald should confront her, but decided it was smarter to hang fire.

'She's not going to admit it, is she?' McCloud had said. 'And at the moment this is only hearsay. We haven't got any proof.'

'And as soon as she realises we're on to her, she'll be careful to stay away from him.'

'Exactly,' McCloud had said. 'Let's back off for a while, make her feel safe and see what happens next.'

Gerald swallowed the last of his pint. Was Sadie Wise in a relationship with Stone or had she just employed him to get rid of her husband? Whichever way you viewed them, things weren't looking good for her. No, they weren't looking good at all.

26

Sadie, turning her head to peer through the darkness at the green luminous dial of the alarm clock, saw that it was four o'clock. Her stomach sank. This was the loneliest time of the night, she thought, when dawn still felt like an eternity away. She longed for the daylight but dreaded it too. When morning came she would have to go to the police. She should have gone last night after the party. She should have gone as soon as she got home and pulled out the drawer in the bedside table and found . . .

A cold wave of fear swept over her as she remembered opening the plastic bag and seeing the gun that Mona had left for her. Small and black and deadly. The girl must have slipped into the bedroom while she was here. How had she done it? Asked to use the bathroom, perhaps, and taken a detour on the way back. Joel wouldn't have suspected anything. He was the trusting kind.

She could hear Joel's steady breathing as he slept beside her, oblivious to the panic that was streaming through her body. As soon as she had found the gun she should have told him about it. She should have told him everything, but she hadn't. Instead she had taken the bag and hidden it beneath a pile of jumpers on the shelf in the top of the wardrobe. It had been an instinctive reaction and a foolish one.

She had a sudden urge to shake him awake, to beg for his help, to spill all the secrets that were crowding in on her. 'I'm screwed,' she wanted to say. 'I'm scared. I'm terrified. I'm in a hole and I don't know how to get out of it.'

Her hand reached for his shoulder, but she quickly withdrew it. To tell him now would be to disturb the last restful sleep he might get in a while. There was no rush. She should allow him some peace before burdening him with it all. It was the very least she could do.

As she lay there, Sadie wondered how she'd managed to get through Emily's party. She had smiled and nodded and drunk too much. Perhaps if she'd stayed sober, she'd have had more sense when it came to the gun. The police would want to know why she hadn't contacted them immediately. Jesus, the police would want to know all kinds of things and for most of them she didn't have any adequate answers.

The very worst thing she could have done was to take Mona to the party. How would she explain that? You didn't socialise with someone you believed to be a killer; you didn't take them with you to celebrate your future mother-in-law's birthday. No, she was going to look guilty as sin. By midday she'd be locked up in a cell and they'd be throwing away the key.

Sadie's chest tightened with fear. She felt as though she had stumbled into a Kafkaesque nightmare, a sinister menacing maze from which there was no escape. Whichever path she took would be the wrong one. If she came clean and Mona was arrested, the cops would hear a completely different story from the girl, a tale of collaboration and evil intent. And she'd follow through too. Sadie had no doubt about it. Mona would be prepared to stand in the dock and swear that the two of them had planned the murders together.

'So what can I do?' she mouthed silently into the darkness. 'What the hell can I do?'

Sadie reached out her hand again and touched the reassuring warmth of Joel's back. He stirred slightly in his sleep but didn't wake up. Usually he was the one person who always made her feel safe, but now he was powerless to help. She had lied to him, withdrawing into a shell of secrecy. She had passed over each and every opportunity to tell him the truth and now it was too late.

At six o'clock Sadie climbed carefully out of bed, picked up her clothes and tiptoed into the living room. It was still dark and misty outside but the light from the streetlamps cast a glow over the furniture. She went to the bathroom, took a quick shower and got dressed. Today she was supposed to be returning to work after a week off but if she went to the police she was unlikely to make it.

Back in the living room Sadie wrapped her arms around her chest and rocked gently back and forth. It occurred to her suddenly that there was an alternative to spilling her guts. It wasn't a good alternative and it certainly wasn't a moral one, but the option was still open to her: she could, if she chose, do absolutely nothing.

She frowned, aware that taking this route would be both cowardly and unprincipled. It would mean Mona getting away with murder, and Eddie's death going unpunished. Could she live with that? She didn't know. She lifted a hand to her mouth and chewed on a fingernail. To do nothing had its own risks. She would, in effect, be covering up a crime and should the truth come out at any point she would probably go to jail as an accessory.

She wondered how Mona would react when she simply

refused to go through with the killing. Not well, she was sure of it. But then what could the girl do without implicating herself? She could hardly go to the cops to complain about Sadie not sticking to her side of the bargain.

Sadie sat down at the table, switched on the lamp, grabbed her bag and found the papers Mona had given her. She smoothed them out and gazed at them. The address was written across the top of a plan of the garden: 12 Constance Avenue, Hampstead. A black arrow pointed to a gate where she could gain access. From the gate, a route had been mapped out to a summer house, and from there another path to the back of the house where a window had a large asterisk beside it.

She shuddered at the map and pushed it aside. There was also a two-page letter, written in a childlike scrawl. Rapidly, she scanned through the words, repulsed by Mona's coldness when it came to the despatch of her own father. She wondered what he'd done to make Mona loathe him so much.

The plan was ridiculous, a fantasy full of holes. There was no way of knowing that her father would even be in the study on the night that was chosen. Or that he wouldn't see or hear an intruder crossing the lawn. How had Mona thought, even for a moment, that this could possibly work? But the answer to that was plain as day: because she was crazy, because her mind was sick and twisted.

Sadie took a few deep breaths, knowing one thing at least – she had no intention of going anywhere near Hampstead. She screwed up the letter and the map and shoved them back in her bag. She didn't dare put them in the bin in case Joel found them. She thought about burning them in the sink but was worried about a lingering smell. What she didn't need at the moment was any awkward questions.

As all this went through her head, Sadie realised that she'd finally come to a decision. She was going to call Mona's bluff, lie low and hope it would all go away. Leaning forward, she covered her face with her hands feeling the shame roll through her. She knew who'd killed Eddie and was going to let them get away with it. But what else could she do? She didn't trust the police when it came to rooting out the truth and she didn't want to spend the next twenty years of her life in jail.

'Sorry,' she whispered. 'Sorry, Eddie.'

A short while later Sadie crept back into the bedroom and retrieved the Beretta from the wardrobe, unsure as to what she was going to do with it. Throw it in the sea? But that was risky. What if the tide brought it straight back in again? But she couldn't bear to keep it any longer than she had to. Perhaps she could dump it in a bin in town. But that was chancy too. She had no idea of where Mona had got the gun or whether it could be traced back to her.

Sadie put the weapon in her bag, slipped on her coat and then scribbled a quick note to Joel. *Couldn't sleep. Have gone for walk before work. See you later. S x* As she left the house, she glanced to the left and the right, as edgy as a fugitive. The gun, although it was only small, felt heavy as lead in her bag.

27

The morning seemed to drag on for ever. Sadie tried to concentrate as she stood at the counter, placing the books into bags and smiling blandly at the customers. From the moment she had arrived at work, she'd been aware of an atmosphere. Her colleagues had all heard about what had happened but seemed uncertain as to what to say or how to react. In her absence, she had obviously been the subject of gossip. *Had Sadie Wise murdered her husband? Had she lost her rag, picked up a kitchen knife and stuck it into his chest?*

Their curious eyes were constantly on her, their gaze following her every move. She was suddenly different, altered, tainted with suspicion. Unsure as to what to believe, they shot her quick glances when they thought she wasn't looking. She had not worked there long enough – it had only been six months – for them to trust her implicitly. No smoke without fire, they were probably thinking, and to some extent they were right. It might not be of the crime they suspected, but she was still guilty.

At lunchtime, eager to avoid any awkward questions, Sadie

collected her coat and bag and headed for the beach. On the way she stopped at a sandwich bar and picked up a ham roll and an apple. The mist had lifted and a thin gleam of sunshine was breaking through the clouds. Despite the cold, she chose a bench, sat down and gazed out at the sea. It was calmer today, the grey waves rolling gently against the shore. Above her a noisy flock of gulls circled and swooped and dived towards the water.

Sadie was halfway through lunch when a man sat down beside her. She glanced over, her heart sinking. It was Peter Royston, the reporter from the local paper.

'Hello there,' he said cheerfully. 'Fancy bumping into you. Small world, eh?'

Not that small, she thought, undeceived by his friendly manner and wondering if he had followed her from the book-shop. Her gut instinct was to get up and walk away, but she forced herself to stay put. Such a response was likely to make him more interested in her rather than less. She gave a thin smile. 'Hi.'

'Nice to see the sun for a change.'

'Yes,' she replied shortly.

Royston shifted his bulk on the bench, making the old weathered wood creak a little. He lifted a hand to sweep back a long skinny strand of hair that had come adrift from his balding pate and was flapping about in the wind. 'On your own today, then?'

Sadie, who had no desire to engage in conversation, simply gave a nod.

'Has your friend gone back home?'

Thinking of Mona, Sadie instantly flinched and then tried to cover it up by feigning a shiver and playing with the collar of her coat. 'Yes,' she said again.

'I must say, I enjoyed the Hunters' party. They certainly

know how to put on a good spread. And your friend – Anne, was it? – yes, she was a fascinating girl. Have you known each other long?'

Sadie began stuffing the remains of her sandwich and the half-eaten apple back into the brown paper bag, making it clear that she was about to leave. 'Sorry to rush off, Mr Royston, but I really have to get back to work.'

'Peter, please. And actually, I was wondering if I could have a quick word.'

'I don't want to be late.'

Royston, ignoring the comment, sat back, stretched out his legs and gazed towards the horizon. 'You see, I've been giving it some thought, this whole tragic business with your husband, and I thought you might like to put your side of the story.'

'And what side would that be?' she retorted sharply.

'Well, you did see Eddie shortly before he was murdered. And now that you're no longer a suspect ...' He paused, glanced slyly at her and asked, 'You're not a suspect, are you?'

'You'd have to ask the police about that.'

'You see, our readers like a good human-interest story, something they can relate to. I mean, you were just in the wrong place at the wrong time and that can happen to anyone. Why don't you let me put your side of the story? If we could just—'

'No,' she said firmly. Sadie could imagine the sort of article he was likely to write, nothing libellous of course, but full of sly suggestions and innuendo.

'Perhaps you'd like to think about it.'

'There's nothing to think about.'

'Only it would give you the opportunity to clear your name, to lay all those suspicions to rest. That's the problem with a small town like this, word gets around and before you know it—'

'There's nothing to tell. If people are talking, that's their problem not mine.'

'So that would be a "No comment", then?'

Sadie glared at him. Despite the cold, his face was covered in a light sheen of sweat. 'Don't put words in my mouth.'

'I'm only trying to establish the facts.'

'Really? Only that's not what it sounds like to me. To be honest, Mr Royston, I just want to be left alone. That's not too much to ask, is it?'

Royston lifted his plump shoulders in a shrug. As he rose to his feet he took a business card from his pocket and offered it to her. 'In case you change your mind.'

'I won't,' she said, ignoring his outstretched hand.

He laid it on the bench beside her. 'You can call me any time.'

Sadie turned her face away and gazed along the front as he walked away. It wasn't smart to make an enemy of Royston but the man was loathsome. He dealt in other people's misery and didn't give a toss about the pain he caused. And what had Mona said to him at the party? Something, perhaps, to arouse his suspicion: a hint, a clue as to what had really happened to Eddie. She had no way of knowing what had passed between the two of them.

She didn't touch the card and after a while the wind caught it, whipped it off the bench and sent it dancing along the promenade. She watched it flick and turn until it came to rest against the base of the low wall. 'Good riddance,' she murmured, but the words were only an act of bravado. As if she didn't have enough to worry about, she now had to add Peter Royston to the list.

Sadie made her way back to the bookshop and for the rest of the afternoon she tried to keep her mind on her job. And yet it seemed like God was mocking her. Every book that was passed over the counter served as a reminder of her wrongdoing. *Perfume: The Story of a Murderer, Postmortem, Killing Orders, Dead Man's Ransom.* She rang up the sales and, with slightly shaky fingers, slipped the novels into carrier bags.

It was a relief when she was finally able to leave at a quarter past five. As she headed for home, she kept her eyes peeled for good places to dump the gun, but didn't spot anywhere suitable. Again and again, she looked over her shoulder, worried now that Royston might be tailing her.

The town was busy but Sadie felt utterly alone as she tramped back to Buckingham Road. Whenever she saw a woman with dark hair, she jumped, thinking it was Mona. She prayed that the girl had gone back to London. But what if she hadn't? And what if Royston tracked her down, trying to get the inside story?

As she opened the door to the flat, she could hear Joel on the phone. She hung up her coat on a peg in the hall and went through to the living room. 'Oh, hold on, that might be her now. Let me check.' He put his hand over the receiver and said softly, 'It's Eddie's dad. Do you want to talk to him?'

Sadie pulled a face. He was the last person she wanted to talk to, but she would have to do it. She gave a nod and reached out her hand.

'Okay, she's here. I'll pass you over.'

Sadie took a deep breath and put the receiver to her ear. 'Hello, Stan.'

'Sadie,' he said gruffly, clearing his throat before proceeding. 'I thought you might like to know that Eddie's funeral is on Friday.'

'Oh,' she said.

'In case you wanted to come.'

Sadie was surprised by the invitation. Her relationship with Eddie's parents hadn't exactly been cordial since the split. 'Er . . .'

'It's up to you. We just thought you might like to pay your last respects.'

'Yes, of course. I mean, I wasn't sure if you'd want me there. You know with . . . I'm so sorry about Eddie and everything. It's all been such a shock.'

'It's up to you,' he said again. 'St Luke's in Kellston at ten o'clock.'

'Thank you.'

He hung up without saying goodbye.

Sadie put the phone down and looked at Joel. 'Eddie's funeral,' she said. 'It's on Friday.'

'Are you going to go?'

'I don't know. I suppose I should, shouldn't I?'

'Not if you don't want to.'

'I don't know what I want,' she said wearily.

Joel put an arm around her shoulder. 'You don't have to make up your mind straight away. Sleep on it and see how you feel in the morning. I don't mind coming with you.'

'You didn't even know Eddie.'

'You shouldn't be on your own. Not for something like this.'

Sadie leaned her head against his chest, trying to figure out what to do. If she didn't go, it would look like she was guilty, like she had something to hide. Perhaps that was why Stan had asked her. Perhaps it was some kind of test. But if she did go, how would she look him and Marcie in the eye? How would she stand there, lie through her teeth and claim she knew nothing about their son's death?

'How was work?' Joel asked.

'A bit weird. You know, everyone wanting to ask stuff but no one daring to.'

'I guess they're not sure what to say. It'll get better. Just give it time; in a week or two they'll have forgotten all about it.' He held her close, kissing the top of her head. 'Don't worry. Everything's going to be okay.'

But Sadie wasn't so sure. She was a liar and a fraud. She was tied up in knots she couldn't escape from. She had a gun in her bag along with three screwed-up pieces of paper, plans for yet another murder. How could it get better? If anything it was only going to get worse.

28

Wayne Gissing flicked on the light, a low-voltage bare bulb that hung by a tattered wire from the ceiling. As he went down the flight of steps into the cellar he was aware of a heavy sour odour, an unpleasant mixture of damp and mould and whatever darkness smelled of. When he reached the bottom he turned on another light, this one a little brighter, and looked around at the bare brick walls. There were two interconnecting rooms, both full of junk and covered with cobwebs.

The larger room, the one he was standing in, had once been used to store coal and the floor was still covered in the black gritty remains. It crunched underfoot as he walked around. Old, rusted tools lay in a heap on a table, along with bits of wood, nails, screws, tins of linseed, paintbrushes and bottles of turps. Crates were stacked against the wall, their contents long forgotten.

He went through to the second smaller, windowless space which contained some unused furniture – a couple of broken chairs, a lamp with no shade and a coffee table with a broken glass top – as well as a mildewed single mattress. There was no bulb in here and the heavy shadows gave the room a spooky feel.

Wayne peered into the dark corners, a smile twitching at the corners of his lips. Yes, it would do, he thought. There were some changes that would need to be made but otherwise it was pretty much perfect. He retreated into the main room and stared hard at the doorway between the two. He would have to find a way of disguising that, a set of shelves perhaps or some sort of false wall. The trouble was he didn't have much time. The funeral was on Friday and it needed to be ready by then.

He went over to the table and picked up the mallet, weighing its heft in his hand. He thought of the damage he could do with it, of the soft crunch of wood against bone. He would like to cave in Terry Street's skull; the bastard thought he could do whatever he liked. Maybe he had taken Eddie out in revenge for Vinnie Keane or maybe he hadn't, but either way it was clear that he'd been involved in the killing.

Well, he wasn't going to get away with it. Not this time. A soft hissing sound escaped from between Wayne's teeth. For years Terry Street had been lording it over them all, running the East End as if it was his bloody right. This was where it stopped. He wasn't going to be walked over any more. Already the whispers were going round, rumours that Terry had decided to teach the Gissings a lesson. Street was making him look like a mug and he'd had enough of it.

His mother's voice came from the top of the steps. 'Wayne? Wayne, are you down there?'

'Yeah.'

'What are you doing?'

'Looking for something.'

'Looking for what?'

Wayne raised his eyes to the ceiling. His mum, he knew, would not come down the steps. She hated the cellar. She said it made the hairs on the back of her arms stand on end. 'A screwdriver,' he said. 'The one at the yard's gone missing.'

'Well, wipe your feet when you come back up. Don't go tramping that coal dust all over the kitchen floor.'

'I won't.'

'I'll see you later then. I'm going down the Bell for a drink with Colleen.'

'Yeah, see you later.'

Wayne took one last look round before climbing the steps again. Kelly was sitting at the kitchen table, smoking a fag and drinking from a bottle of lager. He glanced towards the living room and lowered his voice. 'She gone?'

'Yeah, it's all clear.'

He went to the fridge, got himself a beer and flipped off the cap. 'I reckon it'll do,' he said, sitting down opposite to her. 'Needs a bit of work but nothing I can't manage.'

'I dunno. What about the filth? They're going to be searching for her.'

'They can search all they like.'

'Wouldn't it be better to take her to the yard?'

'That'll be the first place Stone will look.'

'And this'll be the second,' Kelly said.

'He might look, but he ain't gonna find her.' He saw the doubt on her face and said, 'You want to find out what happened to Eddie, don't you? Or do you just want the bitch to get away with it?'

Kelly scowled at him. ''Course I don't. But Mum's going to go ape. She won't have it, Wayne.'

'Well, it's not her bleedin' house, is it? And anyway what she doesn't know won't hurt her. We just need to make sure she's out when we bring the tart here.'

'And then what?'

'And then we get the murderous cow to admit what she did.'

Wayne had big plans when it came to Sadie Wise. If she was being shagged by Nathan Stone – and all the evidence pointed in that direction – then the guy should pay through the nose to get her back safely. He was thinking that twenty grand would be a fair price. Yeah, twenty grand to get the whore back and for Wayne to keep shtum about who murdered Eddie Wise.

'And then what?'

'Whatever you want. It's down to you. Eddie was your man; you can decide what to do with her.'

She took a long drag on her cigarette and gazed at him through narrowed eyes. 'You mean it? Anything?'

'It's your call, Kel.'

Kelly Gissing settled back in her chair and gave a nod. 'That sounds fair enough.'

29

Petra paid for the two gin and tonics, picked up the glasses and carried them over to a table in the corner. The Bell was quiet tonight; it was a Monday evening and everyone had spent their cash over the weekend. Still, it felt nice to be in her old local again, to see the familiar walls and hear the East End voices.

'Ta, love.' Colleen raised her glass. 'It's good to have you back.'

'It's good to be back.'

'Shame about your Kelly, though. Poor kid. How's she bearing up?'

'Oh, so-so. It'll take her a while, I suppose. You don't get over something like that in a hurry.'

Colleen shifted her bulk on the chair, making herself more comfortable. She'd put on a fair bit of weight since Petra had last seen her and now with her large bosom, bright red cheeks and flowery dress she resembled one of those ladies in the saucy postcards they sold down at the front in Bournemouth. 'And what about your Roy? What does he think of you coming back?'

Petra gave a snort. 'He ain't my Roy no more and I don't give a damn what he thinks. Not much he can do about it, is there? Not when my Kelly says she wants me here.'

'You should never have left, love. Not in my opinion. That house was as much yours as it was his. I couldn't stand it seeing some other woman living under my roof. It's not right, not right at all.'

Petra nodded furiously. It was a relief to have someone she could share her anger and frustration with. Wayne wasn't interested, and she couldn't burden Kelly with it all. 'Especially that little trollop. You should see the state of her. She don't get up 'til lunchtime and then she swans around in her dressing gown, tits hanging out for all the world to see.'

'Well, she's a prize bitch that one. And she'll lead Roy a merry dance, mark my words. That type always do.'

Petra, eager for some dirt on the woman who'd replaced her, leaned forward with a gleam in her eye. 'Why? Have you heard something?'

Colleen gave a shrug of her heavy shoulders. 'You only have to look her, darlin'. She won't last. She's the type who's always around for the weddings, never the funerals.' Then, aware of what she'd just said, she quickly patted Petra on the hand. 'Oh, sorry, love. I wasn't thinking. I forgot about Eddie. I didn't—'

'I know. Don't worry about it. It's on Friday as it happens, the funeral I mean. Ten o'clock at St Luke's in Kellston.'

'Your Kelly's going to be glad to have it over and done with. I know I was when my Jack passed.'

'It's not the same, though, is it?'

'How do you figure that?'

Petra grinned at her friend. 'My Kelly thinks she's lost the love of her life whereas you couldn't stand your Jack.'

Colleen sniggered. 'Well, that's true enough. He was one nasty bastard and I wasn't sorry to see him six foot under. The happiest day of my life was when the old bugger dropped dead. They're all sweet as honey until they get that ring on your finger and then they show their true colours. Ain't one of them worth a jot. Ain't a man in the world worth breaking your heart over.'

'You'd never think about getting hitched again then?'

'Not in a million years. I've got my kids and my grandkids and they're all I need. I mean, Jesus, the dog's better company than that old sod ever was.' Colleen took a slurp of the gin and licked her lips. 'No, there's no way I'd ever walk down that road again. I'd rather stab out my eyes with red-hot needles.'

'You've got a point. I'd be happier doing time than living with Roy.' Petra looked around the pub and sighed. 'Although I do miss London. Bournemouth's nice enough but it's not home, if you know what I mean. I've been thinking of moving back.'

'You should. It hasn't been the same without you. You could sell your place and get a nice little flat.'

Petra wrinkled her nose. 'Oh, I don't fancy some poky little flat. I like a bit of room to breathe. To be honest, I just want my old house back. That's not too much to ask, is it?' She heaved out a sigh. 'Trouble is, I've got to get rid of that tart first.'

'She ain't gonna leave without a fight.'

'Tell me about it.'

'I mean, she's on to a good thing, free board and lodgings and cash coming from the yard. She can do what she likes so long as Roy don't get to hear about it. Course you could just kick her out and change the locks but I reckon that wouldn't go down too well. How about your Wayne? Couldn't he help you out?'

'Fat chance. She's got him wound round her little finger, same way she has Roy. And our Kelly's in no fit state to do anything. No, I'll just bide my time and see what happens. You never know what's round the corner.'

'God will provide,' said Colleen.

'Well, that would be a first. He ain't done much for me up to now so I won't hold me breath.'

The two women stayed chatting until closing time when they left the warmth of the pub, braved the bitter wind and walked together to the corner of Raleigh Road where they went their separate ways. It was almost midnight by the time Petra got to the house, unlocked the door and went inside. She could hear the television and the sound of voices as she hung up her coat in the hallway.

In the living room, she was met with a cosy family scene. Wayne was sprawled in an armchair, and Kelly was curled up on the sofa with her head against Sharon's shoulder. Petra felt a surge of anger seeing her daughter so close to that filthy little tart. It got under her skin. It really rankled. If anyone was going to comfort her daughter, it should be her.

'You all right, love?' Petra asked pointedly.

Kelly raised her eyes and gave a nod. 'How's Colleen?'

'Same as always. She sends her best.'

'We were just talking about the funeral.'

'Oh, yeah?'

'We thought we'd go in Sharon's car. There'll be more room for us all.'

Petra's eyebrows pulled together in a frown. She glared at the bitch before returning her gaze to Kelly. 'She's not coming.'

'Of course she is.'

'No way.'

'Why not?'

'You know why not.'

Sharon looked from one to the other. 'Jesus, I am here, you know.'

'Worst luck,' snarled Petra. 'This is a family funeral and you ain't family. So just keep your nose out of it, huh?'

Sharon's upper lip curled. 'It ain't up to you who goes to

202

Eddie's funeral or not. You can't say one way or the other. If Kelly wants me to go, I'll go, and that's the end of it.'

'I wouldn't be so sure of that.'

'Just grow up, Petra. This ain't about you. Think about your daughter for once.'

Petra put her hands on her hips. Gin usually made her maudlin but tonight it was inflaming her rage and making her feel even more bitter and resentful. 'Oh, yeah? And how much thinking about her where *you* doing when you were shagging my husband behind my back?'

'Christ, you're not still banging on about that, are you? For fuck's sake, it was years ago. It's time to get over it, darlin'.' Sharon smirked. 'And let's face it, if he'd been getting what he needed at home, he wouldn't have had to look elsewhere for it.'

'Look for it? From what I heard you were giving it away.'

Sharon leapt up from the sofa, eyes blazing. 'Shut yer mouth, you old cow!'

'Make me!'

Wayne, sensing that bloodshed might be on the horizon, hauled himself to his feet and inserted his body between the warring women. 'For fuck's sake, can't you two give it a rest for five minutes? What about Kel? This ain't helping her none, is it?'

Sharon pointed a scarlet-painted talon at Petra. 'Tell her, not me. I'm not the one being bloody awkward just for the sake of it.'

'Awkward? You've got a bleedin' nerve. Do you hear that, Kelly? Calling *me* bloody awkward after everything she's done.'

Kelly shook her head despairingly. 'God, I've got enough to worry about without you two going at it. I want you both there on Friday. What's wrong with that? Can't you just call a truce and get on for a few hours? That's all I'm asking.'

'Ain't a problem for me,' Sharon said. 'Not so sure about your mother, though.'

'I ain't getting in a car with *that*,' said Petra, stung by her daughter's words. Since when had she and Sharon got so pally? It wasn't that long since Kelly had hated her guts, since she wouldn't have given her the time of day.

Sharon glared at her. 'Well then, you'll have to walk there or get the sodding bus.'

'Please, Mum,' Kelly pleaded. 'Don't be like that.'

Petra glanced at Wayne, but if she was hoping for any support there she only had to look at the expression on his face to know it wouldn't be forthcoming. He'd gone over to the other side and there was nothing she could do about it. Before she could say something she might later regret, she clamped shut her mouth and marched towards the door.

'Mum?' Kelly said.

'What?'

'You will come on Friday, won't you? Please say you will?'

Petra hesitated. 'If that's what you want.'

'Of course it is.'

'All right, then.'

'Thanks, Mum.'

Petra went out of the room and walked stiffly up the stairs. The rage inside her was so strong, so intense, that it took every effort of will to stop it from exploding. She went into the small bedroom, carefully closed the door and slumped down on the single bed. Sharon's smug face danced in front of her eyes. 'Bitch, bitch, bitch!' she repeated like a mantra. Her hands clenched into two tight fists. Well, the filthy little whore might have stolen her husband, might even have got temporary possession of the house, but she wasn't having her daughter too. No, enough was enough. As soon as the funeral was over she'd find a way to get rid of her once and for all.

30

By ten o'clock on Thursday morning, Sadie had her holdall packed and was physically if not mentally prepared for another journey to London. This time instead of searching for Eddie she'd be attending his funeral. The thought filled her with dread. How was she going to endure it, knowing what she knew? A shiver ran through her. She would have to shake the hands of Eddie's parents, expressing her sympathy while all the time—

Her thoughts were interrupted by the piercing ring of the doorbell. 'Oh, who's that?' she said, glancing at her watch. She had a train to catch in half an hour and didn't want to miss it. 'Can you see?'

Joel went to the window and looked down. 'No worries. It's only the postman. I'll go.' He flew down the stairs and was back thirty seconds later brandishing a small parcel. 'It's for you.'

Sadie's heart sank as she took it from him. The address on the front had been written in the childlike scrawl that was unmistakably Mona's. Aware that Joel was watching her, she opened the package with trembling hands, afraid of what lay hidden beneath the brown paper wrapper. It wasn't heavy but as she tore at the sheet she found her thoughts racing. God, what if it was bullets or something crazy like that? She shifted her body to try and obscure Joel's view.

In the event, she needn't have worried. Inside was a silk print Liberty scarf in delicate shades of blues and greens. She held it up, aware even from the feel that it must have been expensive.

'That's pretty,' he said. 'Who's it from?'

'Anne,' she replied, feeling the blood rush to her cheeks. She hated lying to him. She hated the fact that it was becoming second nature to her. 'There's a card with it. It says: *Thanks very much for taking me to the party. Hope to see you soon.*'

'That was sweet of her.'

Sadie quickly shoved the scarf and card back in the brown paper. 'Yes,' she said, forcing a smile. 'She shouldn't have, though. I mean, there was no need. She didn't even stay long.' She'd had to invent a story about Mona having a headache to explain the girl's abrupt disappearance from his parents' house on Sunday afternoon.

'You should invite her for the weekend. After everything's got back to normal.'

Normal? Sadie couldn't imagine her life ever returning to that halcyon state. It seemed like a place where other people lived, a land of milk and honey from which she'd been permanently excluded. 'Yes,' she murmured. 'Maybe.'

'Are you going to wear it?'

'What?'

'The scarf,' he said. 'You should wear it. It'll suit you.'

But Sadie would rather have put a noose around her neck than the silken scarf. 'Not today,' she said. 'I'll . . . I'll save it for a special occasion.' She went through to the bedroom, opened a drawer and pushed the unwanted gift, still in its wrapping, to the very back where she wouldn't have to look at it. As soon as she got home, she'd return it to Mona.

'Are you ready?' Joel called out from the living room. 'We should make a move.'

'I won't be a second.' Sadie took a moment to try and regulate her breathing. She could feel her heart thumping in her chest. Mona's present, although innocuous enough on the surface, served as an untimely reminder of the 'deal' that was still apparently in place. What if she turned up at the funeral and started making demands? But no, she had no way of knowing when or where it was, unless—

'Joel,' she said, quickly walking back into the living room. 'If Anne rings, you won't tell her about the funeral, will you?'

Joel gave her a puzzled look. 'Why not?'

'Oh, because she just has a habit of turning up out of the blue. I know she means well but tomorrow's going to be difficult enough without . . . Just say I've gone away for a couple of days and I'll give her a call when I get back.' She knew that Joel didn't really get it, that in his world people were always pleased to see friends and never tried to avoid them. 'You don't mind, do you? I don't want you to lie or anything.'

'It's okay, I understand. Sometimes you just need a bit of space, huh?'

'Something like that.'

A few minutes later they were in the van and on the way to the station. Sadie kept her eyes on the side mirror, wondering if they were being followed. Ever since Royston had approached her, she'd been constantly glancing over her shoulder. He was the type of journalist who wouldn't think twice about putting a tail on her.

'Are you going to stay in the same B&B?' Joel asked.

'No, Oaklands is more of a boarding house. They don't rent out by the night. I'll find somewhere else; there are lots of places I can go.'

'At least it'll still be light by the time you get there.'

'I'll give you a call when I'm in Kellston.'

Joel pulled the car into the station, cut the engine and looked at her. 'Are you sure you'll be all right on your own? It's not too late. I can still come with you.'

'No, it's fine. Honestly. There's no point in both of us missing a day's work. Thanks for the offer, though.' She leant in to kiss him, wishing that she didn't have to leave, that she didn't have to face the awfulness of Eddie's funeral alone. But it would be even more of a trial if Joel was with her; she'd be constantly worried about bumping into Nathan Stone, or Mona turning up or some dreadful confrontation with the Gissings. 'I'll be home before you know it.'

'Let me know what time the train's due in and I'll come and pick you up.'

'Thanks.' Sadie got out of the car, shut the door and headed for the platform. She turned round to wave and Joel waved back. As she watched the van leave the forecourt, she had a sudden urge to run after it, to leap into the passenger seat and beg him to take her with him to Buckingham Road. *I've changed my mind. I don't want to go to London.* It was as if there was something final about the goodbye, as if her old world was crumbling around her. She felt a lump in her throat and tears sprang into her eyes.

For a while she stood staring into the empty space that had recently contained the man she loved. It was too late now. He was gone. She just had to get on with it. Pull yourself together, Sadie. Wasn't that what her mother would say? With a heavy heart, she traipsed on to the platform, found an empty bench and sat down to wait.

Her journey to London was long but uneventful. She made a point of not talking to anyone, of keeping her gaze averted from her fellow travellers. She stuck her head in a book and kept it there – apart from the few train changes – until she reached the East End. It was only then that she put the book away and gazed out of the window.

She saw the same grey sky and the same drab houses. As the three tall concrete towers of Kellston came into view her stomach gave a lurch. That was where Eddie had died, where Mona – for her own sick reasons – had decided to end his life. The knowledge weighed heavily on her, a reminder of everything she was doing wrong. She should have had the courage to go to the police and tell them her suspicions while she still had the chance. With every day that passed, the truth receded further into the shadows. Who would believe her side of the story now? No one, she suspected; not even Joel.

It was drizzling when she left the station, a light cold rain that slid down the back of her neck. She crossed over at the traffic lights and began to walk along the road. As she passed Oaklands she gazed almost fondly at its exterior, wishing she could book in there again. It would have been nice to have somewhere familiar to lay her head that night.

After wandering up and down for a while, she decided to try a place called Greyfriars, which had a prominent B&B sign outside as well as a *Vacancies* notice in the front window. She went up to the door, raised her hand and was just about to press the bell when she heard a voice behind her.

'Sadie?'

Surprised, she turned round to find Velma standing behind her. She walked back along the path, pleased to see a friendly face. 'Hi,' she said, smiling. 'How are you?'

Velma, dressed in a short black leather skirt, black boots and fake fur jacket, grinned at her. 'Hello, love. What are you doing here? Not on the run, are you? We heard about your old man. The law were round asking questions and checking out your story. I didn't tell them nothin', said I only saw you to say hello to.'

'No, not on the run. Not yet, at least.' Sadie paused and then added, 'And in case you're wondering, I didn't do it.'

'Don't make no difference to me, one way or the other, love. There are plenty of blokes that I wouldn't have minded . . . Well, let's just say there are times I've been tempted.'

'I don't suppose Mrs Cuthbert was best pleased, having the police round.'

'Are you kidding? The old bat loved every minute. It's the most exciting thing that's happened to her in years. 'Course she'd have preferred it if you were actually guilty. Makes for a better story, don't it, having a murderer staying under your roof.'

'That's me,' said Sadie wryly, 'a constant disappointment.'

Velma glanced towards the B&B. 'So what are you doing here? Oaklands isn't that bad, is it?'

'It's Eddie's funeral tomorrow. I just need a room for the night.'

'So?'

'So, last time I was here Mrs Cuthbert told me that she only rents out by the week.'

Velma slid her arm through Sadie's and started pulling her along the road. 'You don't want to listen to anything the Cuthbert tells you. She makes it up as she goes along.'

'Are you sure? I don't want to—'

'Leave it to me,' Velma said confidently.

Sadie didn't argue. Meeting up with Velma had instantly raised her spirits; she was the type of person who took you at face value and never seemed to judge. 'Well, let me buy you a drink later. It's the least I can do.'

'Ta, I'd like that. We can go to the Fox. It's not so far to stagger home.'

In the slightly musty hallway, Velma yelled along the corridor. 'Mrs C? Are you there?'

After a few seconds, the landlady appeared, wiping her hands on a floral apron. As soon as she saw Sadie she stopped and frowned.

'Look who's here,' Velma said. 'We can squeeze her in for the night, can't we? There's no one in her old room.'

'I don't do single nights,' Mrs Cuthbert said bluntly. 'It's the rule.'

Velma put her hands on her hips and raised her eyes to the ceiling. 'Oh, come on, Mrs C, don't be like that. I'm sure you can bend the rules, just this once. I mean, didn't Sadie pay for a full week last time she was here? And she only stayed for a few nights so I reckon you owe her.'

But Mrs Cuthbert shook her head. 'I don't want any trouble. This is a respectable establishment.'

'Yeah, right,' Velma said. 'Everyone who stays here is white as the driven snow. And what kind of trouble is Sadie going to cause? It's hardly her fault that her old man got done in. It's not as though *she* did it. Come on, give her a break. She's had a tough enough time already.'

Mrs Cuthbert looked from one woman to the other before her gaze finally settled on Sadie. She mulled over Velma's words for a few seconds before finally making up her mind. 'Just the one night then,' she said. 'I suppose it can't do any harm. The room's not locked. I'll leave the key on the hall table for you.'

'Thanks,' Sadie said. 'I appreciate it.'

'Ta, Mrs C,' said Velma, dragging Sadie up the stairs before the landlady could change her mind. 'And don't worry about a thing.'

'That'll be the day,' Mrs Cuthbert muttered as she disappeared down the hall. Her slippers made a soft flip-flop sound on the worn carpet. 'I'm too kind-hearted for my own good, that's the problem.'

Velma waited until they were out of earshot before speaking

again. 'So how did it go with the law? Did they give you the third degree?'

Sadie shrugged. 'They came to see me and asked about the last time I saw Eddie, but that was about it. I've not heard anything since.'

'You're off the hook then.'

'Maybe.'

'You don't sound so sure.'

'I'm not,' Sadie admitted. 'Until they found out who did it, I guess I'm still a suspect.'

They climbed the stairs to the second landing and went into Sadie's room. Velma sat down on the single bed, looking thoughtful. 'What made you decide to go to the funeral? I thought after what you said about Eddie and all . . .'

'I wasn't going to,' Sadie said, dumping her holdall on the floor. 'But then his dad rang me and told me when it was and . . . well, it didn't feel right to say I couldn't.'

'But you'd rather not?'

'Nobody likes funerals, do they? And with all the history Eddie and I had . . . I don't know, it doesn't feel right, but then not going doesn't feel right either.'

Velma gave a nod. 'You should be careful. Those Gissings ain't what you'd call the forgiving sort.'

Sadie stared at her, recalling some fairly similar words that had come from Nathan Stone. 'No one's going to kick off at a funeral, though, are they?'

'I wouldn't count on it, love. That lot aren't renowned for their good manners.'

Sadie gave a sigh. 'You're not doing much for my nerves, Velma. I'm shaky enough as it is.'

'A few drinks will soon put that right, hon. And don't mind me: I've learned to always expect the worst and that way it's rarely as bad as you think.'

'I hope you're right.'

'Where do you have to go, for the service and that?'

'It's at St Luke's at ten o'clock.'

'Oh, that's only down the road. You can walk it from here.'

Sadie opened her handbag and reached for her purse so she could get some change for the meter. As she did so, her fingers touched against the cool metal of the gun. It was probably blasphemous to take a Beretta into church but unless she could get rid of it before tomorrow that's exactly what she'd have to do.

'You okay?' Velma asked. 'I haven't upset you, have I? Me and my big mouth. I never know when to keep quiet.'

'No, of course not. I'm just looking for a fifty pence so we can get some heat in here.' Sadie found a coin and crouched down by the fire. She put the coin in the slot, turned the switch and listened as the gas hissed out of the pipes. A second later the flames came on, pale blue and yellow before they gradually changed to orange. She was reminded suddenly of the flames of hell. Perhaps that was where she was heading. But she'd chosen her path and there was no turning back.

31

Sadie thought the interior of the Fox looked vaguely familiar. Perhaps she'd been here with Eddie all those years ago when he'd brought her to Kellston. There was always alcohol involved in any day out with Eddie Wise. This place was particularly nice with a clean wood floor, comfortable chairs and a blazing log fire. The pub, filled with the sound of talk and laughter, had a pleasant, relaxed atmosphere.

Sadie glanced over towards the bar where Velma was waiting to be served. They'd had a few drinks already and the wine was having a soothing effect. She knew she shouldn't drink too much or she'd be nursing a hangover tomorrow morning. Funerals were hard enough to deal with without the added pain of a thumping headache.

Earlier, she'd given Joel a call to tell him she'd arrived safely and managed to get a room at Oaklands. The line had been bad and she'd struggled to hear. The sound of his muffled voice had exaggerated the feeling of distance, a distance that was more than just the miles that lay between them. Why had she ever lied? It had created a barrier that she didn't seem able to overcome. She wondered if Joel felt it too or if he simply put her recent distraction down to the shock of Eddie's death.

Sadie was still mulling this over when a man walked past the table. He did a double take and came back to stare at her.

'Sadie Wise! What the hell are you doing here?'

She looked up at the scowling face of Nathan Stone. 'Thanks for the welcome. It's nice to see you too.'

'What do you expect after what you did, a bleedin' brass band?'

'It never hurts to be civil,' she replied stiffly. 'And what exactly have I done that's upset you so much?'

'You know what.'

Sadie shook her head. 'If I knew I wouldn't be asking.'

Stone made a quick scan of the surrounding tables before sitting down beside her and lowering his voice. 'Thanks to you, lady, we've got a bloody war with the Gissings on our hands.'

'And how do you figure that?'

'How do you think? Someone saw us together down the dogs and now Wayne Gissing has got it into his head that I'm involved in Eddie's killing. His little sister's heartbroken and he wants someone to pay.'

Sadie stood her ground and said stubbornly, 'So? I still don't see how any of that's my fault.'

Stone's eyes took on an even colder shade of grey. 'I'm sorry, but weren't you the one who came to me wanting Eddie's address?'

'Yes, and weren't you the one who wouldn't hand it over unless I went with you to the dogs? I'd say if this is anyone's fault, it's yours. If you'd just given me the address, then there wouldn't have been any bother. Well, not for you at least.'

The corners of Stone's mouth twitched although whether it was in a smile or a sneer was impossible to tell. 'Yeah, well, I didn't know Eddie was going to end up with a knife in his chest.'

'And you think I did?'

'I've no idea,' he said.

Sadie glared at him. 'I didn't have anything to do with Eddie's murder. Why would I want him dead?'

'I've no idea, but then I wasn't married to him.' Stone pulled a face. 'And you never did answer my question. What exactly are you doing back in Kellston?'

'Is that any of your business?'

'Just wondering if you're likely to cause me any more grief.'

'Perhaps you should stay away from me,' Sadie said. 'That way you'll be nice and safe.'

'Bit late for that.'

'So maybe next time you'll think twice about forcing women into random nights out.'

Stone raised his eyebrows. 'You can be sure of it, although I don't recall much forcing going on. But I'll certainly think twice about doing anyone a favour again.'

'It's hardly a favour when you demand something in exchange.'

Stone hissed out a breath. 'Tell me you're not going to the funeral.'

'Why shouldn't I?'

'You got some kind of death wish or what? Don't you know the Gissings are going to be there?'

Velma came back with the drinks and looked at them both. 'Not interrupting, am I?'

'No,' Sadie said. 'Mr Stone was just leaving.'

Nathan Stone stood up, his face looking grim. 'Just watch your back, Sadie. If you've got any sense you'll stay well away from that funeral.'

Sadie stared as he walked off and moved through the crowd towards the bar. 'That man,' she muttered.

'He likes you,' Velma said.

Sadie reached for her drink and gave a snort. 'Like a hole in the head.'

'Oh, believe me, *Watch your back* is about as close to a term of endearment as Nathan Stone gets. He's not what you'd call the emotional sort.'

Sadie glanced across the pub to where Stone was chatting to the red-haired woman behind the bar. Some men, she figured, were just born arrogant and he was certainly one of them. 'It's not my back he's bothered about, it's his own. He's just worried in case I stir up more trouble.'

'Maybe he's right about the funeral, though. Are you sure you should go?'

'No,' Sadie said, 'but it's too late now. I told Eddie's dad I'd be there so I can't change my mind. Anyway, I'm only going to the service, not for drinks or anything after. There'll be lots of people at the church. Nothing's likely to . . . I mean, a church is pretty safe, isn't it?'

'Yeah, I'm sure it will be. Just keep an eye on that Wayne Gissing.'

'I don't even know what he looks like.'

'You can't miss him, love. He's a short, ugly fucker with a face like the back of a bus.'

Sadie sighed. 'Sounds like a dream. I'll watch out for him.'

'And his sister's no shrinking violet either. She'd rip your eyes out soon as look at you. All those Gissings are trouble, but Wayne's the worst. Ever since his old man went down he's been giving it the big I am. Thinks he's got something to prove now that he's running things. There was another bust-up last night over at the Hope. It's one of Terry Street's pubs and Wayne knows better than to go anywhere near it. Didn't stop him, though; place was wrecked apparently.'

'I suppose Stone's blaming me for that too.' Sadie gazed towards the bar again, noticing for the first time the smart grey suit he was wearing. Grey suit, grey hair, grey eyes. 'Mr Grey,' she muttered at exactly the same moment as his gaze suddenly shifted and met hers. Quickly, she looked back at Velma, embarrassed to have been caught in the act of staring.

'He's not that bad,' Velma said. 'Considering.'

'Considering what?'

'Well, you know, after everything that happened.'

Sadie didn't know. 'And what was that?'

'With his wife and all.' Velma shot Nathan Stone a sideways glance, and then leaned forward partly covering her mouth with her hand as if he might be able to lip read. 'Leah, her name was; a real looker – she'd turn any man's head – but completely nuts. Led him a right old dance. She wasn't what you'd call the faithful sort.'

'So?' Sadie said. 'We've all been there. Eddie wasn't able to keep it in his trousers for more than five minutes.'

'So that's something you've got in common.'

'I don't think so. Half the world's had someone cheat on them at one time or another.'

Velma gave a nod. 'Sure they have, hon, but not everyone's partners have been murdered.'

Sadie frowned. 'What are you saying? That Leah—'

'Yeah, someone put a bullet through her head … God, it must have been about seven years back now. 'Course Nathan was first on the list of suspects, especially as they'd had a very public row earlier in the evening. He reckoned he hadn't seen her again after that but Old Bill thought different. And then they found the gun at his flat and …'

Sadie snatched another quick glance and shivered. Of course he was bad. She'd recognised that from the first time she'd met him. 'So why isn't he locked up?'

'Oh, he was. Got life for it, didn't he? 'Cept then it turned out that the cops who nabbed him were bent and made a habit of planting evidence. After three years, the conviction was overturned on appeal and Nathan walked free.'

'But was he innocent?'

'Your guess is as good as mine. Maybe he was, maybe he wasn't. Anyway, it was while he was inside that he met Terry Street. Terry was on remand for something or other – I can't remember what – and the two of them palled up. The rest, as they say, is history. Nathan's been working for Terry ever since he got out.'

Sadie felt her chest tighten. It was a scary thought that she had spent the evening with someone who could be guilty of murder. Although, she supposed, he could say the same thing too, although she didn't imagine that Nathan Stone was scared of much and especially not of a woman. If you'd spent time inside and survived it, there probably wasn't much that could frighten you. 'I wonder if he did it,' she murmured.

Velma raised her eyebrows. 'Best not to go there, hon. Judge not that ye be not judged. Ain't that what the holy folk say? Maybe a few people wondered about you too.'

'They still do,' said Sadie, thinking about the inspector and all his questions, thinking about Peter Royston with his sly, suspicious eyes.

'Well then.'

Sadie gave a nod. Velma was right: she shouldn't be too quick to judge. 'I just wondered why he went to work for someone like Terry Street.'

'Jobs ain't that easy to come by, love, especially when you've been inside. Doesn't matter if some court says you're innocent and lets you go, there's plenty who'll still believe there's no smoke without fire. You can't blame a man for wanting to make a living.'

'No, I guess not.' But Sadie, even though she understood this, still couldn't bring herself to like him. Stone wound her up.

He was like an itch under her skin – constantly annoying – and no amount of scratching was going to ease the irritation. Her gaze slid back to the bar where he was now perched on a stool, smoking a cigarette. She had the feeling that his pose was deceptively casual, that in fact he was aware of everything and everyone around him.

'He still hacks me off though.'

'I can see, hon. That's one almighty scowl on your forehead.'

Sadie made an effort to smooth out the frown. 'I can't help it. Do you think he was deliberately trying to scare me? About the funeral and all?'

'Why would he do that?'

'Why does Nathan Stone do anything?'

Velma didn't get the chance to answer. At that moment a young, peroxide blonde woman who was almost definitely a prostitute – low-cut blouse, a miniskirt barely covering her backside and enough slap on her face to start a Revlon factory – came over to the table. She put her right hand on her hip and pouted.

'Velma, love, you in tonight?'

'No, babe. I've got Sandra covering for me. What's wrong?'

'I'll tell you what's wrong: you have to do something about Dexter. It took him ten bleedin' minutes to get up the stairs after I rang the alarm last night. Ten minutes, hon! I could have been dead meat by then. It ain't right. He's a lazy fucker. And that Sandra's not much better either. All she does is sit on her arse and watch the box; bloody place could be burning down and she wouldn't notice.'

'Okay, I'll have a word.'

'You'll get it sorted?'

'I just said, didn't I?'

'But you'll do it soon, yeah? And that gas fire's been playin' up again. Icy it's been for the past few nights. It ain't good for business having the punters freezing their bollocks off.'

Velma heaved out a breath. 'Anything else, hon, or can I get on with my drink now?'

'Oh, pardon me. Didn't know I was interrupting something important.' The girl threw Velma a hostile look before flouncing off.

Sadie gazed after the prostitute, her brain rapidly digesting the words she'd just heard. She hadn't got around to asking Velma what she did for a living and now she didn't need to. Her jaw must have dropped because Velma gave a light laugh.

'Not shocked are you, love?'

Sadie quickly shook her head. 'Why should I be shocked?'

Velma smiled wryly. 'Because you're a nice middle-class girl who's just discovered that she's out with a tom. Wouldn't blame you for feeling a bit—'

'I don't,' Sadie insisted. And then, seeing the sceptical look in Velma's eyes, she shrugged and admitted, 'A bit surprised, I suppose, but that's only because I'd never have guessed. I mean, you don't look like . . . ' It was true that Velma maybe dressed a little young for her age, but plenty of women did that. 'I just thought you worked in a shop or an office.'

'To be honest, I pretty much hung up the fishnets a few years back. You reach a certain point and . . . ' Velma gave a resigned kind of sigh. 'Well, Terry has a couple of houses down Albert Road and I help look after the girls. It don't bring in a fortune but it keeps me going. Every little helps, as they say.'

Sadie gazed curiously at Velma. She had never met what her mother would call 'a lady of the night' before and found herself fascinated. 'So you're a sort of madam now?'

'Ah, I wouldn't call myself that. No, I just book the punters in and make sure they behave themselves. I ain't no Cynthia Payne, that's for sure.'

Sadie remembered the name. Cynthia, a middle-aged so-called party hostess, had made the headlines when she'd been charged with running a brothel in Streatham. There had been lurid tales of elderly men dressing up in lingerie and being spanked by young women. And something faintly farcical about payment being made with luncheon vouchers. 'She was in the papers, wasn't she? Didn't she go to jail?'

'Six months, hon, although the judge gave her eighteen at the end of the trial. There was talk of lawyers and MPs being clients, not to mention a vicar or two. That's what really got up their noses. Still worried about all that Profumo shit, you see. The sentence was reduced on appeal though; she only served six.'

'Don't you ever worry about being raided?'

'There's no chance of that. Terry makes sure that all the right palms are greased. Old Bill pull a few girls off the streets every now and then, just for appearance's sake, but then Terry pays the fines and everyone's happy.'

Sadie, although she'd heard about police corruption, about bent coppers, had never been sure how widespread it was. 'Really? Is that how it works?'

'Sure. The law knows it can't get rid of prostitution, love. It ain't called the oldest profession for nothing. They can move the girls on for a while, clear a street or two, but they can't make it go away. For as long as there are men willing to pay, there'll be girls prepared to take the cash.'

Sadie took a sip of her wine while she thought about this. 'It must be scary, though,' she said. 'You don't ever know who's going to walk through that door. Do you get much trouble?'

'Some, but nothing I can't deal with. And it's safer for the girls being inside than out. Mainly it's regulars, same guys turning up again and again. It's the strangers you got to watch out for, the unfamiliar faces; you're never sure how they're going to behave.'

Sadie couldn't imagine what it would be like to have sex with a stranger, to have a man pay you money to ... The very

222

thought made her flesh crawl. And what about when one of them turned nasty? She recalled what the blonde had said about Dexter, about being dead meat, about how long it had taken him to get up the stairs. 'Gruesome,' she murmured.

'I need a pee,' Velma said. 'This vodka's going straight through me.'

It was less than thirty seconds before her place was taken by Nathan Stone. He slid into Velma's chair and said, 'So, have you made up your mind about the funeral?'

Sadie looked at him, frowning again. 'I thought we'd already had this conversation.'

'Having it and resolving it are two completely different things.'

'And how would you like it to be resolved?'

Stone gave her a long steady look. 'By you seeing sense and getting on the first train out of here tomorrow morning.'

'I can't do that,' she replied stubbornly. 'I've said I'll go and I will. Anyway, what would it look like if I didn't? They'd all reckon I had something to hide. I didn't kill Eddie so why should I act like I'm guilty?'

'Do you know who did?'

The question surprised her and she struggled to maintain her composure. 'Of course not! What makes you think ... How would I know?' She felt the blood burning her cheeks as she thought of Mona, as she thought of the plans that had been made and the small black gun that was lying in her bag. 'I hadn't seen him in years. I don't know what he was up to or ... or who he hung around with.'

'You sure?' he asked sharply.

'For God's sake,' she said, desperate to be rid of him, 'can't you just leave me alone? I'm going, okay? That's the end of it.'

Nathan Stone rose to his feet, shaking his head. 'I doubt that,' he said. 'I doubt it very much.'

As he walked away, Sadie wondered if he really had killed his wife. Was he the kind of man who could put a bullet through a woman's skull? She felt her stomach shift with fear and revulsion. Quickly she reached for her drink and took a gulp. It didn't matter, she told herself. Nothing about Nathan Stone mattered. After tonight she'd never have to see him again. Tomorrow she'd attend the funeral and then she'd go back home to Joel.

Velma returned and sat down again. 'You all right, love? You look kind of pale.'

'I think I'll make a move,' Sadie said. 'Do you mind?'

'Ain't you going to finish your drink?'

'No, I've had enough. I'm really tired. I think I'll have an early night.' Suddenly, she wanted to be out of the pub, away from everyone and especially Nathan Stone. She got up and patted Velma on the shoulder. 'You stay. I'll be fine. I've only got to walk across the road.'

'Okay, love. Take care. I'll see you tomorrow.'

When Sadie reached the door, she glanced back but Stone had disappeared. The place where he'd been sitting by the bar was empty. His words, however, continued to revolve in her head. *Just watch your back, Sadie.* She swallowed down her fear and hurried out into the cold night air.

32

Petra Gissing stared at her son, who was examining his face in the living-room mirror. His left eyelid, the colour of dark ochre, was almost closed, and a more purplish shade of bruising had spread down to his cheek. His upper lip was split and swollen. 'Don't expect any sympathy from me,' she said.

Wayne's focus shifted slightly. 'Did I ask for any?'

'What were you thinking, going back to the Hope? Begging for it, that's what. And now look at you! It's not going to get any better by the morning. You're going to look a right mess for the funeral.'

Wayne sneered and winced almost simultaneously. 'Eddie ain't going to care. It don't matter to him.'

'What were you thinking?' she asked again, her voice sounding peevish. 'You were just asking for trouble.'

'Terry's the one doing that. It ain't right what he did and you know it.' Wayne turned away from the mirror and sat down on the sofa. His hands with their large red knuckles rested on his heavy thighs. 'He had it coming and you can't say different.'

'Yeah, right. Except I don't see Terry walking around with his face all smashed up.'

Wayne sniggered. 'Maybe not his face, but his pub ain't looking so good.'

'And you think he's going to lose any sleep over that?' Petra couldn't figure out why the filth hadn't charged that Sadie girl yet. She'd made the call to Cowan Road and had been hoping that a quick arrest might put an end to all this bother. But then Terry had friends in high places. Maybe he'd paid the bastards off, got them to leave Nathan Stone and his tart alone. 'He'll have the Hope all fixed up by now, but you won't be able to see proper for days.'

'It's nothin', a few bruises, that's all.'

'And next time?'

Wayne gave her a nasty look. 'Next time I'll make sure that it's more than the pub that gets done over.'

Petra pulled a face, but decided to drop the subject. There was no reasoning with her son when he was in this kind of mood. 'And what have you been doing down in that cellar?'

'What?'

'The cellar. You've been tramping coal dust all over the kitchen again. What are you doing down there?'

'Nothin',' he said. 'I told you. Looking for a screwdriver.'

'That was days ago. Ain't you found it yet?'

'If I'd found it, I wouldn't still be looking, would I?'

Petra reckoned he was lying. He was up to something, but she didn't know what. If she didn't hate that place so much, she'd nip down and take a butcher's, but the cellar with its dim light and shadowy corners creeped her out. She always felt like she was being watched, that a bogeyman was waiting to pounce on her. Even the thought of opening the door made her go all cold and shivery. 'Well, just think on.'

'What's that supposed to mean?'

'It means don't go getting yourself in even more bother.'

Wayne lit a fag, sat back and smiled thinly at her. 'I suppose you'll be making a move once the funeral's over.'

'You trying to get rid of me?'

'No.'

'Sounds like it.'

'Just wondering, that's all. You could take Kel with you for a while. Yeah, a bit of sea air would do her the world of good.'

'The law might have something to say about that. She's supposed to stay in London, ain't she?'

Wayne gave a shrug. 'I don't reckon she's a suspect any more. So long as we let them know where she is, there won't be a problem. Yeah, she could do with a break, get away from here. Why don't you ask her?'

'Maybe she doesn't want to leave. She's got all her friends in Kellston.'

Wayne frowned at her. 'So? It's not like it's for ever or nothin', just a week or two.' He took a drag on his cigarette and squinted with his one good eye through the stream of smoke. 'She stays here, Mum, she's going to get in bother. I'm sure of it. You know what Kel's like when she goes off on one. Don't want to see her banged up, do you? No, you're better off taking her away, least in Bournemouth she'll be safe and you'll be able to keep a check on her.'

'I can keep a check on her here.'

'Not really. What if she flips, decides to have a go at Nathan Stone?'

Petra narrowed her eyes. 'She doesn't know about that girl and Stone. Shit, tell me you haven't told her. You haven't, have you?'

'Course not. But you think she ain't gonna find out? People talk. She stays here and she'll hear about it soon enough.'

The front door slammed and a few seconds later Kelly came in. 'What?' she said, glancing from one to the other as a silence fell over the room.

Petra smiled at her daughter. 'You okay, love?'

'I was,' she said, staring at them both suspiciously. 'What's going on?'

'We were just chatting. Your brother here thinks it might be a good idea if you came back with me to Bournemouth.'

Kelly shot him a look. 'I ain't going nowhere.'

'You see?' Petra said smugly to her son. 'I told you so.'

'Just for a few days, a week,' Wayne said. 'Why not?'

'You know why not,' Kelly snapped back. 'I ain't leaving here until I find out who killed my Eddie.' She stormed through to the kitchen, her face full of anger. Shortly afterwards there was the sound of the kettle starting to boil followed by the noisy clatter of mugs and spoons.

Petra started to get to her feet, but Wayne waved her back down. 'I'll have a word with her,' he said. 'You want a brew?'

'I wouldn't say no.'

As soon as he closed the kitchen door behind him, Wayne knew he was for it. Kelly turned, her eyes blazing, and hissed, 'What's your fuckin' game? What are you playing at?'

'I'm just trying to get shot of her,' he said. 'It's the only thing I could think of. She's been asking about the cellar. I reckon she knows something's going on.'

'So? She ain't going to go down there, is she?'

'You don't know that for sure. It'll make everything a damn sight easier if she just goes back to Bournemouth.'

'Well, I ain't going with her so you can forget it.'

'You could go for a few days and then come back. The tart's still going to be here. What difference does it make?'

Kelly jabbed at his chest with her index finger. 'Ain't you listening to a word I say? No! No way! You got it? I'm staying right here until we sort that filthy murdering cow.'

'Okay,' Wayne said, raising his hands palm out. 'I get it. Keep your voice down, huh? You want Mum to hear?'

Kelly stared at her brother, her teeth bared. 'That Sadie is going to pay for what she did. The bitch is going to fuckin' pay!'

33

Sadie woke with a jolt from a bad dream she'd been having. Rushing from room to room in a strange house full of men and women she had never met before, she'd been searching desperately for Joel. Where was he? Why couldn't she find him? It was important, essential, that she tracked him down. There was a party going on, music playing, people dancing and laughing. She ran upstairs and downstairs, panic rising inside her. Have you seen Joel? He had gone, someone said, he had already left. She was too late.

Sadie lay peering into the darkness, feeling her heart racing in her chest. A dreadful sense of loss swept over her, as if Joel was the one who had died rather than Eddie. She thought of the funeral that was still to be endured and wished the day was over and that she was back in Haverlea. If only she could turn her head and see Joel sleeping. If only she could hear his steady breathing she would know that everything was going to be all right.

Despite the blackness that surrounded her, she was certain it was morning. Outside there was already a steady flow of traffic in the street. Rain fell against the window, making a hard smattering sound and causing the glass to rattle. She recalled the night before, her drink with Velma in the Fox, and the unwelcome interruption from Nathan Stone. There were things that she had meant to ask him, about the Gissings, about Eddie's murder, but they gone clean out of her head when she was face to face with him. Had he sensed that she wasn't entirely innocent? There had been a look in his grey eyes, something like suspicion, but perhaps that was just her guilty conscience.

Sadie reached out and flicked on the lamp. She looked at her watch – it was almost eight o'clock – and quickly pushed back the blankets. Instantly, she was aware of the cold. She got dressed hurriedly, pulling on the black trousers and the black polo neck sweater she had chosen to wear for the funeral.

After padding along the corridor to the bathroom, Sadie returned to her room and stared at her reflection in the mirror as she combed her hair. Her face was pale, its almost ghostly pallor exaggerated by the darkness of her clothes. She put on some lipstick and then wiped it off again; the colour seemed too bright against her skin.

How was she going to get through the morning? There was a stone in her stomach the size of a boulder. She shouldn't have come. It was wrong, a mistake. It didn't matter what people thought of her; she should have stayed in Haverlea and sent a wreath. She was tempted for a moment to follow Stone's advice and get on the first train out of Kellston. But she wouldn't, she couldn't. She owed it to Eddie to at least attend his funeral.

Down in the breakfast room, she had the impression of time standing still, of everything being exactly as it had been on the last occasion she'd been here. Even the rain seemed to be falling with the very same speed and intensity. The room was empty apart from the middle-aged man sitting in the same place, reading what could have been the same copy of *The Times*. He glanced up and gave her a nod.

'Good morning.'

'Morning,' she replied.

Sadie sat down at the same table she had chosen last time. She was still not fully awake and things had a vaguely dreamlike quality to them. Her gaze floated over the box of cornflakes, the sugar bowl and the jug of milk. The white tablecloth was stained in places, pale beige patches where something – probably tea or coffee – had been spilt in the past and not come out in the wash.

Mrs Cuthbert shuffled in and placed a small pot of tea and a metal rack containing four quarters of lightly browned toast in front of her.

'Thank you,' Sadie murmured.

The old woman grunted and shuffled back to the kitchen without a word. Sadie wasn't sure if this response was a sign of disapproval or if she was equally taciturn with everyone at this time of the morning.

'Dreary day for it,' the middle-aged man said.

Sadie looked over at him. 'Yes, I suppose so.' She wasn't sure if he was referring to the funeral – did he even know about it? – or just to life in general. Not wanting to get into a conversation about Eddie she busied herself with the toast and butter and marmalade.

'You brought the rain with you,' he said.

Sadie gave him a nod, a faint smile, before returning to her breakfast and hoping he would get the hint. *Please leave me alone*, she wanted to say. *Leave me in peace. I don't want to talk to anyone.* She needed this time to get her thoughts in order, to prepare for what was to come.

A silence followed, broken only by the sound of the man clearing his throat and then the gentle rustle of his newspaper. Sadie felt her shoulders tense as she waited for him to speak again. She nibbled on the toast, wondering what she would say to Eddie's parents. *I'm so sorry for your loss.* Wasn't that what people usually said? And she was sorry, but she doubted if they would actually believe her. There was too much history, too much bad feeling.

At a quarter to nine Sadie went back upstairs and put on her coat. She would have to leave the holdall here and collect it later; she could hardly turn up for a funeral toting her luggage. Yes, she would come back when it was over, pay Mrs Cuthbert what she owed and jump on a train. It was still early but she wanted to check out exactly where the church was. Velma had given her directions and they seemed simple enough, but the last thing she wanted was to show up late.

As it turned out St Luke's wasn't hard to find. It was a small, pretty stone building with a modest spire and a few old tomb-stones scattered around its grounds. She stood in the street and stared at the arched door. At the moment there was no sign of activity; it would be a while before the undertakers and the mourners arrived. She thought of Eddie lying in his coffin and gave a shudder. Gone. Gone for ever.

Sadie moved away and crossed the road to Kellston Cemetery where she intended to wait until it was time for the service to begin. She walked down the main thoroughfare, along the wide tarmac path, avoiding the wet grass. The rain was still falling heavily, splattering against the canopy of her umbrella.

Occasionally, she stopped to peer at one of the gravestones and to read the inscription. What had their lives been like? Happy or sad? A bit of both, she supposed. But how many of them had gone to their graves with unspoken secrets on their lips? She wondered how long she could keep quiet about what she knew: a month, a year, a lifetime? Already the guilt was eating away at her.

There were narrower side paths leading off into the far

reaches of the cemetery, winding round to what looked like older, wilder parts. In the distance she could see tall obelisks and grey stone angels with their hands clasped in prayer. For a while she took shelter under a willow tree and watched the people – mainly office workers, judging from their appearance – hurry past her on their way to the station.

Every few minutes she glanced down at her watch, unsure as to whether she wanted the time to speed up or slow down. Anxiety fluttered in her chest. She took deep breaths of the damp winter air, trying to steady her nerves. The cold seeped into her bones as she waited.

Eventually, at a quarter to ten, Sadie made her way back to the main gate and began to walk towards St Luke's. She could still change her mind. It wasn't too late. She didn't have to go through with it. But already she could see the hearse and a few black-clothed mourners gathered in front of the church. If she was going to retreat she would have to do it quickly.

Sadie was tempted; there was no denying the fact. Now that the moment was almost upon her, she wasn't sure if she could go through with it. Why hadn't she let Joel come with her? Safety in numbers was what they said, and here she was, utterly alone.

'It's a funeral,' she muttered to herself. 'Not a battleground.'

Still she held back, searching for friendly faces in the small group by the door, but seeing none. And the longer she stood there the harder it became for her to move. She felt, suddenly, like one of those stone angels in the cemetery, doomed to stand for ever in the same position.

It was only the appearance of Stan Wise that finally jolted her into action. He glanced over in her direction but gave no acknowledgement that he had seen her. Yet she was sure he had, sure that his eyes had rested on her for a moment. And then she knew she had no choice. She took one last deep breath before crossing the road.

34

Sadie slipped into a pew at the very rear of the church, sat down and stared along the central aisle towards the mahogany coffin covered with lilies. Her gaze lingered there for a while – her head full of memories of Eddie – before moving up to the stained-glass window. Despite the greyness of the day, the colours shone through with a shimmering beauty.

It still did not seem possible that Eddie was dead, that his body was lying in a box. It was unreal, hard to grasp. She kept thinking that someone would say that it was all a big mistake. She shivered as the priest's words flowed over her: 'We meet in the name of Jesus Christ, who died and was raised to the glory of God the father. Grace and mercy be with you.'

Sadie's eyes raked the congregation, finally seeing a few faces she recognised, old drinking buddies from the past, people who seemed like strangers to her now. Stan and Marcie Wise were at the front with their daughter, Denise, and several other members of the family. Behind them was Eddie's girlfriend, her long fair hair tied back in a ponytail and held with a black velvet ribbon. An older woman, her mother perhaps, was to Kelly's right, and to her left were a short thickset man and another blonde in her thirties.

As the service progressed, hymns were sung and prayers were said. Sadie found herself assailed by a number of emotions, by sadness, by pity and guilt, but most of all by shame. She should have been honest about Mona Farrell, about what she knew. She should have thought less about her own position and more about the truth. And yet the truth lacked a certain appeal when the end result could be a prison sentence.

While the priest was talking, Sadie became aware of being watched. She shifted her gaze and saw that the thickset man had turned and was glaring at her. Wayne Gissing. It had to be. He was as ugly as Velma had said, and his looks weren't improved by a black eye and a split lip. Was that down to the trouble with Terry Street? Stone's warning echoed in her mind and she felt her body tense.

As Gissing turned back to face the front, Sadie glanced to her right, to the two guys who were seated at the other end of the pew. One of them, the one nearest to her, caught her eye and gave a thin smile. Mates of Eddie's? She didn't think so. They were too smart, too clean-cut. The next thought that sprang into her head was *police*.

Now she had something else to worry about. If they were cops, what were they doing here? Checking out the mourners, perhaps, seeing who showed up at the funeral. And she must still be on their list of suspects when it came to Eddie's murder. Were they observing how she behaved, making a note of her body language? Instantly she became self-conscious, overly aware of what her hands were doing, of how she was standing, even of the expression on her face.

Sadie's intention had been to have a few words with Stan and Marcie and then leave before the burial – she presumed Eddie was going to be interred in Kellston Cemetery – but now she began to have second thoughts. Would it look like she was running away? That she was scared of something? Well, she was. She was afraid of the Gissings and what they might do.

As she stared at the back of Wayne Gissing's head, her heart began to thump. She could feel a prickle of sweat on the nape of her neck. But then if the cops were present what could he do? The officers might make her feel uncomfortable, as if she was under scrutiny, but they also provided protection. So long as they were around, she was safe.

The service came to an end and the coffin was carried out of the church. Sadie shuffled out of the pew and joined the other mourners who were congregating in front of the building. She immediately realised there wasn't a hope of talking to Eddie's parents at this point; they were already climbing into a sleek grey Bentley to follow the hearse to the cemetery.

Most people, she could see, were simply going to walk and she stood for a while trying to decide whether to follow them or not. The two men – she still didn't know for sure whether they were cops – had already set off. Stay or go? She shifted from one foot to the other while she tried to make up her mind. A few of Eddie's old friends glanced over in her direction, gave a nod but didn't come over to talk to her.

As the space in front of the church began to clear, she wondered if anyone would actually notice her absence. Well, Wayne Gissing probably would, but by the time he realised it would be too late. In less than fifteen minutes she could get back to Oaklands, pick up her holdall and be in the station waiting for a train to take her home.

Sadie decided that, on balance, it might be smarter to make herself scarce. There was no point in looking for trouble. She was on the brink of leaving when she felt a tap on her shoulder and turned to see the blonde woman who'd been sitting with the Gissings.

'Hello, love,' she said. 'I'm Sharon, Kelly's stepmum. Walking over to the cemetery, are you?'

Sadie shook her head. 'No, I don't think so.'

'Oh, that's a shame. Our Kelly was hoping to have a word with you later.'

'What for?' asked Sadie with a defensive edge to her voice. 'I don't know anything more than I told the police.'

'We know that, dear. We're not blaming you for anything. But it would really help if you'd have a little chat. Put her mind at rest about a few things. Five minutes, that's all she's asking. You can spare that, can't you?' Sharon smiled warmly and linked her arm through Sadie's. 'Come on, we can walk there together.'

And suddenly Sadie found herself being swept down the path and into the street, her protestations falling on deaf ears. 'I'm not really sure if—'

'Miserable old day, isn't it? Shame we didn't get a bit of sunshine. Still, at least it's stopped raining. We should be grateful for small mercies, I suppose. Mind, that graveyard is going to be muddy as hell. I knew I should have worn my boots; these shoes are going to be ruined.'

Although there was nothing threatening about Sharon's demeanour or her words, Sadie still felt ill at ease. She didn't fancy any kind of 'chat' with Kelly Gissing and had no desire to be any closer to Wayne than she'd been in the church. But somehow, now that they'd set off, it seemed impossible to break free of the woman. Before long they had caught up with the rest of the mourners and a few minutes later were passing through the tall wrought-iron gates of the cemetery.

The chosen burial place for Eddie was away from the main thoroughfare and halfway along a narrow path that led towards the older part of the graveyard. They turned left at the willow tree under which Sadie had sheltered earlier, and up a slight slope. When Sharon saw where the others were starting to gather – about ten feet off the dry path – she gave a sigh.

'What did I tell you? That ground's going to be a bleedin' quagmire. If these heels get stuck, love, you'll have to pull me out.'

'Perhaps we could stay here,' Sadie suggested. 'We won't be that far away.'

Sharon looked at her. 'You think?'

'Why not?'

And so it was decided. Sadie was more than happy to keep her distance, but her pulse had started to race at the thought of what would happen after the burial was over. 'So . . . er, what is it that Kelly wants to know exactly?'

Sharon glanced at her and gave a shrug. 'I'm not sure, to be honest. She's pretty cut up about it all. She and Eddie were close, going steady and all . . . but she's not looking to cause any bother. I'm sure of that. You don't have to worry. Only you were there, just before . . . I mean, I think she needs to get things sorted in her head. It's hard for her. She's a nice kid, though. You'll be fine.'

Nothing of this put Sadie at her ease. Sharon's description of Kelly Gissing was in direct contrast to Velma's. What was it Velma had said? Something about Kelly being happy to scratch your eyes out soon as look as you. And then there was Wayne to worry about too; brothers could be overly protective of their little sisters. She scanned the mourners until she found the two guys who might be cops. Like her and Sharon, they were standing off to the side, apart from the main group.

'Do you know those men?' Sadie asked. She gestured with a tilt of her head. 'Those two over there.'

'Old Bill, love,' Sharon said. 'You can smell 'em a mile off.'

'Ah, I thought they might be. What are they doing here?'

'Poking their noses in where they're not wanted, that's what.'

Sharon looked closely at her. 'Maybe they reckon Eddie's killer will show up. Maybe they're hoping someone's conscience will get the better of them and they'll break down and confess.'

Sadie lifted her eyebrows, trying to make it appear as though her conscience was whiter than white. 'What are the chances?'

'Slim,' Sharon said. 'Still it gives the bastards something to do, don't it? If they weren't with us, they'd only be hassling some other poor sods.'

Sadie stared over at the two officers again. They seemed bored and disinterested, as if they knew they were wasting their time. One of them kept glancing at his watch as if there was some place he had to be. Were they paying her any particular attention? She didn't think so, but she could be wrong.

She shifted her line of vision to the group gathered at the graveside. Stan was standing with one arm around his wife, the other hanging loose by his side. His hand, a tight fist, thumped relentlessly against his thigh. Kelly Gissing leaned against the older woman. Wayne stood staring hard at the hole in the ground.

The voice of the priest floated on the air. 'We have but a short time to live. Like a flower we blossom and then wither; like a shadow we flee and never stay. In the midst of life we are in death.'

Sadie, even if she wasn't entirely comfortable in Sharon's company, was glad to be away from the main group of mourners. She was sorry that Eddie was dead, truly sorry, but she still felt as though she didn't belong here, that she was intruding on the family's grief.

'It's a crying shame,' Sharon said. 'And he was no age at all, not really. Why would anyone do such a thing?'

'I've no idea.'

'So were the two of you, you know, on good terms when it . . . it happened?'

Sadie threw her a quick sideways glance. The woman was fishing and not with much subtlety. 'We weren't on any sort of terms. I hadn't seen him in years.'

'He was an easy-going sort, though, wasn't he? A good laugh.'

As the coffin was lowered into the ground, Sadie thought of the first time she'd met Eddie Wise, their eyes meeting across a crowded bar in Kentish Town. He'd been everything her mother had warned her against: a good-looking older man with a wandering eye and a bucketful of charm. Love at first sight? Perhaps. She suspected now that it had been more of an infatuation than anything deeper. She'd been too young to understand what true love was.

'Someone with a grudge, that's for sure,' Sharon said.

Sadie didn't reply. The priest was intoning those familiar words: 'Earth to earth, ashes to ashes, dust to dust . . . '

There was a general shuffling among the mourners and then the dull thud of soil falling against wood. Sadie imagined Mona going round to Eddie's flat, a bright smile on her face as he answered the door. What had she said to him? Nothing to cause any alarm because he must have invited her in. But of course the worst Eddie had ever had to fear from a woman was a paternity suit.

'That's it, then,' Sharon murmured. 'Let's hope they catch the bugger who did it.'

The two police officers leaned in towards each other, speaking softly. One of them gave a nod. Sadie felt a sudden impulse to walk over to them, to admit what she knew, to unburden her soul. Why not? It was better, surely, to face her demons in the company of the law rather than the Gissings.

'There's a nice little caff on Paladin Street,' Sharon said. 'We'll go there, shall we? We can have a nice cup of tea and a warm-up while we wait for Kelly.'

The group around the grave began to disperse, their heads

bent, their voices barely more than a whisper, until only the Wise family and the Gissings remained. Sadie glanced towards the cops again. They were walking back down the slope, heading straight for where she was standing. She felt her heart skip a beat. Jesus, maybe it was too late to confess. Maybe they were going to arrest her. Perhaps they had just been waiting until the funeral was over before they made their move.

Sharon hissed out a breath as they drew alongside. 'Pleased with yourselves, are you? Can't you even leave a family in peace when they're burying their loved ones?'

The shorter one, the watch watcher, lifted his eyebrows. 'Just doing our job, love.'

'Oh, yeah, and what would that be exactly?'

Sadie found herself wishing Sharon would shut up. Her desire to confess had drained away. There had to be a better way of bringing Mona to justice than blurting out the story of a random meeting on a train. She waited, her heart in her mouth, but the cops said nothing else. They just grinned and walked off towards the gates.

'Typical!' Sharon said. 'Mugs, the lot of them.'

Sadie watched them leave, feeling nothing but relief. Then she looked back towards the two families still huddled round the grave. But now Wayne Gissing was gone. She gazed all around but couldn't see him anywhere. She wondered whether she should go and talk to Stan and Marcie. There would never be a good time to express her condolences but this, she suspected, would certainly be the worst. 'Let's go and get that tea,' she said.

'Yeah, let's do that.' Sharon raised her voice a little so the departing cops could hear. 'I've got a bad taste in my mouth.'

They retraced their steps to the willow tree where Sharon, instead of turning right along the main thoroughfare towards the exit, took a left instead.

'Oh,' Sadie said. 'Isn't it the other way?'

'No, love. It's up the other end. Paladin Street. Didn't I say?'

Sadie was less then happy to find herself walking in the opposite direction to Oaklands and away from the safety of the busy streets. Most of the other mourners, including the cops, had already passed through the wrought-iron gates and disappeared from view. She kept glancing over her shoulder but the path behind them remained empty. 'Should we wait for Kelly?'

Sharon shook her head. 'Best meet her there, hon. She won't be long, though. Her mum will probably give her a lift, save her walking.'

By the time they were in sight of the other set of gates, Sadie could no longer see Eddie's grave. The view was obscured by a line of yew trees. The path at this end of the cemetery was deserted; the morning commuters had come and gone and everything was quiet. It occurred to her that there must be other cafés much closer to the main entrance, like the one she'd visited last time she was in Kellston.

'We could have gone to Connolly's,' Sadie said.

'It's always busy there, hon. Can't hear yourself speak. No, it's better where we're going.'

'And how far is it exactly?'

'Just round the corner. We're almost there. It won't take us more than two minutes now.'

Sadie felt a flutter of anxiety in her chest. Why had she agreed to this? Surrounded by other people, she'd felt that nothing really bad could happen but away from the grave, away from the other mourners, she was aware of how vulnerable she was. Ahead of them, to their right, an empty red Capri was parked up on the side of the thoroughfare. Further on she could see the road through the smaller set of gates. The odd car went by but there wasn't much traffic. Still, it was a road at least, a public place where there would be witnesses if the Gissings had more in mind than a friendly chat.

Sadie upped the pace, eager to escape from the graveyard.

'Hey!' Sharon protested. 'Hold yer horses. I can't be jogging in these heels.'

It was just as Sadie drew adjacent to the Capri that it happened. The back door was suddenly flung open and a man leapt out. She stifled a scream, the breath catching in her throat. It only took a split second for her to recognise Wayne Gissing. After the black eye and the split lip, the next thing she noticed was the glint of metal from the knife he was holding.

35

It was fortunate that Wayne's timing was off and he stumbled as his feet made contact with the concrete path. Sadie took the opportunity to try and make a run for it, but Sharon grabbed hold of her coat and held on tight. The two of them struggled with each other, teeth bared, arms flailing wildly, before Sadie finally managed to break free. With her route out of the cemetery blocked, she sprinted across the grass and between the graves. Where was she going? She had no idea. Instinct had taken over and she was simply running for her life.

Her heart was racing, the adrenalin coursing through her veins, as she sidestepped the tombstones and scanned the horizon. There must be someone, somewhere . . . Jesus, where was everyone? Panic and fear swept through her body. It didn't occur to her to scream or shout; she needed every ounce of energy to keep on going. Her bag slipped from her shoulder and fell to the ground. She left it there, abandoned by a black marble headstone.

And now she was aware of the footsteps behind her, of the thick boots squelching down into the earth. She tried to pick up speed but the ground was soft and wet and slippery. Faster, she had to go faster, but already her lungs were pumping, her breath coming in short shallow gasps.

Sadie had barely covered thirty yards when he caught up with her. She heard his heavy panting, his muttered curses, just before she felt his hand clamp down on her shoulder. The pressure spun her around and she went tumbling on to the grass. Instantly he was on to her, yanking her up and wrapping his arm around her throat.

'Bitch!' he spat into her neck.

Sadie lashed out, trying to free herself from his grasp. She wasn't going to die in this damn graveyard. Not today. Not like this. She wouldn't, she couldn't. She dug her fingernails into the soft flesh of his arm and heard him yelp. Seconds later she felt a sharp stinging pain along the back of her hand.

'Do that again,' he hissed into her ear, 'and I'll slice your bloody throat open.'

It was only then that Sadie realised she'd been cut. She stopped struggling, went limp and stared down at her hand. The knife had traced a diagonal line from the knuckle of her forefinger to the bone of her wrist. It was bleeding profusely, long scarlet ribbons running down between her fingers and dripping on to the ground.

'Please,' she begged as she felt the cold steel of the blade press against her throat.

'What's the matter, hon? I thought you liked knives. Isn't that how you wasted Eddie?'

'It wasn't me. I swear it wasn't.' She was trying to speak without moving, terrified that the blade might slip. Her chest was heaving, her heart thumping furiously. 'I didn't do it.'

'You, Stone, one of Terry's goons. It don't make no difference, babe. The end result is the same. Eddie's six foot under and someone has to pay.'

'It wasn't me,' she repeated, her voice a hoarse whisper.

'We'll see. Now are you going to behave, Sadie, or am I going to have to get nasty?'

Sadie let out a groan. Wayne Gissing wasn't a big man but he was a solid one and, as she'd already discovered, he was quick on his feet. She didn't have a chance in hell of getting away of him. 'I will. I swear I will.'

'You'd better, babe, 'cause if you try another stunt like that, you and me are going to fall out big time.'

'I'll do whatever you want.'

'Sure you will.' He released his hold on her and stood back. 'Start walking,' he ordered, brandishing the knife. 'Over to the car. Try and make a run for it again and it's the last thing you'll ever do.'

Sadie gave a nod. 'I won't. I promise.'

Wayne Gissing flicked shut the knife and put it in his pocket. 'Go on then. We ain't got all day. And remember, I'll be right behind you. No second chances, babe. This is it.'

Sadie set off obediently across the grass, retracing her earlier steps. There was no doubt in her mind that he meant what he said; she had seen the cruelty in his eyes, the desire to hurt her. As she walked she raised her hand to her mouth and sucked on the wound. The cut was starting to throb, a hard angry pain that helped focus her mind. This was just the beginning, she realised. Unless she did something fast, there was far worse to come.

When they reached the marble headstone where her handbag was still lying, she glanced over her shoulder. 'Can I pick it up?'

Wayne smirked. 'So long as you ain't got a brick in it.'

'No,' she said, still trying to catch her breath. 'No bricks.' Sadie slowly bent and retrieved her bag. The blood from her hand ran down the soft black leather. Damn it! The handbag had been expensive, Italian, and now it was probably ruined.

She frowned at the irrelevance of the thought, aware of how unimportant it was in the present scheme of things.

In a couple of minutes they were back on the main path where Sharon was leaning against the Capri, smoking a fag. 'Caught up with her then?' she said casually.

'Don't just stand there. Get the bloody door open!'

Sharon pulled a face at Wayne and then turned her attention to Sadie, looking her up and down with nothing but contempt in her eyes. 'Get in then,' she said, swinging open the back door.

Sadie didn't move. She had a plan. It was a sketchy one, risky, but what choice did she have? The second she set foot in that car she was doomed. What she was about to do could be the craziest thing ever – or the smartest. She glanced hopefully along the length of the path, but it was still empty. And then, very carefully, she reached for the zip on her bag.

'Oi! What are you doing?' Wayne snarled.

Sadie paused and looked at him, all innocence. 'Getting some tissues,' she said. 'Unless you want me to drip blood all over your upholstery.'

Sharon chucked her fag on the ground and ground it out with her heel. 'She's not bleeding all over my fuckin' car.'

Wayne narrowed his cold nasty eyes, stared suspiciously at Sadie but eventually gave her a nod. 'Make it snappy then.'

Sadie swallowed hard as she delved into the bag, her heart thumping wildly again. Was she really going to do this? But the outcome of the other option, the option of simply going along with their demands, was too terrifying to contemplate. It didn't take a genius to work out that her life was in the balance. The Gissings wanted revenge and she'd served herself up on a plate to them.

Her fingers curled around the Beretta, but she had no second thoughts. It was now or never. As she pulled the gun out of the bag and pointed it at him, Wayne's Gissing's face was a picture. This was something he hadn't been expecting. She saw his eyes widen in surprise, his mouth fall open.

'What the . . .'

'Get back!' she demanded sharply. Her gaze flew quickly between her two would-be abductors. 'Both of you. Stand together.' And then, remembering Wayne's knife, she added, 'And put your hands up! Put your hands where I can see them!'

The Gissings followed her instructions. But now Sadie wasn't sure what to do next. If she ran towards the gates, she'd have to turn her back on them and Wayne might still come after her. Perhaps she should use the car. Yes, that was a much better plan. She could take the Capri and dump it near the station. 'I want the keys to the car.' She stared at Wayne. 'Take them out slowly. Use your left hand and throw them on the ground.'

'And if I don't?'

'What do you think?' Sadie said roughly, trying to sound like the sort of person who wouldn't think twice about putting a bullet through his chest.

Sharon threw him a filthy look. 'Just do what she says, okay? What are you playing at? She's got a bleedin' gun.'

'Yeah, but she's not going to use it.'

'You reckon?' Sadie said.

Wayne's split lip curled with derision. After the initial shock, he was rapidly regaining his composure. 'Do it then,' he said mockingly. 'Fuckin' shoot me.'

Sadie's hand was shaking, the gun jumping up and down. 'I will,' she said. 'You think I won't?'

Wayne slowly lowered his arms. 'Go on then.'

Sadie glanced from him to the gun and back again. Shit, what now? He was calling her bluff and she didn't even know if the damn thing was loaded. Come to that, she didn't have a clue how it worked. It was all very well having her finger on the trigger but there must be some kind of safety device to stop it from firing.

Wayne was grinning now, sure that he was right. 'You should be careful waving that around. It might go off.'

'You're the one who needs to be careful.'

He slowly lowered his arms and began to walk towards her. 'Oh yeah?'

Sadie went into panic. Another few steps and he'd be on her. Manically, she tried to think of what to do. All those films she'd seen, all those cops-and-robbers dramas on TV. There was a lip on the top of the gun, a small piece of metal jutting up. Did she pull it back? Was that how it was done? He was getting closer now, taking his time, grinning from ear to ear. Well, what did she have to lose? Quickly, she slid back the lip and heard a satisfying click.

Wayne Gissing paused for a moment, his eyes glinting. 'That thing ain't loaded,' he said. 'We both know that, babe, so why don't you just pass it over, huh?'

Sadie's voice was shaking as much as her hand. 'You . . . you want to take the chance?'

'Wayne!' Sharon said warningly.

Wayne glanced at his stepmother and laughed. 'She's taking the piss, hon. Look at her. It's pathetic. She can hardly hold the bloody thing!'

Sadie was grasping the gun with both hands, desperately trying to keep it steady. 'Stay back!'

Wayne took another step closer. 'Or what?'

'I'll do it,' she said with an edge of hysteria to her voice. 'Come any closer and I'll shoot.' Her heart was beating so hard she thought it might burst. Beads of sweat had gathered on her forehead. She felt sick, scared and out of control. She couldn't let him have the gun. She wouldn't. The two of them would take her somewhere, a place where no one could find her. And then what? But she knew what. She'd never see day-light again.

Wayne gave a laugh, his mouth opening to reveal a row of brown stained teeth. 'You're finished, bitch.'

'Get back!'

He shook his head and kept on moving forward. 'Finished!'

And it was at that very moment when she could almost see the whites of his eyes that she aimed the gun down towards his legs and fired. The sound was explosive, a sudden loud bang that seemed to shake the very air. She felt the recoil run the length of her arm. She saw the shock on Wayne Gissing's face before he dropped to the ground and rolled on his side, his hands madly clasping his right thigh. A weird thin animalistic noise escaped from his throat.

'What have you done?' Sharon screeched. 'You've shot him! You've fuckin' shot him!'

Sadie stood there, paralysed, unable to move. She could see the blood on his trouser leg, an ever expanding circle. She seemed surrounded by a sudden cacophony of noise: the echo of the gunfire, the sound of the birds rising from the trees, Wayne groaning, Sharon screaming. The gun slipped from her fingers, fell on the concrete and skittered away.

And still Sadie stood there, incapable of running. Her legs had turned to lead. She stared down at Wayne Gissing writhing in agony. Oh God! Horrified she raised her hand and clamped it over her mouth. Was he dying right in front of her? Oh Jesus! Sharon was kneeling at his side, trying to help, trying to stem the relentless flow of blood. Everything had gone into slow motion. Nothing felt real. She had pulled the trigger and now . . .

She was only faintly aware of the man running towards them from the gates. She could hear his pounding footsteps on the path and yet they seemed oddly muffled. It was all like a bad dream, a nightmare she couldn't wake up from. It was the police, perhaps. Yes, the police were coming to arrest her.

'Sadie!'

She stared blankly back at the man, his face gradually coming into focus. Nathan Stone. She didn't understand. What was he doing here?

'Come on,' he said, grabbing hold of her arm and trying to pull her away from the scene.

'What?' she said stupidly.

'Shift it!' he said. 'Run! For fuck's sake, what's the matter with you?'

Sadie looked down at Wayne again. 'I've shot him.'

'I can see that.'

'I can't just . . .'

'Can't just what? Stay here and wait for the bloody law to arrive?' Stone started to drag her along the path. A few feet on, he let go of her arm, bent down, scooped up the gun and shoved it in his pocket. 'Come on,' he urged again. 'Sadie!'

The urgency in his voice eventually got through to her. She gave a start, her survival instinct kicking in, and began to run. He grabbed hold of her hand and together they sprinted to the exit. The Daimler was parked in the street, a few yards from the gates. He opened the passenger door, bundled her inside and then dashed round to the other side. Jumping in, he quickly started the engine, put his foot down and roared away from the kerb.

'Let's get the hell out of here,' he said.

36

Sadie sat huddled in the corner of the Daimler, shaking like a leaf. She could hardly take it in. It had all happened so fast, a moment of craziness, a moment that could never be changed. She had shot Wayne Gissing. This bare brutal fact would never go away. She would have to live with it for ever. A wave of fear and despair washed over her.

'Oh Christ! What have I done?' She wrapped her arms around her chest and began to rock back and forth, her voice rising in pitch. 'What have I done? How did I . . . Christ! What will I do now?'

Nathan Stone kept his gaze on the road. 'You're already doing it.'

Sadie started to cry, huge gulping sobs that racked her body. 'We can't just leave him there.'

'Sure we can. He's not on his own. She can drive him to the hospital.'

Sadie shook her head, not understanding how he could be so calm about it all. 'I don't want him to *die*!' she wailed.

Nathan Stone winced. 'Jesus, can you stop doing that?'

She turned her tear-stained face to look at him. 'What?'

'That noise,' he said. 'That bloody awful squawking noise you're making. It's going right through me.'

Sadie's eyes widened with incredulity. 'How do you expect me to sound?'

'Quieter,' he said.

'But I've just *shot* a man.'

'Yeah, I'm aware of that. But can we skip the histrionics, please?'

'He could die, for God's sake!'

Nathan Stone heaved out a sigh. 'He's not going to fuckin' die, all right? You shot the bastard in the leg. It's going to hurt for a while but it's not going to kill him.'

'Are you sure?'

'Look, if the bullet had gone through an artery, you'd have known about it. Those things spurt; it comes out like a fountain. And, just out of curiosity, where the hell did you get a gun from?'

Sadie was still trying to get her crying under control, taking big deep breaths. She bit down on her lip and stared out of the window. A few seconds passed before she answered his question. 'Someone gave it to me.'

'Someone?'

She gave a shrug. 'It's not important.'

Stone gave her a quick sidelong glance. 'It's a good thing Eddie wasn't blasted or I'd start to wonder.'

'I had nothing to do with Eddie's death,' she snapped.

'Yeah, yeah, you've already said. What happened to your hand?'

Sadie gazed down at it. The blood was congealing now, closing the wound. 'He cut me. He had a knife.'

Stone raised his eyes to the heavens. 'What did I tell you about going to the funeral?'

'Not to do it. Not to go.' She glared at him. 'You really think this is the time for *I told you so*?'

'Can't think of a better one.'

Sadie rubbed at the dried blood between her fingers. 'Yes, well, you were right. Happy now?'

'That's not exactly the word I'd use.'

The exchange with Stone had, she realised, halted her spiral into hysteria. The wild ravings had subsided to be replaced by an aching sense of dread. It settled over her like a shroud, a thick heavy blanket of despair. She was quiet for a while, trying to properly process the morning's events. After several minutes she said softly, 'What were you doing at the cemetery anyway?'

'What do you think? Keeping an eye on things, on you. Making sure that you didn't cause me even more bother.'

'That didn't work out too well.'

Stone barked out a laugh. 'You can say that again. I reckoned I'd got all the bases covered, but then you pulled that damn gun out of your bag and—'

'So you were there all the time?' Sadie interrupted. She threw him an accusing look. 'You saw what was happening and did nothing. You let him . . . How could you? Why didn't you stop it? Why did you have to wait until—'

'And do what? Ride up on my white charger and gallop off into the hills with you?'

'He could have slit my throat.'

Stone grinned as if it was all one big joke. 'To be honest, I was hoping you might outrun him, save me the trouble of getting involved.'

'And what if he'd killed me?'

'He was never going to do that.' Stone left a short pause. 'Not in the cemetery at least. Wayne might not have the brains he was born with but even he's not that stupid. No, I figured I'd see how it panned out and take it from there. But then of course you went all Wild West on me and . . . ' He gave a shrug of his shoulders. 'Shit, I wouldn't have seen that coming in a thousand years.'

'I'm just full of surprises,' she said dryly.

'And all of them bad. How do you manage that? It's quite a talent.'

There wasn't much Sadie could say and so she said nothing. Instead she turned her face away and gazed out of the window. The traffic was choked up and they were crawling along behind a number 73 bus. 'Where are we going?'

'Euston,' he said.

'Why?'

'Why do you think? You're getting on a train and going home.'

She spun her head round to look at him again. 'What? I can't do that! I can't go back to Haverlea.'

'Why not?'

Sadie's eyes widened in exasperation. 'You know why not! The police are going to be waiting there. They'll arrest me. I'll go to prison and . . . God, I shot a man, in case you've forgotten.'

This outburst seemed to cause Stone even more amusement. 'You're not on the run, Sadie.'

'And how do you figure that one out? He's going to tell them, isn't he? He's going to tell them that I shot him.'

'And why would he do that?'

'Why wouldn't he?'

Nathan tapped his fingers against the steering wheel. 'Okay,' he said in the tone of a patient teacher talking to a slightly dense pupil. 'Listen carefully. This is how it works: Wayne Gissing goes to the hospital with a hole in his leg. While the doctors are busy patching him up, a member of staff calls the law. They're obliged to do that, see, it being a gunshot wound and all. So

Old Bill show their faces and what do you think Wayne says to them?'

Sadie, presuming it was a rhetorical question, waited for him to continue.

'Well, I'll tell you what he *doesn't* say. He doesn't say, "Hey, officers, there I was in the cemetery, just quietly attempting to abduct this girl, and suddenly she gets out a gun and tries to shoot my leg off." Not going to sound too good, huh? So he tells them some cock-and-bull story, something he's cobbled together with Sharon on the way to the hospital, a line about a mugging or such like – and there you go.'

'And what if they don't believe him?'

'Of course they won't believe him. Wayne Gissing doesn't open his mouth without a lie coming out of it. But what can they do? Sod all, other than ask Sharon – and she's going to come out with the same pile of bullshit.'

Sadie leaned her head against the window while she thought about what he'd said. A tiny glimmer of hope was blossoming inside her. 'But what if he doesn't? What if he says it was me?'

'Why would he do that?'

Sadie screwed up her face. 'I don't know. Because I shot him? I don't imagine he's going to be too happy about that.'

'No he isn't, but he's still going to cover his back. Believe me, the best thing you can do is to go home and pretend that nothing ever happened.'

'I can't,' she said.

'You have to.'

'And then?'

'And then what?'

Sadie rubbed her face with the palm of her hand. 'He's going to come after me, isn't he? I'm going to be looking over my shoulder all the time.'

'He won't be doing anything for a while.'

'How long is a while?'

'Just go,' he said. 'I'll sort it out.'

Sadie didn't ask how he was intending to do that. She wasn't sure if she wanted to know. The bus in front of them shifted forward and a few minutes later they emerged on to Euston Road. He turned into the station, drove down the ramp to the underground parking area and pulled up.

'You'll be okay,' he said.

Sadie unlocked the car door but didn't get out. 'What do I say if the police ask me about it? I mean, I was there at the funeral. What if they question me? I was standing in the cemetery with Sharon. What if my story doesn't tally with hers?'

'Just keep it simple,' he said. 'Tell the truth as much as you can. You went to the church, you went to the cemetery, you stood with Sharon and then you left on your own. Is there anyone who can say different?'

Sadie thought about it. The two cops had left before her, and most of the mourners had drifted off at the same time. Had there been any witnesses to her leaving with Sharon? The Wises perhaps. Or the priest. 'I don't know. Someone might have seen us.'

'Well, it'll be their word against yours.'

Sadie suddenly thought of something else. 'My holdall,' she said. 'It's still at Oaklands. And I haven't even checked out. I still owe for last night.'

'I'll get Velma to sort it. Is there anything important in the bag?'

She shook her head. 'Not really. Just clothes and make-up and stuff.'

'No worries, then.'

Sadie opened her bag and took out her purse. 'I'll give you the money,' she said. 'You can pass it on to Velma.'

He waved the offer away. 'Keep it. I'll square up with her.'

But Sadie didn't want to be in his debt any more than she already was. 'No,' she said firmly, taking out a couple of notes and pressing them into his hand. 'You have to take it.' She went to get out of the car but then hesitated and turned back to look at him. 'And thanks,' she said. 'You know, for . . .'

'For saving your arse?'

'Yes.'

'It's a pleasure. Oh, and before you go you might want to . . . er, fix your face. No offence, babe, but I've seen you looking better.'

Sadie flipped down the sun shield, stared at herself in the mirror and grimaced. 'God,' she murmured. Her mascara had run, leaving dark circles under her eyes and long grey streaks down her cheeks. She found a tissue, put it to her mouth, dampened it and set about trying to repair the damage.

While she was doing this, Stone got out of the Daimler, went round to the back of the car and opened the boot. He came back with a first-aid kit and took out cotton wool, antiseptic cream and plasters. 'You need to clean that cut,' he said. 'You don't want it getting infected.'

Sadie glanced across at the small white box with the red cross on the front. 'Are you always this organised?'

'Be prepared,' he replied. 'Isn't that what they say?'

'Like you were ever a boy scout.' Sadie, having done the best she could with her face, turned her attention to the wound on her hand. The antiseptic stung as she applied it and she drew in a breath. 'How am I going to explain how this happened?'

'Just say you caught it on something. I don't know, a nail, a piece of glass. It'll heal up in a couple of weeks. Shouldn't leave too much of a scar.'

She laid a long thin plaster along the length of the cut and gently pressed it down. She thought of Wayne Gissing and the knife and a shudder passed through her. 'This isn't over, is it?'

she asked, her eyes widening as she looked at him again. 'This isn't going to go away.'

'Let me worry about that. Might be best to cover that hand up,' he said. 'Have you got any gloves?'

Sadie nodded, pulled them from her pocket and slipped them on. 'What if he comes after me? Or tries to hurt Joel?'

'Is that the boyfriend?'

'None of this is his fault.'

'Is any of it yours?'

The question caught her off guard and she quickly glanced away, unable to meet his cool grey eyes. 'No,' she lied. 'Why should it be?'

Stone gave a shrug. 'If there's anything you want to tell me?'

'There isn't,' she said.

'You'd better be going then.'

Sadie got out of the car and leaned down to look at him. She had a sudden urge at that moment to get back in, to tell him everything, to let it all spill out of her in one almighty torrent. How much longer could she keep her secret? It was gradually tearing her apart. She needed someone to talk to, someone to confide in.

Stone raised his eyebrows. 'Was there something else?'

She hesitated, the words on her lips, but then shook her head. Even after today, she wasn't sure that she could trust him. He might have saved her skin, but was that for her benefit or his own? Nathan Stone was the kind of man, she suspected, who always had an agenda. 'No,' she said. 'Just thanks, thanks again for what you did.'

'Have a safe journey.'

Sadie shut the car door and walked away. She heard the smooth purr of the Daimler as the engine started up and was tempted to look back, but didn't. She was too scared of changing her mind.

37

Petra Gissing sat back in the chair and lifted the glass of whisky to her lips. She had been on a rollercoaster of emotions since hearing that her son had been shot. First there had been the shock, the horror, the disbelief, quickly followed by the fear that he would die. Then came the relief – the wound wasn't a serious one – and then the pity, the confusion and anger. On top of all that had been her frustration at the endless questions from the filth. Now she was left mainly with a feeling of indignation. Wayne was lying to her and it pissed her off big time.

'What do you think I am?' she said, glaring at him. 'A bloody mug? You can say what you like to Old Bill, but don't try it on with me.'

Wayne gazed back at her, scowling. 'Do we really have to do this now? I'm in bleedin' agony, in case you hadn't noticed.'

'There's nothing wrong with your mouth. You can still talk, can't you?'

'I've already told you what happened. How many times? Jesus, just leave it alone.'

But leaving it alone was the last thing Petra was going to do.

'Who was it? One of Terry Street's goons, I bet. I told you about stirring up trouble. And do you ever listen to me? No, of course you don't, because Wayne bloody Gissing always knows best.'

'Give it a rest, can't you? I'm sick of it.'

'I'll give it at a rest when you tell me the truth.'

Wayne tipped back the bottle of beer and took a long pull. 'They jumped me, right? In the cemetery, by the car. Three of them. Coloured geezers. I ain't never seen 'em before. Well, not so I'd remember. They all look the same, don't they? They wanted cash and I wouldn't give it to them. Junkies, maybe, after a fix. How would I know? One of them had a shooter; the thing went off and . . . ' He gestured towards his leg. 'Then they scarpered, did a bunk. That's it. That's the goddamn truth.'

Petra curled her lip. 'You wouldn't know the truth if it slapped you in the face.'

'Oh, leave him alone, Mum,' Kelly said. 'He's been shot, for Christ's sake. He doesn't need all this aggro.'

'And you're no better,' Petra retorted, turning to her daughter. 'Covering up for him. You think I haven't seen the two of you plotting and scheming this past week? I'm not bleedin' blind. If it wasn't for the fact that we buried Eddie today . . .' She raised a hand and dropped it into her lap. 'It ain't right, lying to your own mother.'

'It's all in yer head,' Wayne said stubbornly. 'There ain't been nothin' going on.'

Petra made a clicking sound with her tongue. 'Yeah, right, and I'm the Queen of flaming Sheba.' What really got her goat was that she knew Sharon had been in on it too. She'd seen her cosying up to that Sadie, walking with her to the graveyard. And where had they disappeared to after the burial? One minute they'd been there and the next . . . And then Wayne saying he was going to get the car, and Kelly suggesting that he take it straight to the Fox instead of coming back for them, that she wanted to walk to the pub, that she needed the fresh air.

'It's Wayne you should be worrying about,' Kelly said. 'Those bastards could have killed him.'

Petra opened her mouth, about to say something on the subject of Sadie Wise, but at that very moment the phone started ringing. No one else moved and so she put down her glass and hauled herself to her feet. 'I'll get it, shall I?'

Wayne gestured towards his leg. 'What do you want me to do, hop there?'

Petra raised her eyes to the ceiling and went out through the door to the hall. She picked up the phone and put it to her ear, hearing the pips go before she could speak. She waited until the caller came on the line.

'Sharon?'

It was Roy ringing from the nick. Hearing his voice again made her wince, reminding her of times she'd rather forget. 'She ain't here.'

'What do you mean, she ain't there?' he asked roughly.

'What do you think I mean? It's plain English. It ain't that hard to understand.'

'Where is she then?'

'How should I know? I'm not her keeper. Out with her fancy man probably.'

Roy sucked in an audible breath. 'Just can't help yourself, can you? Even at a time like this. The screws told me about Wayne. He's all right, yeah? They said he'd been released from the hospital.'

'About an hour ago. I reckon he'll live.'

'So what the fuck happened?'

Petra, aware that the conversation was probably being recorded by the prison, had the nous to stick to the story that her son had told the law. 'Tried to mug him, didn't they? Three

263

of them, the cowardly bastards. 'Course Wayne wasn't having any of it. He put up a fight and one of them took out a shooter and ... Anyway, it ain't as bad as it might have been. A few weeks and he'll be back on his feet again.'

'Put him on. I want to talk to him.'

'And how am I supposed to do that? He can't *walk*, for God's sake. You want him to crawl into the hall?'

'I want to make sure he's okay.'

'I just told you he was. You want a word with Kelly?'

'How's she doing?'

'She's had better days.'

'Yeah, put her on.'

Petra called out through the open door, 'Kelly, it's your dad,' before laying the phone on the table and going upstairs for a pee. She grinned as she thought back to what she'd said about Sharon. The tart had only nipped out for a takeaway but he wasn't to know that. Roy knew she was stirring, trying to cause trouble, but that wouldn't stop him from thinking about it. She had planted a seed of doubt and when he was banged up this evening, when he had too much time to dwell on stuff, he might just start to wonder ...

She looked in the bathroom mirror, made some adjustments to her hair and gave her reflection a friendly nod. Perhaps, all in all, the day hadn't worked out so badly. What did they say about every cloud having a silver lining? Now that Wayne was temporarily laid up, she had the perfect excuse for staying on in Shoreditch.

38

Wayne gritted his teeth, trying to contain the rage that was bubbling up inside him. It wasn't just that he'd been shot – that was bad enough – but that he'd been shot by a fuckin' woman. It was wrong, humiliating, and he'd be a laughing stock if anyone on the street got to hear about it. Sharon had better keep her big mouth shut. In his head, he replayed the fateful moment over and over again; he'd been convinced that the tart was bluffing, sure that the gun was a replica, some fake piece of plastic shit that couldn't even be fired.

And then, as if things hadn't been bad enough, he'd had the filth on his back, bombarding him with bloody questions. The story – which he and Sharon had thrown together on the way to the hospital – was flimsy, full of holes, but the best they could manage in the time they had. And he hadn't exactly been thinking straight. Still, there wasn't a whole lot the law could do about it. They might suspect it was a pile of bullshit, but they couldn't prove a thing.

Before going into A&E he'd had the nous to pass the knife over to Sharon. You couldn't trust the filth when it came to going through your things. Now he took it from his pocket, flicked it open and stared at the blade. He should have cut the crazy bitch's throat when he had the opportunity. Still, he wouldn't make the same mistake twice.

Wayne looked up as Kelly came back into the room. They hadn't had a chance to talk properly since the funeral and he could see the frustration in her eyes. She closed the door, hurried over to the sofa and sat down beside him.

'What the hell happened today?'

Wayne closed the knife and slipped it back into his pocket. 'What do you think fuckin' happened? The crazy bitch had a shooter, didn't she?'

Kelly's jaw dropped. 'What? It was Sadie Wise?'

'Keep it down. You want Mum to hear?'

'I thought it must have been Stone or Terry Street or—'

'It was a set-up,' Wayne said. 'They must have guessed that we were planning something. Stone was there too, keeping out of sight. He fucked off with the tart as soon as . . .' His hands balled into two tight fists. 'It was a fuckin' ambush, Kel. The bitch could have killed me.'

'Jesus,' she murmured, her face growing pale and tight. 'So what are we going to do now?'

Wayne thought about all the hours he'd spent down in the cellar getting the place just right. All that work for what? Well, he sure as hell wasn't going to let it go to waste. And then there was the ransom money he'd been expecting to get. He deserved that fuckin' money, every penny of it and more. 'What do you think? No one puts a bullet in my leg and gets away with it. No one!'

39

Sadie was holding her breath as she got off the train at Haverlea, convinced that the police would be waiting there. Nervously, she glanced along the length of the platform. She had spent the entire journey in a heightened state of anxiety, terrified that at any moment she would look up to find an officer standing over her, his eyes cold and accusing, handcuffs at the ready. Even the ticket collector had made her jump, the sight of his uniform causing her heart to miss a beat.

Although Nathan Stone had insisted that Gissing would say nothing, she still couldn't bring herself to believe it. People didn't think rationally when they were in pain. They lashed out. They let their mouths run away with them. Already he could have made a statement, pointing the finger directly at her. What then? She gave a shiver, thinking of what the future might hold.

Slowly she walked towards the exit. Others hurried past, eager to get home after a day's work in the city. As she approached the barrier, her gaze raked the area beyond. Were the police there? Perhaps, because of the gun, they wouldn't try and approach while other people were around. She passed over her ticket with a shaking hand and went through the gate.

Sadie's pulse was racing as she crossed the forecourt. Her lips were dry, her stomach churning. But by the time she reached the street she realised that nothing bad was going to happen. And then it occurred to her: if they were going to pick her up, they were more likely to do it at the flat. What if they were waiting for her there? She was tempted to turn around, to jump on another train and keep on going until she was miles away.

Sadie stopped on the corner, shifting the cheap holdall she'd bought at Euston from one hand to the other. It wasn't physically heavy – all it had in it was a magazine and a new toothbrush – but it seemed to contain the weight of all her secrets. She had known it would look odd if she returned home without any luggage. Joel would ask questions and she would need to tell more lies. Well, she would need to tell lies anyway, but some were easier than others.

There was a bus stop close by and a taxi rank in front of the station. She instantly dismissed both modes of transport. And she didn't want to call Joel either. Even though she'd been on the train for hours, she needed more time to think. She decided to walk back to the flat. If the police were there, these could be her last twenty minutes of freedom.

It was that time of day, just before dusk, when everything was starting to merge into greyness. The briny smell of the sea floated on the air and she breathed it in, filling her lungs. Even though a drizzly rain was falling, she walked slowly, savouring the sights and sounds. She paused at shop windows, gazing at the displays. She stared up at the darkening sky. She looked at the faces of the people passing by.

It was only when she moved from the bustle of town to the quieter surroundings of the back streets that the events of the morning began to press down on her again: the coffin in the church, the priest intoning, Sharon Gissing taking her arm, Wayne Gissing's hand clamping down on her shoulder, Nathan Stone dragging her along the path towards the car.

Sadie half closed her eyes, wishing she could wipe out the past few weeks and start again. She felt like she had become a different person, shedding a skin to reveal a woman she barely recognised. So much had changed. One small lie had turned into a bigger one, that bigger one into an enormous one, until she had reached the point where her entire existence was governed by deceit.

And now she had shot a man.

She drew in a breath. How was that possible? What had happened to the happy, contented Sadie Wise who'd found love with a man who would never let her down? It was only now, faced with losing everything, that she realised how truly blessed she'd been. If only she had shown more patience and not been in so much of a hurry to sever the ties to Eddie. If only she hadn't gone to London. If only she'd never set eyes on Nathan Stone.

As she turned the corner into Buckingham Road, Sadie felt her chest tighten. She stuck to the side that was darkest, skulking in the shadows like a fugitive. Peering through the gloom, she searched for unfamiliar cars, for policemen waiting to pounce. As she carefully advanced, she heard Nathan Stone's voice whispering in her ear. *I'll sort it out.* She wanted to believe him, but in her heart she knew it was an impossible task. The knot was too big, too tangled, to ever be unravelled.

By the time she reached the house, her nerves were stretched to their limit. The lights on the ground floor were on and she could see Joel at work through the slatted blinds. She stood looking in, feeling suddenly as if she was staring at a stranger. She was reminded of those times she'd walked by other people's houses in winter, observing rooms where the curtains were still open, catching a snapshot of someone else's life and wondering what it was like.

Sadie stayed there for a while, watching Joel move around inside. At any second she expected to hear the sound of a car door slamming, of footsteps pounding along the pavement, but everything remained quiet. She waited until her heart rate had slowed before pushing the gate open and walking up the drive. She unlocked the door, stepped into the hall and put down the holdall.

'It's only me,' she called out. 'I'm back.'

Joel came striding out of the workroom, his mouth widening into a smile as he hurried over to take her in his arms. 'You're all wet,' he said, holding her close and speaking into the crown of her head. 'Why didn't you call? I'd have come and picked you up.'

Sadie leaned into his chest, breathing in his scent, taking the opportunity to feel safe again – even if wasn't going to last for ever. 'It's not far. I just fancied a walk.'

'Are you okay? Was it awful?'

She screwed up her eyes and sighed. *Awful.* The word barely began to describe the horror of the morning. 'It was ... well, I've had better days.'

'It's over now,' he murmured.

Sadie wished that was true. She wished she had the strength, the courage, to look him in the eyes and tell him the goddamn truth. He would be shocked, confused, upset. He would probably feel betrayed, but it was better that the truth came from her than from someone else. She lifted her head, intending to speak, but the words lodged in her throat. Once she spoke out, everything would change. The thought of it was unbearable.

'I missed you,' he said.

'I've only been gone for a day.'

'It felt like longer.'

Sadie stood on her toes, reached up and kissed him on the mouth. 'I know.' Yes, she would tell him, she decided, she would tell him every vile and dreadful detail, but not right now. Just for a while she wanted her old life back. She wanted to push away all the fear and bury all the horror. She wanted to pretend that everything was fine.

'Come on, let's get you upstairs,' he said. 'You look worn out.'

They separated and as Joel reached down for the holdall, he noticed that it wasn't the same bag she'd left with. 'This is new,' he said. 'What happened to the other one?'

'The zip broke,' Sadie said, quickly intercepting him and picking up the bag herself. She didn't want him to feel how light it was. 'I had to chuck it.' She frowned even as she was speaking. Lie number one. She'd only been home for five minutes and already she was making up stories.

'I'll take it,' he said, holding out his hand.

'No, I can manage. It isn't heavy.' She started up the stairs before he could insist, climbing at a brisk pace while she tried to change the subject. 'So what's been happening? Any news since I've been away?'

'Your London friend called.'

Sadie felt her heart sink. 'Mona?'

'Who?'

Sadie flinched. The name had been out of her mouth before she'd had time to think about it. Of course he didn't know her as Mona. It was a good thing she had her back to him or he'd be able to see the red flush burning her face. She rapidly tried to cover up her mistake. 'She's an old friend, just someone I bumped into at the funeral. I haven't seen her for years. She said she might call and ...'

'No, I meant Anne.'

'Oh, right. Anne. What did she want?'

'Just a chat, I think. I told her you were away, that you'd give her a ring when you got back.'

'Yeah, I'll do that. Did she . . . did she say anything else?'

'To be honest, she sounded like she'd had a drink or two. She kept rambling on about the fairground, about how you'd promised to take her there. And then there was some weird stuff about her father. It didn't make much sense.'

Sadie sucked in a breath and glanced over her shoulder. 'What kind of stuff?'

'I didn't really get the gist. She kept insisting that she had to speak to you, that it was urgent and that you were the only one who understood. I take it she and her dad don't get on.'

'I've no idea,' Sadie said, flustered. She swung round the banister on the first floor, her hand gripping the polished wood, and headed up towards the flat. 'It was probably just the drink talking.'

'Oh, yes, and she said I was to tell you that before Christmas would be better than after. I'm not sure what she meant but she kept repeating it over and over, insisting that I pass the message on.'

Sadie reached the second floor, walked along the landing, turned the handle, pushed open the door and went inside. Her heart had started up its hammering again. 'I-I think she means a visit. She was talking about coming to Haverlea for a few days.' How many lies was that now? And all she was doing was digging a bigger and bigger hole for herself. She cleared her throat, aware that her voice sounded hoarse and odd. 'Did anyone else ring?'

'No. Were you expecting someone?'

Sadie was wondering if the police had called to find out when she'd be back. 'Not really. I just . . . I thought Mum might have been in touch.'

'You didn't tell her you were going to the funeral?'

'No. Well, she never liked Eddie. She wouldn't understand.' Sadie gave him a thin smile. 'And she certainly wouldn't have approved.' She took off her gloves and hung up her coat on a peg in the hall.

'What happened to your hand?' Joel asked.

Sadie glanced at the plaster that was covering the knife wound. 'It's nothing, a scratch. I just caught it on something.' And then before he could ask any more awkward questions she took the holdall through to the bedroom. She dumped it in the bottom of the wardrobe, took a moment to steady her breathing and then went into the living room. Trying to act normal. As if everything was as it should be. 'Anyway, what have you been doing with yourself? Did you go out last night?'

'I was finishing off that cabinet for the Finlays.'

'You work too hard,' she said.

Joel inclined his head to one side and gazed at her. 'You're the one who looks exhausted. Sit down and I'll put the kettle on. Are you hungry? I've made a stew so all we need to do is heat it up.'

'You're an angel,' she said, even though she wasn't hungry. She had a sour, sick feeling in the pit of her stomach. He went through to the kitchen and she watched him moving around, fixing his image in her mind as if she might never see him again.

It was another two hours before the front doorbell rang.

40

Sadie visibly jumped as the sound cut through the living room. Her hand gave a jolt and some red wine spilt out from the glass she was holding. A few drops fell on to the carpet, tiny spots of scarlet as bright and distinctive as blood. 'Damn,' she murmured. She put down the glass and looked at Joel, who was already standing up and heading for the door.

'Who can that be?' he said, glancing at his watch.

Leave it! she wanted to shout. *Don't go down there. Don't let them in.* Because she knew who it was, who it had to be. And she also knew that it was too late now to tell Joel the truth about anything. She had meant to talk to him, to try and explain, but as usual she had bottled it. Her last chance and it was gone for ever.

As Joel disappeared, she jumped up, dashed over to the window, pulled back the curtain and gazed down on the street. Her knees were shaking, her whole body trembling. The panda car was parked by the curb and two officers were standing on the path. Inspector Frayne stared up at the lighted window and, although he must have been able to see her quite clearly, he gave no indication of having done so. Instead, he lowered his head and said something to his companion.

Sadie retreated, letting the curtain fall back into place. She didn't sit down but stood and waited, bracing herself for what was to come. So this was it. Finally, it had all caught up with her. They would take her down to the station and charge her with . . . with what? Attempted murder perhaps. Or would she be able to persuade them that she'd shot Wayne Gissing in self-defence? Either way, they'd put her behind bars.

Sadie waited, her heart in her mouth, as the three men climbed the stairs and entered the flat. She heard the click as the door closed. Aware that her hands had clenched into two tight fists, she quickly uncurled them. But what was the point of pretending that she wasn't afraid? It must be written all over her face.

Inspector Gerald Frayne was the first to enter the living room. He gave her a genial nod. 'Sorry to disturb you like this,' he said. 'I hope it's not too inconvenient.'

'That's okay,' Sadie said, giving a nervous laugh. 'Is everything . . . How can we help? Sorry, would you like to sit down?'

Frayne sat in the armchair. The other officer, the constable whose name she couldn't remember, pulled out a chair from beside the dining table and immediately got out his notebook.

'Would you like a drink?' Joel asked. 'Tea or coffee?'

'Not for me,' Frayne said.

The constable shook his head. 'No thanks.'

Sadie sank down on to the sofa and Joel sat beside her. They were all, she noticed, sitting in exactly the same position as the first time the police had visited with the news of Eddie's death. She had one of those odd déjà vu feelings, a tingling down her spine, as if all of this had happened before.

'Do you have some news?' Joel asked. 'About the murder?'

'I'm afraid not,' Frayne said. He looked at Sadie. 'I understand you attended Mr Wise's funeral today?'

'That's right,' she said. Her voice had got a croak in it again. 'What's this about?'

'We're here regarding an incident that happened at the cemetery this morning.'

'An incident?' she repeated. 'What sort of incident?'

Frayne watched her closely. 'A man was shot in the leg. Wayne Gissing. Do you know him?'

Sadie tried to look shocked. 'Shot? What? Is he all right?' She paused for a moment and then added, 'No, not really. I mean, I know who he is. Kelly's brother, right? I've never spoken to him though.' She puckered her forehead into a frown. 'I saw him at the church. Why would anyone want to . . .'

'That's what we're trying to find out.'

'I'm not sure how I can help.'

'The police are talking to everyone who attended the funeral, trying to piece together a picture, see if anyone saw or heard anything.'

Sadie held on to his words like a drowning woman clinging to a lifebelt. Would he be saying these things if he knew she was responsible? But maybe it was a trick, a ruse to try and make her relax and let down her guard. 'I see. Well, of course.'

Frayne left one of his short unsettling silences before he continued. 'So when was the last time you saw Wayne Gissing?'

'It must have been at the burial.' Sadie gave a light shrug. 'He was standing with Kelly near the grave.'

'And how did he seem?'

'Seem?' Sadie repeated.

'Agitated, upset, angry?'

'I-I don't know. I wasn't really looking at him. I don't think so. I mean, I didn't notice anything in particular. I wasn't standing that close.'

'You weren't at the graveside then?'

Sadie shook her head. Recalling the presence of the two London detectives, she knew better than to lie about this. They would have already written their reports, detailing where all the mourners were positioned. 'I was standing back, on one of the paths. I was with Sharon Gissing.'

Frayne's eyebrows shot up as if he was surprised. 'Sharon Gissing?'

'Yes, we got talking as we left the church. We walked to the cemetery together. I suppose it was a bit awkward for both of us. I was the wife Eddie was separated from and she was the girlfriend's stepmother. I think Kelly's real mum was there so . . . anyway, we hung back a bit. We didn't want to intrude.'

'And when the service was over?'

'I left.'

'Alone?'

'Yes. Sharon was waiting for the others.'

'So you didn't go over and talk to Eddie's parents?'

'No. I meant to but . . . I don't know, it didn't seem like the right time.' Out of the corner of her eye she could see the constable scribbling in his notebook, taking down everything she said. 'I picked up my stuff from Oaklands, went to the station and got on a train.'

Frayne took out a large tissue and blew his nose noisily. 'Sorry,' he said. 'I can't get rid of this cold.' He shoved the tissue back in his pocket. 'Going back to the cemetery,' he said. 'Did you happen to notice a red Ford Capri parked at the far end of the thoroughfare?'

Sadie shook her head. 'No.' Keep it simple, she warned herself. Don't embellish. Don't say anything you don't need to.

'So you left straight after the burial. Was that by the main gates?'

'Shortly after, yes.' Had anyone seen her leave? Not Eddie's

277

family – they'd had had their backs to her. And she didn't have to worry about the Gissings; they weren't about to admit that she'd been lured to the far side of the graveyard. No, she was pretty sure that Sharon would be telling much the same story as she was.

'And who was still in the cemetery at this time?'

'The priest,' she said. 'Eddie's parents and his sister, Kelly and her mother. A few others I didn't know.'

'And what about Wayne Gissing?'

Sadie wrinkled her brow as if she was thinking about it. 'I'm not sure. He might have gone by then. To be honest, I can't remember.'

'But you didn't hear the shot?'

'No.'

'You left and went straight back to the guest house?'

'That's right.' Sadie reached out for Joel's hand, took his warm fingers between hers and softly squeezed them. 'I was tired. It was . . . an emotional morning. I just wanted to come home.'

'Did you see anyone at Oaklands?'

'No, sorry, there wasn't anyone around. I went up to my room, got my holdall and went to the station.'

Frayne gave another nod. 'There's just one more thing,' he said. 'Do you know a man called Nathan Stone?'

Sadie's pulse began to race. She had to battle to keep eye contact with him. Jesus, how should she answer? How much did he already know? She didn't want to get caught out in a lie, but the truth might be even more dangerous. The denial was out of her mouth before she had proper time to consider it. 'No, I don't think so. The name doesn't sound familiar.'

Frayne looked towards the constable. It was a quick conspiratorial glance but Sadie still caught it. 'Are you sure?' he said, leaning forward to place his palms firmly on his thighs. 'Only we've been informed that you had a long conversation with him in the Fox last night.'

'What? Who told you that? No, that isn't ... that can't be ...' Sadie frowned hard as if she couldn't understand it and then produced what she hoped was a look of enlightenment. 'Ah, do you mean the tall guy with the grey hair? Was that his name? I don't think he introduced himself. He came over to the table and said that he was sorry to hear about Eddie. He didn't stay for long. A few minutes at the most. Was that him?'

Frayne gave her a long hard stare. 'You've never met him before?'

'No.'

'You're sure about that?'

Sadie, who was still holding Joel's hand, wondered if he could feel the dampness of her palms. 'Absolutely. I went for a drink with Velma – she's a woman I met at the guest house – and the guy just ... he just came over.' She gave a shrug. 'Sorry, is it important? I'd forgotten all about it.'

'You didn't see him again at the church or the cemetery?'

'No.'

'You think this man had something to do with the shooting?' Joel asked.

Frayne didn't answer directly. 'We're still making enquiries.'

Sadie felt her stomach shift. Had someone seen Nathan Stone at the cemetery? Or maybe his car parked by the gates? But it didn't matter, she thought, so long as Wayne Gissing kept quiet about who had really done the shooting.

Frayne rose to his feet and smiled at her. 'I think that's all for now. Thank you for your time. If anything else occurs to you ...'

'Yes, I'll let you know,' Sadie said. She jumped up, eager to see the back of him. Relief was washing over her. A short while ago she'd felt like a woman on the way to the gallows. Now

279

she'd been given a last-minute reprieve. She wasn't stupid enough to feel that she was safe, but at least she wasn't being escorted off the premises in handcuffs.

'I'll see you out,' Joel said.

He went to the door and the constable followed him. Frayne was on the point of leaving too when he stopped and gestured towards Sadie's hand. 'You've hurt yourself.'

'Oh, this?' she said, waving her hand in the air and trying to sound casual. 'It's nothing, a scratch. I caught it on a nail.'

'Was that here or in London?'

Sadie might have lied to him, might have said that she'd done it downstairs in the workroom, if Joel hadn't still been within earshot. 'At the guesthouse,' she said. 'It was my own fault. But it's fine, nothing serious. It will have healed up in a day or two.'

Frayne continued to stare at the plaster for a few seconds as if he was trying to form a link in his head between the wound and the shooting of Wayne Gissing. He lifted his eyes to stare directly into Sadie's. What did he see there? Fear, hope, deceit? She was the first to look away, uncomfortable under the scrutiny of his gaze.

'Well, I'll leave you in peace,' he said. 'Have a nice evening.'

Sadie forced her mouth into a shaky smile. *In peace?* She sensed a hint of mockery in the words as if Frayne could see right into the darkness of her soul and knew that her days of freedom were numbered.

41

Nina Frayne could hear the rain lashing against the window as she poured hot water over the whisky and added a teaspoon of sugar and the juice from half a lemon. She gave the whole lot a stir, carried the mug through to the living room and placed the hot toddy on the table beside her husband.

'Here, drink this before it goes cold.'

'Thanks, love.'

'Are you sure you don't want something to eat? It won't take a minute.'

'No, I'm fine. I grabbed a sandwich at the station.'

Nina placed a hand on the back of his chair. She always worried about him – it had become a habit over the years – but she became even more anxious when he immersed himself in a complicated case. It was as if he lived and breathed every little detail until some form of resolution was eventually arrived at.

'It's turned nasty out there. Pouring down. You won't need to go out again, will you?'

'Let's hope not.'

Looking over his shoulder she saw that the file on his lap

was open to a rough sketch of Kellston Cemetery. It included the main thoroughfare, both sets of gates and a few side paths. Eddie Wise's grave was marked with a tombstone and there was a series of stickmen with initials placed neatly beside them.

'Is this the funeral?'

Gerald pointed with his forefinger to a tiny figure with SW printed beside it. 'Sadie Wise,' he said. 'She was standing right here with Sharon Gissing. That's odd, don't you think?'

Nina studied the diagram, trying to see what he was getting at. 'Odd?'

'Well, there's no love lost between the Gissings and Sadie Wise. It's not that long since they were accusing her of murder. So why would the two of them choose to stand together like that? It doesn't make any sense.'

'Maybe the family changed their mind, decided she's innocent after all.'

'That's not what I've heard.'

'So maybe Sharon was trying to prise some information out of her. You know, the softly-softly approach? What did Sadie say when you asked her?'

Gerald picked up the glass and took a sip of the whisky. 'Not much. Only that they got talking outside the church and walked together to the cemetery.'

'Perhaps she wanted to clear the air. It's not very nice having people think you're a killer.'

'Except the Gissings aren't what you'd call the rational sort. And they're hardly the type to talk things through either. No, that family do most of their talking with their fists.'

'What, even the women?'

'You'd be surprised,' Gerald said. 'Both Kelly and Sharon have been charged in the past with assaults on other females. Not to mention numerous counts of affray. It's usually over some bloke or another; they don't take kindly to having their toes stepped on.'

'So you think Sharon was up to something?

'Possibly.'

'But Wayne Gissing was the one who got shot.'

'Yes.'

Nina thought about this for a while. 'You don't think she did it, do you? Sadie Wise, I mean.'

'I haven't ruled it out. She claims she left shortly after the burial, went out through the main gates and back to Oaklands, but there aren't any witnesses. Nobody can back up her story. No one saw her at the guest house either.'

'Where would she even get a gun from?'

'It might not have been hers. Perhaps it was Wayne's. There could have been an argument, a scuffle and the thing went off accidentally. But I'll tell you something, she looked white as a sheet when we turned up at the flat this evening.'

'Lots of people are nervous of the police. It doesn't necessarily mean anything. And it must have been a difficult day for her with the funeral.'

'It was more than that. Her body language . . . She was tense, defensive. It was all wrong. I've got a feeling she's hiding something. I'm sure she is. I just can't figure out what. And then there's all this business with Nathan Stone. I told you about him, didn't I?'

'The man who works for Terry Street, the one she was supposed to have gone to the dogs with?'

'That's him. So she claims they've never met, that she's never heard of him, but one of McCloud's men saw them talking in the Fox last night. When I pulled her up on it she said he was a complete stranger who came up to her in the pub to express his condolences over Eddie.'

'But you don't believe her.'

Gerald shook his head. 'I'd swear on it. She knows him all right. So why is she lying?'

'Well, if there was ... *is* something between the two of them she's hardly going to admit to it in front of her boyfriend.'

'She could have come down to the station at any time, talked to me in confidence. Better that, surely, than being a suspect in a murder case.'

Nina, who felt that part of her job in these exchanges was to try and put the opposing point of view, chipped in with, 'True, but why would they even talk to each other in the pub? If they are involved, wouldn't they be more likely to keep their distance?'

'Maybe he had something important to tell her, something that couldn't wait. Maybe he's not very smart. Or maybe he's so arrogant that he thinks he can do whatever he likes and get away with it.' Gerald drummed the fingers of his free hand on the arm of the chair. 'Cowan Road had a tail on him – that's how they knew about him seeing Sadie Wise – but he gave them the slip this morning. Disappeared for hours and didn't turn up on the radar again until the early afternoon.'

'So he could have been involved in the shooting. What's Ian McCloud's take on all this?'

Gerald swirled the whisky and lemon around in the glass and gave a weary sigh as he thought about his former colleague. 'I think he's leaning more towards the gangland idea, some kind of feud that's got out of hand, an eye for an eye and all that. He can't see any real motive for Sadie Wise wanting her husband dead.'

'There doesn't seem to be one – on the surface. I guess you just have to follow your instincts. I mean, McCloud's never spoken to her, has he? He hasn't seen what you've seen.'

Gerald was quiet for a moment, pondering. 'Peter Royston's got his suspicions too. He's been sniffing around, looking for an angle.'

'I don't like that man. He's a scandalmonger . . . and a creep.'

'Doesn't mean he's wrong, though. The guy's got a nose for a good story.'

Nina bent and kissed the top of his head. 'Well, I'll leave you to it. I'm going to have a bath and go to bed. You won't stay up too late, will you?'

'I won't. Goodnight, love.'

Gerald finished off the whisky while he slowly perused the contents of the file. He checked out Sharon Gissing's statement again, trying to read between the lines. She claimed that after the burial Sadie Wise had left the graveyard while Wayne had gone to collect the car. The other two, Kelly and her mother, had decided to walk to the Fox and so she'd stayed and waited for Wayne alone. She had heard the shot as she was walking towards the main gates but presumed it was just a car back-firing.

Gerald flipped over the page and continued reading. After a while, when Wayne still hadn't come back, Sharon had started heading up the main path. She could just about make out the red Capri at the far end, but was short-sighted and couldn't tell if Wayne was actually inside or not. It was only when she reached the car that she discovered he'd been shot and was lying in front of the bonnet. She hadn't wanted to waste time by calling for an ambulance and instead had driven him straight to A&E.

Gerald raised his eyes to the ceiling and gave a snort. It was nonsense, the whole damn lot of it, but impossible to prove. A cock-and-bull story invented to prevent the police from discovering who the real assailant was.

Wayne's statement naturally tallied with Sharon's except for the embellishment of his three black muggers. Petra and Kelly Gissing had nothing useful to add; they had left with Eddie's family and didn't know anything about what had happened

285

next. The statements from the two plain-clothed officers, sent to keep an eye on proceedings, were next to useless too. They had gone to stand just outside the gates, but were unable to confirm or deny that Sadie Wise had left when she said she had. Within a minute or two a brawl had broken out in the street and by the time it had been broken up the mourners had dispersed.

Gerald frowned. A deliberate ploy or an unfortunate coincidence? The former, he decided. Whoever put a bullet into Wayne Gissing had made sure that the police would be distracted at the time of the assault. And, standing on the street with the sound of the traffic and the shouting of the brawlers, the officers would have been less likely to hear the gunshot.

Leaning his head against the back of the chair, Gerald yawned. His eyes felt sore and scratchy. He knew he should go to bed and try to get some sleep, but too much was going through his mind. He thought about the cut on Sadie Wise's hand and wondered if it meant anything. He thought about her face, pale and pinched and drawn. It was true to say that bad things happened when she was around.

Gerald moved his head and looked down at the file again. He flicked over a few more pages until he came to a photograph of Nathan Stone. He stared long and hard at the picture. With some villains you could read their personalities in their features – the cocky smile, the hard eyes or the mocking mouth – but this was a harder face to fathom. There was something closed about it, something impenetrable. Nathan Stone was a man who, according to McCloud's notes, had probably murdered his wife. And Sadie Wise was a girl who might have had her husband killed. Perhaps the two of them had more in common than he'd originally thought.

42

Peter Royston ate the last of his chips while he stared out at the grey stormy sea. He had taken shelter from the rain in one of the covered benches on the front but the wind still whipped around his ankles, causing the bottom of his trousers to flap and a chill to gather in his toes. He checked his watch again and saw that he still had five minutes to wait. The graveyard shift didn't start until ten.

The promenade was virtually empty. It was too late for the dog walkers and too early for the pubs to be kicking out their customers. The sky above was starless, full of clouds, but there was plenty of light from the streetlamps. He watched the waves smash their way on to the sand, rushing up the shore before quickly retreating again.

At this time on a Friday night he'd usually be in the White Swan, sipping on a pint and keeping his ears pricked for any local gossip. Still, he'd easily make last orders if his bit of business ran smoothly. And even if he didn't make it, it would be worth the sacrifice if he managed, eventually, to dig the dirt on Sadie Wise.

Royston scratched his chin and grinned. The chances of a scoop in a place like Haverlea were few and far between and he wasn't about to let this opportunity slip through his fingers. There could be big bucks to be made by selling the story on to the nationals, but that wasn't the only reason he wanted it so much. For years he'd had to put up with the likes of Frank Hunter and his cronies poking their noses in where they weren't wanted and dictating what could or couldn't be printed in the local paper. Middle-class, conservative and influential, they yielded an excess of power and even had his spineless editor in their pocket. Thatcher's puppets, the whole bloody lot of them. Just for once he'd like to wipe those smug smiles off their faces – and what better way of doing it than exposing Frank Hunter's future daughter-in-law as a murderer.

Royston rose to his feet, screwed up the vinegary chip paper and chucked it in the litter bin. As he crossed the road towards the hotel, he thought about the girl Joel Hunter was planning to marry. On the surface she might seem whiter than white, but he wasn't taken in; he reckoned there was a dark streak running through her. He'd been tipped the wink that she was involved with a Kellston villain called Nathan Stone, but as yet hadn't been able to corroborate the rumour.

When he'd approached her in town, Sadie had been . . . what was the word he was looking for? Evasive, perhaps. Certainly not cooperative. Since then, things had moved on. Today's news about the shooting at Eddie Wise's funeral had stoked the fire, adding to his suspicions about her guilt; he was kicking himself now that he hadn't bothered to make the trip to London.

Royston rubbed his hands together as he climbed the steps to the Bold, pushed open the door and walked inside. The place was deserted and it wasn't much warmer inside than out. He strode over to the desk, leaned on the counter and dinged the bell. While he waited he gazed around the foyer at the faded wallpaper and slightly shabby furniture. The hotel, built in the Victorian era, had once been a splendid building and a fashionable place to stay, but its glory days were long over. Now they struggled to fill the rooms even in the summer months.

It was another few minutes before Derek Pugh, the man on night duty, shuffled out from the back. He was in his early sixties, grey and morose with a face like a slapped arse. 'Ah, Mr Royston. I haven't seen you in a while. What brings you here?'

'I need some information.'

'And what kind of information would that be?'

'The useful sort. You had a girl staying here last weekend, Anne something. Early twenties, slim, short black hair. I'd like an address if you've got it.'

Pugh's eyes turned sly. His tongue darted out and slid along his upper lip. 'Not sure if I'm allowed to do that, Mr Royston. I think it's against the rules.'

Royston leaned against the counter and held up a folded five-pound note between his fingers. He watched as the older man's eyes flicked down towards the money. 'Well, what do they say about rules? They're there to be broken, right?'

Pugh, possibly hoping for an increase in the bribe, wasn't immediately forthcoming. 'The boss wouldn't like it.'

'There are lots of things your boss wouldn't like, a copy of your criminal record being one of them.' Royston always made a point of knowing other people's business, of rooting around in the shadows; he was an expert on dirty laundry and skeletons in the closet. 'I mean, what if he got to hear about those cautions you've had for—'

'Aw, Mr Royston, you know I don't do that any more. It's all in the past.'

'Of course it is. Still, people aren't always quick to forget or forgive. Be a shame to lose a good job like this over something that happened years ago. Personally, I'm all in favour of second chances, but then I'm a liberal-minded sort of person.'

Pugh glared at him for a moment, but when he realised that his indignation was wasted, he lifted his shoulders in a shrug. 'I suppose it won't do any harm, not just this once.' He reached out for the fiver, but it was quickly snatched it away.

'Anne something,' Royston said. 'Last weekend.'

With a sigh, Royston reached down under the desk, picked up a large red leather-bound book and placed it on the counter. He flipped back through the pages until he came to the right days and ran a finger down the short list of bookings. 'No,' he said, 'no one by that name.'

'Try the Friday.'

But Pugh shook his head. 'Sure you've got the right hotel?'

All Royston knew was what the girl had told him at the party. 'You don't remember her?' He gave the description again. 'Young, in her early twenties, short black hair.'

'Unless she came back after ten or left early in the morning I wouldn't have seen her.'

Royston reached out for the book, but Pugh clamped his hand down on it. 'I'm telling you there's no one called Anne registered here.'

'Any women at all, women on their own?'

Pugh went through the list again. 'Just the one,' he said. 'A Mona Farrell. She booked in on the Saturday and left on the Sunday.'

'Let me see,' Royston said impatiently. This time Pugh gave in and let him take the book. He turned it around and stared at the name and the London address. Was it her? He flipped back through the previous week. Well, there were no other women booked in on their own. Maybe Anne was a diminutive of Mona. Or maybe . . . He had a sudden flashback to the party, to Sadie Wise dragging her friend away from him. She'd seemed

290

on edge, nervous, alarmed even to find the two of them talking together. Maybe Anne wasn't the girl's name at all.

Royston scribbled down the Hampstead address and pushed the book back across the counter along with the five-pound note. 'Let me know if she shows up again. I'll make it worth your while.'

Pugh palmed the note and slid it into his trouser pocket. 'Always a pleasure, Mr Royston. Have a nice evening.'

Royston left the hotel with a spring in his step and a good feeling in his guts. If 'Mona Farrell' and Anne were one and the same person then it could be the break he needed. Something was off and all he had to do now was follow the smell.

43

If it hadn't been for the Christmas decorations springing up around town, Sadie wouldn't have been aware of November passing into December. As she walked home from work, her gaze took in the shop windows with their artificial snow, plump red Santas, swags, garlands, trees and garish baubles. There had been a sudden explosion of glitter and glitz.

Despite the colourful show, she still felt devoid of any festive spirit. It was two weeks now since Eddie's funeral and she'd spent the entire fortnight in a state of distraction, constantly worried that the police would turn up again. Instead of getting less fearful as time passed by, she was growing increasingly anxious, sure that they must be gathering evidence and the net was gradually closing around her.

To make matters worse, Mona Farrell had embarked on a campaign of letter writing. These letters, which came through the post almost every day, were long and rambling, often threatening, sometimes pleading and always thoroughly disturbing. *If you don't stick to your side of the bargain, then I'm going to tell everyone what you've done. Don't think that I won't. I don't care if I live or die. I've got nothing to lose, you've got everything.*

Included with the letters were more roughly drawn plans of the Hampstead garden with instructions on where to wait, where to go to and the exact position she should be standing in when she raised the gun and fired through the study window at Mona's father.

This had all started on the Saturday after Eddie's funeral. Joel had been working downstairs when the phone rang in the flat. As soon as Sadie had heard the voice on the other end of the line, her heart had sunk.

'Why are you calling me here? I thought we'd—'

'You haven't been in touch,' Mona had said peevishly. 'It's been over a week. What's going on? You said you'd call.'

Sadie had taken a deep breath, pressing the phone close to her ear before delivering her answer. 'I think it's better if we don't . . . if we don't talk any more. I can't do what you want me to do. I *won't*. Do you understand?'

There had been a short silence. 'You can't renege on a promise.'

'I didn't promise anything.'

'Yes, you did. Why are you doing this? It's not fair. It isn't.'

'Please don't call me again. It's over, all right? I can't do this any more.' And then before she could say anything else, Sadie had hung up. The phone had rung again almost instantly, but she hadn't picked up. She had turned the answer machine off too. When Mona had continued to call, over and over again, Sadie had got down on her hands and knees and pulled out the lead. While she'd been sat on the floor with her arms wrapped around her legs the harsh sound of the phone had continued to echo in her ears.

Joel had been bemused by her refusal to take any further calls off 'Anne' and Sadie had had to offer up a feasible explanation.

'She wants to talk about Eddie all the time. I can't . . . I don't want to think about it any more.'

'Can't you tell her that?'

'She never listens.'

And so Joel had continued to say that Sadie wasn't in and a few days later the letters had begun to arrive. Sadie was in the habit now of always going down to pick up the post – she didn't want him to know how often Mona was writing – and every time she saw that childlike scrawl her heart would skip a beat.

'No,' she would groan. 'Not again.'

After she'd read the letters, she would tear them into tiny little pieces and shove them in the bin under the leftovers and the wet tea bags. It was crazy, mad, but she didn't know what else to do. A part of her realised she should be keeping them as evidence of Mona's guilt – these were clear plans for the murder of her father – but she was too afraid that they would make her look guilty too. If the police ever got hold of them, they would jump to the obvious damning conclusions.

There was Joel to worry about as well. How long before Mona started dripping her poison into his ear? If she was drunk and angry, there was no knowing what she might say. Sadie had returned the gifts, the book and the scarf, without any sort of note. But if she'd been hoping that Mona might get the message and stop harassing her, those hopes had been quickly dashed.

As she reached Buckingham Road, Sadie slowed her pace, not wanting to get home any faster than she had to. There was an awkward atmosphere between her and Joel at the moment. None of it was his fault. It was all entirely hers. She had chosen to lie, to deceive, and now every day she felt a little more distant as if she was being carried on the tide and gradually drifting away from him.

Joel was in the kitchen, sitting at the table. He looked up as she came in and from the expression on his face she knew that

294

something was wrong. Immediately she thought the worst, that the police had been back or that Mona had called and told him about the imaginary 'pact'.

'What's happened?'

He hesitated, his mouth twisting. 'It's . . . well, I wasn't sure if I should tell you or not but—'

'Tell me what?'

'I don't want you to get upset.'

Sadie felt a jolt of alarm. 'Oh, just tell me, Joel. Please.' She pulled out a chair and sat down opposite to him. Her lips were going dry, her throat tightening. 'I'd rather know, whatever it is.'

Joel took an audible breath, glanced down at the table and then up again. 'My mum rang earlier. They got a letter this morning, an anonymous one. It was about you.'

'What?'

'Just some rubbish accusing you of . . . of being involved in Eddie's murder. They know that it's nonsense. They don't believe a word of it. It's just some crank trying to stir up trouble.'

Sadie put her elbows on the table, lifted a hand and chewed on a knuckle. She instantly guessed that it was Mona, but couldn't say it out loud. 'My God, why would anyone do that?'

'Don't worry about it. Some people . . . they're just . . . they've got nothing better to do. Nobody believes it, not for a minute.'

Sadie jumped up, went over to the sink and poured a glass of water. She took a sip and then, with her back still to him, asked, 'What else did it say? The letter?'

'Nothing much.'

She turned to look at him again. 'What's nothing much?'

Joel pulled a face. 'Some jibes about how you couldn't be trusted, that you were using me, that all you care about is money – or, to be more precise, my parents' money.'

Sadie shook her head. 'So now I'm a murderer *and* a gold digger. Was there anything else?'

'That was pretty much it, I think. Look, I know it's cruel and nasty, but you just have to put it out of your mind.'

But that was one thing Sadie couldn't do. Mona wasn't going to stop until she got what she wanted. 'Are they going to take it to the police? Did your mum say?'

'I don't think so. Do you think they should?'

Sadie gave a shrug, wondering how careful Mona had been. There would be a postmark on the letter, maybe even finger-prints. What if they managed to trace it back? She shivered at the thought, aware of how unstable the girl was. A rush of panic made her hands shake and she quickly put down the glass on the side of the sink. 'I suppose it would be a waste of time. I doubt if they could find out who sent it, could they?'

'I shouldn't think they'd even try.'

'No,' Sadie said, hoping he was right.

Joel stared at her, his eyes full of concern. 'Are you okay? I feel really bad about ... I mean, you've got enough to deal with without this as well. I wasn't sure if—'

'It's not a problem,' she lied, attempting to keep her voice steady. 'Like I said, I'd rather know.'

'At least we can get away from it all tomorrow.'

'Huh?'

'The Lake District,' he said. 'You hadn't forgotten, had you?'

Sadie had forgotten. It had gone clean out of her head. Every year, before Christmas, Joel's parents rented a large rambling house in Grasmere for a week. During that time friends and relatives came and went and the house was always full to over-flowing. Although she'd enjoyed it in the past, this December the thought of all that socialising, all that endless smiling and chatting, filled her with dread. 'I was wondering ... would you mind if I gave it a miss? After everything ... I just fancy a quiet weekend.'

Joel looked disappointed, but gave a nod. 'Yeah, I understand.

If that's what you want. It's been a tough few weeks. I'm sure they'll be fine about it. We can just stay here and take it easy; maybe we could catch a film or go for a meal.'

'No, you should still go. I want you to. Your mum and dad will be really disappointed if you pull out now.'

'I can't leave you here on your own.'

'Why not? I'll be fine, honestly I will.' Suddenly the prospect of solitude, of having time to think, filled her with a wondrous sense of relief. She wouldn't have to worry about saying the wrong thing or letting something slip. Just for a while, she'd be able to breathe and maybe get her head in order.

'It's not because of the letter, is it? Because if it is—'

'It isn't,' she insisted. 'I promise.' Although that wasn't strictly true. The subject was bound to come up at some point and she couldn't bear the strain of lying. She'd be under scrutiny at the Grasmere house and that was the last thing she wanted. 'I might go and see Mum on Sunday. She's been worried, you know, after all this stuff with Eddie.'

Joel sat back and folded his arms his arms across his chest. 'Are you sure you won't come? It won't be the same without you.'

'I just feel . . . I feel really tired, exhausted, like I want to sleep for a year. I wouldn't be good company. You'll apologise for me, won't you?'

Joel opened his mouth as if he was going to try and persuade her to change her mind, but then almost immediately closed it again. Perhaps he realised that the decision had been made and that it was pointless to argue. He left a pause and then said, 'Everything's all right, though, isn't it? I mean, between us?'

'Of course,' Sadie said, a bit too brightly. 'That's not why I don't want to come. It's not that at all.' All her instincts told her to lean across the table, put her hand over his and make some physical contact, but instead she looked away. Somehow, when it came to it, she just couldn't give him the reassurance he needed.

44

Sadie felt a twinge of regret as she waved Joel off the following morning. She'd had a restless night full of strange disturbing dreams in which she was constantly trying to find her way home but never succeeded in getting there. Wisps of those dreams still lingered as she stood on the doorstep and watched him leave.

Over breakfast she had come close to changing her mind – perhaps it would be good to get away, to try and forget about things for a while – but she knew it was hopeless. She had gazed at his face and her stomach had twisted. How could she go on deceiving him? Eventually the truth would come out and he would see her in a different light. He would find out that she'd shot a man, that she'd known who murdered Eddie, that she'd lied to him and to the police. How would he reconcile this Sadie with the one he thought he loved?

'I'll call you,' he'd said.

'Have a good time. Give my best to everyone.'

Sadie went back upstairs and sat at the table for a while. Then she picked up her bag, went through to the kitchen, took out the latest letters from Mona Farrell and burned them in the sink.

Once she had cleared away the ashes, Sadie put on her coat. Despite the cold, she walked down to the front, hoping that the sea air would clear her head. She braced herself against the wind as she strode along the promenade. It was the doing nothing that was getting to her. She felt helpless, out of control, as if she was simply waiting for things to happen.

There was a red phone box next to the boating pond and she was tempted to step inside and call Nathan Stone. Had the police talked to him? What had they said? Had he got rid of the gun? What was going on with the Gissings? There were so many questions and only one way of finding out the answers. But she knew he wouldn't be at the bar – it was far too early – and she had no other way of contacting him.

For a while she stood by the pond and watched the wind whip across the surface, rippling the water. There were no kids playing here today. There were no boats bobbing about, no tiny yachts with graceful white sails. The bad weather was keeping almost everyone indoors.

Sadie glanced over at the phone box again, but knew it was pointless. Even if she did manage to reach him, he wouldn't tell her anything. *I'm not talking about this over the phone.* Wasn't that what he'd said last time she'd called? No, he'd be tight-lipped about it all, wary in case the police were listening in. She sucked in a breath. She didn't want to think about Inspector Gerald Frayne and his cool, suspicious eyes.

It was only when the cold started seeping into her bones that she began walking again. She went past the swimming baths with their wafting chlorine smell and then the arcades with their flashing lights and music until she reached the end of the prom-enade. Here she turned and headed for home. The rain started on her way back and by the time she reached the flat she was drenched. She went upstairs, ran a bath and stripped off her clothes.

While she lay in the hot water, Sadie reviewed her options. When it came down to it there were only two: either she went to the police and came clean about everything, or she kept her mouth shut and waited to see what would happen. Except in her heart she already knew what would happen: at some point the truth would come out and her world would fall apart.

Sadie was still racking her brains for smarter ways to address the situation when the doorbell rang. She closed her eyes and sank down under the water. Whoever it was would have to come back another time. It rang again and again, but she continued to ignore it. What if it was the police? She said a silent prayer that it wasn't. *Please God.* She wasn't ready for them yet. She wasn't sure if she would ever be ready.

Half an hour later, Sadie got out of the bath, dried herself off and pulled on her dressing gown. She opened the door to the flat, went out on to the landing and peered down the two flights of stairs into the hallway. A white envelope was lying on the floor and she wondered if it had been the postman who'd rung the bell.

Sadie padded downstairs in her bare feet and picked up the letter. The minute she saw the handwriting on the front, the breath caught in her throat. She'd know that scrawl anywhere. *Mona Farrell.* What made it worse was that there wasn't a stamp – it had been hand-delivered. Quickly, with her heart thumping, she tore open the envelope and read the contents:

Dear Sadie,

Meet me tonight at the fairground by the Big Wheel at eight o'clock. If you don't come, you'll be sorry. I won't keep quiet – you know I won't. Come on your own and don't bring Joel. Please come. I need to see you.

Your dear friend,

Mona

Sadie stood for a long time staring down at the note. Her hands shook as she read and re-read it. She didn't have to go. But Mona would come round again if she didn't show up. Well, so what? She could turn off all the lights, pretend she wasn't in – but she couldn't hide for ever. The girl would keep trying until she got what she wanted. No, it was time to stop running, to turn and face things head on. It was time to take back some control.

45

Mona gazed into the mirror as she carefully styled her hair, gelling it up into short neat spikes. After the disappointment of finding that Sadie was out, she had spent the day exploring Haverlea. In truth, she didn't think much of it. It seemed a slow, sleepy sort of town, although that was maybe due to the time of year. The place was one of those touristy seaside spots, busy in summer but dead in winter. Hopefully, it would perk up a bit at night.

If the town was dull, the hotel wasn't any better. The only other guests were virtually geriatric, old women with tight blue-rinsed perms and disapproving faces. She gave a shudder and reached for the red pill on the dressing table. Quickly she popped it in her mouth and washed it down with a gulp of vodka.

Sometimes it was hard not to get angry at Sadie; she was forever saying one thing and then doing another. In Hampstead, Mona had checked the post every day waiting to hear from her, waiting for a single reply to any of the letters she'd sent. And then there were all the phone calls she'd made. Well, no one likes being ignored, do they? In the end she'd had no choice but to write to the Hunters. She hadn't wanted to do it, but Sadie needed reminding of the promise she'd made. It had been the only way, the last resort.

Mona put on some lipstick and sat back to view the effect in the mirror. She inclined her head and smiled at her reflection. Even though Sadie drove her mad at times, she wouldn't be without her. And everyone had their faults. The trouble with Sadie was that she was too kind, too forgiving. Take Eddie, for example. Why should a man like that be allowed to get away with what he'd done? She recalled the way he'd looked at her when he'd opened the door to his flat, the quick appraising glance that had raked her body from head to toe.

'Yeah?'

'Are you Eddie?' she'd asked, smiling sweetly. 'Eddie Wise?'

'What's it about?'

'My name's Anne Faulkner. I'm here about your wife, Sadie.'

'Oh, you've just missed her.'

'I know,' she'd said. 'It's you I want to talk to. Could we do this inside? It won't take long.'

And just like that, he'd stood back and let her in, even taken her through to the kitchen and offered her a coffee. She wondered what he'd been thinking about in the last few minutes of his life. Nothing much, she imagined, and certainly nothing of importance. Men like Eddie Wise only ever thought about themselves.

Mona had no regrets about what she'd done. His worthless, pitiful existence had been snuffed out in a matter of seconds. What had she felt as she'd slid the knife between his ribs? Very little. It had been an act of mercy, like putting down a rabid dog. When she looked back, which wasn't often, the whole event had a slightly surreal quality to it, sharp in places, misty in others. Anyway, she had simply done what she had to do and now Sadie was free of him for ever.

As the effects of the pill kicked in, Mona's mood started to lift. She glanced at her watch. Soon it would be time to go. She felt the same stirring excitement as a child would feel as she anticipated not just the lights and the rides, but the joy of sharing those things with a friend. It would be good to see Sadie again. This evening she would make her see sense and persuade her to go through with her side of the bargain.

'It's only right,' she whispered. 'It's only fair.'

Yes, it was time for Sadie to face up to her responsibilities. Paul Farrell, like Eddie, had to be swept from the face of the earth. Mona jumped up, eager to be off. Tonight was going to be a good night, a *great* night, a night to remember.

46

Peter Royston had got the message at eleven o'clock the previous evening. He had come back from the pub, somewhat the worse for wear, to find the red light blinking on his answering machine. Swaying slightly, he'd jabbed at the button and waited to see if anyone would start speaking. More often than not, all he got was a long pause and then the click of a phone going down. People didn't like talking to machines. But on this occasion, the caller went ahead.

'Er ... Mr Royston? This is Derek, Derek Pugh. I just thought you might want to know that the Farrell girl booked in again today. She's here for two nights. So ... er ... yeah, that's it really.' There was a short silence. 'You'll call by some time, huh? Like we discussed. Yeah, okay.'

Royston grinned as he sat across the road from the Bold and replayed the message in his head. This could be just the break he needed. In the two weeks that had passed since he'd dropped in at the hotel he'd been doing extensive digging on Mona Farrell and what he'd discovered made for interesting reading.

The girl was the daughter of a leading industrialist, an arms manufacturer called Paul Farrell. She was twenty-three, an only child, and still lived with her parents in Hampstead. That wasn't the fascinating bit, though. No, what had really triggered his interest was Mona's history: she'd been expelled from numerous schools, been arrested during a couple of political demonstrations and was generally the subject of untold rumour and gossip.

The latter had come from Royston's contacts in London, other reporters who had heard stories and were willing to share them. The best of these was that a blaze at the family home was thought to have been deliberately started by her. The affair had been hushed up by her influential father, and Mona was still receiving psychiatric treatment.

For all his research, Royston hadn't been able to establish a firm connection between Sadie Wise and Mona Farrell. They obviously knew each other – that much had been established at Emily Hunter's party – but where they had met and why Sadie was so jumpy in her company remained a mystery. He recalled the look on her face as she'd dragged the other girl away from him. On the surface the two of them seemed to have little in common, but that was what made it all the more intriguing.

When he'd first heard about Mona's return, Royston's intention had been to come here and confront her, to talk to her, to maybe try and back her into a corner about why she was using a false name – from his digging there was no indication that she'd ever been referred to as Anne – but then he'd decided on a different tack. Instead, he'd opted to wait for her to emerge from the hotel, knowing that at some point she was bound to get in touch with Sadie. He wanted to see them together one more time before he made up his mind about what to do next.

Royston shifted on the hard wooden bench and pulled a face. He'd been sitting in the same place for hours now and his backside was killing him. Darkness had fallen, it was after seven, and he was growing colder by the minute. Earlier, in the morning, he'd thought he'd hit pay dirt when Mona came out of the Bold and made her way to Buckingham Road. He'd trailed behind at a safe distance, making sure he wasn't spotted, but in the event it had all come to nothing. She had stood ringing the front doorbell at number 67 for over five minutes but no one had come down. Finally, he had seen her take an envelope from her bag and slip it through the letterbox.

Although he'd been disappointed in the outcome, the walk hadn't been a complete waste of time. He had discovered two things: the first that Sadie wasn't in (or wasn't answering the door) and the second that she wasn't expecting Mona Farrell. Which begged the question: why wouldn't Mona have phoned ahead if she was coming to Haverlea? It was a long journey from London. There was only one answer that sprang instantly to mind and that was that she'd intended to take Sadie by surprise.

'But a good surprise or a bad one?' Royston murmured to himself.

He was still pondering on this when the door to the Bold opened and Mona Farrell stepped out. He could see her clearly in the light from the foyer but she wouldn't be able to see him. Quickly he got to his feet and moved round to the side of the shelter, keeping to the shadows. Was she going to meet Sadie Wise? There was only one way to find out.

Royston followed her along the promenade. There were plenty of people around – no matter what the weather, the front was always busy on a Saturday night – and so, taking care to keep her in his sights, he mingled with the crowd. She was wearing the same outfit as this morning: jeans, a black suede jacket and gloves, but her short hair was spikier.

It didn't take him long to realise that she was heading for the fairground. The average age of the crowd dropped by a decade as he walked up the path and through the turnstile. Instantly he was hit by the sweet smell of popcorn and candyfloss. The place was noisy, hectic, ringing with the mechanical sounds of the rides, screams and laughter and music.

He kept his gaze firmly fixed on Mona Farrell as she wandered between the stalls. She stopped occasionally to stare at this or that, but didn't talk to anyone. She bought a hotdog from a vendor and ate it as she walked. He was tempted to buy one too – it was hours since he'd had anything to eat – but was too worried about losing her in the crowd. If she disappeared from view he might never find her again.

Royston reviewed everything he knew about Mona as he wound through the fairground, following in her footsteps. The girl had a troubled background, maybe even a psychological disorder. She was wild, anti-authoritarian and a possible arsonist. And then something else came back to him. Hadn't she been talking about fairs at Emily Hunter's party? Yes, she'd been going on about scenes in old films before Sadie Wise had shut her up. He bounced this around in his head but wasn't sure if it had any relevance. He stored it away for future reference.

There was no connection, so far as he'd been able to discover, between Mona Farrell and Eddie Wise. And yet . . . well, it all seemed too much of a coincidence, this odd girl turning up, using an alias, shortly after the murder. And there had been something strained, even forced, about the way Sadie behaved towards her. Was it blackmail? Could Mona be . . . But no, that didn't add up. She came from a wealthy family and her weekly allowance was probably more than Sadie Wise earned in a month.

So what the hell was going on?

Royston, with his journalist's nose, knew instinctively that there was a story here, something tangled, something dark and sinister. Unfortunately, at the moment, he couldn't see the wood for the trees. He couldn't be certain, either, that Mona was actually meeting anyone tonight; she could have simply decided to come out for a stroll.

After half an hour, Royston's patience was starting to wear thin. He'd been hanging around all day with nothing much to show for it and didn't fancy another hour or two of the same. With no sign of Sadie Wise putting in an appearance, he decided to go ahead and make the move.

Mona was standing by the Big Wheel when he sidled up beside her. The ride was circling round slowly, the seats swaying, the bright lights blinking against the blackness of the sky.

'Ah, back in Haverlea, I see.'

Mona turned her head, frowning, but almost instantly her forehead cleared. 'Mr Royston! Hello. Fancy seeing you here.'

'Peter, please. And you're Anne ...' He made a pretence of groping through his mind for her surname. 'I know it. Just give me a moment and it'll come back to me.'

'Faulkner,' she said. 'Anne Faulkner.'

He noted how easily the lie slid from her lips. 'Well, it's very nice to see you again. I didn't realise you'd be back so soon.'

She gave a shrug. 'You can get tired of the city. I didn't know you liked fairgrounds.'

'No, well, not especially. I just came out for a walk.' He nodded towards the wheel. 'Thinking of taking a spin?'

'I prefer to watch.'

'Can't say I blame you. I don't have much of a head for heights.' He paused and then said, 'You've come back to give Sadie some support, I suppose.'

Mona narrowed her eyes. 'Support?'

'You need your friends at times like these. It must be hard for her. First of all her husband getting murdered and then all this business at the funeral ... The police haven't got the most vivid imaginations in the world. When it comes to suspects she'll be up there at the top of the list.'

Mona gave a snort. 'Nobody can think Sadie did it. That would be ridiculous.'

'Nobody with a brain,' he said. 'So how did you two meet? Have you known each other for long?'

Mona's cat-like eyes focused on him. She took a cigarette from a pack in her pocket, raised it to her lips, struck a match and lit it. There was nothing hurried in her movements, nothing to suggest that she was in any way anxious about this unexpected encounter. She exhaled the smoke in a long narrow stream. 'If I didn't know you better, Mr Royston, I might think you were squeezing me for information.'

He grinned amiably. 'Not squeezing, just asking. I like to get my facts right.'

'And what "facts" would those be?'

'A small town like this runs on rumour and gossip. And poor Sadie is the main topic at the moment. You'd be surprised at how much speculation there is.'

Mona took one last glance at the Big Wheel and then started to walk away. 'People shouldn't listen to gossip.'

Royston stuck by her side, determined to get something out of her before they parted company. 'Maybe not, but they do. It's human nature. We like to think the worst of each other.'

'So you're trying to dig the dirt on Sadie.'

Royston feigned a look of horror. 'Not at all. Why would I do that? No, you've got me all wrong. If anything, I think she's the victim in all this. And it's a shame, a crying shame.' He rubbed his hands together. 'The *truth*, that's what I'm after. That way we can stop all the wagging tongues.'

Mona gave him a quick sidelong glance. 'Or get them wagging even faster.'

'Ah, now, don't be cynical.'

'What do you expect? You're a journalist, aren't you? The only side you're on is your own.'

'Don't you want to help Sadie?'

'Sadie hasn't done anything wrong. Why should she need help?'

'It's not always that simple.'

'Not for you, maybe.'

Mona continued to manoeuvre her way through the crowd. The lights of the rides flashed brightly, and garish neon signs threw out invitations to shoot the ducks, throw some hoops or have their fortune told by the famous Madame Romany. The rumble of the roller coaster sounded like distant thunder.

Royston continued to stay close, trying to read her body language. She was confident at the moment, sure of herself. She might not like him but nor did she see him as any kind of threat. He would need to change that if he was going to shake any useful information out of her.

'Has Sadie told you not to speak to me?' he asked. 'Is that what's going on here?'

Mona stopped and raised her eyes briefly to the sky before lowering her gaze to stare at him. 'It's been nice to see you again, Mr Royston, but I think we're finished here.' She dropped her cigarette butt on the ground and killed it with the heel of her boot. 'Goodnight.'

Royston let her have the satisfaction of thinking he'd been dismissed. He gave a nod. 'Goodnight then, Anne. Enjoy the fair.'

She gave a small triumphant smile before walking away. 'I will.'

Royston kept his eyes fixed on the back of her head as he tagged along behind, taking care to keep out of sight. She glanced over her shoulder several times as if to reassure herself that he was really gone and then went over to a stall and bought a coffee. He waited a few minutes, giving her time to feel secure, before approaching her again. She was sipping from a paper cup when he called out from behind. 'Mona?'

The girl spun round, her face instantly twisting as she saw who it was and realised her mistake. She glowered at him from over the rim of the cup, her eyes cold and angry.

'Just one more thing,' he said, strolling up to her. 'I really couldn't leave without asking. Why exactly are you calling yourself Anne Faulkner?'

'Oh, my,' she said sarcastically. 'We have been doing our homework, haven't we?'

'It's a reasonable question.'

'It's none of your business.'

Royston smiled thinly at her. 'You think? Only it makes me curious, and when I'm curious my mind starts going off in all kinds of fascinating directions.'

'Fascinating?' she replied mockingly. 'I doubt that very much.'

'All right, then. Let's call it a loose end – one of many when it comes to Sadie Wise. Now you can't blame me for wondering why—'

'You're seeing mystery where there isn't any,' she interrupted sharply. 'It's quite straightforward really.'

Royston scratched at his chin while he scrutinised her. 'Is it?'

'Very,' she said. Mona gave a sigh and lifted her eyes to the heavens again. 'Haven't you ever got tired of who you are, wanted a change? It's just a bit of fun, a chance to escape and be someone different for a while.'

But Royston wasn't buying it. 'And Sadie's happy to go along with this charade?'

'Why not? It's not harming anyone.'

'A bit careless, though, signing into the hotel under your own name.'

Mona gave a snort of derision. 'It would only be careless if I was trying to hide something.'

'I just can't see the point of it, that's all.'

'Okay, I'll explain, but not here. Let's go somewhere quieter.'

As she started to walk again, Royston fell in beside her. She was playing for time, he thought, trying to come up with a more convincing explanation. 'So, you're Paul Farrell's daughter,' he said as they veered away from the rides and headed towards the far end of the fair.

Mona said nothing.

'I hear he might be expecting good news in the New Year.'

Again she said nothing.

'So you and Sadie: how long have you—'

Mona finally broke her silence. 'God, don't you ever get tired of interfering in other people's business?'

'Not really. It's only tiresome when other people lie to you.'

'And you think that's what I'm doing?'

'I have no idea,' he said. 'You haven't really told me anything yet, at least nothing substantial. How can I draw any conclusions before I've got the facts?'

'Somehow I can't imagine a few facts getting in the way of a good story.'

'Is it?'

'Is it what?'

'A good story,' he said.

While she walked Mona raised the plastic cup to her lips and blew across the surface of the coffee before taking a few fast sips. 'No,' she said. 'It's a very boring one.'

Gradually they were leaving the crowds behind and moving into the less populated part of the fairground. The noise levels began to drop, distant rattles merging with the tinkling of the music. They left the bright lights and moved into the gloom. Eventually they reached a perimeter wall where there was nothing more than a few shabby caravans, a scattering of metal and some long coiling cables that snaked back towards the centre of the fair.

'So,' she said, turning to look at him. 'What's on your mind exactly?'

'You were going to explain why you're using a false name.'

'Why not? If you were Paul Farrell's daughter, you'd hardly want to advertise the fact. I like to be my own person. It's easier that way.'

'You don't get on?'

'You could say that.'

'Does he know you're here?'

Mona scowled at him again. 'I'm twenty-three. It's none of his business where I am or what I do.'

Royston decided to go for it. Some opportunities only came around once in a lifetime and you had to grab them with both hands. 'Oh, come on. You might have fooled the rest of them but you don't fool me.'

Her eyes widened a little. 'I haven't got a clue what you're talking about.'

'Sure you do. You're up to your necks in it, you and Sadie. Why else are you in Haverlea?' Royston had no real idea where he was going with this; he was just following his instincts and hoping she'd believe he was more in the loop than he actually was. 'I know all about Eddie Wise.'

Mona visibly flinched, but then quickly shook her head. 'Eddie? What about him? You've lost me.'

'I don't think so.'

'And how do you figure that out?'

Royston had Emily Hunter's party in the back of his mind, where Mona had been talking about fairgrounds and films. There was something niggling, a possible connection he still couldn't grasp. 'It's obvious,' he said. 'Do I need to spell it out for you?'

'You don't know anything,' she said smugly.

'Anne Faulkner,' he retorted quickly. 'Now where have I heard that name before?'

Mona's expression showed that he'd hit home. The smile that had been playing on her lips immediately disappeared. 'You're just pathetic, a grubby little journalist with a sewer for brains.'

'Sometimes you need a sewer when you're dealing with shit.'

She came up close to him, her eyes blazing. 'You're disgusting. You know that?'

'I might be disgusting but at least I'm not—'

Royston never got the chance to finish his retort. Although aware of the sudden action, of the girl drawing back her arm, it was too late to dodge out of the way. As the hot coffee splashed all over his face he squealed out in pain.

'Bitch!' he yelped. 'Fuckin' bitch!'

With his eyes tightly closed he reeled back and stumbled, falling to his knees. He bent his head and covered his face with his hands, clawing at the burning flesh. He couldn't see, couldn't think, couldn't breathe. The crazy bitch had blinded him! Frantically, he tried to rub off the hot liquid. He needed cold water. Where was the water? He needed . . .

Royston was in too much agony to register the movement behind him. Beyond the sound of his own groans, his own agonising pain, nothing else existed. The blow, when it came, sent him sprawling across the concrete. With his nose pressed against the ground, he was faintly aware of the sweet smell of popcorn. A thumping raged inside his head and then there was only blackness.

47

It was a quarter to eight when Sadie arrived at the fair. She stopped by the turnstile, almost having second thoughts, but then a group of girls came up behind her and she had no choice but to push on through. Instantly she was aware of stepping into a different world. Gone was the calm, quiet order of the promenade, replaced by an almost physical assault on the senses, a swirling world of colour, sound and movement. Even the air smelled different.

She passed a candyfloss stall, the floss like sweet pink cotton wool, and walked on to the carousel with its distinctive barrel-organ music. The ride, probably viewed as too childish by the predominantly teenage crowd, was almost empty. There was something eerie about the painted horses going round on their own, their wide eyes staring into the dark. She gazed at them for a while, remembering the part in *Strangers on a Train* where Bruno rides on the carousel, watching his intended victim.

Sadie shuddered and turned away. She didn't want to think about it, but suddenly it was all she could think about. Bruno had gone on to commit murder, to put his hands around

Miriam's throat and squeeze the life out of her. Bruno had been mad, sick in the head, obsessed with death – or, to be more precise, the death of his father. Just like Mona, she thought. It wasn't hard to see why the girl identified so closely with the character.

As she walked on, Sadie breathed in the cool night air. Her heart was already starting to beat faster. How would Mona react when she told her straight that she wasn't going to do it? There would be no journey to Hampstead, no hiding in the garden, no shooting of her father. And anyway, there was no longer a gun to do the shooting with.

Her thoughts took a sideways shift as she wondered again if Nathan Stone had got rid of the Beretta. Her fingerprints must be all over it. But he'd wipe it clean first, wouldn't he? Just in case it was found. She was relying on him, but that might not be the smartest move. Still, there was nothing she could do about it now.

Sadie went past the Hall of Mirrors where groups of girls nervously giggled at their distorted reflections – fat, thin, tall, small – while probably adding to whatever neuroses they already had about their body shape. She could clearly recall hanging around the fair when she was younger, wanting to be cool but knowing that she wasn't. She'd always had the wrong clothes, the wrong face, the wrong attitude. She'd been awkward and defensive, uncomfortable in her own skin. The boys' eyes would roam over her, linger for a second and then quickly move on.

Sadie felt a rush of sympathy for that somewhat tragic adolescent version of herself. It was only when she'd gone to London that she'd found her confidence. Suddenly she was no longer a shy, cautious girl afraid of her own shadows; she had blossomed into someone who actually believed in herself. And then she'd met Eddie . . .

The thought dragged her back to the present. In her head, she went over what she was going to say to Mona. She had to be firm, determined. She had to hold her ground. And if Mona threatened to tell Joel or go to the police? Then she had to call her bluff – and act as though she meant it.

The Big Wheel loomed over the fair, a glittering circle of flashing lights. As she approached, Sadie looked around for Mona but couldn't spot her. She glanced down at her watch and saw that it was now five to eight. She was early but only just. While she waited she tried to prepare herself. The problem was that it all felt so hopeless. Nothing could change what had already happened; Eddie's murder couldn't be undone and it would haunt her for the rest of her life.

The minutes ticked by. Eight o'clock came and went and there was still no sign of Mona. Sadie began to pace impatiently; now she was here she wanted it over and done with. Where was she? What was she playing at? Maybe she'd changed her mind, but somehow that didn't seem likely. She wouldn't have come all the way to Haverlea to back out at the last moment.

While Sadie stood waiting, she gradually became aware of a disturbance. As if pulled by an invisible force, people were starting to drift towards the far end of the fair. A murmur was passing quickly through the crowd, a ripple of excitement. She stood on her toes, trying to see what was happening, but her view was blocked by the wall of spectators.

A group of uniformed police officers came striding down the central path and Sadie shrank back at the sight of them. For one terrifying second she thought they were coming for her, that Mona had confessed everything and set her up for an easy arrest. She heaved a sigh of relief as they passed straight by.

A couple of girls came sauntering over from the direction of the crowd and stopped by the Big Wheel to gaze up at the lights.

'Excuse me,' Sadie said. 'I don't suppose you know what's going on over there, do you?'

318

The older of the two – they looked like sisters – shifted a wad of chewing gum from one cheek to the other. 'It's some old bloke. Reckon he's collapsed or whatever.' There was a hint of disappointment in her voice as if she'd been hoping for something more dramatic. 'We couldn't see properly, mind. There were too many people in the way.'

'Oh, right,' Sadie said. 'Thanks. I was just wondering.'

The girls walked on and Sadie continued to look around. It occurred to her that Mona might have spotted the police on her way in. Had she turned tail and fled, afraid that she was walking into a trap? It was possible. She could have had the same knee-jerk reaction as herself, and if that was the case then there was no chance of her turning up.

Sadie glanced at her watch again, wondering how much longer she should wait. Five more minutes, she decided, and that was it. There was no point hanging around in the cold if Mona wasn't going to show. She gazed in the direction of the crowd again. Even though she knew the police hadn't come for her, their presence still made her feel jumpy. That was the problem with having a guilty conscience.

An ambulance crew hurried past, carrying a stretcher. For Sadie, the atmosphere of the fair had changed now, its former frivolity overlain by a darker note. She felt a thin shiver run through her. No, she wasn't going to wait any longer. Mona had said eight o'clock and it was now twenty past. She turned away from the wheel and headed for the exit.

As she walked, Sadie glanced over her shoulder a few times, half hoping, half dreading that she would spot the familiar black spiky hair. The courageous part of her wanted to get the confrontation over and done with, but the more cowardly part was relieved at the reprieve. She took one final look round before passing through the turnstile and on to the promenade.

An ambulance was parked up by the gates along with a

couple of panda cars. Sadie lowered her head and dodged round them. As she cut down towards the town, she wondered if Mona was staying at the Bold again. She slowed, debating whether to retrace her steps, return to the promenade and ask at the hotel, but decided against it. If Mona had been spooked she wouldn't hang around; she'd get out of Haverlea as fast as she could. Anyway, all Sadie wanted to do now was to get back to the relative safety of the flat.

It began to drizzle as she drew closer to home, thin spits of rain that settled on her head and shoulders. She picked up the pace as she turned the corner into Buckingham Road. It crossed her mind that Mona might be waiting for her at the house, but she instantly dismissed the idea. No, if the police had scared her off at the fairground then she'd hardly show her face here.

Still, Sadie kept her eyes peeled as she drew closer. She was so focused on number 67 that she took no notice at all of the white van that was parked a few yards from the gate. And that, as it turned out, was a big mistake. The side door of the vehicle slid quickly open as she drew adjacent to it and two women jumped out. They hurled themselves at her, grabbing her arms. Taken by surprise, Sadie only registered a flash of blonde hair, a hissing of breath, before she was bundled into the back of the van.

There was no time to shout or scream. It was over in seconds. Her first instinct was to struggle, to try and fight, but her efforts were useless. Quickly she was thrown to the floor and pinned down by a third assailant. He straddled her back, sitting heavily on the base of her spine. He grabbed her hair and yanked back her head. As he leaned forward she could feel his hot angry breath on the back of her neck.

'It's over, bitch! It's payback time.'

Sadie felt her blood run cold as she realised who it was.

48

Sadie was all alone in the back of the van. It was dark and cold and it stank of exhaust fumes and oil. Her feet were bound at the ankles, her hands tied behind her back. A wide piece of gaffer tape had been placed across her mouth. Her body ached from the bad suspension, the muscles in her legs going into spasm every time the vehicle hit a bump in the road. Afraid of being sick and choking, she had managed to manoeuvre herself into a sitting position but the motion of the van still made her feel nauseous. Although maybe it wasn't just the van. Wayne Gissing's threatening voice still echoed in her head:

'Enjoy the journey, babe. It could be your last.'

Sadie's stomach twisted with fear. Although she didn't know how long they'd been travelling – three, four hours? – she was pretty sure from the straight line they were going in that they must be on the motorway. This meant they were probably heading towards London. She closed her eyes, trying to blank out the horror. She couldn't decide what was worse, being stuck in the back of the van for another few hours or arriving at their destination.

They had stopped only once so far and that had been at a service station. She'd heard the sound of the cap coming off the petrol tank, the click as the nozzle was put back in place on the pump. There had been silence for a while – perhaps the Gissings had gone off to the toilets or to get a coffee – but then the side door had slid open and Wayne had looked in and grinned.

'Still breathing, then?' he'd said. 'That's a shame.'

She'd tried to peer around him, but could only see a brick wall. She could hear cars coming and going in the background, but the van must have been parked up in a corner away from prying eyes.

'Where's Nathan Stone when you need him?' Wayne had asked, clearly enjoying himself. 'Oh, hey, nowhere to be seen. Looks like you're on your own, babe.' And with that he'd given a snort and slammed shut the door again. A few seconds later the van had started up and they were back on the road.

Sadie continued to think about Nathan Stone. His attempt at 'sorting' the situation obviously hadn't gone too well. Still, she couldn't blame him for that. When push came to shove, the only person to blame for all this was herself. She'd made mistake after mistake until she'd become trapped in a web of lies and deceit . . . and now she was reaping the reward.

She shifted her arms and flexed her fingers, trying to loosen the rope that was wrapped around her wrists, but only succeeded in making the ties dig even deeper into her flesh. Her whole body was filled with pain and every time she moved the agony increased. Although struggling only made it worse, she couldn't stop herself from trying. It was better than doing nothing.

It was another hour or so before she became aware that they had come off the motorway and were now driving on ordinary roads. Her heart began to thump in her chest. A dull feeling of

322

dread seeped into her bones. What was going to happen next? Where they going to kill her when they arrived at their destination? Maybe they were taking her to a forest or a wood, somewhere lost and lonely where they could dig a shallow grave and . . .

Sadie took a few deep breaths, trying to prevent herself from toppling into panic. Why would they bring her all this way just to kill her? No, it didn't make any sense. They could have stopped anywhere and put a bullet through her brain. But what were they planning, then? She thought of Wayne Gissing's angry eyes and her blood ran cold. He was going to make her suffer.

By the time the van pulled in and the engine was turned off, Sadie had sunk into a deep pit of fear. She heard the front doors opening and closing, the sound of footsteps and then voices.

'Nip inside, Kel, and make sure the coast is clear.'

'There's no need. The lights are off. She's in bed.'

Wayne Gissing's voice took on a harder edge. 'What are you, fuckin' psychic? She could be sitting in the kitchen for all you know.'

'She'll be dead to the world. She was out with Colleen tonight.'

'Just do it, okay? Just fuckin' do it.'

Sadie heard a sigh and then more footsteps, the click of heels on a hard surface. There was a short silence before a voice she recognised as Sharon's chipped in.

'There's no need to bite her head off. Petra probably has crashed. She'll be dead to the world; you know what she's like when she's been on the gin.'

'It doesn't hurt to check.'

'And what about *her*? How are we going to get her inside?'

Sadie flinched, bracing herself for what was going to happen next. She didn't have long to wait. The door slid open and

323

Wayne clambered in, bringing with him a cool breeze and a thin orangey light from the streetlamps. He winced as he dragged his leg over the edge of the van, the discomfort no doubt reminding him of the bullet she'd put through his shin.

He crouched down and started untying the rope around her ankles. 'We'll keep this simple, right? You try anything, make a move, and you're dead. Get it?'

Sadie nodded, making a grunt of acknowledgement through her taped lips.

'And not a fuckin' sound. If I so much as hear you fuckin' breathe, you'll be sorry.'

Sadie gave another nod.

When the rope was off her ankles, Wayne looked over his shoulder and said to Sharon, 'Is it all clear? Is the door open?'

'Yeah, all clear,' she replied softly, poking her head inside the van. 'You ready?'

Wayne dragged Sadie over to edge of the van. Her feet had pins and needles and her legs, full of cramps, felt they might collapse at any moment. He put his head out and glanced up and down the street. 'Check the other houses,' he ordered Sharon.

'There's no one watching. Come on, quick.'

Wayne got out of the van, roughly yanking Sadie after him. With her hands still tied behind her back, her balance was off and she almost stumbled. Wayne grabbed hold of her arms, keeping her upright. Even as her feet touched the pavement, he was pushing her forward, propelling her through a gate and along a short driveway. It was all over in a matter of seconds. She had no time to look around, to take in any of her sur-roundings, before she was inside the house.

With Wayne on one side and Sharon on the other, she was frogmarched through a hall and living room to a kitchen at the back. The bright overhead light made her wince and she half closed her eyes against the glare. Almost immediately she was plunged into gloom again as her abductors pushed her through another door to the rear and down a flight of old stone steps to the cellar.

Kelly Gissing was waiting at the bottom, her face like thunder, her teeth bared. She glared at Sadie, her eyes flashing with anger. 'This is for Eddie,' she hissed. And before Sadie could even think about trying to move out of the way, the girl slapped her hard across the face. The blow sent a shot of pain through Sadie's cheek and sent her reeling back against Wayne.

'Take it easy, Kel,' he laughed. 'You don't want to kill the bitch.' He left a short pause before adding, 'Not right now, anyhow.'

Sadie, still in shock from the blow, barely had time to think before Wayne was shoving her forward again. She felt something hard and gritty under her feet. She had only a few fleeting impressions – blackened brick walls, the smell of damp, shelves full of old paint pots – before she was thrust through another door leading into a smaller windowless space. Here there was only a meagre light casting shadows into the corners of the room.

'Welcome to your new home,' Wayne said.

Sadie turned and stared at him.

He stared back, grinning from ear to ear. 'Enjoy your stay.' Suddenly he reached out and twisted a handful of her hair around his left hand. He pulled hard on the roots, pushed his face into hers and said, 'This might hurt a bit.'

Sadie let out a gasp of pain as he ripped the tape from her mouth. 'Jesus!'

'Best not to speak, babe,' he said. 'You might say something to annoy me.'

Kelly glared at Sadie and then looked at Wayne. 'You should

finish her off. You know what she did to Eddie. She's a murdering cow.'

'I didn't kill him,' Sadie protested. 'I swear I didn't.'

Wayne suddenly spun her round so she had her back to him and she heard the flick as the blade of his knife shot out. 'What did I say to you?' For a second, convinced that he was about to kill her, her heart stopped. She closed her eyes and prayed. *Please God. Please God.* And then, miraculously, she got a reprieve. Instead of slicing her throat, Wayne cut through the ties on her wrists. She heard the rope fall to the ground and felt the blood rush into her hands again.

'Over there,' he ordered, gesturing towards the single mattress on the floor. 'Sit down and shut the fuck up!'

Sadie quickly did as she was told.

'Come on,' Sharon said. 'Let's get out of here before your bloody mother wakes up.'

Wayne continued to glare down at Sadie, his look cold and sadistic as if he was weighing up the best possible method of inflicting pain. 'Don't get lonely,' he said mockingly. 'I'll be back.'

'Wayne!' Sharon urged.

Finally, he shifted his gaze and walked away. Sadie stayed very still as the three of them left. She watched the door close and heard a key turn in the lock. After that there was an odd scraping sound that she couldn't make any sense of. She rubbed her hands together trying to get the circulation back and let out her breath in a long slow sigh of relief. She wasn't exactly happy to find herself locked up, but at least she was still alive.

Left alone, she raised a tentative hand to touch the place on her cheek where Kelly had slapped her. It was sore and throbbing. She gazed around her prison. The cell was about fourteen foot square with a single bare bulb attached to the wall. The flex ran back through a badly drilled hole into the larger room beyond, which meant that she couldn't turn the light off. Not that she wanted to; she had no desire to be plunged into darkness.

Other than the bed, there was no furniture at all. The single mattress was thin and worn and smelled of mildew. It was covered by a green blanket and an old eiderdown patterned with roses. The walls had grey silvery cobwebs clinging to the brick. On the bare stone floor were three bottles of water, a roll of loo paper and a plastic bucket. There was no food.

Although there was little to see, Sadie continued to focus on the room. She was trying to push away a niggling question at the back of her mind. But try as she might she couldn't keep it at bay. Why hadn't they put a blindfold on her as they'd led her from the van and through the house? The only logical answer made her guts spasm with fear: they didn't have to worry about what she might have seen because she wasn't getting out of here alive.

49

Mona Farrell paced from one side of the room to the other, raking her fingers through her hair and swigging from a bottle of vodka. 'Damn, damn, damn,' she muttered. Why had that scumbag had to come along to ruin everything? Her face creased in disgust as she thought about Royston and his sly, accusing eyes. 'You're up to your necks in it, you and Sadie . . . I know all about Eddie Wise.' She was glad he was dead; he bloody well *deserved* to be dead.

But what now?

She was still trying to figure it out, but her thoughts wouldn't run in straight lines. What day was it? Sunday, of course it was Sunday. She recalled checking out of the Bold last night, going straight to the station and catching a train to Liverpool and then another one to London. The journey was blurred, a hurtling through darkness. Her head had been spinning; it was still spinning. Back in Hampstead, she'd felt safe, but the feeling hadn't lasted long. Worried that the police might be on her tail, she'd taken off first thing this morning, telling her mother that she was going to stay with friends for a few days.

What were the chances of anyone remembering her from the fairground? She had bought a hotdog and a coffee, but lots of people must have done the same. Just one more face in the crowd. But someone might have noticed her walking with Royston. And what would the cops find when they searched his home or his office desk? The bastard had been digging the dirt on her – there'd be notes, documents, maybe even his suspicions written down in black and white. And then there was the hotel register, proof that she'd been in Haverlea on Saturday. How long before they found out about that? Shit, everything was starting to fall apart.

After returning to Hampstead, Mona had tried calling Sadie over and over again but there had been no reply from the flat. She had wanted to warn her about Royston. If Sadie had come to meet her at the fair then she was in the frame too. Being local there was more chance of her having been recognized.

It hadn't been until this evening that she'd finally got through to Joel. 'Hi, it's Anne. How are you?'

'Anne,' he'd said, his voice sounding tight and anxious. 'Have you heard from Sadie at all?'

'What? No. That's why I'm calling. Are you all right? Has something happened?'

'I don't know where she is. She … she seems to have gone missing.'

'I don't understand.'

'You don't know where she might be?'

'What do you mean, missing?'

Joel had taken a deep breath as if he was trying to get his thoughts in order. 'I went away for a few days and then the police … I've just got back but she isn't here. There's no note or anything and she hasn't rung. They're looking for her, for Sadie.'

'The police? Why? What for?'

'I'm not sure exactly,' he'd said, suddenly coming over all coy.

'It's something ... I think it's to do with Eddie. But I have to find her. Do you have any idea where she might be?'

'No. Sorry. I haven't a clue.'

'Are you sure?'

'Yes, of course. I'd tell you if I did.'

'Okay, thanks, yes, I'm sorry. I'm just ... Look, I'd better go.'

'Let me know if you hear anything.'

Mona had stepped out of the phone box with a smile on her face. So Sadie had done a runner too. That was good news. It was a relief. She must have heard about Royston and guessed that she'd be a suspect. Or maybe she'd even been at the fair when his body had been discovered.

Mona stopped pacing for a moment and gazed out through the window on to Station Road. She had chosen this B&B because it was almost opposite Oaklands and she could see everyone who came and went. She had a feeling, a gut instinct, that this was where Sadie would come. To Kellston. Of course she would. Where else? Sadie wouldn't dare call Hampstead in case the police were monitoring the phone. No, she'd come here, hoping that Mona would too.

'She'll remember,' Mona murmured, pressing her face against the glass. Yes, Sadie would remember that Mona had followed her during all that silly business with Eddie, that she knew about Oaklands. It was the natural place for them to meet up again. It was only a matter of time. She'd be here soon, tomorrow or the day after. And then what?

Mona had money that she'd withdrawn from a savings account, over a hundred quid. She had some gold jewellery too, a watch, three pairs of cufflinks and a tie pin, all of which she'd nicked from her father's bedroom. Once they were sold, the cash would keep them going for a while. They could go over to France and ... She frowned. Would Sadie have brought her passport? Maybe she wouldn't have thought of it. Or maybe she hadn't even had time to go back to the flat. Well, it didn't matter. There was Ireland or Scotland, plenty of places they could hide until the fuss died down.

'Plenty of places,' she said out loud.

Mona gazed down at the Sunday traffic, getting sparser now as night drew in. She shifted her gaze to focus on the door of Oaklands. The inside of her head was starting to feel odd, muffled, like it was wrapped in cotton wool. But that didn't matter. She lifted the bottle to her lips and drank. Everything was going to be all right. Sadie needed her help and she was here to give it. She'd keep on waiting until she came.

50

Inspector Gerald Frayne sat back in the chair and studied the man in front of him. He felt sorry for Joel, who reminded him, in some ways, of his own son. They were of a similar age and had the same trusting eyes. Those eyes were filled with confusion at the moment – it was clear that he had no idea at all where Sadie Wise had gone or why she'd disappeared.

Gerald kept his voice calm and reassuring. 'Try not to worry. I'm sure we'll soon get to the bottom of this. When exactly was the last time you saw her?'

'Early in the morning,' Joel said. 'Yesterday. She'd decided not to come to the Lake District. I think . . . I don't know, I think maybe she was worried about all the people who'd be there, that they'd be gossiping about her and Eddie. She was upset about it all.'

'And she didn't mention going anywhere while you were away?'

Joel pushed the palms of his hands down his thighs. 'Only her mum's, but I've checked and she hasn't heard from her. I don't understand. This isn't like her, Inspector. She wouldn't just . . . And the bed wasn't slept in last night; we made it before

I left and it's still . . . No, I'm sure it hasn't been. Something bad must have happened. It must have.'

The 'something bad' Gerald suspected was the murder of Peter Royston but it wasn't a thought he was going to share with Joel. 'Let's not go jumping to any conclusions. She hasn't been gone that long. Is it possible that she's just gone to see a friend, someone in Haverlea perhaps, and stayed over for the night?'

'She's never done it before. And I can't think of anyone she's that close to round here. I mean, we've got friends but . . . Anyway, I've rung round and none of them have seen her.'

Gerald gave a nod. It had taken them a while to track Joel Hunter down. The house in Grasmere had no phone and so the local police had been enlisted to pass on the information that Sadie Wise appeared to be missing. Joel had driven straight back to Haverlea, arriving at about six fifteen. It was now almost seven o'clock. 'What about friends in other places? London perhaps. She used to live there, didn't she?'

'That was years ago. No, I can't think of . . . ' Joel paused, frowned a little and then said, 'Well, there's Anne. She called me earlier, just after I got back, but she was trying to get hold of Sadie too.'

'Anne?'

'Yes.'

'Do you know what her surname is?'

Joel shook his head. 'Sorry. Sadie might have mentioned it but . . . '

'An address then.'

Joel shook his head again. 'I didn't really know her that well. I've only met her once, a few weeks back when she turned up out of the blue. It was my mum's birthday and there was a party so we all went to it together. She didn't stay long though, only half an hour or so. Sadie said she wasn't feeling well.'

'Does Sadie have an address book?'

Joel, as if eager to be doing something useful, jumped up off the sofa. 'Yes, it's by the phone.' He crossed the room, retrieved a small pale blue book, walked back and gave it to Gerald. 'This is it.'

Gerald in turn passed the book to PC Turner. 'Have a flick through this, John, see if you can find an Anne in it.' He waited until Joel sat down again before asking his next question: 'Has Sadie ever mentioned the name Mona Farrell to you?'

'No, I don't—' Joel stopped abruptly as if something had just occurred to him. 'Hold on, yes, she might have mentioned a Mona. I'm not sure. When she got back from London. A friend she'd bumped into at Eddie's funeral? I think so. I couldn't swear to it, though.'

'Only we've not been able to track down Mona Farrell either. She told her mother she was going to stay with friends for a few days but we don't know where.'

'What, you think Sadie might be with this Mona? Is that what you're saying?'

Gerald didn't tell him that Mona Farrell had booked into the Bold hotel on Saturday. He thought about the papers they'd found at Peter Royston's flat, a few press cuttings about the death of Eddie Wise and some basic stuff on Sadie. There had, however, been a virtual dossier on Mona Farrell with information on her history, her family and her connection to Sadie. At the very end of this file, a question had been posed in Royston's small neat handwriting: *Mona = Anne?*

PC John Turner closed the address book and put it down on the table. 'No Anne in it,' he said. 'No Mona Farrell either.'

Gerald paused for a second before asking Joel, 'Do you think it's possible that Mona Farrell and the woman you know as Anne are one and the same person?'

Joel looked bemused. 'What? Why would they be? Look, what's going on here? I don't get it. I don't understand.'

'Do you know a journalist called Peter Royston?'

'Yes, of course. I mean, I don't know him well or anything. He's a reporter on the local paper.'

'Did you know he was looking into the murder of Eddie Wise?'

'No, but I can't say it surprises me. He likes scandal, likes writing about it. He's not a particularly pleasant man.'

'You haven't heard then?'

'Heard what?' Joel asked.

Gerald leaned forward a little, keeping his eyes fixed on the other man. 'Mr Royston was found murdered at the fairground on Saturday night.'

Joel flinched, his face paling. 'He's dead?'

'I'm afraid so.'

'I can't believe it. Do you know who … how? Why? Have you arrested anyone?' It took a few seconds for his brain to make the necessary connections and then the leap as to why the police were so eager to find Sadie. 'God, you can't think Sadie had anything to do with it. That's crazy! She wouldn't. She *couldn't.*'

'We're not making any accusations, Joel. We simply want to talk to her. Does she often go to the fair?'

'No, never.'

'Well, we're pretty sure she was there on Saturday night. We have a witness, a local woman, who claims she saw her standing by the Big Wheel at about eight o'clock. She looked as though she was waiting for someone.'

Joel gave a shake of his head and stood up again. He paced over to the window and stared out for a moment. 'I don't know why she'd go there. Maybe they're wrong … this witness. Are they sure?'

'Yes,' Gerald said. 'Does Sadie have a passport, Joel?'

Joel spun round, startled by the question. 'What?'

'A passport,' Gerald repeated gently. 'Please don't be alarmed. It's just procedure. One of those things we have to check when people go missing.'

'Yes, she keeps it in the bedroom.' Joel, as if he didn't know what to do with his hands, put them in his pockets and then took them out again. 'I'll go and get it, shall I?'

'If you would.'

Joel returned about thirty seconds later, brandishing the passport. 'Here,' he said, thrusting it into the inspector's lap as if its presence in the flat was proof positive of Sadie's innocence. 'I knew it would still be here.'

Gerald flicked it open, checked that it hadn't expired, gave a nod and passed it back. 'Thank you.'

'She didn't have anything to do with the murder,' Joel said insistently. 'Even if she was at the fair, that doesn't mean . . . Maybe she saw something and it scared her. Maybe she's in danger or . . . my God, what if the same person who killed Royston has done something to her too?'

'Why don't you sit down,' Gerald said. 'Please try not to worry too much. We've got no reason to suspect that she's been hurt in any way.' He waited until Joel was back on the sofa before continuing. 'How has Sadie been lately? I mean, in herself?'

Joel briefly lifted his hands before letting them drop back again. 'As you'd expect. All this business with Eddie has knocked her for six. And it's not easy being under suspicion, especially in a small town like this.'

'You didn't feel she had anything else on her mind?'

'Isn't that enough?'

'Yes, of course. It must have been very hard for her. For both of you. This type of thing can put a strain on relationships.' Gerald saw a flicker in the younger man's eyes and knew that he'd hit a nerve. Perhaps the relationship wasn't quite as rosy as

336

it appeared on the surface. He thought of the rumours about Sadie Wise and Nathan Stone. 'Any unusual phone calls, anything like that?'

'Unusual?'

'You know, people putting the phone down when you answer it. Not speaking.'

Joel shook his head. 'No.' And then he frowned. 'Well, maybe there was something.' He hesitated as if weighing up in his mind any possible disloyalty to Sadie. A few seconds passed before he said, 'The girl, Anne – Sadie was trying to avoid her.'

'In what way?'

'She didn't want to take her calls. I had to keep telling her – Anne, I mean – that Sadie wasn't in.'

'Did Sadie tell you why?'

'Only that Anne kept going on about Eddie. She didn't want to talk about him. It was too much for her. I don't think Anne was being deliberately unkind, just a bit insensitive.'

'How often did she call?'

'Quite a lot, almost every day.' Joel ran the palms of his hands along his thighs again. He stared down at the floor before slowly lifting his gaze to look at the inspector. 'Why do you think that Anne and Mona are the same person?'

'I can't really say at the moment.'

'But you think Sadie might be with her?'

'It's possible.'

Joel pondered on this for a while. 'But if that's the case, then why did Anne call me earlier? Why would she be looking for Sadie if they were together?'

Gerald suspected that the girl had called to squeeze some information out of Joel, to try and suss out what was happening this end. 'What did she say exactly?'

'Nothing much, only that she didn't know where she was.' Joel screwed up his face, trying to remember the details of the conversation. 'I told her the police were looking for Sadie and she asked me why. I said . . . I said I thought it was something to do with Eddie. I mean, I didn't know about Peter Royston then.'

'Did she mention Royston at all?'

'No.'

'And how did she sound?'

Joel gave a shrug. 'Normal, the same. A bit worried, I suppose. She said to let her know if I heard anything. Oh, and she was calling from a phone box – she doesn't usually. I heard the pips go when I picked up the phone.'

'Any noise in the background?'

'No, I don't . . . I'm not sure. I can't really remember. I don't think so.'

Gerald gave a nod and, having decided that he'd gleaned as much information as he could from Joel Hunter, rose to his feet. 'Well, thanks for all your help. As I've said, try not to worry too much. Obviously if you hear from Sadie, you'll let us know?'

Joel stood up too. 'What are you going to do?'

'Keep on looking. I'm sure she'll turn up.'

'She hasn't done anything wrong, Inspector. I'd swear to it. Sadie isn't . . . She's a kind person. She wouldn't hurt a fly. This is all . . . ' Joel's mouth twisted as he struggled to come up with the right words. 'You have to find her. She'd never just leave like this, she wouldn't, not without, not . . . She just wouldn't.'

Gerald, feeling sorry for the guy, reached out and gave him a paternal pat on the shoulder. 'We'll keep you informed. If you think of anything else, anything at all that might be useful, just give me a call.'

A few minutes later the two police officers were back in the car. 'Poor bastard,' Gerald said as he pulled across his seatbelt. 'He hasn't got a clue.'

Turner put the key in the ignition but didn't immediately turn it. 'Do you think Sadie could be with Nathan Stone?'

'It's possible. The Kellston lads have paid him a visit and he says not. But if she doesn't want to be found, he's hardly going to point them in the right direction.' As he sat back and gazed along the road, Gerald was starting to revise his theory about why Anne/Mona had called the flat. 'Maybe our two girls have got separated or had a falling out. Mona went home to pick up some things – we know that for a fact. What if she was supposed to meet up with Sadie later and Sadie didn't show?'

'So she rang to see if Sadie was here.' Turner bowed his head a little to gaze up at the top windows. 'The two of them killed Royston, did a runner to London, split up and . . . maybe Sadie *is* with Stone and doesn't want Mona to find her.'

In his head Gerald quickly reviewed all the paperwork they'd found at Royston's place. 'But why kill him? Royston didn't have any evidence to link either of them to the murder of Eddie Wise. Nothing solid, at least. He was certainly digging, but that's about the sum of it.'

'Well, you know what these reporters are like, devious sods the lot of them. Perhaps he gave the impression of knowing more than he did.'

Gerald gave a nod. 'You could be right.' The autopsy, which had been done this morning, hadn't told them much more than they'd already been able to gather at the scene, that Peter Royston had died from a blow to the back of his head at around eight o'clock and that his skull had been fractured. There'd been no need for any conjecture about the murder weapon: the piece of lead pipe had been found by his side, still covered in blood. Forensics had confirmed that there were no fingerprints.

The pathologist had provided one interesting fact, however: a cup of coffee had been thrown in Royston's face shortly before he'd died. Had that been an angry response from someone who'd just heard something they didn't like? It struck Gerald that this was more likely the action of a woman than a man, although he didn't voice this opinion out loud. These days you had to be careful about making what could be perceived as sexist comments.

Turner switched on the engine and pulled away from the kerb. 'The trouble is no one actually saw Royston and Mona Farrell together at the fair. Or the two girls come to that.'

'It's early days,' Gerald said. They were still trying to track down all the fairground workers – as well as the visitors who'd been there last night – but it wasn't an easy task. It could be days before they got statements from everyone.

'It couldn't have been planned, could it? I mean no one with any sense would actually choose to kill in a place like that. There's too much chance of being seen. They could have gone to his flat or lured him to a quiet spot.'

Gerald dug out a tissue from his pocket and blew his nose. He felt like he'd had this cold for ever. Why couldn't he get rid of the damn thing? It kept him awake at night, making him tired during the day. He fought to stifle a yawn. 'Planned or not, Royston's still dead.'

'He's that all right.'

Gerald scowled and pressed his lips together. Sadie Wise was out there somewhere – probably in London. Hadn't he had a hunch about her right from the start, a feeling in his guts? After all his years in the force he could spot a liar when he saw one. He balled up the tissue, his hands closing around it in a tight, determined fist. Well, she might have got away with murder once, but she sure as hell wasn't going to do it twice.

51

Sadie was already starting to lose track of time. How long had she been here for? Three, four days? When she looked at her watch she was no longer sure whether it was day or night. The bulb attached to the wall was always on, a constant dim glow casting shadows across the room. She lay on the mattress and gazed up at the ceiling.

There were extended periods when no one came at all, when she would begin to fear that they had left her there to rot, and then she would hear that strange scraping noise again, followed by the sound of the key in the lock. She didn't know which felt worse, the sick horror of abandonment or the sight of Kelly looming over her with all that hate in her eyes.

Sadie could feel a throbbing in her left eye, half closed from where the girl had punched her hard in the face. It was always the same routine, the same endless questions, the same lashing out.

'So who was it, you bitch? Who did you get to kill Eddie?'

'No one,' Sadie would plead. 'I didn't. I swear I didn't.'

'You're a fuckin' liar! Tell me! Tell me, you bitch!'

'I didn't do anything.'

Wayne Gissing would watch with that sly, sadistic smile of his while his sister laid into her. And there was nothing Sadie could do to protect herself. If she tried to fight back, it only made it worse. Anyway, it was two against one; she hadn't got a hope in hell. There was nothing she could say either; if she admitted that she knew who'd killed Eddie, Kelly would kill *her*, and by continuing to deny it . . . well, the outcome would probably be the same eventually.

Sadie lay very still, trying not to move. Whenever she changed position her body cried out in protest. She had bruises on her back, her chest, her arms and legs. Her face hurt too, a constant ache that wouldn't go away. She longed for sleep, for release, but at the moment it simply wouldn't come. Whenever she closed her eyes she would see Kelly looming over her again.

And then there was the hunger. Sadie was trying not to think about the empty pit in her stomach. Since being snatched off the street in Haverlea she'd only been given two sandwiches. The first had been in the afternoon after the night she'd arrived, and she had eaten it greedily, stuffing the bread and cheese into her mouth. It had been another thirty-six hours before she'd been provided with another. This time she had been more careful, tearing off small pieces in order to make it last and savouring every morsel. There was still water, but she was taking care to ration it. She drank only a limited amount every day in case it was not replaced.

Sadie could feel the four walls of the room closing in on her. Already she knew every inch of her prison, every brick, every cold slab on the floor, every cobweb. The door was firmly locked and didn't even have a handle on this side. She had examined the lock over and over again as if by constant scrutiny she might discover a means of getting it open. But no, there was no way out.

She wondered if Joel had realised she was missing. He would have tried to ring from the pub at Grasmere, but would not have been worried when she hadn't picked up. She had told him she might be visiting her mother and he wouldn't know that number off the top of his head. Would he be home yet? It was only then, when he flicked through her address book and made the call, that alarm bells would start going off.

Maybe the police were already looking for her. She held on to this hope, needing something to cling to. But in the back of her mind the little voices were chattering away: Why would they check out the Gissing house? Why would they look for her in London? Would they even take her absence seriously? People failed to return home every day. She would just be one more girl in a long list of missing people.

Sadie's gaze slid over the ceiling as she tried to fight off her despair. She made an effort not to breathe too deeply; there was a stench emanating from the bucket in the corner. Nobody ever emptied it. She must stink as well; she hadn't been able to have a wash or brush her teeth since she'd got here.

She had time, too much time, to dwell on all the mistakes that had led her to this God-forsaken hole in the ground, but feeling sorry for herself wasn't going to achieve anything. She had to figure out a plan, a way of getting out of here before she became too weak to act. But what? Wayne was always guarding the door, creating a barrier between her and the cellar beyond.

It was cold in the room, but that wasn't why she shivered. Just the thought of Wayne Gissing made the hairs on the back of her neck stand on end. The last time he'd come, he'd leaned over her before he left and whispered, 'I could do anything to you,

343

anything at all.' And of course it was true. He had all the power and she had none.

Sadie forced herself to sit up. She leaned forward and wrapped her arms around her knees. *Think.* The idea that she might die here filled her with horror. It was better to die fighting, she decided, than to just lie down and give up.

52

Wayne Gissing limped into the hall as Sharon was pulling on her leather jacket. He frowned at her. 'What are you doing?'

'Going to work.'

'You can't.'

Sharon started doing up the zip. 'Huh?'

'Kel's already gone out and I've got a bit of business. I told you.'

'So?'

'So we can't all be out at the same time.' He lowered his voice and glanced up the stairs, knowing that his mother was in the bathroom. 'Who's going to keep an eye on things?'

Sharon gave a careless shrug. 'Well, not me, that's for sure.'

Wayne took hold of her elbow, propelled her back into the living room and closed the door. 'Someone's got to stay here. What if she decides to go poking about in the cellar?'

'She won't.'

'Oh yeah, and you know that for a fact, do you?'

'I know she can't stand the place. And no offence, babe, but

345

I'm not spending the evening alone with her. She's got a bloody screw loose. You'll have to change your plans.'

'It's too late for that.'

'And I've got to go to work so that's that.'

Wayne, who had been looking forward to a few pints down at the Dog, raked his fingers through his hair in frustration. 'So give it a swerve. It's not as though you need the cash. Shit, we're going to be rolling in it in a couple of days.'

'A couple of days is a couple of days. I need money now, love. I can't live off air.'

Wayne tried again. 'Twenty grand,' he said. 'That's plenty to go round.'

'If he pays up.'

'Course he'll pay up. Wants the tart back in one piece, don't he?' The ransom note had already gone off, delivered in the dead of night to the Hope. Nathan Stone might not have all the money, but his boss certainly would. Terry Street was rolling in it. Twenty grand would be a drop in the ocean to him. And how could he refuse to help? Stone was a smart bastard, the brains behind most of the firm's investments. Terry relied on him and couldn't afford to have him pissed off.

'And what if he doesn't? Maybe he doesn't give a fuck about the girl.'

'Then we'll send her back a piece at a time until he changes his mind.'

Sharon glared at him. 'What? You're kidding, right? I didn't—'

'Yeah yeah, keep your knickers on. I'm only messing. Look, he's going to pay. Trust me, he will. So are you staying or not?'

'I've already told you. I can't afford it.'

Wayne didn't want to leave Sadie Wise unattended, but he didn't relish a night in with his mother either. She probably wouldn't venture down into the cellar, but was it worth the risk?

There was only thing for it. He took his wallet from his back pocket, slipped out a fiver and offered it to Sharon. 'Come on, help me out here.'

She screwed up her face, ignoring his outstretched hand. 'A fiver? That's not going to go far. Make it a score and I'll think about it.'

'Are you having a laugh?'

Sharon gave another shrug and made as if to leave. 'It's not worth me skipping work for less. See you later.'

'Okay, okay,' he said, reluctantly taking out a twenty. The woman was robbing him blind, but he didn't have a choice. It was worth paying just to escape from an evening of soap operas and game shows, not to mention his mother's endless nagging. There was only so much a bloke could take.

'Ta,' Sharon said, quickly snatching it from his fingers before he could change his mind. 'And believe me, you're getting a bargain.'

'You reckon?'

'You know it.'

Wayne smirked, put his wallet in his pocket and went back through to the hall. He took his heavy winter overcoat from the peg and left the house. As he limped towards the Dog, he thought about what he'd spend the ransom money on when he got it: a holiday first of all, a fortnight on the Costa, and then a new motor, something flash to pull the birds in. He could do with some new threads too.

It was a shame he was going to have to share the cash. With a three-way split it would be just under seven grand each. Not bad, but not a fortune either. Really, he should be getting more than a third. After all, he was the one who'd taken the bullet. He scowled as he thought about that moment in the graveyard when the mad cow had pulled the trigger. Jesus, he deserved to get at least half for the pain he'd been through – he'd earned it.

Wayne glanced casually over his shoulder, certain that one of Street's goons would be lurking in the shadows. They would have guessed by now – although they couldn't be a hundred per cent sure – that the Gissings were behind the abduction, and they'd be trying to find out where Sadie was being held. Would they even think of looking in the house? Well, if they did, they wouldn't find her. She was securely hidden and you couldn't hear a damn thing through the thick walls of the cellar.

He was still trying to figure out exactly how and where they were going to do the exchange. It was going to be tricky, a time when things could go badly wrong. After all, once Stone got the tart back there was nothing to stop him and Street from blowing their fuckin' heads off.

Wayne pushed open the door to the pub and stepped into the warm smoky interior. He went over to the counter and ordered a drink. By the time he was on his third pint, his mood was starting to get even darker. The more he thought about what Sadie had done to him, the more resentful he became. What was seven grand compared to a bullet in a leg, a leg that would probably never be the same again? Yeah, he'd like to chop the crazy bitch into pieces and post them back to the Hope. And maybe he would. Maybe he'd do just that.

53

It was rare that Petra Gissing ever got the house to herself but with both the kids out for the evening it was her intention to put her feet up, watch the telly and make the most of the peace and quiet. Which was why she wasn't best pleased to find Sharon comfortably settled on the sofa, already in her dressing gown and studying a copy of the *TV Times*.

'Not working tonight, then?'

Sharon gave her a disdainful look. 'What do you think?'

Petra scowled back at her. 'You always work on Wednesdays.'

'So this Wednesday I'm not. Got a problem with that?'

Petra did have a problem, a big one, but she bit her tongue. She knew the best occasions to pick a fight and this wasn't one of them. No, there was no point wasting her energy on idle bickering. If she was going to get shut of Sharon, she would need to use her nous, play it cool and outwit the evil cow. She wasn't, however, prepared to spend any more time in her company than she had to and so she grabbed her coat and headed down the road to Colleen's.

Inevitably the two of them ended up at the Bell. Petra had

only meant to stay for a couple, but by half eleven she was still there drinking her seventh gin and tonic behind closed doors. It was a long time since she'd been at a lock-in and she wasn't complaining. Well, not about the extra drinking time, but she had plenty of other things to get off her chest.

'There's something going on, Colleen. I'd bet my bleedin' life on it. All three of them whispering together in corners or shutting up the minute I walk into a room. There's something brewing, mark my words.'

'What about Kelly? Won't she tell you nothin'?'

'No,' Petra said resentfully. 'She's as bad as the other two. And Wayne's being as shifty as they come. Not that he isn't always — that boy's got sly bones, just like his dad — but he's ten times worse right now. He's got that look in his eye, you know what I mean? I don't like it, Col, stuff going on behind my back like this.'

'Can't say I blame you. I'd be the same myself.'

What really irked Petra was that Sharon was also in on the secret, that the three of them had formed a tight little unit from which she was excluded. It made her feel pushed out, ostracised, as if she wasn't really part of the family. She didn't deserve to be treated like this. 'And do you know what that evil slut Sharon said to me this morning?'

'What did she say, love?'

Petra put on a high-pitched voice, mimicking the younger woman. 'Oh, I suppose you'll be wanting to get home for Christmas. Don't worry about your Kelly, she'll be fine. I'll take good care of her.' Her eyes narrowed with anger. '*She'll* take good care of her, as if *she's* her bloody mother. It ain't right, it ain't right at all.'

'It's downright criminal,' Colleen said, backing up her friend. 'You've got no idea what they're up to then?'

'It'll be something to do with this Eddie business, bound to

350

be. Kelly doesn't talk about nothin' else. The poor guy's six foot under and the filth still ain't made an arrest. It's been weeks, Col. At this rate they'll never find out who done it.'

Colleen swigged on her gin and gave a rueful shake of her head. 'It ain't proper, not your own flesh and blood hiding stuff from you. You need to have a word, get it all out in the open.'

'And I'll tell you what else,' Petra continued, 'since the weekend I've not been alone in that house, not for five minutes. Most times they're all out somewhere, at work or down the pub, but not for the past few days. There's always been one of them there. It's like they're keeping an eye on me.' She frowned down at the slice of lemon floating in the gin before lifting her gaze to meet Colleen's again. 'Oh, I know that sounds daft, like I'm paranoid or something, but I'm telling you it's the God-honest truth. I can't get five minutes on my own, not for love nor money.'

Colleen raised her eyebrows, perhaps not entirely convinced that Petra was under any kind of surveillance, but too much under the influence to try and offer up a more rational explanation.

'Everyone needs a bit of quiet, don't they? It ain't too much to ask.'

'No, it ain't, not too much at all.'

'So how do I sort this out? Wayne's up to something. I can see it in his eyes. I said, didn't I? He's got that sneaky look about him. He was just the same when he was a kid. I could always tell when he was lying, and that was most of the time so I had plenty of practice.'

Colleen gave a snigger. 'And since when did you ever let a bloke get the better of you? You're getting soft in your old age.'

Petra frowned, wondering if this was true. She sipped at the gin and placed the glass back down on the table with a solid thump. 'Oh, I'll get to the bottom of it, you see if I don't.'

Colleen gave Petra's elbow a nudge. 'That's more like it. Come on, drink up and I'll get us another.'

It was almost midnight when the two women finally staggered out of the pub and headed for home. They said their goodbyes at the corner and went their separate ways. Although Petra could normally hold her drink, tonight she'd had more than usual. The gin washed through her veins, making her feel both maudlin and resentful. Where had all the good years gone? It didn't seem that long since she'd been young and carefree, looking forward instead of always looking back. What had she done to deserve this? She was lonely in Bournemouth and that was the truth of it; she missed her kids, Colleen, the familiar streets of London. Shoreditch was where she belonged and where she wanted to spend the rest of her life.

The chill night air cut through her bones, making her shiver. She pursed her mouth, partly in response to the cold, but mainly in protest at the way she was being treated by her family. 'It ain't right,' she muttered as she walked up the path to the house. She fumbled in her bag for her key, took it out, placed it in the lock, turned it and quietly opened and then closed the door. Unlike other members of the household she had some consideration for people who might be sleeping.

From the jackets hung up in the hallway, Petra could tell that both Wayne and Kelly were already home. She went through to the kitchen and put the kettle on. It was late but she didn't feel sleepy; there was too much rattling around in her head. She needed a brew and a chance to think.

Five minutes later, she was sitting down with her elbows on the table and a big mug of tea in front of her. She spooned in a couple of sugars and gave the tea a stir. It wasn't easy to concentrate – the gin was blurring the edges of her thoughts – but as she drank she tried to make sense of what had been happening recently: Eddie's murder, Kelly's grief, the funeral, the shooting of Wayne at the cemetery. She felt there must be clues somewhere and she glanced around the kitchen as if one might be lurking in the cupboards or in between the pots and pans.

Petra's gaze eventually drifted towards the cellar door. Her brow wrinkled as she recalled Wayne's recent forays into its depths. A screwdriver, that's what he'd claimed he'd been looking for, but he'd been down there more than once. Anyway, there were always tools lying around at the yard. No, he'd had another reason. She was sure of it.

If it hadn't been for the booze, Petra would never have set foot inside the cellar. As it was, she still hesitated as she opened the door, flicked on the light and peered down into the gloom. With the slanting ceiling she couldn't see further than the base of the steps. She didn't want to go down, feared going down, but knew she had to.

Tentatively she made the descent, her left hand trailing along the dusty wall. When she reached the bottom, she drew in a breath, her eyes widening in confusion. Everything was different to how it had once been. Although it was an age since she'd last been here, she hadn't forgotten what the place looked like.

The door leading off into the second smaller room was now completely obscured by a wide set of steel shelves covered in paint pots, boxes, tools and other random items. Bemused, she moved forward and stared at them. Why would anyone choose to put shelves here when there was plenty of other wall space? It didn't take a genius to work out the answer. Wayne was hiding something he didn't want anyone else to find.

Petra's first guess was a stash of drugs. Roy had dealt on and off through the years, coke and weed and shit like that, and now that he was banged up Wayne was probably trying to step into his shoes. But then she thought of all the whispering that had been going on lately, the exchange of glances, the secrets that were being kept from her. Maybe it was something else.

At first sight the unit looked too heavy for her to move, but as her gaze dropped to the floor she saw that it was actually on wheels. She wrapped both her hands around the edge and pulled. It shifted quite easily, sliding away from the wall with a thin scraping sound. She held her breath, wondering whether the noise had travelled upstairs. She listened for any movement but there was none. No, they'd all be fast asleep by now.

Once the unit was out of the way, the door was exposed. Petra reached for the handle and pressed it down. Damn, it was locked! Frustrated, she rattled the handle again. It was no good; she wasn't going to get in without a key. First, she checked all four shelves of the unit, poking in between the old tins of paint and the tools, and then moved on to other parts of the cellar. As she searched, the tips of her fingers became blackened with dust. Then, just as she was starting to give up, she suddenly realised where it would be.

Petra flew up the steps, passed through the kitchen and living room and walked quietly into the hallway. She went straight to Wayne's jacket hanging on the peg, slipped her fingers into the right-hand pocket and pulled out a large set of keys. Success! Taking care not to let them jangle, she retraced her steps and went back down to the cellar.

There were about twelve keys on the ring – some of them for the yard – and she tried the most likely-looking ones first, the ones that were old and tarnished. The first two failed, she couldn't even get them in the lock properly, but the third slid in easily. As she began to turn it, she thought she heard a noise, a faint mewling sound like an animal in pain. Startled, she stepped back. What was that? She waited a while before moving forward again and pressing her ear against the door. There was nothing but silence.

Petra wondered if the gin was playing tricks on her hearing. She was getting nervous now, her heart starting to thump in her chest. Maybe this wasn't such a good idea after all. Sometimes ignorance was bliss. But then, as she was thinking of making a hasty retreat, she remembered those words uttered by Colleen: *And since when did you ever let a bloke get the better of you?*

Before she could change her mind, Petra quickly turned the key and pushed open the door. Nothing could have prepared her for what she found inside. She gasped at the sight of the girl sitting with her arms wrapped around her knees, her face cut and swollen, her hair matted with blood. Jesus! Jesus Christ! It took a moment for her to realise that this was the girl in the newspaper, the girl she'd seen at the funeral – this was Eddie Wise's wife.

Their eyes met and Petra instinctively stepped back. No, she couldn't cope with this. It was too much. She had walked into a nightmare. She went to slam the door, to shut off the dreadful vision, but Sadie Wise quickly jumped to her feet.

'Please,' she begged. 'Please help me. Don't leave me here!'

54

Sometimes you only got one chance and Sadie knew that this was it. If the door closed again, it would be shutting on her only hope of escape. A few seconds ago, she'd been bracing herself against the next round of punches, but now suddenly there was a glimmer of hope. She could tell straight away that her presence in the cellar was a complete shock to Petra Gissing.

'Please,' Sadie begged again, trying to engage with the older woman. 'You have to help me. I can't take it any more. They're going to kill me. I don't want to die in this place.'

Petra continued to stare, her mouth gaping, her eyes filled with disbelief.

Sadie made no attempt to move towards the open door – she didn't want to spook the woman – but instead sat back down on the mattress. 'They think I killed Eddie, but I didn't. I didn't have anything to do with it.'

Petra glanced over her shoulder before returning her gaze to Sadie. She lifted her hands and rubbed at her face as if she still couldn't believe what she was actually seeing.

Sadie's mind was racing, the adrenalin rushing through her

body. What next? Should she jump up again, try and shove Petra out of the way and make a run for it? Quickly she weighed up the odds: she was younger but in her current state probably not stronger. And what if Wayne and Kelly were upstairs? She might not even make it to the front door. No, she had to play it smart. She had to try and talk her way out of here.

'They got it all wrong,' Sadie insisted, keeping her gaze firmly fixed on Petra. 'It was a mistake. It wasn't me. I'd never do that. Please let me go. I won't say anything, I promise. I just want to go home.'

Petra's gaze roamed around the cellar, taking it all in. She wrinkled her nose as if the bad smell had only just reached her.

Sensing that her pleading wasn't having much of an impact, Sadie changed tack. 'They'll go to jail if I die. You know they will – your son *and* your daughter. They'll be in prison for years. Is that what you want? And what about you? They won't believe you knew nothing about it.'

'Don't threaten me,' Petra hissed.

'I'm not. I wasn't. I'm sorry. I'm just saying it like it is. It's going to look bad, isn't it? And the police will be searching for me; I've been missing for days. They'll think of here eventually. Maybe they already have. They could be on their way. They could be here any minute.'

Petra chewed on her lower lip, thinking about it. 'They've got no reason. Why would they?'

'Sure they have,' Sadie said. 'What about Kelly's accusations? Everyone knows what she's been saying about me.'

But still Petra didn't seem convinced.

Sadie decided on more radical action. Leaning forward, she clutched at her stomach and groaned.

'What is it?' Petra asked. 'What's wrong?'

'It hurts,' Sadie said, rocking back and forth. 'I need help. Christ, I need a doctor. *Please*, you have to get me out of here.'

Alarm passed across Petra's face, fear that Sadie was going to croak in front of her. Her fingers tightened around the door handle. 'And then what? You'll go running straight to the law.'

'No, I won't. I swear I won't.' Sadie racked her brains, trying to come up with a convincing argument. 'I can't, can I? I was the one who shot Wayne. If that comes out, I'll go to prison too. I was carrying a gun, for God's sake.'

This was clearly news to Petra. 'It was you? You shot him?'

'I didn't mean to,' Sadie said quickly. 'It was an accident. He grabbed me in the cemetery. It . . . it just went off. I never meant to. I didn't even know the damn thing was loaded. But don't you see? It means I *can't* tell the police anything. I was carrying a gun, for God's sake. They'll lock me up too.'

Petra remained silent.

'Please,' Sadie begged. 'I'll say I was mugged. They can't prove I wasn't. I won't breathe a word about all this. I swear on my life. I mean, we're quits now, right? I understand why they did this. I hurt your son and he hurt me. That's it, finished. But I really need that doctor.'

Petra shuffled from one foot to the other. 'I don't know. I have to think about it.'

'There isn't time to think.' Sadie clutched at her stomach again, laying it on thick. 'Do you really want me to die here?'

Perhaps it was this thought that finally galvanised Petra into action. Having a corpse lying around in the cellar was hardly a prospect to be relished. 'All right, all right then.'

'You'll let me go?'

'But if you tell anyone—'

'I won't, I swear I won't.' Sadie slowly rose to her foot, terrified that the woman would change her mind. 'Thank you.'

Petra pulled a face, her thin lips turning down at the corners. 'I'm not doing this for you, love. Don't think that for one minute.'

Sadie opened her mouth but then promptly closed it again. Sometimes it was better to keep quiet. Instead she simply gave a nod.

'Stay there,' Petra said. 'I need to check upstairs.'

The next sixty seconds were the longest in Sadie's life. What if she didn't come back? What if Petra went to fetch Wayne and . . . She stared longingly at the open door, tempted again to try and make a run for it. It took every ounce of will power to stay put. If she blew it now, there wouldn't be any second chances.

Eventually she heard the soft tread on the stone again. Petra came to the door, put a warning finger to her lips and beckoned her out. Sadie's heart was pounding in her chest as she left her prison and began the long walk up the steps. Was it a trap? Maybe this was just another play in some sick game of revenge. Maybe she would get to the top and . . . she swallowed hard. No, she couldn't bear to think of it. One foot in front of the other, one step at a time. It hurt to walk, but it was the kind of pain she could endure if it meant she was heading for freedom.

She emerged, blinking, into the brightness of the kitchen. Quickly she looked around but the room was empty. Although she'd checked her watch while she was waiting – it had said a quarter to one – she hadn't been sure whether it was day or night. Now, from the dark squares of the window, she knew it was the latter.

Petra came up behind her, went straight to the back door and opened it. A rush of cold air flooded into the kitchen. Sadie realised, suddenly, that she had no idea where she was. In East London probably, but whereabouts? She had no coat and no money; both had been taken off her by Wayne Gissing. But none of these things mattered as she gazed hungrily at the outside world. She would have walked the streets naked if it meant getting out of here.

But as she took a step forward, Petra blocked her way. She looked Sadie up and down as if she was seeing the full extent of her injuries for the first time. And now she was obviously having second thoughts. To release Sadie in this state was too big a risk. She might collapse on the street and be picked up by the law. 'No,' she muttered, 'you can't go out like that.'

'I'll be fine,' Sadie said softly, afraid of wakening anyone else who might be in the house. 'I will.' She gazed over Petra's shoulder to the small yard beyond. One lunge, that was all it would take, and she could be free. She could push past her and ... but was the gate locked? It was too dark to tell. And it was far too tall for her to climb over. She felt her heart sinking. She couldn't let this happen, not when she was almost there. '*Please*, I'll be fine.'

'Where are you going to go?'

Sadie wondered where she could go. Only one place sprang to mind. 'Kellston,' she said, thinking of Velma. 'I've got a friend there. She'll take care of me.'

'Where in Kellston?'

'A guest house. It's called Oaklands. It's opposite the station.'

Petra pondered on this for a moment and then said, 'Wait here,' before moving past her and disappearing into the living room.

Sadie wasn't sure what was going on. She gazed longingly towards the gate. Here she was alone in the kitchen with the door open. Was it worth the gamble? There was nothing to stop her from ...

But the thought had barely entered her head before Petra was back. She had a set of car keys in her hand. 'We'll drive. It'll be quicker.' She gave Sadie a small push on the shoulder. 'Come on, then,' she said roughly. 'Don't just stand there.'

Sadie stepped out into the chill air, walked along the path to the gate and waited while Petra pulled across two bolts. The

360

woman did it slowly, trying not to make a noise. Every now and again she stopped, glancing back over her shoulder and up at the top windows of the house. Sadie, impatient and fearful, looked too but saw nothing but blackness.

It seemed an age before the gate was open and they passed through into a dark narrow alleyway. The only illumination, and it was meagre, came from a house that still had its lights on. Petra went first, weaving her way past dustbins, heaps of tin cans and other accumulated rubbish. Sadie stuck close to her heels, terrified of bumping into something and creating a racket.

After twenty yards, the path took a sharp right-angle turn and emerged on to the street. Petra hurried towards the red Ford Capri parked under a streetlamp. She unlocked the driver's side, got in and leaned across to open the passenger door.

It was only in the confined space of the car that Sadie became aware of the pungent smell of alcohol. It drifted off Petra in waves so strong they almost made her gag. Jesus, the woman was pissed! She had to be. But Sadie was past caring. She'd rather take her chances with a drunk driver than with Wayne bloody Gissing.

Petra put the key in the ignition, started the car and instantly stalled it. 'For fuck's sake!' she muttered as the Capri gave a lurch. She tried again and this time succeeded in getting away from the kerb.

Sadie said a silent prayer, hoping they weren't too far from Kellston. It would just be her luck to escape from a dungeon and end up wrapped around a lamppost. She gazed out of the window, trying to figure out exactly where they were. Nothing looked familiar. She saw a few street names but they didn't ring any bells.

Petra, hunched over the wheel, shot her a quick sidelong glance. She was, perhaps, starting to have some regrets about what she was doing. 'You open your mouth about all this and you're dead, you get it? No second chances.'

'I get it,' Sadie said. 'I've told you, haven't I? If I blab to the police, I'll be going down too.'

'Just remember that, huh?'

Sadie kept her eyes on the road ahead. Petra was steering erratically, frequently veering over to the right. Fortunately, there wasn't much traffic about. 'How far is it?' she asked.

'Not far.'

Sadie gave a nod. Her teeth were gritted, her hands clenched tightly in her lap, partly in response to the driving but mainly because freedom was so close and she was terrified that something might still go wrong. She wondered how Wayne and Kelly would react when they found she was gone. Not with equanimity, she imagined. Still, Petra was their mother; if anyone could deal with them, she could.

Five minutes later everything was starting to appear more familiar. There was a building she recognised, an old factory with two tall chimneys that she'd seen from the train. They must be getting close. She uncurled the fingers of her right hand and ran them through her matted hair. God, she must look a state. But that didn't matter right now. All she wanted was to get there, to be safe, to be free.

Petra took a left on to Station Road and slowed down, her eyes darting to the left and right as she searched for the guesthouse. 'Where is it, then?'

'On the other side,' Sadie said, gesturing towards the long line of Victorian houses. 'It's just opposite the station. You can drop me there or by the Fox.'

But Petra didn't seem too keen on this idea, worried perhaps that Sadie wasn't going where she said she was going. 'Before the Fox or after?'

'Just before.'

When they got to the pub, Petra swerved into the car park, did a careless three-point turn and, turning right, exited back on to Station Road. A few seconds later she pulled up outside Oaklands. 'Okay, we're here. Remember what I said? You call the filth and you'll be sorry. I'll make sure of it.'

'I won't.' Without another word, Sadie opened the car door, stepped out on to the pavement, closed the door behind her and walked quickly up the short drive to the guesthouse. The house was in darkness and she pressed hard on the bell, hoping that someone would answer. As she waited, she glanced back over her shoulder. Petra was still watching her.

'Come on, come on,' Sadie urged. *Please*'.

She was about to press the bell again when a light came on in the hall and a figure appeared through the frosted glass. There was the sound of a bolt being pulled across and then the door swung open.

Velma, who was still dressed, stared at her for a moment. And then her jaw dropped as she realised who she was – and what state she was in. 'Jesus Christ! What the—'

What happened next would remain forever engraved on Sadie's memory. Almost simultaneously she heard the sound of the Capri moving off and a shout coming from the direction of the Fox.

'Sadie! Sadie!'

She turned to see Mona Farrell hurtling across the street at exactly the same time as the car accelerated. There was a screech of brakes, a dull thump, a single piercing cry. She had a sense of time standing still before Mona was thrown into the air like a rag doll, her body twisting as she fell on to the bonnet of the Capri, bounced off and landed heavily on the pavement.

At first, paralysed by shock, Sadie couldn't move. It was Velma who ran to help, Velma who knelt down beside the girl. Sadie stood watching, her gaze flicking between Mona and the car. And then, without much more than a second's hesitation, Petra put her foot down and the red Capri shot off.

Sadie's legs felt leaden as she forced herself to walk. She couldn't understand it. What was Mona Farrell doing here? Where had she come from? Not that any of those questions really mattered any more. As she reached the end of the drive, Velma turned and shook her head.

'We need to call an ambulance,' Sadie said.

'It's too late, love. She's dead.'

Sadie dropped her gaze to the limp, lifeless body of Mona. The girl was lying on her back. Her eyes were glassy, partly open. A thin trickle of blood was running from the corner of her mouth.

55

Despite the late hour the street suddenly began to fill. People seemed to appear from nowhere until a small crowd had gathered. Like moths drawn to a flame, they fluttered round, their voices hushed, their eyes drinking in the tragedy. A soft murmur rippled through the air. An elderly woman brought a blanket and placed it over Mona's body.

Velma stood up, moved away and took hold of Sadie's arm. 'Come on,' she whispered. 'We have to go.'

Sadie gazed at her, bemused. 'We can't just leave her.'

'There's nothing more we can do, love. The ambulance will be here soon, and so will the law.'

'Which is why we have to stay,' Sadie protested. 'They'll want to know what happened. They'll want statements and—'

'You do know they're looking for you?'

'Yes . . . no . . . I don't know. I thought they might be. Joel must have told them I was missing.'

Velma gave her an odd look. 'You don't have a clue, do you?'

'What do you mean?'

Velma shook her head. 'Wait here a sec.' She walked briskly

365

up the drive, closed the door to Oaklands and came back to join her again. 'We have to get away from here.'

Sadie didn't understand what was going on. She was still reeling from the shock of the hit-and-run, still dazed, still in a state of partial disbelief. Her brain couldn't fully register the reality of Mona lying dead on the pavement. 'We can't. I mean, it doesn't feel right, leaving her like this.'

But already Velma had taken hold of her arm and was propelling her gently forward. 'Don't say anything. Just trust me, okay?'

Sadie, who was in no state to argue, allowed herself to be manoeuvred round the crowd. As they walked up the street, her confusion increased. Where were they going? Why were they leaving the scene of a crime? Petra Gissing had been drunk; she had killed Mona and just driven off. *Mona Farrell was dead.*

It wasn't until they were a good ten yards from the accident that Velma finally spoke again. Her voice was low and anxious. 'What happened to you, Sadie? Where have you been?'

'The Gissings happened. They grabbed me on my way home, shoved me in a van, brought me to London and ...' Sadie shrugged, knowing that the rest was self-evident. Suddenly her experiences in the cellar seemed far away and distant, overlain by the more immediate horror of Mona's death. 'Wayne's mother let me out. She drove me to Kellston and ... I don't understand what Mona was doing here. What was she doing here?'

'I've no idea, hon.'

'She was drunk, really drunk. Petra, I mean. I could smell it on her. She could barely drive in a straight line.' Sadie paused and then, recalling what had been said earlier, asked: 'What did you mean about me not having a clue?'

'The police, love, that's what I meant. They've been looking for you – they came to Oaklands – but not because your boyfriend reported you as missing.'

Sadie frowned. 'I don't—'

'Have you ever heard of a guy called Peter Royston?'

'He's a reporter in Haverlea.'

'Was,' Velma said. 'Not any more. I hate to tell you this but he was murdered on Saturday night.'

Sadie stopped dead in her tracks and stared at her. 'What?'

'Don't stop,' Velma said, glancing nervously over her shoulder. She tugged on Sadie's elbow again. 'Come on, we're almost there.'

Sadie, who had become used to doing what she was told over the past few days, obediently began walking again. 'Dead? How ... what ... I don't ...' But she could barely string her thoughts together, never mind a sentence.

'And you went AWOL at the same time and no one knew where you were so ...' Velma sighed into the cold night air, her breath emerging in a small steamy cloud. 'Well, you know what Old Bill's like, always putting two and two together and making five.'

Sadie shuddered as she started to realise the kind of trouble she was in. Royston was dead and she was in the frame. 'Where?' she asked.

'Huh?'

'Royston. Where was he ...'

'Oh, at a fairground,' Velma said. 'Someone caved his head in, apparently.'

Sadie swallowed hard. She'd been supposed to meet Mona Farrell at the fair, had waited for her by the Big Wheel. Someone must have seen her and told the police. 'And they think it was me?'

Velma veered left into Albert Road, pulling Sadie along with her. It was empty apart from two prostitutes standing hopefully on the corner at the far end. One of them was tugging on a cigarette, thin plumes of smoke rising from her mouth. Sadie found herself staring at the smoke as if it meant something, as though if she concentrated hard enough some answers could be found in a world that had gone mad.

'Here we go,' said Velma. She stopped by one of the old three-storey redbrick houses and pulled out a set of keys from her pocket. A few seconds later the door was open and they were inside. Velma reached for the light switch and the hallway lit up. She turned to gaze at Sadie. 'Jesus Christ, look at you! You need a doctor.'

'I'm all right.' Sadie's eyes met Velma's and she quickly looked away. 'Okay, I'm not all right but it's just cuts and bruises. They're the least of my problems from the sound of it.'

'You need to get cleaned up,' Velma said. 'There's a bathroom upstairs.'

Sadie looked around. Off the hallway, to the right, was what looked like a waiting room with two sofas and a coffee table heaped with glossy magazines. 'Where are we exactly?'

'Work. It's all right, you'll be safe here.' Velma started walking up the stairs. 'You can have a bath, or a shower if you'd rather. There's plenty of hot water. There's shampoo and soap on the shelf and clean towels in the cupboard.'

On the first-floor landing were four rooms, all with numbers painted on them. Velma went into Number 1 and emerged shortly after with a blue-and-white-striped dressing gown. 'Here,' she said, passing it to Sadie. 'Don't worry, it's clean. The bathroom is down the far end.'

Sadie followed quietly behind, not knowing what to say or do. She had switched to automatic pilot. Was Mona Farrell really dead? Royston too? And then there was Eddie . . . except that seemed like an age ago, more like years than weeks.

Velma opened the door to the bathroom and ushered her inside. 'Take as long as you like. Do you need anything else? Just leave your clothes here and I'll sort them out later.'

Sadie shook her head. 'Thank you.'

Velma gave her a rueful smile. 'I'll wait for you downstairs. Try not to worry, love. I know it all seems like . . . but we'll sort it out. We'll find a way.'

Sadie went into the bathroom, closed the door and leaned against it. A short while ago, when she'd stepped out of the Capri and walked up the drive to Oaklands, she'd been convinced that the worst was over. But she'd been wrong. The memory of Mona Farrell falling through the air came back to haunt her. She squeezed shut her eyes, trying to block out the image. No, it wasn't over. This nightmare would never be over.

56

Petra's hands gripped the wheel as she headed back towards Shoreditch. Her body was rigid, her teeth chattering. There was nothing she could have done. She told herself this over and over again. Even if she hadn't been drunk, she wouldn't have been able to stop in time. Not that the filth would see it that way, which was why she'd had to take off double quick. Why hadn't the silly cow looked where she was going? What was wrong with her? The road had been virtually empty, for Christ's sake, and she'd chosen to run straight into the Capri!

Through the shock and the alcohol, she was struggling to think straight. She had to come up with a plan before she became paralysed by panic. As she drove, using every remaining ounce of will power to keep within the speed limit, she attempted to reconstruct the scene in her head. Apart from Sadie and the woman who had answered the door at Oaklands, had there been anyone else around? Could someone have seen her face or taken down the registration of the car? It seemed unlikely. It was late and it was dark. But Jesus, that was the least of her worries! The big question was whether or not Sadie Wise would grass her up to the law.

Petra glanced in the rear-view mirror, dreading the appearance of a flashing blue light. In truth, it was years since she'd been behind the wheel. She didn't have a licence because she'd never passed her test. After her third fail she'd given it up as a bad job and left all the driving to Roy. She raised her eyes to the heavens, cursing her bad luck. She could be looking at a manslaughter charge. She wondered if the girl was dead. *Please God, don't let her be dead.* But there had been something about the way she'd twisted in the air, the way she'd fallen, that didn't bode well.

It was only when she got close to home that she realised she couldn't possibly leave the car where she'd found it. There might be blood on the bonnet and there would certainly be damage, dents, evidence of the accident. But where to dump it? It couldn't be too far away or she'd have a long walk back.

She circled round for a couple of minutes, the sweat running down the nape of her neck, until she found an empty spot. In her eagerness to get away, she was halfway out of the Capri before she thought about fingerprints.

'Damn it!' she muttered.

Quickly she drew back in, pulled off her cardigan and used it to wipe down the wheel and the inside door handles. Had she touched anything else? Had Sadie Wise? She didn't think Sadie had been wearing her seatbelt – she hadn't been wearing her own – but just in case she cleaned the metal parts of that too.

Petra got out of the car, put her cardigan back on and looked around at the surrounding houses. There were no lights on. With her right hand in her pocket, she used the corner of the cardigan to surreptitiously wipe the outside handle and the edge of the door before walking around to the passenger side. She made another rapid survey before repeating the procedure.

It was too dark to properly assess the damage to the car. She glanced over at the bonnet, but didn't look too closely. Whatever was there, she didn't really want to see it. It hadn't been her fault. She hadn't meant to do it.

Then, with the keys grasped tightly in her left hand, she hurried home with her shoulders hunched and her head bowed. It felt like an eternity before she finally made it back to her own front door. She let herself in, her breath coming in fast short pants. What now? She listened out for any sound from upstairs. There was only the noisy rumble of Wayne's snoring.

Petra went into the living room and put the car keys back on the table. Then, remembering that her prints would be all over these too, she snatched them up again and wiped them clean. When this was done, she walked through to the kitchen and pulled a bottle of whisky out of the cupboard. She poured herself a shot with shaking hands, downed it in one and immediately poured another. It was only then that she finally began to calm down.

The big question, however, still remained: would Sadie Wise keep her mouth shut? The girl's earlier argument, that she had more to gain by keeping quiet, had been persuasive. But the accident might have changed everything. What were the odds? Petra rubbed at her forehead, trying to get her thoughts in order.

There was, she eventually decided, nothing to be done about that particular problem other than to cross her fingers and hope. There was, however, plenty she could do about the evidence of Sadie's abduction. Jumping to her feet, she grabbed a bucket from under the sink, filled it with hot water and added several hefty squirts of bleach. If the law did turn up on the doorstep, they wouldn't find anything amiss downstairs. She was going to scrub that cellar top to bottom and she wasn't going to stop until every trace of Sadie Wise's presence had been removed.

57

Sadie didn't look in the mirror until after she had taken the shower. She spent a long time under the hot water, trying to slough off the dirt and the blood along with all the misery of the past few days. She soaped and scrubbed, wincing as her fingers came into contact with the damaged flesh. Her skin was mottled with bruises, old and new, plum-coloured, ochre and brown. After the cleansing was over she stood very still, tilted back her head, closed her eyes and just let the water run over her.

When she was finished, the room was full of steam. She dried herself off and put on the dressing gown. It was only then that she finally got the courage to wipe clear the mirror with the back of her hand. She was astonished, even disgusted, by her own reflection. It was like staring at a stranger. The whole left side of her face was swollen, her cheek raked with scratches, her left eye half closed.

'Sadie Wise,' she murmured. 'Look at the state of you.'

It was a minute, maybe two, before she got the energy to move again. There was a comb on the window ledge and she pulled it through her hair, getting rid of the tangles. Next she tackled the problem of the bad taste in her mouth. There was toothpaste in a mug and a couple of used toothbrushes. She was tempted to risk one of the toothbrushes, but somehow couldn't bear the thought of it. Instead she squeezed the toothpaste onto her finger and spread it around her teeth. She rinsed out her mouth and repeated the procedure until the only thing she could taste was mint.

When she was done, Sadie left the bathroom and walked down the stairs. 'Velma?' There was no response. She passed through the hall and headed for the room she had seen when she'd first entered the house. When she reached the open door, she gave a tiny jump. There was a man sitting on one of the sofas. He lifted his head and gave a thin smile. It was Nathan Stone.

'What are you doing here?'

'Velma called me,' he said.

'Why would she do that?'

'Because she's a friend. Because she knows you're up to your neck in it and you need some help.'

Sadie couldn't dispute either of these things, but she still didn't welcome his presence. 'I see,' she said tightly.

'Are you coming in or are you just going to stand there all night?'

Sadie hesitated – did she really need this on top of everything else? – but with little other choice she finally ventured into the room. She perched on the end of the unoccupied sofa and glanced at him. 'Where's Velma?'

'She's gone to Oaklands to pick up some clothes for you. She'll be back later.'

Sadie could see his gaze roaming over her, examining, probing, taking in the extent of the damage. Feeling self-conscious, she lifted a hand and pulled the top edges of her dressing gown together. 'Why don't you just come out and say it?'

'What?'

'That you've seen me looking better.'

'Wouldn't that be a touch insensitive?'

'Since when did that stop you?'

Stone's eyebrows shifted up, but he let the jibe pass. 'Velma thinks you should see a doctor. I can get one if you want, someone discreet. He can come here, look you over.'

Sadie quickly shook her head. 'I don't need a doctor.'

'He won't go blabbing to the law, if that's what you're worried about.'

'I don't need one,' she repeated, repelled by the thought of some stranger, doctor or not, examining her battered body.

'So you want to tell me what's been going on?'

Sadie gave a shrug, not sure where to start even if she wanted to. She looked around the room, studying the dark red walls and the chipped cream woodwork. A pair of heavy black drapes was drawn across the window. On the coffee table were neat piles of magazines – *Mayfair*, *Playboy*, *Penthouse* – and she stared at the covers for a while before shifting her gaze again. There was a potted palm in the corner, the tips of its slender green fronds turning brown. 'It's a long story.'

'When was the last time you ate?'

'I don't know. Yesterday? The day before?'

Stone rose to his feet, went over to a door at the back of the room and opened it. 'Okay, you talk while I make something to eat.'

Sadie hesitated but then stood up too and followed him through to a shabby-looking kitchen, smelling of stale cooking and dope. A layer of magnolia paint was peeling off the walls to reveal a pale bluey-green colour underneath. In the centre of the room was a table with four chairs. She pulled one out and sat down. 'I don't think I can,' she said.

'Eat or talk?'

'Both.' Sadie pushed an overflowing ashtray to one side, placed her elbows on the table and cupped her chin with her hands. 'Either.'

Stone took a loaf of bread from one of the cupboards and placed it on the counter. He opened the fridge and peered inside. 'Then you'll just have to force yourself.' He pulled out a tub of margarine and a carton of eggs and put them beside the bread. 'Poached or scrambled?'

Sadie didn't have the strength to argue. 'It doesn't matter. Scrambled.'

Stone took three eggs from the carton and broke them into a small glass bowl. He whisked them up with a fork and added salt and pepper. He dropped two slices of bread into the toaster and then lit the gas ring on top of the cooker. He placed the pan on the stove and put a knob of margarine in it.

Sadie watched him while he worked. His movements were brisk, efficient and oddly comforting. He was wearing a pair of dark blue trousers and a navy sweater. His grey hair, swept back from his forehead, was slightly mussed as if he'd rolled out of bed and forgotten to comb it.

'I'm listening,' he said, glancing over his shoulder. 'Just start at the beginning.'

58

Sadie's account was stumbling at first, full of pauses and reversals, until she finally got into her stride. Even as she was telling him about her first meeting with Mona Farrell, the words sounded odd and fantastical, more like a fairy story than a real-life event. By the time the scrambled egg was placed in front of her, she had reached the point where Mona had turned up at the flat in Haverlea. She stopped and stared down at the plate.

'Eat!' he ordered. 'Or at least try.'

Sadie picked up the knife and fork. She took one mouthful and then another. She had thought herself beyond hunger, but her body had other ideas. In three minutes flat she had the plate cleared of everything but a sprinkling of crumbs.

While she was eating, Stone had been pottering round the kitchen. Now he brought two mugs of tea to the table and sat down opposite to her. 'You take sugar?'

Sadie shook her head. 'No, thanks.'

'Can I ask you something?'

'If you like.'

'Why didn't you tell Joel about Mona Farrell?'

It was a question Sadie had asked herself a thousand times. 'I don't know. I'm not sure. I suppose it didn't seem that important at the time, not after I first got back from London, and then Eddie was killed and . . . When the police asked me if I could think of anyone, anything, I just thought it sounded crazy, like a tale I'd invented so they wouldn't suspect me.' She rubbed at her eyes, momentarily forgetting the bruises and flinched at the pain. 'It was only when Mona sent the book that I really began to wonder if she could have had something to do with it. And then it felt like it was too late to tell anyone, that it would look like I'd been deliberately hiding something.'

'Okay,' he said. 'Go on. Tell me the rest.'

While she continued with the story, he made only an occasional interruption to clarify this point or that before giving her a nod to carry on. She told him about the phone calls, about Emily Hunter's party, Peter Royston, the gun left in her bedside drawer and all the letters Mona had sent with the details of how her father was to be murdered. Glossing over the events of the funeral – 'You know all about that' – she finished with Mona's note pushed through the door asking for a meet at the fairground.

'I take it she didn't show up?'

'No.'

'But Peter Royston did.'

Sadie gave a low moan. 'The police think I killed him. I was there, wasn't I? I was at the goddamn fair. I went there and I waited and . . .' She could hear her own voice rising in pitch, the upper notes edged with hysteria. 'How am I ever going to prove I didn't?'

Before she could completely lose the plot, Nathan Stone

brought his palms down firmly on the table. 'Hey, calm down. You don't need to prove a thing. It's all circumstantial. They're the ones who have to prove it.'

Sadie took a few deep breaths before she spoke again. 'But it doesn't always work that way. You know it doesn't. Innocent people go to jail.' She gave him a penetrating look. 'You of all people should know that. If they stitched you up, they could do it to me too.'

Stone sat back and folded his arms across his chest. 'Ah, I see someone's been talking.'

'It wasn't Velma,' she said too quickly, a red blush rising to her cheeks. 'I just . . . just heard it somewhere.'

Stone lifted his shoulders in a shrug that was perhaps a little too careless. 'It doesn't matter. It's hardly a secret. Everyone knows round here.'

Sadie fell silent for a while. She sipped on her tea, watching him over the rim of the mug. Perhaps she shouldn't have said anything but it was too late now. 'Sorry,' she murmured.

'What for?'

'I don't suppose you like being reminded.'

'Like I said, it doesn't matter. You learn to live with it. What else can you do? There's no point crying into your beer for the rest of your life.'

'I guess not.'

'And in case you're wondering, the answer is no, I didn't. I may have loathed and despised my wife, but I didn't put a bullet in her head.'

In that moment, despite the scepticism she'd once had and for reasons she didn't entirely understand, Sadie found herself believing him. There was something in his eyes, a depth of hurt that made her feel he was telling the truth. However, she was hardly in a balanced state of mind so her instincts could be way off course.

'Let's get back to your story,' he said. 'The Gissings grabbed you in Haverlea, right?'

'Yes. When Mona didn't turn up, I went home and there they were, waiting in a van just near the house. They brought me back to London, locked me in the cellar and . . .' She made a vague fluttery gesture towards her face. 'Well, what can I say? They wanted payback for Eddie. Kelly reckoned I was responsible and so . . .'

'Jesus,' he said. 'We had no idea. I swear to God. We just thought they were holding you. If we'd known what they were doing, we'd never have—'

'Hang on,' she interrupted, astounded. 'What the hell are you saying? You knew they had me? You knew all along?'

'Sure. You don't think Wayne kidnapped you just for the fun of it, do you? He wanted twenty grand for your safe return.'

'What?'

'Yeah, he thought that with me being your fancy man and all, I'd be more than willing to pay up.'

And now a red raw anger was rising in her. She could feel the tightness in her chest, the banging of her heart, as she glared across the table at him. 'You knew? You bloody well knew and you didn't even bother telling the police? You just left me to rot in that vile stinking cellar. What's the fucking matter with you?'

Stone's eyebrows went up again, but his voice remained calm. 'And would that be the same Old Bill who have you firmly in the frame for Peter Royston's murder?'

Sadie, who was on the verge of delivering the next instalment of her tirade, opened her mouth and then smartly closed it again. She paused, thought about it, swallowed hard and then said, 'Well maybe I'd have rather faced the police than have the shit kicked out of me every day. Did you ever consider that? And if you knew where I was, why didn't *you* come and get me?'

Stone leaned forward again and put his elbows on the table. 'Look, we knew he had you, okay, but we didn't know where. We didn't think he'd be so bloody stupid as to keep you in his own damn cellar.'

Sadie gave a snort. 'This is Wayne brain-dead Gissing we're talking about.'

'Fair point,' he said.

'And who's this "we", for God's sake? Did Velma know about it too?'

'No, Velma didn't know anything. It was just me and Terry. The note, the ransom note, was delivered to the Hope. It was addressed to both of us.'

Sadie shook her head in confusion. 'I don't get it. Why should Terry give a toss about what happens to me?'

'He doesn't,' Stone replied blithely. 'But villains take care of their own – at least the smart ones do – and I don't have that kind of dosh. Wayne must have figured that Terry would give me the money.'

'And would he?'

Stone gave a low mirthless laugh. 'What do you think? But Terry's not a complete bastard. He was prepared to play along until we sussed out where you were.'

Sadie didn't even want to think about how long that might have taken. 'I could have been dead by then.'

'Wayne was never going to kill you. You weren't worth anything to him dead.'

Suddenly it all felt too much for Sadie. She'd been to hell and back and there was still no light at the end of the tunnel. Feeling a sudden urge to cry, she bit down on her lip and covered her face with her hands.

'Sadie?'

'I can't do this any more,' she mumbled. 'I can't.'

Stone was quiet for a while. The only sound in the room was the loud tick, tick, tick of the clock on the wall. 'The way I see it, you've got three choices: you can just sit around feeling sorry for yourself, you can go on the run or you can front it out with the law.'

Sadie moved her hands away and stared at him. 'You'd be feeling sorry for yourself if you'd just ruined your entire life.'

'It's not ruined,' he said. 'It's in a bit of a mess, that's all.'

'A bit of a mess?' She barked out a mirthless laugh. 'That's an understatement if ever I heard one. And how on earth can I go on the run? Go where? Do what? I've got family, a home, I've got—' She'd been about to say 'a boyfriend' but somehow Joel seemed very distant to her now, like someone she'd known a long time ago. 'I can't just disappear.'

'Which only leaves the third option.'

Sadie lifted her arms in frustration. 'I'm wanted for murder,' she said. 'They'll lock me up and throw away the key.'

'You're only a suspect because you disappeared straight after Royston was killed. That's going to look suspicious to even the most pea-brained plod. What we need to do is to come up with a story that explains your absence. Why you went away, what you've been doing, why you didn't come forward earlier.'

'Why are you doing this? I don't even understand why you're here.'

'Maybe I just like interfering in other people's business. And anyway, as you pointed out to me in the Fox, if I'd never invited you to the dogs, the Gissings wouldn't have been convinced that you'd hired someone to waste Eddie.'

'It was hardly an invitation. If I remember rightly you—'

'God, let's not go there again.'

Sadie bowed her head, swirling the dregs of tea around in her mug while she tried to sort things out in her mind. Could she trust him? The question was, she realised, completely irrelevant. She had reached the end of the road. She had run out of choices. Slowly, she lifted her head to look at him again. 'So, what are you thinking?'

59

Stone got up, paced silently around the kitchen for a few minutes and then sat down again and began to talk. 'For starters,' he said, 'I think you'd better skip this whole "strangers on a train" malarkey. It's not going to wash with the law. No, I reckon you need to stick with Mona's own story, that you two knew each other way back and that you just bumped into each other again. Maybe she . . . I don't know . . . maybe she developed some kind of weird obsession with you, started calling all the time, sending gifts, turning up unannounced.'

'And then?'

'And then she started dropping hints that she might know something about Eddie's death.'

'So why didn't I go to the police?'

'Because you didn't believe her. Why should you? The girl's a raging fantasist. And you were aware that she had big problems, psychological problems. You didn't want to make things worse by involving the law.'

'But that doesn't explain why I said nothing to Joel.'

'It's not Joel you have to convince.'

Sadie gave a sigh, knowing this wasn't entirely true.

'If the cops ask,' he continued, 'just say that you didn't think much about it, that you thought it would all blow over, that it was just in Mona's head.' He scratched at his chin, at the stubble that was casting a dark shadow across his jaw. 'You have to keep things simple, straightforward. It's the detail that trips you up.'

'So what about the fair? I was there. People must have seen me.'

'For sure, but that doesn't prove anything. Tell it like it was, that you got a note from Mona, went along to the fair, but she didn't show up so you just went home again. You weren't especially worried because she wasn't what you'd call the reliable sort. Anyway, next morning you decided you wanted to get away for a few days so you took a train to London and—'

'Hold on,' Sadie interrupted. 'If I wanted to get away, why wouldn't I have gone to the Lakes with Joel?'

Stone waved her objection aside. 'Maybe you didn't want to spend time with Joel. Maybe things haven't been too good between you lately. I don't know, maybe you just fancied some shopping in Oxford Street. But the point is that when you leave, you haven't heard anything about the death of Peter Royston. You come to Kellston and—'

Sadie stopped him again. 'So what about the Gissings? They kidnapped me, for God's sake. They locked me in a cellar. They beat me up.'

'Do you really want to go there with the law? You shot Wayne, remember. Even if it was in self-defence, they're still going to question why you were carrying a gun. It's against the law, in case you hadn't heard.'

'So they just get away with it?'

'He's got a hole in his leg. I wouldn't say he's got away with anything.' Stone rubbed his fingers over his chin again.

'Anyway, you ever heard that phrase: *What goes around comes around*? I'm sure the Gissings will get what they deserve.'

'And what does that mean exactly?'

'It means you've got more important things to worry about at the moment.'

Sadie knew that he was right. If she wanted to get off the hook, she'd have to do some clever wriggling. 'Okay, but if I came to Kellston on Sunday, where have I been staying for the past few days? And why do I look like I've gone ten rounds with Henry Cooper?'

'Yeah, I've been thinking about that. How does this sound? You turn up at Oaklands, bump into Velma and she offers you a place to stay – somewhere cheaper than the guesthouse, some-where more private. She works for Terry and he owns a lot of properties round here. She keeps a check on the flats that are empty and she offered to let you stay in one. That way she'd be making a few quid and you'd be saving money too.'

Sadie gave a nod. 'All right, but what about the bruises? How am I going to explain why I look like this?'

'You were mugged,' he said, echoing what she'd suggested earlier to Petra Gissing. 'A group of girls, five or six. It was dark, you were on your way back to the flat and they tried to grab your bag, but you held on to it. Something disturbed them and they ran off.'

'I don't have my bag – or my coat, come to that. The Gissings took them.'

'You will have,' he said. 'You'll have them by the morning.'

Sadie didn't ask him how. She didn't want to know. 'Why didn't I report it to the police?'

'Because you'd had enough of the cops, enough of all their questions about Eddie – and as you didn't think there was much chance of the girls getting caught, you decided to let it drop.'

Sadie's head was starting to spin. Panic rose into her chest, squeezing the breath out of her lungs. 'I can't remember all this, I can't! I'll make a mistake. I'll get something wrong.'

'You won't.'

'I will!'

Stone reached across the table, put his hand over hers and looked into her eyes. 'Do you trust me, Sadie?'

She stared back at him, feeling confused, afraid and defensive – and something else too, although she didn't want to admit it. Grateful, perhaps. Relieved. Glad that he was here. 'Why should I?'

He moved his hand away, sat back and grinned. 'Do you know what I like about you?'

'I shouldn't think it's a long list.'

'You're right,' he said.

She waited but he didn't elaborate. 'Well?'

But Stone just shook his head. He folded his arms across his chest, his face suddenly taking on a different, more matter-of-fact expression. 'Let's go back to the beginning. Let's start with when you first met Mona Farrell . . .'

They went over the story again and again, adding and taking away, moulding and shaping until Stone was finally satisfied with her version of events. By the time they'd finished it was after three and Sadie was exhausted.

'So what now?' she asked wearily.

'Now you go to bed and get some sleep.'

'Where's Velma? You said she was coming back.'

'She is, but not until the morning. I thought we needed time to sort things out.'

'And tomorrow?'

'She'll take you down to Cowan Road and you'll tell your tall tale to the police.'

'And you think they'll believe it?'

'Not all of it,' he said, 'but it should be enough to keep you out of jail.'

Sadie traced a finger across the surface of the table. She thought about it, looked up and gave a small nod. It might not be perfect, might not be ideal, but at least there was hope. At the moment she was prepared to settle for that.

Epilogue

It was five days now since Sadie had turned down the invitation to have Christmas dinner with the Hunters and had gone instead to her mother's house. There had been nothing very festive about the occasion. They had sat across the table from each other, picking at the turkey and making small talk while they tried to skirt around any subject that might cause an argument. As this was pretty much everything – politics, religion, the state of Sadie's relationship with Joel – there had been a generous amount of dull, heavy silences. When the day had finally come to an end, they had parted with obvious relief on both sides.

Sadie paused in her packing, her hand resting on the clothes piled into the suitcase. Sometimes, out of nowhere, she would feel that sick dread pressing against her chest again. It came in the dead of night, waking her from bad dreams, and in broad daylight too. A shudder of what might have been ran down her spine.

The memories of her time in the cellar, her escape, Mona's death and the long exchange with Nathan Stone were always with her. Some of it was blurred at the edges, other parts so sharp and focused she could feel them cutting like a blade through her mind. Her thoughts drifted back to the morning she had faced the police.

Sadie had woken, washed, put on the dressing gown and walked down the stairs to the room with the sofas and the magazines. Velma had been waiting for her. There was no sign of Stone, but her coat and bag were lying on the coffee table. Beside them was the holdall that she'd left behind in Oaklands after Eddie's funeral.

'How are you, hon?' Velma had asked. 'Did you get any sleep?'

'I think so, thanks.'

Velma had brought a set of clothes – a pair of jeans, a T-shirt and a pale yellow sweater – everything slightly too big but gloriously clean. There was brand new underwear too. After breakfast, she had got dressed and they had strolled the short distance to a ground-floor flat just round the corner in Meckle Street.

'Walk around, take a good look. This is where you've been staying for the past few days.'

And Sadie had wandered through the sparsely furnished rooms, trying to commit it all to memory: the magnolia walls, the tiny galley kitchen, the bathroom with its cracked bath and rust marks running from the taps. There were sheets and blankets, pillows and a gold-coloured eiderdown on the double bed.

They had left the holdall in the flat along with toiletries, more clothes and a Sunday newspaper dating from the day she'd allegedly arrived. Milk was placed in the fridge along with eggs, butter and a packet of ham. Teabags and bread were put in the cupboard.

'Do you think the police will check?' Sadie had asked.

'There's no way of knowing, hon.' Velma had placed the key in her hand. 'Best to be on the safe side, huh?'

There had been a tall Christmas tree in the foyer of Cowan Road Police Station, awash with tinsel, the fairy lights blinking. While she and Velma had waited, sitting on hard plastic chairs, Sadie had found her eyes drawn continuously towards it. It had seemed out of place, incongruous, in the otherwise cold and clinical surroundings.

Sadie's recollection of the actual interview was broken and disjointed. She had done her best to play the part: a girl who had only just discovered that the police were looking for her, a girl who'd been mugged, a girl who flinched and became wide-eyed at the shocking news of the deaths of Mona Farrell and Peter Royston.

There had been a lot of toing and froing, officers entering and leaving the room. She had the sense of phone calls being made behind the scenes, of information being confirmed, details being checked, before the next set of questions was thrown at her. Why had she come to London? Where had she been staying? What had her attackers looked like? Why did she think Mona Kellston had come to Kellston? She had held her nerve. She had kept it simple. She had stuck to her story.

Eventually, she'd been released, but this had only been a reprieve rather than an ending to the affair. Back in Haverlea, she'd had to go through it all again, this time under the cool, judgemental eyes of Inspector Gerald Frayne. He had not believed her; she had seen it in his gaze and in the tight, straight set of his mouth. Over and over he had tried to catch her out, phrasing the same questions in different ways.

'Why did Mona Farrell call herself Anne?'

'When we bumped into each other on the train, she told me that she didn't like the name, that everyone called her Anne now.'

'Really?' Frayne said. 'Only her family claim that no one ever referred to her that way.'

'It's what she told me.' Sadie had given a light shrug. 'I hadn't seen her for years so ...'

'You didn't think it was odd?'

'Not everyone likes the name they've been given.'

It had gradually become clear to Sadie that the inspector had nothing on her. Oh, plenty of suspicions, that was for sure, but nothing he could prove. There were witnesses to her being at the fairground, but no one had seen her with Mona Farrell or Peter Royston. In the end, unable to charge her with anything, Inspector Frayne had let her go.

Although Sadie had finally managed to walk free, she had not escaped unscathed. Sometimes there was damage that could never be undone. The twisted mind of Mona Farrell had left a legacy and nothing could ever be the same again.

She remembered the look in Joel's eyes, the horror and the pity when he'd seen her again for the first time. But over the next few days, as the initial shock subsided, his concern had been replaced by confusion and an endless barrage of questions: What had she been doing in London? Why hadn't she told him about Mona Farrell and 'Anne'? Why hadn't she called to let him know that she'd been attacked?

'I was only away for a few days. None of this makes any sense, Sadie.'

And he was right. It didn't. It was a tissue of lies, but she had no choice. She couldn't tell him the truth. To do that would have meant asking him to keep secrets, to scheme and deceive, to go against everything that made him who he was.

Joel had known that she was hiding something and the knowledge was a barrier between them, a wall that grew higher by the day. Her silence only made things worse. By refusing to talk, to explain, she fed his suspicions, creating a distrust that ate away at their relationship. As Christmas approached it had become clear to both of them that something had been broken – and could never be fixed.

Sadie finished her packing and took a final look round. Was there anything she'd missed? Her gaze skimmed the room, alighting on the framed photo on the dresser: her and Joel standing in the back garden with their arms round each other. She crossed the room and picked it up, a pain pulling at her heart as she ran her thumb across the glass, a final touch of his face before she left for ever.

Before the tears could start, Sadie put the picture down again. She fastened the suitcase, took it down the stairs and left it by the front door. Then she went back up to the flat, stood by the window and waited for the taxi to arrive.

Only a fraction of Gerald Frayne's attention was on the *Nine O'Clock News* – unemployment down, a new Honda factory to be built in Sunderland; most of it was focused on the file balanced on his lap. He glanced up at the TV, sighed and returned his attention to the thick sheaf of papers.

Nina looked over at him. 'You'll wear that file out. How many times have you been through it this week? I thought the case was closed.'

'There's something we've missed. I'm sure of it.' Frustrated, he flicked back a few pages. 'It doesn't add up. I mean why would Mona Farrell kill Eddie Wise? There's no rhyme or reason to it.'

'But you said they found her fingerprints in his flat. And wasn't there a receipt for a knife in her purse?'

'Oh, I'm not disputing that she actually killed the man, I just can't figure out why. I mean, Peter Royston I get – he was sniffing round, threatening to expose her – but Eddie? What did she have against *him*?'

'Did she need to have anything against him? I thought she had a history of psychiatric illness.'

'Yes, but nothing like this. And he wasn't just some random victim. According to Sadie Wise, she and Mona bumped into each other on the train, had a brief chat, a bit of a catch-up and then went their separate ways. That was on the Friday evening. By Sunday afternoon, Eddie Wise was lying dead on the kitchen floor with a knife through his chest.'

Nina took a sip of cocoa while she pondered on this. 'Maybe, in some kind of twisted way, Mona thought she was doing Sadie a favour. There were problems, weren't there, over the divorce? Hadn't Eddie been avoiding the issue for quite a while?'

'Years, apparently.'

'Well, there you go.'

'But how did Mona even know where he lived? London's a big place. And fine, Sadie might have told her that she was starting the search in Kellston, but at the time – or so she claims – she didn't even know where he was living herself.'

'You think she's lying about that?'

Gerald gave a snort. 'I think the truth and Sadie Wise parted company a long time ago. None of it adds up. According to Joel, Sadie was trying to avoid Mona Farrell, refusing to take her calls, and yet she still went to meet her at the fair. Then there was all that business at the funeral. And why did she suddenly take off for London as soon as her boyfriend's back was turned? No, it stinks; it's rotten to the core.'

'What's Ian McCloud's take on it all?'

Gerald's old colleague at Cowan Road had kept him in the loop as the London side of the investigation had progressed. 'His theory is that Mona had some kind of obsession with Sadie. There were press clippings found in a shoebox in her bedroom, pictures of the happy couple on their wedding day, except Eddie had been cut out of them all. And there were other items that had been taken from the Haverlea flat – not valuables, just personal stuff, an empty perfume bottle, a lipstick, strands of fair hair pulled out of a comb.'

Nina inclined her head, gazing at her husband. 'But if Mona was fixated on her, it's hardly Sadie's fault.'

'Unless she used that obsession to her advantage.'

'Which was what, exactly? Even if she did somehow manipulate Mona into murdering Eddie, then why turn up at his flat? Why go and talk to him about the divorce? She was putting herself in the frame when she didn't need to.'

'Maybe it was too late by then.' Gerald pressed on his temples with his fingertips, feeling the start of a dull, throbbing headache. 'She was already in London and people knew she was looking for him. By getting Eddie to sign the papers, it would look like she didn't have a motive. And maybe ... maybe the timing was off. Perhaps Mona made her move earlier than she was supposed to. Another few hours and Sadie Wise would have been completely in the clear.'

'But if she had his signature, she had her divorce – so why have him killed at all?'

'Bitterness, revenge? Your guess is as good as mine. The guy walked out on her, don't forget, and fleeced her in the process.'

'Years ago,' Nina said. 'Do you really think she'd risk everything she's got now, a home, a fiancé, a future, just to get her own back? It seems pretty extreme.'

Gerald's gaze floated back towards the TV for a moment. He stared at the screen, but all he was really seeing was Sadie Wise sitting in the interview room. Her face might have been battered and bruised, but her eyes were full of grim determination. 'So perhaps there was another motive, something we don't know about.'

'Like what?'

But Gerald was at a loss. All his instincts told him that

Sadie was lying, that he couldn't believe a word that came out of her mouth, but proving her guilt was a different matter entirely. It always got under his skin when he had a case with loose ends, and this one was virtually unravelling at the edges. There were too many unanswered questions, too much left up in the air.

The only part of the investigation that he'd had any real control over was the murder of Peter Royston and, other than the fact that she'd been at the right place at the right time, there was no solid evidence that Sadie had actually colluded in the killing. Witnesses had come forward to confirm that she'd been standing by the Big Wheel for over fifteen minutes, that she'd gone nowhere near the back of the fairground and that she'd left alone after the police and ambulance arrived.

Gerald looked at his wife again. 'And Mona Farrell being knocked over. You don't think that's a touch coincidental? The one person who could have filled in the gaps and suddenly she's dead.'

'You think it was deliberate?'

Gerald briefly dropped his gaze, staring down at the papers as if by a sheer effort of will he might be able to read between the lines. He looked up again and shrugged. 'Let's just say it was convenient for Sadie.'

'So they haven't found the driver yet, the person who did it?'

'It's still under investigation.'

Nina yawned, lifting her fingers to cover her mouth. 'So what now?' she asked. 'What are you going to do?'

Gerald shook his head. The more he thought about the case, the more his temples ached. 'What can I do?' It seemed to him that the end of the story was as shrouded in mystery as the beginning: Sadie's trip to London, the mugging, the hit-and-run. Nothing was clear. It was all smoke and mirrors. 'Unless some new evidence comes to light, the case is closed.'

'And can you live with that?'

Gerald gave her a wry smile. 'I'm going to have to, aren't I?' He allowed himself one last glance at the page, his eyes quickly scanning the list of items found in Mona's bedroom in Hampstead. It included a Liberty silk scarf and a paperback copy of a novel called *Strangers on a Train*. He shook his aching head. No, there was nothing to help there. He closed the file and placed it neatly on the table beside him.

Petra Gissing stood at the sink, gazing out at the back yard. Her arms were wrist-deep in the bowl, but she'd forgotten all about the washing up she was supposed to be doing. Sometimes, without any warning, it all came back to her – the girl appearing out of nowhere, the screech of brakes, the dull thud as Mona Farrell's body hit the car – and suddenly she was back on Station Road with the panic coursing through her veins again.

She swallowed hard, her jaw clenching. But it hadn't been her fault. Already she had dismissed the version where her eyes were on Sadie Wise instead of the road, where she didn't even bother to look before she put her foot on the accelerator. No, that wasn't how it had happened. The girl had run straight out in front of her. It had been a done deal. There hadn't been a chance of her stopping in time.

Anyway, there were rumours flying round that Mona Farrell had been sick in the head and that she was the one who'd killed Eddie. It wasn't public knowledge yet – her family were rich and influential and busy trying to sweep it all under the carpet – but if it was true, then surely Petra had done the world a favour. One less nutter on the streets had to be a good thing.

Wayne came in through the back door, interrupting her thoughts. He brought with him a gust of chill winter air and the attitude of a sulky schoolboy.

'Don't start,' she said.

He stamped his wet boots on the mat and glared at her. 'I didn't say nothin'.'

'You don't need to. Just get over it, huh? It's been weeks now and you've still got the bloody hump. You can't change what's done so just grow up and deal with it.'

'Yeah, right,' he said, pulling out a chair and sitting down at the table. 'Twenty fuckin' grand you cost me. Do you know what I could have done with that?'

Petra raised her eyes to the ceiling – she'd heard it all before – and let her breath hiss out through her teeth. 'Frittered it away on beer and fags, probably. Jesus, you should be thanking me, not having a go.'

'And how do you figure that out?'

'Because if it wasn't for me, you'd be six foot under by now. Do you really think Nathan Stone was going to pay up? Well, I've got news for you – he wasn't. What he was going to do is come round here and blow your bloody head off your neck!'

'Says you,' he grunted.

'Says anyone with half a brain.' Petra didn't have any regrets about releasing Sadie Wise. The girl, as she'd promised, hadn't gone to the law, not about the kidnap and not about the accident either. At about eight o'clock on the morning after she'd let her go, Petra – who hadn't been to bed yet – had received a phone call from Stone. His instructions had been curt and to the point.

'There's going to be a car arriving in ten minutes, a grey BMW. Give Sadie's coat and bag to the driver.'

Petra didn't have a problem with that. She knew where they were. While she'd been cleaning out the cellar, she'd found them stuffed into a crate in the bigger room. 'And then what?' she'd asked. 'What happens next? I don't want more trouble. I didn't even know about . . . She shot Wayne, don't forget. She could have killed him. Why don't we—'

But Stone had hung up before she'd had the chance to finish. The BMW had duly arrived and Petra had hurried out to hand the things over. She'd thought about asking the driver to pass on a message to Stone, but had second thoughts when she saw the evil look in his eyes.

The rest of the morning had been equally tense for her, trying to act normal when the kids got up while all the time stressing over what Stone might do next and wondering whether the law would come knocking on the door.

Petra took her hands out of the bowl and dried them on a tea towel. She gave her son an impatient, irritated glance. 'And don't ask me to say I'm sorry 'cause I'm not. I've got better things to do for the next ten years than stare at the four walls of a prison cell.'

'Yeah, yeah,' he said dismissively.

'And don't "yeah, yeah" me. That girl could have bleedin' well died in that cellar. Then what? You'd have had a bloody corpse to deal with. Don't you ever think about anyone but yourself? We'd have all gone down for it, the whole damn lot of us!'

Wayne curled his lip, the loss of the money still rankling with him. 'She wasn't going to croak, for Christ's sake. A few more days and he'd have paid up. That's twenty grand you flushed down the toilet.'

'I saved your bloody skin is what I did. Try showing some gratitude for a change.'

'Thanks for nothing,' he said sarcastically.

Petra made a tutting noise and got on with making the lunch. While she peeled the spuds a small triumphant smile tugged at the corners of her lips. It was good to know that she was still in charge, still in control. She'd played a smart game and got away with it. Not one of them, not Wayne, Kelly or Sharon, had managed to suss out what had really happened that night.

Petra's thoughts slid back to the morning after. She recalled Sharon going out – it must have been almost midday by then – before stomping back into the house, waving her arms about. 'It's gone! It's bloody gone! Some thieving toerag has nicked my car!'

'Are you sure?' Wayne had asked.

'Of course I'm bloody sure.'

'Maybe you didn't park it where you thought you did.'

Sharon had put her hands on her hips, her eyes flashing. 'I know where I parked it. I'm not a bleedin' idiot. I'm calling Old Bill.'

'You can't,' Wayne had said sharply.

The two of them had exchanged a look. At this time, of course, they hadn't even realised that Sadie Wise wasn't in the cellar any more.

'Why can't she?' Petra had asked. 'She'll have to report it or the insurance won't pay out.'

'All I'm saying is there's no point in being hasty.' Wayne had got up off the sofa, gone into the hall and put on his coat. 'Let's have a scout round first, see if we can spot it.'

It had been a while, well over an hour, before they'd come home again. Petra had later learned that they'd found the Capri in a matter of minutes, panicked at the state of it and decided to get rid. The car had obviously been in an accident and there were smears of blood on the bonnet and front bumper. Knowing that the filth would have them all down as suspects – apart from Petra who didn't drive – they had taken the car to the yard and reduced it to scrap metal. A decision had been made to wait a few days, until after they'd got shot of Sadie, before reporting it as stolen.

Petra put the potatoes in a pan, added cold water and placed the pan on the hob. Her son had done her a favour, although he didn't know it. With the car destroyed, the evidence of the hit-

and-run had gone too. With no eye witnesses to the accident –
at least none that were prepared to come forward – she was off
the hook.

Wayne sat back and glared at his mother as she moved
around the kitchen. 'I still don't get it,' he said.

'What don't you get?'

'It's a bit of a coincidence, ain't it, the Capri getting nicked
like that on the night you let Sadie Wise go.'

Petra assumed an innocent expression – she'd had plenty of
practice over the past few weeks – and met his gaze head on.
'Well, it wasn't the girl, if that's what you're thinking. The keys
were still here, weren't they, and the car wasn't broken into.
Anyhow, I took her to the high street and put her in a cab.' She
left a short pause and then added slyly, 'Perhaps you should be
looking closer to home.'

Wayne frowned, not getting her gist. 'Huh?'

'Well, where was Sharon on the night in question?'

'She was here, for God's sake, she didn't even go out. You
know that.'

Petra gave a snort. 'I don't know nothin' and nor do you. She
says she was here. She *says* the car was nicked. How do we know
she's being straight? I reckon she knows more than she's letting
on.'

Wayne opened his mouth as if about to protest, but then
slowly shut it again. Petra could see the cogs turning in his
brain, an effort that gave his face a strained, constipated look.
No one liked being taken for a mug, least of all her son.

'Still, it don't matter now,' Petra said. 'All done and
dusted, ain't it?' She turned her attention back to the potatoes,
stirring the pot as the water bubbled. Divide and rule, that
was the trick. If she could drive a wedge between Sharon and
the rest of the family, she was halfway to getting what she
wanted. It might take time but she had plenty of that. Already

she was making plans for how she'd redecorate the master bedroom.

Sadie Wise placed her suitcase on the bed and glanced around a room that was already familiar. Her heart sank a little, knowing that this would be her home for the foreseeable future. How had it come to this? But in her heart she knew exactly how and there was no point in going over it all again. When she'd turned up at the front door, Mrs Cuthbert's face had fallen. No one liked trouble and Sadie seemed to carry it around with her.

'Oh, it's you. I'm sorry but if you're looking for somewhere to stay—'

'I am,' Sadie had interrupted quickly, 'but not just for the night. I'm after something more long-term, a few months maybe.'

'A few months?'

'At the very least. I'm moving back to London, you see, so I need . . . The room I had before would be fine if it's still available.'

Mrs Cuthbert had hesitated, torn between an inclination to refuse – at her age she didn't need any unnecessary bother – and the prospect of a regular income from a small shabby room that was always hard to let. Eventually the latter had won out and she'd stood aside, albeit with a show of reluctance, to allow Sadie across the threshold. 'I don't want any trouble, mind.'

'There won't be any, I promise.'

Sadie opened the suitcase and started to empty it. She wasn't entirely sure why she'd come back here. It was, she suspected, because she lacked the energy to go anywhere new. With so much changing in her life, she craved some kind of familiarity, even if was only in the form of a small single room with peeling wallpaper and a pervasive smell of damp. Anyway, it wouldn't be for ever. Once she was back on her feet, she'd be able to get a place of her own.

Having left most of her stuff at her mother's house, the process of unpacking didn't take long. Once it was done, she shoved the case on top of the wardrobe and wondered what to do next. It was almost six o'clock – too late for job hunting – but she felt that kind of restlessness that comes with the hope of making a fresh start.

She went over to the window and stared down at the street. Inevitably, she was jolted back to that traumatic night when she'd finally managed to talk her way out of the cellar only to witness the gruesome sight of Mona Farrell being mown down in front of her. She wrapped her arms around her chest, shuddering at the memory.

Sadie closed her eyes and waited a moment before opening them again. She had to find a way to deal with it, to move on, or she wouldn't have any kind of future at all. The first step, she decided, was to tie up the loose ends. Quickly she turned away from the window and pulled on her coat.

Outside the rain was coming down heavily, hammering on the pavement and running in fast streams along the gutters. She put up her umbrella, began to walk and then made a zigzag dash across the road when the cars slowed for the red traffic lights. As she went past the Fox, the door opened and she heard the clink of glasses, a snatch of laughter, before the door swung shut again.

Sadie hesitated, wondering if Velma was in there – she wasn't in her room – but knew that now wasn't the right time for a detour. Although she wasn't looking forward to seeing Nathan Stone again, it was something that couldn't be avoided. Living in Kellston, she was bound to run into him at some point and she preferred to get it over and done with.

However, as she rounded the corner and saw the blue neon

sign for Ramones, her resolution began to fade. Did she really have to do this now? Maybe it could wait until tomorrow or the day after. There wasn't a rush. It wasn't as if he was going anywhere. But she was aware that if she put it off, she'd probably never do it, and it was better, surely, to have the meeting on her terms rather than his.

Sadie slowed as she drew closer to the bar. It wasn't a comfortable feeling being beholden to someone you didn't like. But sometimes, she thought, you just had to swallow your pride and get on with it. If it hadn't been for Nathan Stone, she wouldn't be here now, a free woman, if not a particularly happy one.

Before she could change her mind, Sadie pushed open the door and stepped inside. It was quiet apart from the soft strains of jazz playing in the background. There was only a handful of customers, early drinkers who'd come straight from work and were busy demolishing their first bottle of wine. The barman gave her a glance, but went back to polishing his glasses as she walked past and went to the rear of the bar.

A part of her had been hoping that Stone wouldn't be around, but there he was, sitting at the same table, his grey head bent over what could have been the same set of books. She had one of those déjà vu moments, recalling how she'd hesitated the last time she'd come and wondering what would have happened if she'd just turned around that day and walked straight out. There would have been no need for the lies she'd gone on to tell Joel, no need to try and hide the truth.

Sensing her presence, Stone looked up. His cool grey eyes narrowed at the sight of her, his brows shifting up. If he was pleased to see her, he was doing a good job of hiding it. 'Well, if it isn't Sadie Wise.'

'Hello,' she said.

There was one of those awkward silences before he waved a

hand towards the chair on the opposite side of the table. 'Are you going to sit down?'

Sadie glanced at the chair, but then shook her head. 'I'm not staying. I just . . . I just came to say thanks, you know, for helping me out and everything.'

'Right,' he said.

Sadie pulled a face, unsure what to say next. She shifted from one foot to the other. 'So thanks,' she finally managed to utter again. 'I appreciate it.'

Stone sat back, folded his hands on the table and gazed at her. 'And that's it? Not even a drink for all my troubles?'

She looked back at him, trying to read his face but getting nowhere. Was he serious or just teasing? 'I'm sorry,' she said dryly. 'My manners are atrocious. Would you care for a drink?'

'I would. Trouble is, I don't like drinking on my own. It's a bad habit, don't you think, and I've got enough of those already. Why don't you stay and have one with me?'

'I can't. I've got things to do.'

'What sort of things?'

Sadie thought of Oaklands and the long empty evening stretching out ahead. It wasn't an appealing prospect. She may as well spend ten uncomfortable minutes with Nathan Stone as spend them staring at the four boring walls of her room. 'I suppose they could wait.'

Stone smiled for the first time since she'd arrived. 'In that case, thank you, I'll have a Scotch.'

Sadie went over to the bar, ordered the drinks – a Scotch for him, a small red wine for herself – and took them back to the table. She pulled out a chair and sat down.

'Cheers,' he said, raising his glass. 'Here's to . . . what would you suggest?'

Sadie gave a shrug. There was, she thought, something artificially casual about him, as if she'd caught him off guard and he was trying hard to hide it. Perhaps it wasn't just her that was feeling ill at ease. 'Moving on?' she suggested.

Stone chinked his glass lightly against hers. 'Moving on,' he echoed. He took a sip of the whisky and put the glass back down on the table. 'I take it things went all right with the boys in blue?'

'A picnic.'

'Somehow I doubt that, but you're still a free woman so you must have been reasonably convincing.'

'Convincing might be too strong a word. But yes, as you see, they haven't locked me up.'

'That's always a good sign. So what brings you back to Kellston?' He inclined his head and grinned. 'Other than the more obvious attractions.'

Sadie wrinkled her nose. 'Oh, please. Anyway, I think the clue was in the toast.'

'I take it things didn't work out in the cold wasteland of the north, then?'

Something like that.' Sadie took a few quick sips of wine, wondering what it was about him that always made her feel defensive. He got under her skin, but she couldn't explain exactly why. The only time she'd felt any real connection was the night Mona Farrell had died, although then she'd been so exhausted she could barely think straight. 'But it's not a problem. I'll be fine.'

'So what's the plan?'

'Plan?'

'What are you going to do next?'

Sadie lifted and dropped her shoulders again. 'Start again. Get a job, get a life. You know, the usual.'

'So you'll have some time on your hands.'

Sadie wasn't sure what he was getting at. 'Will I?'

'Until you get a job, I mean.' He picked up his glass and

swirled the Scotch around. 'I'm taking Barry and his missus out for lunch on Thursday. Why don't you come along? For some obscure reason, Cheryl seems to like you.'

Sadie gave him an incredulous look. 'You're kidding, right?'

'Yeah, there's no accounting for taste.'

'Very funny. You know what I meant.'

Nathan grinned at her again. 'Have a think about it.'

'I don't need to think about it.' She waited for him to try and persuade her, to maybe even say that she owed him, and was surprised when he didn't. 'That's what got me into trouble in the first place, remember?'

'That wasn't the mistake,' he said.

'No?'

'No. The mistake was talking to a stranger on a train.'

Sadie lifted her glass and sighed into the wine. She thought of Mona Farrell walking along the carriage and sliding into the seat opposite to hers. Why hadn't she kept her mouth shut about Eddie? Why hadn't she put the file away? If only she could turn back time, but she couldn't. 'That may be true,' she said, 'but there's still no such thing as a free lunch.'

'No point in going hungry either. I take it you're back at Oaklands? I'll pick you up at twelve.'

Sadie gave him a long steady look. 'I haven't agreed to anything yet.'

'Well, while you're thinking about it, shall we have another drink?'

wouldn't have to do anything, he would be protected from difficult contact with outsiders, anything he wanted would be provided for him without question, and so on.'

Vogel tried not to show too much astonishment. He supposed he shouldn't be that amazed. Sir John Fairbrother had clearly thought he was near immortal and could get away with anything. He also, equally clearly, had immense powers of persuasion.

'And the homeless man agreed to all of this, just like that?'

Fairbrother shrugged. 'You're living rough, out in the cold, drinking meths and cider. Somebody offers you warmth and comfort, champagne and fine brandy. Bit of a no brainer, some might say.'

Vogel supposed Freddie Fairbrother had a point.

'When did your father tell you all this?' he asked.

'He came to see me about seven or eight months ago. Just turned up in Brisbane, complete with beard and bald head. A simple but excellent disguise. I almost didn't recognise him at first. But, of course, I hadn't seen him in eighteen years.

'The substitute Sir John was already installed at Blackdown. Bella knew all about it from the beginning. She and my father had staged their fall-out, you've probably guessed that, and she quit the board of Fairbrother's so that she would be able to disassociate herself from the mess the company was in. Pa told me he wanted me back in the fold because he was afraid the board still wouldn't accept Bella without the presence of a male Fairbrother. I was going to be the prodigal son. The thing is, Mr Vogel, I found that I rather wanted my birthright back. I really did. And it seemed like the perfect plan, in which everyone would be a winner.

'The bank would be saved. As far as the world was concerned my father would die with his blessed reputation still intact, but actually he would be living on this exotic island he secretly owned in the Middle East, under the protection of his chum Sheik Abdul whose family fortune has been greatly enhanced by many years of involvement in Pa's dubious international financial dealings. Pa was totally confident he would never be found there, and that he would be able to continue pulling the strings at Fairbrother International. Bella and I would each get exactly what we wanted, the top job at Fairbrother's, or more or less, for her; all the trappings that come with being head of the Fairbrother clan for me, without doing the work, and the homeless man got a standard of living and a level of care he could never have dreamed of.'

'But then it all went wrong. What happened, Freddie?'

'Well, Pa's poor sap responded rather too well to the care he was receiving. Pa had told me in Brisbane that he would be dead in weeks. Eight months later he was still going strong. Or reasonably strong. Meanwhile the affairs of the bank were becoming more desperate, critical in fact. My father realised something had to be done, things had to be speeded up or the whole plan would fail.'

'And your father told you that, did he? That he had decided to speed up his impersonator's death?'

Fairbrother looked furtive, as if realising he may have inadvertently revealed rather too much about his own involvement. 'Uh no, he didn't tell me anything like that,' he said quickly. 'I thought the fire was an accident. I still thought that when I arrived in the UK. I knew it was being investigated, but I was confident that no evidence of arson would be found.'

I'll bet you were, thought Vogel, who already realised that Freddie's capacity for self-deception was probably greater than his capacity for deceiving others. Unlike his father.

'Do you know who this man was, the man who, in effect, died in your father's place?'

'No idea,' said Freddie casually.

'Do you not even know his name?'

'No, why would I? He was just some homeless jerk. Pa used to refer to him as Johnny Two.'

Freddie laughed humourlessly.

'I see,' said Vogel, who was fighting an almost overwhelming urge to slap Freddie Fairbrother across the face. Instead he stood up, keeping his hands loose at his sides, and asked Freddie to do the same.

'Frederick John Fairbrother, I am charging you with conspiracy to murder your sister, Christabella Ann Fairbrother, and also conspiracy to fraud. You do not have to say anything. But it may harm your defence . . .'

Freddie did not seem to hear the caution. He stood with his mouth slightly open and an expression of disbelief on his face. He'd heard the first bit all right.

'You're charging me?' he asked ingenuously. 'But you told me you weren't going to. You told me I could go home. Home to Australia . . .' His voice tailed away.

'I have absolutely no recollection of that,' responded Vogel deadpan.

'But I've only been in the country for forty-eight hours,' Freddie continued.

'Yes, and look what you've achieved,' said Vogel, equally deadpan.

'And you said yourself, I'm barely involved, never have been, not with any of it,' Freddie continued. 'These charges are nonsense. No court will convict me.'

'Mr Fairbrother, I feel confident we shall be able to prove that you phoned your father yesterday morning, straight after Bella had undoubtedly told you she had arranged to meet me at her home. You knowingly sent your sister to her death. Oh, and you have just confessed that you were fully aware of your father's fraudulent attempt to fake his own death for both personal and professional gain. I am quite confident that we will gain convictions against you.'

'You've tricked me, you bastard,' said Freddie.

'Not at all, Mr Fairbrother,' said Vogel.

A small satisfied smile twitched at the corners of his mouth.

EPILOGUE

Sir John Fairbrother was made of stronger stuff. He pleaded that he had been suffering from amnesia and could remember next to nothing since disappearing from his home. He knew nothing of the imposter who had taken his place at Blackdown Manor. He knew nothing of the catastrophic fire at the manor. He knew nothing about the death of George Grey, nor of his dear daughter, Bella. Jack Kivel was clearly responsible for all of it, and Sir John had no idea why.

His solicitor Peter Prentis arrived from London and, although not entirely able to hide his shock at the events which had been brought to his attention, went through the motions of taking control of the situation. His client, he said, would answer no more questions, and would be pleading not guilty to all charges.

A second search of the grounds of Blackdown Manor and the immediate area, following the break-in at The Gatehouse, revealed signs of recent habitation in an old keeper's cottage, on Fairbrother land, which had previously been dismissed as derelict. A camp bed, tinned food supplies, and a small portable generator were found in an upstairs room with boarded-up windows.

It seemed incredible that Fairbrother would have chosen as a hiding place somewhere actually on his own property, but he was clearly a man conditioned to thinking outside the box. A man not only without morals, scruples, conscience or almost any normal human emotions, but also without a great deal of fear. Vogel reckoned that is exactly what he had done, that he had vacated his barge in Brentford and high-tailed it there right after killing George Grey. The one murder Fairbrother had surely committed himself, whether or not that could ever be proven. It therefore appeared likely that it had been Sir John himself, with or without the assistance of Jack Kivel, who had broken into The Gatehouse, presumably with the intention of silencing Janice Grey. He had, after all, almost certainly been more or less on the spot, camping out in the old keeper's cottage less than a mile away. And he had once been an elite soldier – of an age, but doubtless still more than capable of dealing with a small frightened woman.

Vogel was determined that Fairbrother would pay for his truly horrific series of crimes. He considered the man to be every bit as much of an evil monster as any violent criminal he had encountered in his career, and there had been a few of those.

There was considerable evidence against Sir John, albeit much of it circumstantial. But Vogel was aware that the key to it all might be the evidence of his own son.

Vogel had thoroughly enjoyed charging Freddie Fairbrother and watching the man's somewhat smug and confident demeanour change to one of shocked and fearful disbelief. However, a little plea bargaining might eventually be called for, because it was imperative that Freddie should be prepared to give evidence against his father in court.

Martha Kivel claimed to have been totally ignorant of all her husband's nefarious activities, in spite of a number of items of value from Blackdown Manor, including, somewhat incredibly, the Gainsborough worth millions, being found in Jack's shed in the Kivels' back garden. Vogel found it difficult to believe that Martha hadn't had at least an inkling over the years of the lengths to which Jack was prepared to go on behalf of his employer and boyhood and army friend. However, he had little choice but to give her the benefit of the doubt.

Further inquiries into the military careers of both Kivel and Fairbrother revealed that, whilst stationed in Germany, Kivel had been suspected of killing a taxi driver during an argument over the fare following a drunken night out. Fairbrother had given Kivel an alibi, which the military police had been obliged to accept even though they'd believed it to be false. Fairbrother had saved Kivel's life, in a way, but only in facilitating him to continue to live in freedom. And, as Vogel had half guessed following the brief exchange between the two men which he had witnessed at Bristol airport, it seemed that Fairbrother's hold over Kivel might have been down as much to a kind of blackmail as comradely love and loyalty.

The response of airport police and the apparent lack of communication at Bristol Airport on the night Kivel took his own life there and the two Fairbrother's were arrested, was the subject of a Civil Aviation Authority Inquiry.

Janice Grey was charged with conspiracy to commit arson. She steadfastly maintained that, whilst she now realised that her husband must have been hired by the real Sir John and been fully aware of the whole intrigue, she'd had no idea that the man she had cared for to the best of her ability had been an imposter. And that whilst she had been aware of the plan for George to set fire to Blackdown Manor, she'd believed, as she thought George had too, that this was merely in order to obtain insurance money, and that there had been no intention to harm anyone. Except, of course, George! Vogel thought the woman was probably telling the truth, also that George had been ultimately little more than a scapegoat, and that it had almost certainly been Jack Kivel who had tampered with the gas tank and caused the explosion at the manor. But this was now unlikely ever to be known for sure.

Nobby Clarke pulled all the strings she could in the Met and at the Palace of Westminster in order to bring some sort of retribution against Sheik Abdul. It was of course a lost cause. The sheik's lawyers asserted that his private jet had been made ready at Bristol Airport to transport a very important passenger who could not be named for diplomatic reasons. When this VIP had failed to turn up it had returned empty to the Middle East.

Sophia Santos' remains were flown back to her distraught family in the Philippines, where she would be buried with due Catholic honours. Vogel hated it when foreign nationals died violent deaths on British soil. He always considered that the British forces of law and order, if not the whole country, had let them down.

Another innocent victim of the whole debacle was Bella Fairbrother's fourteen-year-old daughter Kim. Victim support and social services were involved in assisting the understandably devastated girl. But it transpired that Kim had for a couple of years, and unbeknown to her mother, been seeing the father who had played no part in her upbringing. Sean Reardon had been her mother's fitness instructor when he and Bella had had a brief affair. It seemed there'd been no question of Bella wanting him in either her or her daughter's lives. But Reardon had been delighted to later have the chance to get to know Kim, and upon learning of her mother's death and all the horrors surrounding it, had promptly offered the girl a home.

Vogel asked Nobby to launch a major inquiry in London to try to discover the identity of the man Sir John Fairbrother had so cynically plucked from the streets of the city in order to take his place. Johnny Two was eventually identified as Roland North, originally from Chelmsford, Essex, who had ended up on the streets following a series of broken relationships and an inability to hold down any sort of employment, possibly due to a drink problem. It turned out that he had a son, Wayne, who spoke with rather a distinctive accent which Vogel believed was known as estuary English, a blend of Cockney and Essex. It seemed likely that Wayne's father had probably had much the same accent, and been advised to talk as little as possible, blaming the ravages of Parkinson's for his poor speech. Wayne had apparently over the years made a number of attempts, albeit ineffectual, to find his errant father, and at least wanted to give Roland North, or what remained of him, a proper funeral. This was duly arranged in Sampford Arundel Church, not far from the manor house which had been home to Roland for the last months of his life. The only home he'd had in years.

Janice Grey, on bail, asked if she could attend. Vogel, Nobby, Ted Dawson and Saslow also attended. Tom Withey, not totally able to fight back a tear or two, and Bob Parsons were there, representing Wellington Fire Service. A small wake was held at the Blue Ball. Fiona, the landlady, provided some complimentary food. Nobby bought the first round of drinks.

Vogel offered to join in. Nobby glanced scathingly at his ginger ale, the DI's favourite tipple.

'Never, ever, will I let you near a bar,' she said. 'We could all end up drinking that stuff.'

'It might do you good, boss,' said Vogel.

'When I want you to tell me what will do me good, Vogel, I'll let you know,' said Nobby, downing her usual double malt in one.

Vogel grinned.

'Decent of you to come, boss,' he said quietly.

'Poor sod,' commented Nobby Clarke. 'He had a bloody awful life and a bloody awful death.'

'Yes, well, at least we've got that bastard Fairbrother banged up where he belongs.'

'On remand, Vogel. He's not been convicted yet.'

'If this one walks, I shall personally burn down the court he stands trial in,' said Vogel.

'Fighting talk, DI Vogel.'

Vogel grunted.

'Don't worry, I'll provide the petrol,' said Nobby.

Lightning Source UK Ltd.
Milton Keynes UK
UKHW011558171019
351785UK00004B/67/P